The Deadly Kiss

A Gripping Crime Mystery

The DI Hogarth Deadly Kiss series book 1

Solomon Carter

Great Leap

Prologue

It wasn't right. Nothing about it was right.
The way she looked at him. The way she would no longer smile when she spoke. There was no warmth in her anymore. Something had changed and he didn't like it. When he tried to tell her about his hopes, his fears, she shut him down, putting him in his place. Back in his box. True, he'd never had the knack with women. Never. He could become friends with women, yes, but things never went any further. It had been this way for far too long. It was galling. Painful. Humiliating. But with this young one, he knew he'd come close. So close. But now, even with this one, he had been robbed at the very last. Why? Because the girl had revealed another face, played her hidden card, and the result? He found himself torn apart yet again. This was a torment he didn't deserve. It was only right that he directed all that pain back where it came from. But not right away. Not before he had tasted what had been stolen. Tonight, he was going to get what she had promised. So many promises had been made by those eyes, so many sweet possibilities, and he would not leave empty-handed. No matter what it took. This evening walk on the sand, these soft words of pity and apology, they would be her last. It was a desperate shame, of course. But this time he would not be the one wearing it. He would make her wear it. Maybe then the torment would be gone. And if not gone, at least it might fade – providing some relief from the endless ache inside. They walked side by side on the dark beach, passing the coloured wooden huts

as the tide lapped ever closer towards their feet. He listened as the girl tried to explain herself, but all the while he was admiring the pretty eyes behind those glasses. He was biding his time. Choosing his moment. His heart was already beating faster, his loins stirring. Tonight, everything would change. There would be an end to empty words. An end to torment. Finally, there would be release.

Two weeks later...

Hogarth sipped his malt whisky and tried to focus on the soothing fire in his throat. Usually, it comforted him. The taste of earth, the sweetness of caramel, fire of black pepper, and the slightest hint of the sea. Hogarth knitted his eyes shut and tried to keep his mind still. But as he sipped, the face of young Helen Brimelow came to mind. Pale as chalk. Eyes softly shut, face pristine, like the statue of an angel depicted in heavenly rapture. So pale in fact, her skin was almost blue...but in the morning moonlight, her lips had seemed grey. There had been a dark spatter of still-damp blood across her slender throat, then the terrible gash which began between her collar bones and just kept on going down her torso. The poor girl's life had been stolen before it had even really begun. Stripped naked, her youthful dignity broken as she died... It was one more reason why Joe Hogarth could never bring a child into the world. Not that he was suited to the task. The latest bottle of malt sitting on the corner of the fireplace confirmed he wasn't fit for a normal life. And having seen the body of young Helen, he suspected he would never be the same again. He sipped his whisky, but this time all he could smell was blood. He scowled, raised the glass and downed the rest in one. He stood and grabbed his jacket from the back of the armchair, and buttoned up his shirt which had been undone almost down to his belt, his pale, soft, hairless chest exposed. He shouldn't have been going anywhere. He was due for bed. Another long day would start tomorrow. Another day of trying to fix the unfixable. The grim discovery of the girl's body in an abandoned beach hut – two weeks back – was still fresh as the dark morning when he'd first seen it. And they were still no closer to catching the killer. The photographs on the murder board hung on the wall by his desk, taunting him daily. He could have moved the board, but DS Palmer might have guessed his reasons. A little bit of face would have been lost and, besides, Hogarth reckoned he needed the horror to drive him on. But the horror he felt was nothing compared to the horror of the girl's bereaved father. He knew he owed it to the man to find the killer. If seeing those images meant a little extra suffering as motivation, then so be it. But twenty-four-hour suffering was not something Hogarth had reckoned on.

Tonight, he wanted at least a short respite before he faced the treadmill once again. He listened to the rush of the electric shower still on in the bathroom down the hall then blinked and looked at his whisky bottle. Dalwhinnie. A fifteen-year-old malt, a present to himself to be saved for Christmas, a birthday or bar mitzvah. But not anymore. He poured himself another oversized helping, drained it down, and sucked his teeth. He set the tumbler down and turned for the living room door. It would be cold outside, but he still shunned his overcoat. He was in a hurry to escape. With any luck, the booze would do its job and would keep him warm. And maybe the walk along by Prittlewell Brook would purge him of his memories before they could turn into nightmares. Maybe. But he doubted it. The method hadn't worked so far, but it was all he knew.

"I'll be back soon!" he called over his shoulder before he thumped down the stairs. The shower clicked off, and the bathroom door swept open, releasing a cloud of billowing steam as Hogarth's head dipped below the horizon of the staircase. A buxom woman wrapped in a towel leaned out of the mist. She blinked and pulled the towel tight around her.

"Joe? You're not going out again, surely?"

The downstairs door slammed. He was already gone.

Hogarth pulled his jacket lapels high about his neck and stuck his hands into his pockets. He started on his walk down the road of terraced houses, heading towards the busy Fairfax Road at the bottom. He would cross at Fairfax slowing only when he neared the brook. Then, as he often did these days, he would peer down at the trickling black water set in the concrete cutting, before making a loop and following the narrow waterway back on his return. The walk could take him twenty minutes or an hour, depending on how he was feeling. Tonight, Hogarth needed a long one.

His phone buzzed as he moved between endless Wi-Fi hotspots. He grunted. He should have turned the damn thing off. He slid the phone from his pocket and eyed the screen as his thumb hovered over the off switch. He saw there was a fresh WhatsApp text from Palmer. After a long time, Palmer had pushed him onto WhatsApp, and that was enough of the future for him. He'd tried Insta, and it had almost got him into some unwanted woman trouble, so he'd deleted it. These days, texts were enough. His text chats with Palmer were a mixture of work, discussions about drink and television, and of Palmer's latest personal ordeal – having her teenage niece foisted on her – after the relationship between Palmer's sister and daughter had broken down. To his mind,

Palmer had been very unwise to take the girl on. On top of the usual work drama and lack of partner or social life, his deputy now had a problem teenager to deal with. If Palmer had been struggling to get a bloke before, she had zero chance with somebody else's problem child indoors. Hogarth double-checked Palmer's text for anything important, but he saw nothing new about the Brimelow case. Just another gripe about the teenager helping herself to Palmer's wine.

"Kick her out then," spat Hogarth, without bothering to type it. He switched the phone off and got walking. It was freezing, but the temperature suited his mood.

It had been a rotten fortnight.

The murder had started it. Ed Quentin, the pathologist, had given them little to go on. Despite the evidence of sexual assault, the killer had been careful. Quentin said there was evidence that a condom had been used, and it was possible the killer had worn gloves throughout. There were no witnesses. Then came the meetings with his superior, DCI Melford – getting dragged into the headmaster's office for another rollicking for ruffling some important feathers. Melford had received letters – letters requesting that the brass consider transferring Hogarth to another branch altogether. If a member of the public had penned the letters, they wouldn't have been a problem. But they had been sent by the town's MP – part of his slow-burn campaign to get Hogarth out of his hair. They had a history. A bad one. And on top of the MP's letters came another serious complaint.

Lately, Hogarth had taken to spending a few extra hours keeping an eye on one Simon Drawton. In the last six months, Simon Drawton had been accused of indecent assault by two different young women of similar ages and appearance. Both times, just as the case was beginning to get traction, the allegations against Drawton had been dropped, and both victims said they had been mistaken about the whole affair. Mistaken. Hogarth had been angry and reprimanded both girls for wasting police time. But he knew his anger had been misplaced. Where there was smoke there was fire... And when it came to Drawton, he smelt plenty. After the Brimelow murder, Simon Drawton was an obvious suspect. Just a shame DCI Melford hadn't agreed... then, one night, after Hogarth had gotten a bit too enthusiastic in trying to get Drawton to admit what he'd done, Melford had threatened Hogarth with suspension. The same old threat. Even so, Hogarth knew he needed to be on guard. Drawton had influence... that, together with the MP's poison pen letters, and he was in serious danger of getting kicked to some remote part of the Essex force. Trouble was, after all these years, Hogarth wasn't about to become cautious. Not when a monstrous killer was on the loose... it was enough to give anybody nightmares.

Hogarth stopped and leaned over the wall by the brook. He stared down into its blackness, listened to the trickle of water and the sound of an owl nearby. He heard a shuffling sound below in the black thicket by the brook. Probably some hobo fixing up his bed for the night or a couple getting their rocks off in the bushes. Not his concern. Especially after a few whiskies. Hogarth pressed on. He passed the endless lighted windows of the sprawling Southend hospital before he doubled back through the long alleyway by the local school. He rejoined the brook, but much further on. Here there was a footpath along the edge, and he followed it back home. The walk and the cold air were working through him

now. He was beginning to feel drunk. Again he heard the rustling of branches near the last section of the brook and felt someone watching him, but he ignored the feeling and strode home. Back in the warmth, he poured a final glass of malt, downed it in one, then stripped off and slipped between the sheets. The warm body of WPC Andi Bromley formed a warm and tempting mound in the bed beside him. But as Hogarth slid closer, the woman promptly turned away. "It's too late, Joe. I'm up early, and so are you."
He knew she would lie there, silent and angry. But from experience, he knew he would be awake the longest. He folded his arms underneath his head and stared up at the ceiling; it was as pale as the dead girl's skin. It was all no good. The whisky, the walks, even Andi. All he could think of was Helen Brimelow, and all the while Drawton was on the loose. When Andi's first snores pervaded the room, Hogarth's temples were still tight as snare drums. He was in for another long night.

One

In the end, Hogarth couldn't bear to lay in bed a minute longer than he had to. He was up and showered long before Andi, yet she was the one with the journey ahead of her. Hogarth toasted a couple of barely edible dry old crumpets. He drowned them in butter to soften them and was out of the house while Andi was still snoring in his bed. Andi was due for work at Barking police station by nine. Hogarth knew she'd still make it, and if she didn't, it really wasn't his problem. She liked her independence, and frankly, Hogarth liked it, too.

He made the now-familiar drive across town, crossing past the duck-egg blue walls of The Cricketers pub before taking a left down Avenue Road. He carried on until he reached the quiet, snaking little road he knew well. The old red-brick manse at the end of the street belonged to the local Baptist church, while Simon Drawton lived at the nearest end, his big square-windowed Victorian semi overlooking the neat little primary school on the opposite side. The school might have bothered Hogarth, but then Drawton wasn't that kind of predator. It was a good job that children weren't his thing – though Hogarth guessed that the young female teaching assistants probably were. It was something else he needed to keep an eye on.

It wasn't yet seven o'clock, but Hogarth reckoned the man would be up. He looked like an early bird; had a hawkish, pompous face and an almost permanent smarmy smile. A couple of months back, the day after the indecent assault charges against him had been dropped, Hogarth had forced his way into Drawton's house. He had knocked on the door, but as soon as it opened, he had barged Drawton out of the way so he could find anything the bastard had wanted to hide. But the house had been spartan and spotless and he had found nothing incriminating, not even on the array of computer monitors upstairs. The computer screens had flashed endless lists of numbers relating to the Hong Kong Stock Exchange and the Nikkei Dow, with another one showing the front page of the BBC News website. Hogarth had been left glowering at him, knowing the man was a sicko, but still unable to prove a thing. The man's smarmy face had been a red rag to a bull. He'd tried to force Drawton to admit his guilt, but the man only shrugged and smiled. So, Hogarth had done what came naturally. He'd given Drawton three solid punches right in the face. He had drawn blood from the man's mouth and nose and decided to end it there. Every punch had been delivered with a few damning words relating to Drawton's slippery ways and dirty crimes. It wasn't justice, but it had still felt good. Drawton had threatened charges but changed his mind. That was when it started – the hassle from the brass, and the letter-writing campaign to have him transferred out of town. After that, those three punches hadn't seemed like such a good idea. And yet… here he was, stalking his enemy once again. It was early. Drawton's upstairs lights were on.

Hogarth's head was thumping from strong coffee and too much whisky. Maybe following his latest impulses was not such a good idea. The booze was probably affecting his decision making. He got ready to turn tail when another flash of Helen Brimelow's corpse invaded his thoughts. He sighed and yanked up his handbrake. Decision made.

Hogarth smashed the lion-headed brass knocker of the big red front door. A wicked grin settled on his face as a light flicked on in the hallway, and a blurred figure cautiously advanced down the stairs. From the look of him, Drawton was still wearing his pyjama bottoms. There had been no woman at home last time Hogarth called. No boyfriend, either, he noted. Hogarth didn't trust a man who didn't display any signs of his urges or proclivities at home. Everyone had them. The more buried they were, the worse it seemed to be.

Drawton came close to the narrow glass panes on either side of the door knocker, the bevelled glass distorting his face.

"Inspector Hogarth?" he said, in his well-schooled accent. Not far away, a light switched on at the manse.

"Surely you don't expect me to open the door?"

"I don't, no," said Hogarth. "But I'd like you to, all the same."

"Dear me. Don't you ever sleep?" said the man.

"Not much these days. What about you?" said Hogarth.

The men stared at one another through the glass.

"Are you going to attack me again?"

"What if I promise to keep my hands to myself?"

Drawton stared at him. The light stained Hogarth's face in bright gold and dark shadows.

"If that's true, then I'll consider not reporting this visit to your superiors."

"My superiors? Got a direct line, have you?"

"With the position you put me in last time, I think I was entitled to use all the resources at my disposal."

"Your resources being senior police officers and politicians, I take it?"

"Are you here for revenge, Inspector? That really would be most unwise."

"I already gave you my assurance. Look – are you going to open the bloody door or not?"

Hogarth heard Drawton sigh before he turned the handle and pulled the big red front door open. Drawton stepped back into the hallway. He was guarded, his dark eyes staring hard at Hogarth through his round-framed spectacles.

"I only opened the door because I'm intrigued, Inspector. What can a man like you want from me, if not blood?"

Hogarth breezed past Drawton, scratching an eyebrow with his fingernail as he went. He strode down the bright wooden-floored hallway and headed for the kitchen at the back.

"I never wanted blood, Drawton. I got carried away, that's all. But not today. Today I'm being civil."

"Civil? You?" Drawton closed the door behind them and followed Hogarth towards the vast kitchen. Hogarth walked into the darkness and Drawton flicked on the light switch. Lights came on in the kitchen and out in the small back garden, illuminating a neat Zen-style space with gravel, grey stone, and sculpted shrubs. Hogarth picked up the kettle from its port and filled it at the sink.

"You're looking worse for wear, Inspector," said Drawton. "Late night?" He stayed back by the kitchen door.

"Whereas you look as chipper as ever, *old bean*," said Hogarth, attempting a posh voice. "Odd how a man like you can sleep so soundly, after everything you've done."

"Those charges were dropped – need I remind you?"

"But that indecent assault was just the tip of the iceberg, wasn't it?"

"No, it wasn't. I was cleared. Those two young women were malicious, unscrupulous, little gold diggers. They saw me as a soft target, I'm sure."

"Two women who didn't know each other? Who weren't friends? Who lived entirely separate lives? Come on! What are the odds on that? In my book that puts *you* firmly in the dock, not those girls. One gold digger might make sense, but two is stretching it."

"I don't care what you believe."

"Okay. So, let's pretend that you're right. It's a lie, but let's go with it. Let's say these two scheming, pretty young ladies just Facebooked each other. They struck some kind of insane money-making pact and came after you, first one then the other. But you still showed them in the end, didn't you? You got a bit rough to prove that you weren't all Jeeves and Wooster. But then… after you slapped them around, what happened? You got a little hot under the collar? You saw an opportunity for more… and you crossed a very dangerous line. You crossed it twice. Now that's what I call form, Drawton. Don't you dare tell me they were up for it, because those two wouldn't have let you put an arm around them if you were their uncle."

"I was cleared."

"No. You were never cleared. The charges were dropped. Must have cost you a fair bit of money in terms of persuasion."

Drawton kept his mouth firmly shut.

"Coffee?" said Hogarth, opening each cupboard door as he looked for the jar.

"No, thank you," said Drawton. "And if this horrid little fantasy of yours is the only reason you came here this morning, then you won't be staying."

Hogarth set a cup on the worktop and found a coffee jar to go with it. It was a gold jar with a picture of a mountain top on the front. Incan Gold. Pretentious and fake, just like Simon Drawton.

"No," said Hogarth. "It's not the only reason."

Drawton nodded. "I thought not."

The kettle whispered as it began to heat the water.

"You killed Helen Brimelow, didn't you?"

Drawton's eyebrows fell low over his glasses.

"Just tell me. Off the record. Didn't you?"

"Of course, I didn't."

"Those two girls gave you a taste for it. Then you wanted more. After those two, you had to go further. You wanted everything. The works. But the only way a man like you could ever get anything like that from a sweet young girl like Helen was through force and violence. Or did that part turn you on, as well?"

"Inspector!"

"She was sixteen years old, man! Maybe she told you that. Maybe she didn't. Did you know she was a churchgoer? Just like you pretend to be. The only churchgoer in the family it seems. She was a good girl, Drawton. Church isn't my bag, but I haven't got anything against those who want to bring a little hope into the world. She was a hope-giver, Drawton. She helped at the food bank in town. Her social media profile proves that she organised sponsored events for charity. She was a rare one, a doer of the best kind. One day, a girl like that might have ended up making a real difference in the world. At sixteen years old, she was already a role model. But you snuffed that out and butchered her to cover your sick urges. That was the price Helen had to pay on your behalf."

"No, Inspector. I swear it. What happened to that girl was terrible and wrong."

"You were very neat about it. Meticulous, just like your personality. You must have worn gloves. You used a condom. The pathologist found traces of chemicals consistent with a condom."

"Please," said Drawton. "This is abominable. If you carry on like this I'll be forced to call—"

"The police?" said Hogarth, with a vicious grin. He lifted the kettle before it clicked off and poured the steaming water over the coffee granules in his cup But instead of returning the kettle to the port, he kept it in hand. He walked a few steps nearer to Drawton watching the thin man's Adam's apple bob up and down his throat.

"You should know I have influence well beyond the offices of Southend Police station."

"Threats from bastards I don't like don't hold much water anymore," said Hogarth. "No pun intended." Drawton's eyes landed on the kettle in his hand.

"I am aware that our local MP has cause to dislike you," said Drawton. He sounded nervous.

Hogarth narrowed his eyes. His grip tightened on the kettle handle.

"You said you wouldn't threaten me, Inspector. Not this time."

"Yes, I did, didn't I?"

Drawton eyed the kettle, and the plume of steam rising into the air.

"I didn't kill that girl, Inspector. No matter what you think of me, I think it is horrific what happened to her. The person who did that is as far removed from me as the earth is from the sun."

"For crying out loud!" said Hogarth. "You attack young women but you think killing them is wrong? I don't believe you."

Drawton blinked and pushed his glasses back up on his nose.

"I'm only a man, Inspector. A red-blooded male."

"They were still girls, man!" said Hogarth. But he soon changed tack. "So you admit it?"

"I admit nothing. All I am saying is that I have never wanted to hurt anyone, male or female, young or old."

Hogarth bared his teeth. The kettle wavered in his hand. Drawton's lips closed into a tight line.

"You did it, didn't you? You did it all." Hogarth stepped closer and Drawton backed away. Hogarth narrowed his eyes and turned away. He slammed the kettle back onto its base and picked up his coffee. Instead of attempting to drink it, he poured it down the sink.

"If you did kill Helen Brimelow, I will find out, Drawton. And when I prove it, I promise you, I will ensure that you'll never get away with it. No matter who you know. Not this time. Not ever again."

Hogarth started walking. Drawton stepped aside to avoid the inevitable shoulder barge.

"Inspector…"

Hogarth wheeled around and stared at the man, his eyes burning.

"You can threaten me all you like. But I am not guilty of that girl's murder. I had never heard of her before I read her name in The Record. To be frank, I think what happened to her is appalling."

Hogarth ground his teeth.

"The person who did that must be extremely disturbed. Nonetheless, they deserve every bit of the justice you promise. Worse, maybe."

"She was a true believer. A church volunteer, Mr Drawton. You're a churchgoer, aren't you?"

"You already know, I attend Avenue Baptist on a Sunday morning."

"You mean they actually let you in?"

Drawton nodded. "The law says I'm innocent until proven guilty… and we're all sinners in the eyes of the Lord, Inspector. Don't forget, you're a sinner too."

Drawton gave a flourish of his hand.

"Oh, I'm certain of it. But what I'm not, Drawton, is a sick, scheming hypocrite."

Hogarth turned away.

"Inspector," called Drawton, "I really do hope you catch them."

"Don't worry," said Hogarth. With the door in hand, he looked back down the hallway to where Drawton stood. "You know I will."

Hogarth slammed the door behind him. Out on the doorstep, he put his hands on his hips and shook his head. He had achieved nothing and felt even worse than before he had started. After that little escapade, there was bound to be more trouble from Melford. Just what the doctor ordered, he thought. Hogarth noticed a flurry of curtains in the bay window to his right. He looked across as the manse curtains dropped back into place. The pastor, vicar, minister… whatever the Baptists called them these days, they had seen him. Great, he thought. If DCI Melford didn't get a call about him, then the man upstairs certainly would. Hogarth puffed out his cheeks and marched back to his car. It was still early. But he had nowhere else to go, so he went to work. And with that, his working day had begun.

Two

When DS Sue Palmer walked into the small, white-walled room that constituted their office, Hogarth had already been there for an hour and a half. She saw the crushed coffee cup on his desk, alongside the remnants of a canteen bacon roll. She looked up at the murder board above his desk. The grim images of Helen Brimelow's body, with the brutal wound from her throat to her abdomen, was front and centre, along with a list of all of the people they had interviewed. On the other side of the image was a list of the suspects they had drafted at the start. Both lists matched. Some of them had been interviewed three times over. The list of evidence found at the site was the shortest of all, and much of it had been crossed through by Hogarth, as had many of the suspect names. But the name Drawton had not been crossed out. Instead, it had been underlined. Palmer even suspected a new third line had been added beneath the previous two. The room was airless and humid. Palmer made a face and left the door ajar for a bit of what passed for fresh air. "Morning," she said, dropping her handbag down on the small centre table. It was a bleached wood job, a small square Ikea thing for conducting their meetings. Palmer was frazzled after another 'morning chat' with her niece. This time it had been about respecting her home. Her flat was small and needed to be kept tidy. Evidently, tidiness was another part of the parenting puzzle which her sister had chosen to leave to her. But if Palmer was frazzled, she sensed Hogarth was faring worse. His hair looked unkempt and a little greasy. Hogarth knew she was there. He turned around to look her in the eye. He looked disheartened and weary, and Palmer wondered what had been going on.

"Late night?" she said.

Hogarth flicked his eyebrows. "Funny. That's what Drawton said to me."

"Drawton? Please tell me you've not been to see him again?"

"Why not? He's the standout suspect, and the only reason he's still out there is because he's been influencing some people with too much power."

"Even so, I don't think Melford likes him much, either."

"I didn't mean Melford. Even if he's forgotten what it's like, at least he used to do the same job we do. It's those high-office cretins with their uniforms which never see a grain of dirt. They have no idea about the job. I wonder if they ever did."

"You seriously think Drawton's influencing the chief, then?"

"I don't know. Someone higher than Melford, at any rate. It doesn't bloody matter, does it? We're not likely to find out."

Palmer pulled a chair from the meeting table and dropped into one of the uncomfortable wooden seats. She crossed her legs and settled back as best she could. Apart from the Brimelow murder, they had a few lesser crimes on, but they weren't overflowing with work. Which was a blessed relief – seeing as the team had shrunk. It meant the chance for a coffee and a breather which they needed but neither felt they deserved. They had rarely experienced such treats since DC Simmons had transferred to Basildon. The DC had been involved with a young blonde journalist who loved exploiting a little kiss and tell. It was a serious no-no and had almost cost them an entire case. Hogarth could have pushed for suspension, even a dismissal. As it was, Hogarth stayed quiet and allowed Simmons the dignity of a voluntary exit which kept him in the force but allowed him to learn his lesson. Palmer doubted whether she would have been as gracious as Hogarth. The DI was as tough as a pair of battered old boots, but once in a blue moon, the kindness hidden inside made a rare showing for a selected few. They had not been given a replacement yet. There was talk of a DC making the swap back from Basildon, but Hogarth had tried to block it. He'd never liked the staff on the other local team. If forced, DC Faye Gordon was probably the one Basildon would send, but everybody knew Hogarth was a spiky character. Palmer couldn't blame anyone for thinking twice. And as it was, Palmer was enjoying the streamlined make-up of the team. It was like a working partnership, something almost like the cosy bantering duos depicted in US dramas. Except that Hogarth wasn't anything like as slick. In fact, attitude wise, the DI probably had more in common with Johnny Rotten than any of his US counterparts. Either way, Palmer was glad Faye Gordon didn't seem keen. Of course, this had nothing to do with the fact that Gordon was younger, slimmer, and still pretty enough to turn heads.

"You really shouldn't have," said Palmer.

"Paid a visit to Drawton? Of course not. But that pompous bastard deserves some payback for what he did, even if the brass are happy to let him off."

"Even so, it might be time to let it go. You can hardly afford any more complaints, can you?"

"Oh, I don't know." Hogarth's craggy face twitched with a hint of a smile. "They can't get rid of me right now, can they? If they do, this outfit's buggered. I think I've got a little slack yet."

"Maybe," said Palmer. "But I wouldn't hang yourself with it."

Hogarth raised an eyebrow, nodding.

"Drawton mentioned our esteemed MP."

Palmer's face turned serious.

"Hartigan?"

Hogarth gave a slow nod. "Dropped his name like a get-out-of-jail-free card. Shows you the stamp of both men. Of course, they're bum chums. No wonder I got a carpeting the first time."

"You beat the living daylights out of him!"

"I hit him three times. Three punches. That's it."

"You could have been dismissed."

Hogarth shook his head. "Drawton didn't push for it, because he deserved a hiding. That's a guilty conscience for you. He probably even thinks he's paid his debt. But he hasn't. Not by a long chalk."

"He could have had your head on a plate."

"Alright, alright. No need to spook me on a Monday morning. There's plenty to be spooked about already."

"Such as?"

"Melford wants to see me again, later. It can't be about the visit to Drawton. It's too soon for that. Must be Hartigan's poison pen campaign."

"Which is exactly why you need to restrain yourself."

"Yes, ma'am," said Hogarth, with a mock salute. "Hartigan is a villain, though. You do remember that?"

"I do. But he's also an MP."

"Proper little motivational speaker this morning, aren't we?"

Palmer rubbed her forehead with the heel of her palm.

"Sorry. It must be the Aaliyah effect."

"Ali-what?"

Palmer smiled. "My niece, remember?"

Hogarth smiled. "Sounds like a sneeze gone wrong. Or maybe it's a bit Arabic. Your sister a Middle East fan, was she?"

"She named the girl after a pop star."

Hogarth crumpled his chin and shook his head. "Never heard of her."

"The popstar died around the time her daughter was born. Plane crash, I think."

"What a choice. How auspicious!" said Hogarth. He slapped his knees and heaved himself to his feet.

"How long have you been at it?" said Palmer, as Hogarth groaned and stretched.

"Bit personal, isn't it?"

Palmer thought of Hogarth's latest dalliance with the Barking PC Andi Bromley but said nothing. She had Googled the woman's face to get an idea of Hogarth's latest lover. It didn't happen often, after all. Palmer had found Bromley's smiling visage among the many faces shown on the Barking Police website, complete with contact details. The woman looked pretty enough, but totally no-nonsense with it. Palmer had made it her business to discover the woman was only a few months older than herself. Social media showed that Bromley's fortieth had been celebrated on a boozy pub crawl around Leicester Square. Hogarth had somehow hooked up with her a little while later though it was hard to tell how serious they were about each other. Palmer knew they saw each other no more than a couple of times a week, sometimes less. She didn't want him to be unhappy, but Palmer didn't think she was a good match. Hogarth saw Palmer's struggles and decided to put her out of her misery.

"Come on."
"Where?" said Palmer. "I've only just got in."
"Don't worry. I think you'll want to get this one out of the way as much as I do. We've got Gerald Gilmot in interview room one. He rushed in because he said he has something to share. Wish I'd known he was coming in. I would have gone to Poundland to buy some pegs for our noses."
Palmer frowned but dutifully followed.

"So, Gerald, to what do we owe this pleasure?" said Hogarth, as he took one of the uncomfortable seats around the scratched-up interview room table. Gilmot had been left to stew in the waiting area for a while. Hogarth had hoped the waiting experience might dissuade him from making any new ridiculous accusations or false tip-offs. But alas, Gilmot had decided to stick it out. At some point, the desk sergeant had endured enough of the stink and put Gilmot into IR1. As a result, the entire room smelt almost as bad as the man himself. Gilmot was a small man. Five foot six, with a large head on a slight body. He liked to wear black leathers to go with the motorcycle he had probably never owned and never would. The leathers might have been good for sleeping on the streets in winter, but they were also excellent at helping his bacteria to linger and ferment. To complete the look, Gilmot wore a stars-and-bars Confederate flag bandana on his head and sported a pathetic greying beard which reminded Hogarth of wrestler Hulk Hogan.
"Thought you were ignoring me, Inspector," said Gilmot, with his gap-toothed smile and goofy voice.

"As if the thought ever crossed my mind," replied Hogarth. "Funny to see you in here though, Gillie. It's not even raining this morning. Haven't you got an alleyway to get to?"
Gilmot smiled on regardless.
"I'm afraid we can't offer a cuppa this morning. The machine's on the blink again," lied Hogarth. "What's the story, then?"
"The girl killer," said Gilmot, looking smug.
Hogarth stiffened in his seat and tilted his head like a bird. "Come again?"
Palmer narrowed her eyes and bit her lip.
"The church girl who worked at the food bank. The one with the nice hair and clothes and glasses. The pretty young thing. You've not found the killer, have you?"
Hogarth puckered his lips and crumpled his chin then sat back in his seat and folded his arms.
"Not a good subject to pick, Gillie. Like most things, it's well beyond your field of expertise. You should have invented something about one of your hobo chums threatening to shiv your mates. That might have been believable enough to keep you in here a bit longer. But a ratty little rascal like you, trying to rub our noses in it? That was hardly likely to go down well, was it?"
"Hang on. I came in to help the police with their investigation," said Gilmot.
"Get it over with. Spit it out."
Gilmot snorted and his eyes flicked onto Palmer. He grinned a mean little grin. "You look like a good one, miss," he said. "I bet *you'd* like to solve it, wouldn't you?"
"We all would," said Palmer.
"The papers say you're failing though, don't they?"
"The papers always say something," said Hogarth. "It's a rag, Gillie. Nothing more."

Gilmot leaned forward towards Palmer.

"He reeks of a guilty conscience, doesn't he? Don't you ever wonder why?"

Palmer frowned.

Hogarth grinned and shook his head. "There's only one person who reeks in here. What are you talking about, Gillie?"

"Yes, Gerald, what are you talking about?" said Palmer.

"Have you thought that maybe you haven't found the killer because he's too close to home? That's what I reckon. I see things, you know. See things at night. I'm smarter than they think I am."

"Put your money where your mouth is or stop wasting our time," said Hogarth. "What exactly have you seen?"

Gilmot's eyes became arrogant, his mouth almost a sneer. He leaned back in his chair and looked at Hogarth like he had the measure of him.

"I saw you last night, drunk again, staring down at the brook. Like the brook means something. Maybe it's another place you could do someone in."

"What?" Hogarth was wrongfooted. He shook his head and his brow dropped low over his eyes.

Gilmot continued. "You were by Prittlewell Brook," he said, stroking his beard. "I thought you'd seen me, but you didn't. I was a few metres away, but I could still smell that whisky on you. You were there again, like you have been for weeks."

"And? What of it?!" said Hogarth. "Come on, Gillie. Tell us some more. I had no idea you were such a sleuth."

"A criminal always goes back to the scene of the crime, don't they?"

"Got a pen, DS Palmer? I think we should be taking notes."

"You keep going back. You've got guilt written all over you. Coppers like you. You always get away with it. That's why I'm glad you're here, miss. You can't find the killer. Why not? Because it's him. Maybe he killed her by the brook. That's why he goes there. That's why he's drinking too much. He's no better than the people he locks up."
Hogarth lunged out of his seat, sending it skittering back. "That's enough for one morning, Gilmot. You're beginning to sound like someone who's paranoid as well as daft.".
"You believe me, don't you, miss?" His eyes stayed locked onto Palmer. Hogarth stood upright, opened the interview room door, and held it open.
"DS Palmer, to you, Gerald," was her reply.
"Nothing like a bit of blue-sky thinking to change up an investigation, is there, Palmer? Thank you, Gilmot. Now sod off and crawl back under your rock."

When Hogarth got back from escorting Gilmot to the outside world he saw that Palmer had wedged the office door open. Hogarth cupped a hand over his mouth to smell his breath. Coffee was all he smelt. No whisky. He checked his armpits, noticed a trace of sweat, and shrugged. He walked inside and didn't bother to mention the door. His eyes drifted back to the photograph of the girl's body before they settled on Palmer. He found she was already looking up at him.
"What a start to the day," said Hogarth.
"After your early visit to Drawton, I dare say you've had enough of *interesting*."
"You could say that," said Hogarth. "So, you going to arrest me?"
"I'm more likely to have Gilmot arrested for wasting our time."

"Let's save that for when we want Melford and the rest to clear off for the day."

"Or at least until you've invested in those pegs. But it was still enlightening, anyway," said Palmer.

"You already know I like a little whisky of an evening."

Palmer arched an eyebrow.

"I do." Palmer considered how to pitch the idea of Hogarth cutting down, but soon realised it was a non-starter. "I meant those late-night walks…"

"Those walks clear my head," he replied. "I thought I heard some sort of rodent rummaging around by the brook. Turned out I was right. It was Gilmot." Seeing Palmer was still looking at him, Hogarth arched an eyebrow.

"Helen Brimelow wasn't killed in the brook. She was killed in a Thorpe Bay beach hut. You saw it yourself."

"I wasn't thinking about the poor girl. I was thinking about you. Everything alright… at home, I mean?"

Hogarth blanched by a degree. But Palmer saw it.

"You mean Andi, I take it? I'm okay," he said, his words trailing off. He shrugged. "She likes a laugh, so do I. If we split, I won't be topping myself, if that's what you mean."

"I bet she'd be delighted to hear that."

Hogarth shrugged. "My home life is fine, Palmer. How's yours?"

Palmer winced and he changed the subject.

"It's my work life that needs sorting. We need to make some inroads into this case before it drives me insane. If we let them get away with this, they'll only do it again. That's the price of failing. Find that killer, I'll be right as rain again, and no more late-night walks."

Until the next time, thought Palmer. She knew the job was bad for him. But just like the whisky, she suspected he would never give it up.

"Let's hope we get something this afternoon, then," she said.

Hogarth nodded, but the look in his eyes said he wasn't optimistic. The truth was, after two weeks, neither was she.

Three

The Refuge Food Bank had never been top of Hogarth's favourite venues, but in terms of the job, it had always been one to watch. For better or worse, the food bank didn't just offer food parcels. It provided tea, coffee, and plates of hot and cold food salvaged from the waste mountain of the local supermarkets. All of it was prepared by volunteers and staff of a Christian background, and Hogarth knew a lot of love went into every plate, bar the odd grumpy server. He'd seen it in action. Been in there once or twice. But today the venue had been changed from a free café and free shop, into a place of worship. The café tables had been cleared and set against the wall, one on top of the other and the faux-leather dining chairs had been laid out in lines like church pews. At the front, a flipchart frame had been repurposed to display an oversized photograph of a smiling Helen Brimelow. There was a floral tribute tied below the photograph, and a PowerPoint screen was emblazoned with the words 'Farewell Our Spring Blossom'. Not one given to emotion, Hogarth was still stirred by the sentiment. The girl had been a giver and had much more still to give when her life had been taken. It wasn't fair, but such was the nature of murder. Hogarth couldn't bring her back, but he could at least make sure the killer paid their dues for the crime. Seeing the photograph, feeling the palpable grief all around him, Hogarth knew the justice he could provide would never be enough.

The proper church service had already taken place at St Andrews, the cathedral-like C of E across the roundabout. This service was for Helen's friends, her volunteer colleagues, and the local poor and homeless who had known her well enough to pay their respects. Every chair was taken. The homeless and the dubious lingered in every remaining space around the hall. Hogarth was sure a few of them were casing the place for what they could steal. But almost everyone seemed subdued or upset. The front line of seats was filled with people audibly sobbing. There was a man in the front and centre seat; balding, thin, in a brown suede jacket. Hogarth recognised him as David Brimelow, Helen's fifty-one-year-old father, a resident of the houses across the street, and a kind of personal friend. Two seats away were his ex-wife Marie, and her new partner, Phil Dobson. Marie looked rigid with grief. Dobson was doing his best, stroking the woman's shoulder, caressing her face. Hogarth looked at the three of them with the same narrow eyes he'd been using for the last two weeks. No cracks had appeared as yet. They all seemed genuine. But the best murderers had always seemed to be the best actors. And the murderer was generally close to the victim. But generally wasn't good enough. Hogarth was here for evidence. Waiting for a mask to slip. As he gazed around, he found a pair of eyes on him. He looked towards a gang of ruffians to see little homeless man Gerald Gilmot nestled amongst them, giving him a knowing glare at which Hogarth curled his lip. At the front, two men stood up from their seats. One was older middle-aged with greying hair and spectacles, and he was holding some papers. The other one was a little younger, with muscles and a beard. They had interviewed the bearded man before, but not the man in glasses. The two men looked around the gathering while they shared a quiet word. Their eyes betrayed a little nervousness. After a moment of conferring, the older man put the papers down, clasped his hands, and started the service with a deep and sonorous voice. He sounded like a priest but he wasn't dressed like one. He was in a cardigan and jeans, but his face looked vicarly enough. The other man, who Hogarth knew as the venue manager, was styled like a hipster from a London coffee bar. He looked like the kind of overgrown kid who owned a skateboard or a BMX. There were plenty of them around these days. Man-boys in their late thirties and early forties. Hogarth wondered if they all still lived at home with their mummies.

"Good afternoon, everybody. Good afternoon, and welcome to this sad, sad occasion, to mark the passing of our treasured friend and deeply valued volunteer, Helen Brimelow."

As the vicarly man got into his groove, his bearded deputy nodded in support of his wise words before shuffling aside to take his seat. Hogarth met his eyes. His brain whirred through his internal Rolodex of witness names. Freddie Halstead. Interviewed twice. No motive. No evidence. Just like all the bloody rest, he thought. But he didn't know anything about the vicar man, hadn't ever seen him before. Perhaps he had been an influence on the girl… no stone unturned, he told himself.

"Coffee?" whispered Palmer. She offered him a cheap porcelain cup she'd filled with coffee, but he waved it away. "The stuff they serve in here is dreadful."

"Then they must have upgraded for the service."

Hogarth remained sceptical until he sipped it. He wondered if they were using Drawton's Incan Gold brand. Actually, it wasn't too bad.

They listened to the talk and watched the crowds as the first of the church songs were played by a man with a guitar at the front; a man in glasses dressed in a lumberjack shirt.

"Have we spoken to the singer? Or the vicar?" said Hogarth.

"No. I've never seen them here before."

"Get names and add them to the list," said Hogarth.

He was clutching at straws and they both knew it.

Hogarth looked around and was modestly impressed. Over half of those in the hall were following the words on the PowerPoint doing their best to sing along, including some well-known miscreants and addicts from around the town. The speeches resumed with tearful tributes made by volunteers and friends and family. A couple of the volunteers seemed to like the spotlight too much. Their tributes turned into stories which put them front and centre. One of them was a shaven-headed lout with dark-circled eyes and a mischievous grin. The way he spoke, it made Hogarth think the events he described had been made up on the spot. Hogarth grimaced.

"He's a bullshitter. Get his name, put him on the list."

Palmer nodded and made a mental note.

Another song. Another tribute. The process carried on for twenty minutes, by which time Hogarth's back was aching. The bearded hipster, Freddie Halstead, was handed the microphone by the vicar. The hipster cleared his throat and looked down at the tiled floor for inspiration. Not far from where Hogarth and Palmer stood, the door to the main room opened, and a young woman walked in, her eyes aimed at the front of the hall. Hogarth noticed that most of the nearby men turned for a look. The newcomer had become one of the prettier girls at the service.

"That one's fashionably late," observed Hogarth.

But Palmer didn't reply. Hogarth saw the look on her face; one of surprise, irritation, and deep concern. It took him a few second to work it all out, by which time Palmer was busy sidestepping through the crowd, making a less than subtle approach. It was Palmer's niece, the girl with the pop star name. She looked like a handful on all counts. And what the hell was she doing here? He knew murder and death held a fascination for some people, but the girl certainly didn't look like a goth. She was far too well presented for that. She was extremely pretty, and he saw there was a definite look of a younger Sue Palmer about the face. Hogarth wondered if Sue had been this pretty when she was young. Probably. Though, as Hogarth knew all too well, the job took everything in the end.

He eyed Freddie Halstead without listening to his brief streetwise sermon. It was a decent talk, but Hogarth had heard it all before. Despite his hipster ways, he reckoned Halstead might make a decent vicar one day. Template, but effective.

"…hell are you doing here…?" said Palmer. "…really not a place for someone like you…"

Palmer's whispered admonishments were loud enough for a few to hear. Even the usual miscreants were looking around to 'shush' someone. Hogarth stepped through the crowd to join Palmer's side.

"This is your niece, I take it," he said.

The girl seemed glad of the excuse to break out of her telling off. She gave Hogarth a smile that could have melted icebergs and launched speedboats, though Hogarth was wise enough to know that a lot of sass and guile was likely hidden beneath. Palmer was blushing and angry but she sighed and made the introduction.

"This is my boss, Detective Inspector Hogarth," said Palmer. "And yes, this is my niece, Aaliyah."

"The niece she can't wait to get rid of," said the girl, rolling her eyes.

"You know that's not true," said Palmer, struggling. "We've just had a disagreement about house rules."

"Shhhhh!" said someone nearby.

"Let's talk in the corridor," said Hogarth. The prospect of meeting a mini Palmer seemed like light relief after the oppressive atmosphere of the service. These days he felt oppressed enough as it was. They walked into the food bank corridor. The girl wore a cheeky smile on her well made-up face whenever she looked at Hogarth. He felt wary when he looked at those eyes. A girl with that much self-confidence was always going to be trouble.

"Aunty Sue is always on about you," said Aaliyah.

"You never call me Aunty Sue!" said Palmer.

"Always on about me? I'll bet," said Hogarth, raising an eyebrow.

"Not like that. She thinks you're good at what you do. In fact, I—"

"Enough, Aaliyah. Enough."

The girl shut her smiling mouth.

"Odd," said Hogarth. "When we're at work, your Aunty Sue usually only tells me what I've been doing wrong."

The girl's eyes changed as if she might well have heard some bad along with the good. Hogarth noticed Palmer looked distinctly uncomfortable.

"I don't know what's got into you, coming down here. Or how you found the place!" said Palmer. "The Refuge food bank is hardly the most glamorous place to spend your time. Least of all on a day like this. Did the station tell you where we were?"

The girl's smile dropped away.

"You forgot, didn't you? You mentioned it last night. You said you were coming. I thought it sounded fascinating, all the odd characters you get around here, all in one place. We don't get anything like that in Rayleigh."

"Rayleigh? That's only a few miles away," said Hogarth.

The girl shrugged. "It's true all the same. You get nothing in Rayleigh except shops and idiots on skateboards mucking about in the car park."

"Sounds like you're not looking hard enough. If it's culture you're after, just ask anyone at Rayleigh nick," said Hogarth.

"Don't listen to DI Hogarth," said Palmer. "He's not allowed near children for this very reason. He's a bad influence."

"I'm not children," said the girl.

"No. But you're still too young to be here," said Palmer.

The girl's eyes lit up. "But it's a public venue, isn't it? The sign by the door said everyone is welcome."

"Everyone who needs food and can't afford to go anywhere else. Whereas you, madam, are well catered for in all respects."

The girl stood firm, giving Palmer the kind of look every teenager has given their elders: eyelids at half mast, cool disdain and disrespect oozing from her gaze. Palmer's cheeks flushed with another wash of anger, but Hogarth could tell

the girl wasn't going to listen no matter how badly Palmer
lost her rag.

"Listen," said Hogarth. "Aunty Sue here is right."

"She doesn't call me Aunty or Aunty Sue. No one does. She
calls me Sue."

Hogarth and the girl smirked at one another.

"Well, Uncle Joe here says if you're determined to stay
around, the rules are as follows. Watch yourself, have your
fun, but don't ever come back. Take a look around, enjoy
your slumming if that's what you're after, then get off
somewhere else quick as you can. I know DS Palmer here is
trying her best to look after you. Hanging around this lot has
never done anyone any favours… and in case you hadn't got
the message, one young girl who worked here was killed."

The girl gave Hogarth a toned-down version of the same
look.

"I know. It made national news, you know."

Hogarth grimaced.

"All the more reason why we can trust you not to come
back. No one comes here for fun – not even them." Hogarth
aimed a thumb at the gathering on the other side of the thick
glass and wooden-framed fire door.

"But these people, they all look so different though, don't
they?" said the girl.

"They're people, Aaliyah," said Palmer. "They're down on
their luck, that's all."

Hogarth and Palmer exchanged a glance. The girl had some
interesting ways about her. Hogarth realised how much of a
job Palmer had on her hands.

"Right. I need to get back in there," said Hogarth. "You
never know when someone might say something they'll
regret."

"Ooh," said the girl. "Are you here hunting for the killer?"

"In this game, we never stop hunting, do we, Sue?"
"When we get the chance," said Palmer. "I should be in there too, Aaliyah. You've had a look around. I think it's time you left before you attract any unwanted attention." Hogarth opened the heavy door and stepped back inside the main hall.

"Aunty's right," said Hogarth, keeping his voice low. "There's no boyfriend material in here."

The girl smirked again and Palmer gave Hogarth a stare not far off the one her niece had given him a few moments before.

"He's funny," said the girl, as the door slowly swung shut. "Funnier than you are, anyway."

Just as Palmer should have expected, the girl followed Hogarth into the main hall, leaving Palmer with a fresh ache settling around her temples. Palmer walked back into the room, her eyes scanning the crowd for anyone with early designs on her niece. A big local heroin addict known to everybody as Suitcase was giving Aaliyah some noticeable side-eye, and nudging his friends. Suitcase was at least thirty years too old for her, but Palmer knew he wouldn't be past trying. Without realising, Palmer was glaring at him. Suitcase caught her look and turned his eyes to the floor. The last of the songs had finished. The older vicar guy was wrapping up the service with some final words, and plenty of heads in the crowd were already turning towards the table of sandwiches being unveiled from their foil coverings at the back.

"You'd be very welcome to stay with us, have a tea and a chat, reminisce about Helen. If you'd like, there will be tea, coffee and sandwiches. Freddie… would you like to add anything? Helen was one of your team, after all."

The vicar-type stood aside and offered the front space to the hipster who looked awkward, like anyone else put on the spot. For a moment, his job seemed much like any other. He'd been dumped in the deep end by his boss and didn't have a clue what to say. Halstead shrugged, put his hands in his pockets and looked around. His eyes passed over the room.

"What can I say?" he began. "What's not already been said? She was such a sweet girl. Lovely. Innocent. In fact, looking back you could say she seemed angelic. She held no fear of working on the front line with us. She held no fear of giving her all, or loving people who had real, tough, hardened exteriors. She was the best of us. You all know what I mean. She loved it here, and she loved every single one of us. Like you, I can't believe she's gone. I miss her."

There were murmurs of agreement. A few nodding heads and some fresh sobbing.

Like a skilled orator, he changed tone and tack.

"But I can tell you one thing I know for sure. I know where she's gone. And I know one day every single one of us here will see her again. Am I right, people?"

A few people called out 'yes' and 'Amen'. Hogarth's eyes roved across the most vocal of them, narrowing his eyes, checking their faces.

The hipster ended the meeting with another piece of erudite public speaking, this time in prayer – before every man and woman in sight rose to their feet and filled the hall with a jostle of movement. Most headed to form a well-schooled queue for the sandwich table.

Hogarth glanced at Palmer, telling her his intent. He wanted a chat with the vicar, or whatever he was called. Hogarth found the niece was watching him, too. Hogarth wondered if he'd become part of her new pet project. He hoped not.

"Reverend... can I have a word?"

The man in the cardigan was fussing with his papers, getting them into order. He looked up at Hogarth with a benign smile.

"Actually, I'm not a reverend, I'm a pastor. But thanks anyway."

"I'm not au fait with the lingo, I'm afraid."

"Not a churchgoer, then?" said the smiley man, who placed two small fists onto his hips. Hogarth looked at him and guessed he was ten years older than himself, tops.

"Weddings, christenings, and funerals, I'm afraid," said Hogarth.

The pastor chuckled. "I see. I take it you're a policeman?"

"Well guessed."

"You look the type. Pardon me for saying so."

"You're pardoned, Pastor...?"

"Eddie Fellows. I don't tend to use a title. It's a little bit off-putting to some people."

"Understood," said Hogarth. "Nice service."

"Not bad, in such awful circumstances," said Fellows. "But I can't take the credit. This project is run by Freddie and the volunteer team here. It's quite an amazing place. I just turn up and watch it all happen. It works almost as if someone else was in charge."

To make his meaning clear, the pastor gazed up at the ceiling.

"Must be nice to have such certainty about things. Good triumphs over evil, and all that. Repent and you'll be forgiven."

"Hope is essential for all of us, Inspector...?"

"Detective Inspector Hogarth."

The pastor nodded. "Hogarth, like the engravings man."
Hogarth shrugged. "So I hear."
The man regarded him for a moment. Hogarth felt he was being analysed.
"You know, Inspector, the scriptures say that without a vision we perish; it's exactly the same for hope. Everyone needs hope in order to survive."
The pastor's eyes flickered at Hogarth, as if he'd something of the darkness in him. Hogarth narrowed his eyes to close the curtains on the windows of his soul. He added a smile for effect.
"I admit, I've been a bit sceptical of the place. But seeing some of these bad boys and bad girls acting like they've got some manners can't be a bad thing."
"No. It's not."
"But you must know one of this lot could have killed Helen Brimelow. One of them in here now, praying, singing, shaking hands with people, waiting for their sandwiches."
"You haven't found anyone yet, have you?" said the pastor.
"These things can take longer than we'd like. But I guarantee you, we'll find 'em in the end. We always do."
The pastor nodded. "Will you need to question me?"
"Did you have many dealings with Helen?"
"A few. I was impressed by her. She attended our house group a few times. Of course, my wife and a few others were always present."
Hogarth took a moment to make an assessment before he said, "We'll talk again, Pastor. But not today. I'm here to look and listen."
"Not a problem," replied the pastor. "I think I'd better go and help serve the sandwiches. I'll make myself available whenever you like."
"Much obliged," said Hogarth.

The pastor moved into the crowd. Hogarth felt several sets of eyes on him. He made a rapid recce of the hall and saw Gerald Gilmot, Suitcase, David Brimelow and Palmer's niece watching him. Hogarth narrowed his eyes and jutted his jaw in contemplation. He'd seen a lot of sorrow in the food bank hall. Felt a lot of it, too. It felt raw and genuine. The truth was it had moved him. It gave him extra motivation to solve the case, as if he needed any. But as much as he felt the grief in the air, Hogarth also believed one of the fifty or so people in the hall knew something they hadn't let on. Someone must have seen the girl with Drawton. And if not Drawton, then who?

"Any progress?" said a flat, nasal voice. Hogarth turned to see a drawn-looking David Brimelow eyeing him as he approached. The man seemed to be trying to divine an answer from Hogarth's face even before he spoke. What he saw there made the man slow up and shake his head.

"Afraid not. But I assure you, David, we're working flat out on this. It's my sole focus at present."

David Brimelow. The man was known to him through the Naval Club. The drinking establishment Hogarth used rather than the local pubs, places where half the town's residents thought of him as scum, or the filth. He'd seen and felt plenty of genuine hatred over the years. One of the many joys of being a police officer. The Naval offered him the chance of drinking a malt in peace. He did go to a few pubs, but never for long. He rarely overstayed his welcome. David had been a member of the Naval before him and had smoothed out his membership when he had first arrived in town, after his transfer from the Met. Because of such help, for a time David had been the closest he'd had to a friend outside of work. They had never been genuine friends, of course. More drinking acquaintances but after the death of Helen, the man's world had spun off its axis, and Hogarth's role in his life had been revised to that of trusted friend. It was manipulation. Subtle, but effective, and Hogarth couldn't help that his pity for the man's loss had made him susceptible.

"I trust you, Joe," said Brimelow. He slapped a hand on Hogarth's shoulder. Hogarth's mouth formed a downturned line. For a moment, he wondered if that hand belonged to a killer. He dismissed the thought quickly, in case the man saw it on his face, but David was quickly surrounded by people wanting to pass on their condolences. When Brimelow moved on, Hogarth did, too. The visit had been largely fruitless. He'd learned little more than what he already knew. But at least he'd made one more contact. He eyed the pastor as he handed out a sandwich on a plate. Hope? Hogarth's hopes were getting slimmer by the day. But the sliver he had left still kept him working. For now, it was enough. He looked for Palmer and found her with an annoyed look on her face. He followed her eyes to find the niece weaving through the scrum near the sandwich table. The serving volunteers were looking at her, along with Freddie Halstead, Pastor Fellows and one of the volunteers. Hogarth reckoned she was interested in more than the sandwiches. The big sweaty man called Suitcase made a space for her to push into the queue beside him.

"'Ere you go, doll. You get in here with me. I'll protect you from the fuzz."

The big man known as Suitcase laughed out loud at his own joke. When he saw Hogarth and Palmer scowling at him, he laughed all the more.

"Egg and mayo, please," said Aaliyah. Freddie Halstead handed her a plate with a polite smile, and the pastor made a joke. Palmer wasn't laughing. Hogarth slapped her on the shoulder and she turned to face him.

"She'll soon have enough of the place when the smelly ones start cracking on to her," he said. As if to prove his point, for want of a napkin, one of the scruffy guests was wiping his buttery hands on the wall. Hogarth curled his lip. He watched Palmer march across the hall to begin prising her niece away from all the attention.

Palmer broke through the food queue. There were theatrical tuts and complaints from the back, but she'd heard it all before. Even without the town's new killer, she knew paedophiles and those who preyed on young girls were frequent flyers in the food bank – she even recognised one or two among the crowd. There was no way she could leave Aaliyah alone there, no matter the good intentions of the church that ran it. Palmer was offered a sandwich by the pastor but turned it down with a curt shake of the head.

"How about a prayer?" said a kindly faced old man standing beside him. Palmer ignored him. She wasn't in the mood for being polite and she was still a few feet away from her niece, who was busy talking not just to hipster Halstead, but the young man beside him. Both men had stopped serving sandwiches to engage in the conversation. Palmer had seen Halstead plenty of times, spoken to him too, but she had never seen the young man before. He looked odd, and she couldn't tell his age. Palmer decided he looked a little severe, which was odd for a volunteer. Definitely not quite right for a place like this.

"Excuse me," said Palmer, cutting past two *fragrant* customers.

"…I didn't think you looked old enough." They were her niece's words, followed by a chuckle from Halstead and his young companion.

"What do you mean?" said Halstead.

"To have a son his age," said Aaliyah.

"I'm not," said Halstead, raising an eyebrow. "This one is my brother. But I still feel like his dad some days, don't I, Ollie?"

Halstead attempted to ruffle the younger man's hair. Unsmiling, the younger man swatted his brother's hand aside. Palmer looked at them. There was a family resemblance, but it was fractional and mostly hidden by Halstead's beard.

Aaliyah was still laughing with embarrassment as Palmer reached her side.

"Come on, Aaliyah, we really need to go."

"Aaliyah? That's your name?" said Halstead. "Like the singer, right?"

Palmer and her niece took on the same look of surprise.

"Yeah," said the girl. "Not many people remember her."

"I remember. She must have died around the time you were born."

"A bit before that, actually."

"You're a young one, then," said Halstead. "Sounds like your mum likes good music."

"Once, maybe," said the girl. "My mum doesn't have a clue about anything these days."

"That's what Ollie here says about me – there's only ten years between us," said Halstead.

The young man tried to laugh, but it rang false. He didn't seem happy.

"You really are brothers then?" asked Aaliyah.

Halstead nodded.

"Not much resemblance," said the girl.

"Beards and Brylcreem can do that to people," said the brother. His tone was acidic and he still didn't meet their eyes.

"I was thinking of height, as well," said Aaliyah, looking between them. The young man looked up, with a scowl.

"She's teasing you, Ollie," said Halstead.

"Sorry about my niece's manners," said Palmer.

"Sorry about my brother's," said Halstead.

Palmer offered a half-smile. Despite his fashions – and his church associations – Halstead seemed okay. "Come on now, Ali. We've got to go. I can't leave you here."

"Niece?" said Halstead, looking between Palmer and Aaliyah. "Now you mention it, I can see the family likeness. Both got the same pretty face. Though I don't know if I'm permitted to say that to a police officer."

One of the bigger men in the queue, Suitcase, piped up. "Don't get excited, officer. Freddie here is only buttering you up so you'll let him off his parking tickets." Suitcase roared with exaggerated laughter at his own lame joke and winked at as many people as would meet his eye. Palmer frowned and shook her head.

"Come on."

Aaliyah tutted and rolled her eyes and Halstead made a show of laughing before he returned to handing out plates of sandwiches to the hungry crowd. Palmer edged away and her niece followed. A few muted wolf whistles trailed in her wake.

"See what I mean?" said Palmer. "This isn't the place for you. If you want something to do while I'm at work, you could look after the flat, or apply for a job or—"
"*Or* I could volunteer in here. I mean, why not? Look at the place. They must need people. It's heaving in here."
Palmer didn't say a word. She let her eyes do the talking.
"And," said Aaliyah, "they're one down, aren't they?"
"That's not even funny. No. Look for a job or a college course. The last thing you want is to spend time in a place like this. I'm serious. A place like this can drag you down."
But the look on Aaliyah's face said she wasn't listening. Evidently, she was enjoying the attention she was getting as much as Palmer abhorred it. Palmer opened the door to the outer corridor and yanked her niece by the arm.
"You're such a stiff sometimes, Sue," said the girl, but she followed anyway. Back at the food queue, a couple of the men were already making crude jokes. Behind the counter, Freddie Halstead and his brother served sandwiches as fast as the mostly male clientele could take them. Ollie Halstead handed out every full plate as quick as he could and refused to meet any eye. His older brother offered each customer a smile and a word of encouragement. Freddie Halstead's eyes tracked to the door, and through the netted glass he saw the two women, aunt and niece, still talking in the hallway. The pastor laid a supportive hand on his shoulder and drew his eye.
"Quite a day," said Fellows.
"Too right," said Halstead, his eyes tracking back to the door. Beside him, his younger brother was looking in the same direction.

Four

Early evening.

It was a cold grey evening in Westcliff, but inside their flat, the coffee smelt good and Freddie's simple food was shaping up to look delicious. The old-school Roberts red digital radio blared from the top of the fridge freezer. Freddie Halstead tapped his booted toe to the beat and mumbled along with the singer. Freddie sawed through the second bagel and laid it beside the first. He opened the soft bread, humming as he spread a thick helping of cream cheese on one side and then laid a thick slice of pink smoked salmon on the other. He repeated the process with the second bagel, applying the same care he used when combing his hair and waxing his beard. When the bagels were perfect, Halstead opened a bag of cheesy Kettle chips, split them between the plates, then poured the orange juice and coffee. The measures were identical and so neat that the meal might have looked good enough for an Instagram post. But that wasn't the point. Halstead had never bothered with Insta. He was already too old for that game. He strived for perfection because it was in his genes... because Ollie was fussier than he was. They had eaten leftover sandwiches for lunch at the memorial service, and now it was bagels for tea, but Halstead didn't care, so long as Ollie ate something without one of his man tantrums. They weren't just unpleasant. They were almost scary. Halstead laid out the meal in a neat line along the breakfast bar, complete with evenly spaced cutlery. The flat the brothers shared wasn't big enough for a dining table, but the breakfast bar suited them well. Ollie had never been one for face-to-face interaction. Ollie was better at talking, but still not to any great degree. The side-by-side eating arrangement was just fine. With the meal prepared, all Freddie needed was for Ollie to come and enjoy it. Freddie made every meal. If he didn't do it no one else would. Certainly not Ollie. Freddie used the back of his hand to wipe away the sweat from his brow, then peeled off his apron and laid it on the worktop.

"Ollie! Dinner time, pal."

Freddie rinsed the coffee pot while he waited for his brother to arrive. By the time the pot had been thoroughly cleaned, his brother was still nowhere to be seen. Halstead frowned. He turned down the volume on the radio. The flat was dead quiet. Why couldn't he hear the PlayStation? He strained his ears and somewhere he heard the faint sound of a cat meowing. Then a hiss. Bloody cats. Freddie glanced at the open sash window opposite the breakfast bar. He moved across to shut it. The cats were a nuisance around here. Always making such a racket.

"Ollie! Come on, bro. I've made smoked salmon and cream cheese bagels. Your favourite."

He was wasting his breath. He frowned and spent a few seconds arranging the angle of the coffee mug handles before he left in search of his brother. They lived in a two-bed flat. The box room was just big enough for a single bed and a small chest of drawers. This was Ollie's room, of course. From the outside, people might have thought giving him the small room was unfair, but Freddie worked full time and he paid the rent. Most of Ollie's benefits went towards his games habit. Freddie was happy with his side of the deal.

It was hard to say whether Ollie was happy or not with his, because he rarely smiled, but he never complained. The best barometers of his mood were his behaviour, his closedness, his tantrums. His mother, before she gave up on them, used to say that Ollie had a condition. That he was on some spectrum or other. But she had never pursued it. She had said she didn't like labels, but Freddie knew better now. The woman was just plain lazy. It was easier to do nothing and suffer for it. Labelled or not, Ollie still had a serious problem, and without the label, he had never received any help until his brother had got stuck in and made some calls. Once he moved in, life got better for Ollie. But Freddie wasn't certain if his life had.

Freddie knocked on his brother's bedroom door. "Ollie?" he said. There was no reply. Freddie waited a moment to be sure, then plunged the handle. He stepped inside and found the bedroom empty. As ever, it was dark, cramped, and stuffy. Lately, the room didn't smell very good, either. But Freddie didn't have the heart to complain. They had an awkward enough relationship as it was. Freddie closed the door and checked in the front room. The living room was empty too. Ollie's PlayStation had been left on, the game paused, with a loud humming noise coming from the big TV. Halstead tutted, picked up the remote control and switched it off.

"Where the hell are you, Ollie?" he muttered.

A loud mewl came from an open window. The bloody cats were at it again. They were always fighting, or having it off, or doing both at once, and they were loud either way. Perhaps Ollie had gone down to shoo them away. It was a theory, but Freddie didn't quite believe it. It was just after five pm and already getting dark. Ollie was a creature of habit; if they didn't sit down to eat soon, it wasn't going to happen. But dinner was important. The therapist had said that. Routine was essential. Ollie had to be there. Freddie walked to the window. He intended to close the windows, draw the blinds and search elsewhere, but the sound of the cats had disturbed him. They sounded as if they were in pain. He was about to close the window but instead looked down into the garden. There he saw Ollie, swathed in a wash of light. From two floors up, Freddie peered down on the communal garden of the vast old house which had probably once been a school or a boarding house. The house had been carved into flats long ago. And as places went, they occupied a nicer part of Westcliff. Desirable, even. Which was just one more reason why Freddie Halstead was so appalled by what he saw. It took him a moment to be sure of what he was seeing. His heart started to beat harder, his eyes widened. He knew. Maybe he'd known for longer than he cared to admit. Downstairs, Ollie was kneeling on the soil of a border beneath the overgrown trees that lined the large garden. The young man was holding a skeletal looking tortoiseshell cat by the length of its tail like a racket handle. The cat clearly wanted to get away. It struggled and mewled and hissed, frightened for its life. Its eyes were huge and bright; its back arched high. Its front legs clawed at the soil. Freddie's mouth dropped open as he watched Ollie lower a smoking cigarette closer to the fur of the animal's back, slowly and ever closer until Freddie had no remaining doubt. The poor cat hissed in anticipation of the pain it was about to endure.

"Ollie!" roared Freddie. But Ollie didn't let go and he didn't look up. Freddie slapped his hands to his head, turned, and ran for the door of the flat. He didn't want anyone to see, anyone to know... didn't want to even comprehend what he had seen. He heard the screech and yowl from the open window even as he ran down the stairs. He didn't stop running. He opened the heavy front door of the building, flung it wide, and turned left towards the back garden. There he was – Ollie, sitting in the same crouch he had seen him from twenty feet above. Sitting in a crouch by the muddy border, with a smug yet serene look on his face. Ollie smoked his cigarette and breathed deep, letting a long plume of pale smoke billow up into the air. The cat was gone, no doubt running for its life, coping with its pain. Ollie's face showed nothing. No guilt. No shame. No horror. Just peace, and maybe something more. Satisfaction. Freddie swallowed and looked back at the large old house. The ground floor flats were silent, their windows dark. The curtains drawn or the rooms empty. Next, he looked up at the floors above. The higher floors were safe too. Except one. Up at the very top, the single window of the attic flat was open, and the girl with the bright red dreadlocks had her head stuck out of the window, smoking. She looked down at them both, impassive, breathing out smoke. It was impossible to say how long she had been there, or what she had seen. "Hiya," she called. Her voice was jovial, which was a relief. "Hi," replied Freddie, sounding awkward, nervous. He'd thought of asking the girl for a date once, but decided she was too close to home. Now he knew he would never ask at all. She was another 'what if' destroyed by the puzzle of his brother. Halstead and the girl looked at one another for a long moment, before she smiled and withdrew. Ollie remained crouching by the border. He smoked on as if nothing had happened.

"Bloody hell, Ollie, what the hell are you doing?" hissed Freddie.

"Hell?" he said. "You use a lot of bad words for a Christian, Freddie."

"Don't you think I'm entitled?" said Freddie, wiping his face as he shook his head. He took a moment and offered his brother a hand. He left it there until Ollie took it, then he helped Ollie to his feet, laid both hands on his shoulders, gripped hard and looked him in the eye.

"You *can't* do things like that, Ollie. Not ever. You hear me?"

"Why not?"

"You *know* why," said Freddie. "It's not right."

"Isn't it?"

"You know it isn't."

"Because the Good Book says so?" he said, looking away, his voice like a sneer.

"Because it's not right."

"As if we're fit to judge anything."

Ollie was already drifting away. Freddie slapped him on the back, firmly but brotherly and drew him back towards their flat. The rebuke had been given. If they were to remain on speaking terms, that would have to suffice. From now on, he would have to watch his brother closely. More closely than ever.

"I made you bagels, Ollie. Your favourite."

But Ollie didn't say anything at all.

Five

Hogarth crumpled in an unseemly heap on top of Andi Bromley and kissed her neck. She sighed and chuckled before forcing him aside by reaching for her mobile phone from the bedside cabinet. Hogarth tried to ignore it. Andi was forty years old, but as coppers went, she wasn't exactly a serious person. She acted a lot like 'the young people'. For one, she was a phone junkie. Hogarth tried to overlook her phone habits as best he could, but it bothered him all the same. He felt the woman looking at her bright phone screen across his shoulder before she dumped it back on the cabinet. But, she was always warm as toast, her body smooth and soft to the touch, and curvy in all the right places. For the most part, she was just what the doctor ordered. But he knew he still wasn't going to sleep tonight. He wondered if he had satisfied her. Not good, especially if it was true. Eventually, it would be all around Barking nick that he was a duff shag. Not a good look. But when he strained his eyes he saw her rosy cheeks and sleepy eyes and knew he'd done okay. She looked back at him, smiling, and they kissed.
"Now you're calling me round at the drop of a hat – what's a girl supposed to think about that?" she said.
"I don't know?" he said. "You should probably be flattered. I don't chase many people."
"So you chase me, do you?"
"So long as it's fun."
The woman made a joke of slapping his cheek.

"I might have said no, you know. I'm a busy girl. Just because you're a DI doesn't mean you outrank me everywhere."

"I never said it did." Hogarth slid away. He sat on the edge of the bed, the duvet draped over his knees. He looked at the moon through the gap in his net curtains. Behind him, Andi began to stroke his back. Hogarth didn't move, didn't flinch, didn't bat an eye.

"A girl might think," said Andi. "That you were getting more serious."

"Serious?" said Hogarth. He took a half look back over his shoulder, to find Andi leaning on her elbow. His eyes fell to her bosom then rose back to her eyes. They shone at him, reflecting the moonlight and the street lamps outside.

"Yeah. That's twice in two days, now. Four nights in the last six. It's getting a bit more than casual, isn't it?"

"Is it?" said Hogarth.

Her hand stopped stroking for a moment, and then it started up again.

"I think so," said Andi.

"And? What would you think of that?"

"Nothing yet. I was just thinking, that's all. Whether we should let things develop. Whether I should let us get more serious, or just nip it in the bud."

"Well?" said Hogarth.

"I think we'll wait and see, shall we?"

Hogarth grinned and looked back. "Always a good policy," he said.

"You think I'm girlfriend material, then?"

"We're in our forties, Andi."

"Only just, in my case," she said.

"What's the right answer supposed to be?" said Hogarth.

"If you can't figure that out, there's no hope for you."

Hogarth grinned.

"Will you want me around tomorrow night?" she said. "If so, I might as well start leaving a few things here. For convenience."

Hogarth's eyes hardened by a degree. He hoped the lack of light would hide it from her and kept his smile firmly in place.

"Let's just see what tomorrow brings. He leaned back, kissed her, and felt an added passion from Andi's lips. An added pressure, too. He patted her hip and slid away.

"I fancy a nightcap. How about you?"

"No thanks. I've just had one," she chuckled. "I need some sleep."

"Fine. I'll join you in a bit."

Hogarth grabbed his dressing gown from the chair and threw it over his goose-pimpled white body. He belted it and picked up the empty tumbler from by the door. There was the merest hint of malt left at the bottom from his last pre-bed drink. In the living room, he grabbed the Dalwhinnie. He was down to a half bottle. He shrugged and poured a small measure, then made it a larger one. He dropped himself into the armchair, sipped the fiery warmth and sucked his teeth. It was dark. His mind wandered, his eyes staring into space. He thought of the memorial flipchart stand with the girl's photograph and the tied-on bouquet of flowers. He fell into a grim reverie and was grateful to be snapped out of it as his phone vibrated on the coffee table at his side.

"Who the hell—?"

Hogarth picked up the phone and saw the answer on the screen. It was David. David Brimelow. He'd saved the man's

number to his phone nearly three years back. Hogarth frowned and rolled the phone in his hand for a moment. He answered it because he knew any other option would only sabotage another night's sleep. He put the phone to his ear and set the whisky down.
"David? What's up?"
He heard the heavy breathing before anything else. Hogarth narrowed his eyes and stiffened in his chair.
"David?"
"I…I…" the man was stuttering and incoherent.
"David, you're worrying me now. What's the matter?"
"They killed her, Joe. The bastard butchered her, and I can't accept it. Can't handle it. My sweet, sweet girl…"
"I know, David. I know. And I promise you I'm doing everything I can, but you being up this late, doing whatever you're doing, drinking whatever you're drinking, it's not good for you…" Hogarth caught a glimpse of his own hollow-eyed reflection in the mirror above the fireplace. He was a fine one to talk.
"I know… But the trouble is…without her… I've got absolutely nothing. No future. No hope. No reason to live…"
"David… you haven't done anything silly… have you?"
The man's heavy breathing returned to the line. Heavy breathing but no answer.
"David?!"
"I really need to see you, Joe. I need to see another human being who understands how shit this is. I need to speak to someone *right now.*"
"Yes, and you're talking to me now."
Hogarth heard the gentle footfall descending the stairs in the hallway. Andi appeared in the doorway, draped in one of his

work shirts, a blanket draped like a cape around her shoulders.

"What's going on?" she whispered. Hogarth lifted a finger, telling her to wait.

"A phone call isn't enough, Joe. I need to see someone face to face."

"Now?"

"Uh... yeah... Now."

Damn...

Hogarth ground his teeth and his nostrils flared. "Fine," he said curtly. "I'm on my way. But you'd bloody better not have done anything stupid, David. I mean that."

"Yeah... I... I hear you."

"See you soon, then." Hogarth thumbed the end-call button even as David Brimelow mumbled into the mouthpiece. It was the only complaint the situation would allow.

In the doorway, Andi Bromley folded her arms. He looked at her face, her shapely figure. As girlfriends went, she wouldn't have made a bad choice. She had a tough exterior. She was hard faced at times. But when she smiled, she was a different girl. She was mostly fine, apart from that damned mobile phone of hers. Andi shook her head at him.

"You're going out again? Now?"

Hogarth scratched his eyebrow.

"This isn't like last night, Andi. It's the victim's father. He wants to see me."

"You what? He's got your number?! You're bloody mad, you are? A CID detective handing out his personal number to victims? Next you'll be telling me you give your home address to the criminals."

The worst ones already know it, he thought.

"David had my number from before his daughter's murder. It's unfortunate, but there's nothing I can do about it."
"Call him back and tell him you have to draw a line. This is how coppers like you end up burnt out."
"You think that's humane, do you?" he said.
"I call it self-preservation, Joe. What about you?!"
There was a moment's silence as he stood up.
"I know you burnt out once before... didn't you?"
"What's that supposed to mean?" said Hogarth."
He watched as Andi tensed in the living room doorway.
"Nothing. It was just something I heard, that was all."
"Well, now you can get all your gossip direct from the horse's mouth."
"Joe... I was interested in you, that's all. You should be flattered."
Hogarth frowned and put a hand to his forehead.
"Good to hear personal news still reaches far and wide."
"It was about a case. Something involving the MP's wife... You got too close to her. Something like that."
"And she's dead, too, Andi. The woman's dead and this has nothing to do with her."
There was the briefest silence before she spoke again.
"Even so, you shouldn't bring your work home with you. Not ever. A cop has to have boundaries. It's a survival thing."
"Sound advice. Shame I've never been able to take it."
"Joe... you're the one who wanted me here, remember?"
Hogarth looked her in the eye. He nodded.
"Then call him. Tell him to wait until tomorrow."
"I saw his daughter's body, Andi. The killer butchered her for fun. David's a broken man. If I don't go..." Hogarth sighed. "Look, I've got no choice."

Glum faced, Andi stood aside from the doorway, making room to let him pass.

He stopped and planted a kiss on her cheek. Her only response was a brief look. Hogarth nodded, accepting her bad mood as his penance. He pulled a few clothes together as fast as he could and drained his whisky. When he opened the front door, Andi's voice called his attention. "This isn't healthy, Joe. None of it."

"That's the thing about murder, Andi. It's bad for your health." As soon as he closed the door he regretted the comment. It sounded snarky and crass. If he couldn't hold his tongue for a woman like Andi, no wonder he'd been a bachelor for so long. "You're getting the life you deserve, Joe," he muttered to himself as he walked towards his car. Upstairs in the bedroom, Andi Bromley looked out through the net curtains. She turned away. Shaking her head, her eyes trailed back towards her police uniform hanging from a wardrobe door.

Hogarth parked beneath the looming black tower blocks of the Queensway Estate. There, at the centre of three tower blocks, raised on a one-storey platform above a set of empty garages, was the low black box of the Refuge food bank. It was empty and silent, but the sombre mood of the memorial service lingered – in his mind, at least. He'd driven across town, over the limit, but reasonably confident no one would stop him. The night shift cars would be waiting at the town centre hotspots, and the fringes of the fastest roads to catch their prey. He was safe enough. He parked on Coleman Street, just beyond the high fences of the estate. Coleman Street had an odd layout. Before the estate was built, maybe it had been a street with two sides, like all the others. These days the street was made up of one parade of terraced housing with the tower block estate on the other side. Helen Brimelow's family lived in one of the terraced houses. The walk to her volunteering post at the Refuge had been a short one. But he couldn't help wonder how it started. From the little he knew, most of the house owners had no love for the tower blocks and even less for the food bank. He had never asked David his opinion about the Refuge and now wasn't the time. He had only one objective. To make sure David was safe and well enough to survive until the next morning. Hogarth knocked on the door of number twelve and waited, his eyes roving the tower blocks across the street as his ears tuned in to a myriad of different sounds which could have meant trouble. Behind him, the front door popped and the door swung inwards, but not fully open. Hogarth listened to the soft trudge of Brimelow's footsteps as he traipsed away down the hall. Hogarth walked in and closed the door behind him. The house was stuffy, smelly, and heavy with grief. Hogarth trailed past the dimly lit front room, finding the light brightest in the back dining room. He stopped as soon as he entered, seeing the dated dark wood dining table in the middle of the room with a bright pendant lampshade hanging over the middle. On the table was an iPad, a couple of worn-looking family photo albums, a few leather-bound school achievement files, and a mostly empty bottle of Co-op blended Scotch whisky. Hogarth wrinkled his nose at the stuff before he went into the room. David Brimelow sat at the head of the table, his face ashen and white, his back close to the garden door. He looked up at Hogarth and offered a pathetic smile. "Welcome to a feast of memories, Joe. Don't worry. I won't put you through the photographs. I just wanted some company for dessert."

"From the look of that bottle, you need bed more than company."

"Truth is I could do with a little of both. A woman to ease the burden for a time, if you know what I mean?"

Hogarth knew exactly what he meant. Brimelow was describing the situation Hogarth had just been taken from.

"But I'm not as much of a catch as I was. And now, what am I? Nothing but a failure in all respects. I couldn't even protect my own daughter from them. I should never have let her work over at that damned place!"

Hogarth took a seat at the side of the table and planted himself beside the iPad. The device had been in recent use – the screen was still open, set to a gallery of thumbnail images, most of them of Brimelow, his young daughter and his estranged wife.

Seeing his ex-wife was jarring. "Is Esther coming to see you?"

"Esther? She blames me as much as I blame myself. Which is just another reason for her to stay away. It's the excuse she'll use, at any rate."

"How can she blame you?"

"Because she died on my watch!" he snapped. "I was her dad. She was in my care, and I let it happen."

"David, you didn't let anything happen. Whoever took her life never gave anyone the chance."

"But I could have stopped her—"

"Could you?" said Hogarth. "Could you really? She wasn't a child anymore. Okay. Maybe she was still at school, but when they get to that age, who really has a say? You're lucky that she was a good kid. She still loved you. She could have been doing a lot worse than—"

"Than getting herself known by the town's worst criminals?"
"I was there at the memorial service, David. I never even knew she had done such good work. I liked her before, but now I admire her."
"Well, fantastic then. I'll have that engraved on her headstone. That'll make everyone feel so much better."
Hogarth narrowed his eyes. The man blushed and shook his head.
"I'm sorry, Joe. Sorry to have dragged you over here like this."
Hogarth puckered his lips and picked up the whisky bottle.
"How much have you had?"
"Most of it," he said.
"Anything else?"
"Yes," he replied, breaking into a grin. "Some peanuts, and a cheese and onion pasty."
"The old health kick still going strong, I see," said Hogarth.
Brimelow burst out laughing, but the noise was strained and ugly. Hogarth winced inside. The man seemed to sense Hogarth's response and the smile fell from his face.
"I can't go on like this," said David. "Not like this. How am I supposed to live? I have no purpose now. She was it. They took her. They smashed my life to bits! They took whatever future I had left. It's gone."
Hogarth believed him, but couldn't say so.
"Almost all things heal in time, David," he was forced to say.
"I don't want to heal!" he roared, smashing his fist against the table. "I shouldn't ever get over this. She was everything! I want them found, and I want them dead! Dead!"
"David, you're hurting and you're drunk."
"And I'll still be hurting in the morning. Churchill and Nancy Astor, wasn't it?"

Hogarth had no idea what the man was talking about. He shook his head.

"What are you planning to do, David?"

There was a moment's pause before Brimelow lifted his hands. "Look at me. Just look," he said. "I'm five foot seven of string, bone and sinew. I'm in my middle fifties and out of shape. What can I do? If I found them, I like to think I'd kill them stone dead but the truth is—"

"I'm asking you what you *want* to do."

"I want the killer dead. But if I can't have them killed, the least I want is them locked away for the rest of their lives."

Hogarth gave a curt nod. "And my job is to find them. That's all I can do."

"Then do it, for God's sake. *Do it!* Do your job and find them! I'm in hell here. I see your glum old face, I hear you *say* that you're working flat out, but we're two weeks on and there's still no result. Who knows how many girls this bastard has taken?! Please don't let him destroy another family! Please don't!"

"I promise you, I am doing all I can. I mean it. I only stop to sleep. That's all. I live and breathe this case."

"Not like I do, Joe. Not like me."

Hogarth's mouth narrowed.

"I'll find them."

"Just do it," said the man, his voice revealing his contempt and disgust.

Hogarth stood up from the table. He was about to walk around to lay a hand on his friend's shoulder, to tell him to go to bed, to enforce it if necessary. But as he moved, he caught sight of the small white plastic bottles lined up on the sill of the garden window. They were just visible behind the curtains. Hogarth changed course and walked to the window. He pulled the chintzy old curtains aside and saw three bottles, all matching. He picked up one bottle and shook it before he read the label. It was full. The label was old, peeling at the corners. The chemist's printing was fading, but the name and dosage were still clear enough. Mrs E Brimelow. Co-codamol. 30mg of codeine. Hogarth placed the bottle down beside the others and shook the other two in turn. Each was still full.

"Clearing out the medicine cabinet, David?" said Hogarth.

"Something like that," replied David.

"These belonged to your wife."

"She never once needed an excuse for a migraine, my Esther," said David. "She left those behind when she walked out. It's nothing, honestly."

Hogarth scratched his brow. "No, it's something, David. You got me round here to bollock me for not finding the killer. To stick some extra petrol in my engine, right? Then what? Exit stage left. David Brimelow finishes himself off with cheap whisky and super-strength painkillers?"

"I could think of worse ways to go," said David, with a faint sneer.

"So could I. But you're better than this."

Hogarth scooped up the trio of bottles in one hand and started to head for the door.

"Wait! What are you doing? Where are you going?"

"To do you a favour."

David Brimelow leapt up from his seat and knocked a photograph album to the floor. Some snapshots of a newborn baby swaddled in pink and white slipped out. Both men looked down and saw the photographs on the carpet.

Hogarth met the man's eyes and stormed out of the room. Brimelow gave chase. By the time he caught Hogarth, he was already inside the tiny downstairs toilet, one bottle open, lid in hand, a stream of white tablets cascading into the toilet bowl, sinking to the bottom.

"No, those are mine!" said Brimelow, dragging Hogarth back by the shoulder. Hogarth swatted his hand away.

"Strictly speaking, that's not true," he said, opening the second bottle. "We could always phone Esther to ask her permission. I'm sure she'd be pleased to hear that you're playing the role she cast for you. The kind of man who gives up at the first hurdle."

Hogarth emptied the second bottle into the toilet and tossed the empty plastic down to the floor.

"You bastard!" snarled Brimelow, teeth bared, tears streaming. He thumped Hogarth in the kidneys with a stiff but survivable punch, Hogarth grunted and opened the last bottle. He emptied it into the toilet then turned to face his man. He seized Brimelow's fist as he tried to deliver another blow, then looked him in the eye.

"That's it, David. Looks like you've rediscovered your mojo. If I were you I'd save it to get through what's next."

"Next? What *is* next?" said Brimelow, the fight leaving him like wind leaving a ship's sail. His shoulders turned slack, his eyes dead.

"Letting me find the man who killed your daughter. And after we've found him, your big day in court. You want that, don't you? The killer damned for all to see, called out for what he's done, shamed and sent down for life."

"Of course I want to see that," said Brimelow, his voice no more than a whisper.

"Good. So start acting like it."

Hogarth pushed the flush button on the top of the cistern and the water and a hundred or so tablets were swished away.

"They were my way out," said Brimelow.

"No one gets a way out of this. Not you, not me. Especially not the killer. Remember that, David. I give you my word. You already had it, but here it is again. I'll find him, and when I do I want you there to see it."

Brimelow nodded. His eyes looked as sober as Hogarth had seen them since he arrived.

"Thank you, Joe," he said meekly.

"Don't thank me. But friendly advice – that's the last free hit you'll ever have on me. Next time you want to give me a talking to, save it until the morning, okay?"

"Sorry. I thought we were friends."

"We are. When you're sober, you'll probably remember how friends treat one another. Finish the bottle if you need to, then get yourself to bed. You want justice, I'll help you get it. But only if you're alive to see it."

Brimelow nodded. Hogarth slipped past him and stopped at the dining room.

"And, David. Next time you intend to kill yourself with whisky, at least do it with some style. Co-op blended? That's no way to go. A good peaty single malt, maybe."

Brimelow was wide eyed and meek. He took Hogarth's anger without comment, which made him feel ashamed for losing his temper with the man. Hogarth dragged a hand through his hair and walked to the door.

"I'll call you tomorrow, just to check in," said Hogarth.

Brimelow stayed back in the narrow hallway, staring after him.

"But not until late on," he added. "Something tells me you'll be needing a lie in."

Hogarth closed the door and made his way back to his car. The encounter had sobered him up, more than he liked, but a hangover was still on the cards.

By the time he got home, Andi was fast asleep and unmoving on the edge of the bed. She seemed far away. Slipping between the sheets, Hogarth had the distinct impression that reaching out to touch was strictly verboten.

"Sorry, Andi," he whispered. "But I was right. He was going to top himself."

On the other side of the bed, Andi Bromley said nothing. But her eyes were bright. She blinked a few times and forced herself to close her eyes. Hogarth was too wired for sleep, but it was too late for whisky. Whether he liked it or not, he needed to close his eyes until morning.

Six

When he arrived at the police station next morning, Hogarth wasn't in the best of moods. Andi had left early. Not a good sign. He had heard her movements, but as sleep had come so late Hogarth could hardly bear to open his eyes. So instead he'd waited for Andi to come and say goodbye, to plant a farewell kiss as his wake up call, but the kiss never came. Instead, he had heard her thumping down the steps before the front door finally slammed. When he opened his eyes, she was gone without a word, not even a note. At the very least, the woman was pissed off. But there was a very good chance things were a lot worse than that. Thanks a bunch, David.

As soon as he arrived at the station, he went to the canteen for a coffee. The stuff they served wasn't good, but it was better than the hot black vomit the vending machine served. He took the coffee into the office to find Palmer waiting for him. From the once-over she gave him, he saw she had been expecting him to be the worse for wear. From the look on her face, he knew he hadn't disappointed her. He felt rough. Now he knew he looked the part too.

"Yes, I had a late night," said Hogarth.

"I didn't say a word," said Palmer.

"I saw you looking. This time it was courtesy of David Brimelow."

Now he had Palmer's attention. She looked up at him. "Oh?"

"He stretched the notion of friendship a little far and demanded a late-night tête-á-tête."

"And you agreed?" said Palmer, shaking her head.
"Now you sound like Andi."
"She was with you last night…?"
Hogarth didn't reply.
Palmer stiffened in her seat, gaining an insight from Hogarth's awkwardness "I doubt I'd have been pleased, either. What happened?"
"David put on a little show for me. He was about to top himself with whisky and co-codamol. I flushed the pills down the toilet and recommended he splash out on a better whisky."
"You said what?"
Hogarth shrugged. "I'd had enough. I don't think he'll bother me late at night again. And no, I don't think he'll top himself, either. Though he may well have ruined what passed for my love life."
Hogarth pinched his brow before he noticed Palmer's silence.
"Sorry. Too much information. Must be the lack of sleep."
Palmer shrugged. "At least you've got a love life. All I've got is a sulk buddy."
"And look here," said Hogarth, pointing at his own face. "Now you've got another one." He pulled out a chair.
Palmer rolled her eyes as Hogarth sipped his drink and settled back in his chair. When he looked up he saw a strained look on her face.
"What?" He put his cup on the table. "What's happened now?"
"A visitor came looking for you, just before you got in."
"Not Gerald Gilmot, again?"

Palmer shook her head. "Afraid not. It was Melford. He wanted to see you as soon as you got in."

Hogarth sighed and rolled his head to one side.

He stood and hitched his trousers by the belt. "That's it. Another love letter from our local MP. Any more good news coming my way?"

"Who knows?" said Palmer. "Maybe Melford is keeping some back for you."

Hogarth gave the comment the derisory look it deserved before walking out to face the music. A few of the uniforms noticed the look on his face, and his direction of travel. The workshy PC Orton made a point of humming the funeral march. Hogarth shot him a look but got no more than a chuckle in reply. His powers were clearly on the wane.

"Come in, Hogarth," said the weary voice on the other side of the DCI's door. Hogarth did as he was told. The moustachioed DCI was taller than Hogarth, in fact, taller than most of the current crop of officers at Southend, hence the nickname 'Long Melford'. His height was one reason for the nickname. Built like John Cleese, Melford even looked a little like the man in his Hollywood prime, but with a far dourer manner. The other reason Melford had been named after a small Suffolk town famous for antique shops was because of Melford's penchant for old clocks. The wall behind his desk was festooned with at least ten different specimens and probably more, but Hogarth had never bothered to count. The only clock missing, Hogarth regularly thought, was a cuckoo. A cuckoo clock would have suited Melford down to the ground. But DCI Melford wasn't a Ministry of Silly Walks type of cuckoo, he was far closer to Reggie Perrin. Melford had stayed in the job for far longer than was good for him – which was why Hogarth reckoned he had been turned into a human stress ball. Or maybe a punchbag. Hogarth closed the door. He refused to adopt the wide stance and clasped hands of a guilty schoolboy. Instead, he cast a look at the man that some might have thought fractionally insubordinate.

"Sir. DS Palmer said you wanted to see me?"

"Indeed, I do, Hogarth. But I'd say it's need rather than want. Any inkling as to why I might need to see you again today?"

"Something in the post, perhaps?"

Melford lounged back in his seat, letting the creaking leather of his chair do the talking. There was a stack of files on his desk, but Hogarth suspected they were the same files he'd seen last time he'd been in. They were case files which made a man look busy by their weight and volume, but he wondered how often the man had opened them.

"Good guess. It was James Hartigan again."

"Our esteemed MP. I'm not sure how he has any time for constituents in between these letter-writing stints."

"Now you can see you were very unwise to make an enemy of the man. In this town, he's got a job for life. The other lot will never win."

"I never made an enemy of him, sir. He made one of me."

Melford narrowed his eyes. "Not wishing to rake over the past, but you *were* sleeping with his wife!"

Hogarth scratched his brow. "You may remember he threw her to the wolves, sir."

"You have your excuses. My point is that Hartigan will always hold the upper hand."

"Oh, I don't know. The man's a scoundrel and even MPs sometimes get rid of the worst among them. A ritual sacrifice now and then means the rest of them can stick their noses back in the trough with their consciences cleansed."

"I hope you don't make a habit of voicing these opinions. At least not beyond these four walls."

"You know me, sir. Discretion is the better part of valour."

Melford didn't look impressed.

"Don't think I'm the only one receiving these complaints, Hogarth. This feels like part of a campaign. Last week I had a whisper in my ear from the chief. He inquired as to whether you'd settled down."

"Settled down?" said Hogarth, frowning. "What the hell's that supposed to mean?"

"Mind your Ps and Qs when you're in his room, Hogarth," said Melford, sternly. "I should think he's asking if you've stopped causing trouble."

"And how did you reply, sir?"

"So far, so good, that's all. So far, so good," said Melford, his dark eyes still firmly on Hogarth's. "But there isn't anything else I should know? You're not up to any of your not-so-secret watches on Hartigan's house, or getting too close to any of his business associates?"

"Right now, I haven't got the time to waste on him. But, if the man's so paranoid that he's wasting his time on me, then I'd bet he's up to something. That's why he wants me out of the picture. He knows I'm a threat."

Melford paused before he spoke. "Stay clear of the man, understand? As long as you're behaving yourself, I can continue to vouch for you."

"Of course. It's hardly as if we can afford to be a man down at present, can we?"

Melford bristled. "Don't you even think of making my position any worse."

Hogarth bit his lip and narrowed his eyes. Melford noticed and read the gesture for what it was.

"What is it?"

"Nothing, sir."

"Spit it out."

"I was wondering; you've had no other complaints about me in the last day or so?"

Melford's thick eyebrows lowered over his dark eyes.

"Why? What else should I be worried about?"

"Nothing," said Hogarth, rolling back on his heels, a hint of relief showing on his craggy face.

Melford narrowed his eyes. "Simon Drawton…? You've not gone after him, again, have you?"

Hogarth tilted his head to one side. "He could still be a suspect in the Brimelow case."

Melford raised a finger and pointed it at Hogarth.

"You'd best have a rock-solid position backed by plenty of evidence before you go after that man. Without watertight evidence, leave well alone. Do I make myself clear?"

"Crystal, sir. Leave Hartigan and Drawton alone."

It was Melford's turn to narrow his eyes. "You know what I meant, Hogarth. That's all for now."

Hogarth reached for the door and Melford turned his eyes back down to his paperwork. He picked up a pen and clicked it ready for use, but as Hogarth was about to open the door, Melford looked up as if he'd just remembered something.

"One last thing."

"Sir?"

"I've asked DS Palmer to keep an eye on you. For my peace of mind, she will report to me. The information stays with me unless I deem otherwise."

Hogarth frowned and his cheeks reddened. "Sir?!"
"This is for your benefit," said Melford. "You need all the support you can get to stay on the straight and narrow. Think of DS Palmer as your helper."
"I already did, sir."
"Good. Then it really shouldn't be a problem, should it?" Melford made a signal for Hogarth to close the door.
Hogarth left the room and gritted his teeth as he stared down the corridor. He took a moment to compose himself before he marched back to the office. As soon as he was inside, Palmer raised her hands, palms flat.
"When were you going to tell me, eh?" said Hogarth.
"Soon as I got the chance, you must know that?" said Palmer.
Hogarth closed the door and walked to the desk.
"So, what's on the list for you to snitch on? Swearing? Drinking too much? Molesting the WPCs? What is it?"
Palmer gave him a hard look.
"I'm already in a difficult position, please don't make it worse."
"Apparently, everyone's in a difficult position except me," said Hogarth.
"Look, I should think he's on about you steering clear of Hartigan and hassling—"
"Hartigan's a criminal, Sue! No matter who pays his salary, or what title he's got, it's immaterial. He's in with Patrick Ferber and Ferber is a gangster."
"A gangster in a prison cell," said Palmer.
"Yes, for now."
"Let's just agree that we have no reason to discuss Hartigan, then we can move on and forget about it," said Palmer.
"What else did he say?"

Palmer's eyelids lowered to half mast. Her voice took a quieter tone. "Drawton. I didn't say a word, but he either knows or has guessed you've been pushing Drawton around again."

"Pushing him around? The man's a violent pervert, and he could be our killer. Are sexual predators also on my banned list?"

"It's not like that. You must know I didn't tell him anything."

"I gathered that. I shouldn't have to thank you, by the way. Trust like that should come as standard."

"It does," said Palmer.

"Then where will you draw the line?" said Hogarth.

"I only agreed just to get him off my back."

Hogarth puffed his cheeks and grabbed an office chair.

"But you need to be more careful," said Palmer.

Hogarth nodded. "Probably true. Is that it? No more skeletons in the closet today?"

"Almost," said Palmer. "He said he wants continual updates."

"That's what he gets."

"He wants more of them. The brass want a result on the Brimelow case."

"*I* want a result on the Brimelow case. They want a result, so they undermine me to get it? Great stuff. These management people are pure genius. And why didn't he ask me to report to him?"

Palmer shrugged. "I think he knows you probably won't."

Hogarth shook his head. "They're trying to force me out. This is just another little ploy to achieve the same end. Divide and conquer, Sue. That's what this is."

"Then it's not working, is it?"

Hogarth's face turned into a mean grin. "No, it's not. Because I've always been too bloody stubborn to do what other people want."

Palmer nodded. "You don't have to tell me."

Hogarth dragged a hand through his hair. "Right, then. Now I feel all appreciated, I think it's time we got on with the job, don't you?"

Seven

By mid-morning Hogarth and Palmer were back at Coleman Street. This time, they were on the other side of the fence, inside the Queensway Estate, walking the first-floor platform outside the food bank. It was a mild day, and the smokers were out in force, abandoning their empty plates for a quick cigarette.

By Hogarth's estimate there were no less than thirty of the usual suspects malingering outside. The dodgiest ones had taken a seat on a low concrete wall set around a space once intended for a playpark, like the one on the other side of the Refuge, but as it was empty, the drinkers had turned it into an al fresco drinking space. The younger, less addicted clientele had gathered around the play park to gossip. Among them were single mums, troubled young couples, and a few of what Hogarth termed the 'soft ones'. By which he meant 'soft' in the head, as well as in attitude. With staffing stretched, splitting up to talk to different groups was essential if they were to glean any fresh ideas from the people who had been at the memorial service. Funerals were always good to stir the emotions, sometimes providing fresh insights from guilty consciences. Sometimes, a new witness might even appear. Hogarth felt he was still hoping for the impossible, but with no new leads or evidence, there was little else to be done. Palmer took the soft bunch by the playground while Hogarth approached the hardened street drinkers on the other side of the building.

"Fallen on hard times, officer?" said a heavy-set man wearing a market T-shirt with an image of a wolf baying at the moon. Hogarth recognised the man's face, but not the name. The leathery-skinned old fellow certainly wasn't a threat, so Hogarth grinned along with him. "Not yet, but you never know, do you?" As he spoke, he imagined Hartigan's glee if such a fate ever did befall him.

He recalled the faces from the memorial. The ones most affected by the talk and the singing. Big Suitcase had shown no such emotion, but since the man had been involved in at least two suspicious deaths since Hogarth had arrived in town, he was obliged to check. Speaking to Suitcase in public often meant getting ridiculed for the sake of banter. When alone, Suitcase was a different man. His drug habit made him sweaty and paranoid, and his fears about getting set up for a crime often came to the fore. With the big hard men sitting on the low wall, there were no points to be gained through subtlety. They respected only bluntness. Anything else was seen as a sign of weakness, and Hogarth couldn't afford to let anyone on the street think he was scared of them. He stepped over the small concrete wall into the tiny square and stopped opposite Suitcase and his duo of drinking companions. Each was a lesser-known scallywag. Hogarth was sure neither had been present at the memorial service.

"So, how are we today, gentlemen?" he said.

Suitcase looked up at him. As soon as he saw the man's eyes, Hogarth knew he was dead drunk.

"Capital D for Dandy, your highness," said Suitcase, chuckling to himself. Hogarth frowned.

"You were here at the memorial service yesterday," said Hogarth.

"Oh, yeah. Lots of tears. Great sandwiches." Then he snapped his fingers as if he'd just remembered something.

"And then you and your partner happened to bring along that nice little dolly bird. Lovely bit of eye candy."
Hogarth's face darkened by another degree.
"You can show off for your mates, Suitcase, but we both know what it's like when you're alone."
Suitcase's eyes flickered with a vague reaction before he started singing the *Twilight Zone* tune.
"Da-da-da-da, da-da-da-da. This detective has powers to make you talk, boys. It's almost scary."
"Scary?" said Hogarth. "What's scary is that there's a proper killer out there. Someone who preys on young girls like Helen Brimelow. Helen helped you, Suitcase. You know she did. I dare say she helped all of you at some time in the last year or so. Someone here – someone you know from among all these people must have some idea who did that to her."
"Someone always knows something, officer," said Suitcase, smirking.
"Don't be an idiot all your damned life," said Hogarth. "Why not do something good for once?"
Suitcase broke into a fit of wheezy laughter and slapped his thigh. But the man on his right was less amused. He met Hogarth's eye before sipping from his can of Special Brew.
"I remember her. She was a nice girl. Religious, right, like most of 'em. But she never put it on you. She never preached at you. She just helped you and left it at that. Like I say, she was a nice girl."
Suitcase stopped laughing and looked at his companion like he was a traitor. The man met Suitcase's eye.
"What? So, he's a copper, I get it, but he's trying to find a sicko. There's nothing wrong in that."

"As if you'd know anything worth saying," said Suitcase, slurring his words.
"Sometimes people think they don't know anything," said Hogarth, "but by talking, they remember…"
He nodded at the man to continue.
"Helen's dad lives over there, doesn't he? They both did."
The man pointed across the street with his beer can.
Hogarth didn't say a word.
"Nice people, both of 'em. Always friendly."
Hogarth nodded. "Do you have any idea who might have wanted to hurt her? Do you remember anyone talking about her in a weird way? Or maybe you might have overheard one of the other locals or even the volunteers talking about her?"
The man frowned as if to think, then shook his head. "No, man. They're all really tight in there, right. Like family. It's nice to see. It's kind of old fashioned."
Niceties. Fluff. Hogarth had been hoping for much more. His mood was beginning to sour.
"If you can think of anything that might help, let us know, won't you?"
The man nodded.
"Your name is…?"
"Gary. Gary Cooper, like the film star."
Beside him, Suitcase broke out laughing, but Hogarth had the feeling the man was telling the truth. He left the square yard and looked across to the people smoking by the fence. One man caught his eye. Hogarth decided to try him next. Guilty consciences and all that. Hogarth made his move and caught sight of Palmer in the distance. She was talking to a small group of men and women by the corner of the play park fence, and beside her was a small trim female copper in a blue cap and a yellow high-viz jacket. Hogarth strained his eyes. It was Ecrin Kaplan, the PCSO and now a trainee PC.

No doubt Kaplan was on her beat, and Palmer had nabbed her to help. Smart move. And Kaplan was a smart one too. Smart enough to finish with DC Simmons after he jumped into bed with local journalist and man-eater, Alice Perry. Smart enough even to have Hogarth thinking about their manpower problem. Yeah, Kaplan had potential alright.
The short man who had caught Hogarth's eye had now turned away and was heading back to the Refuge doorway. He had an odd shuffling look about him. Probably one of the 'soft ones'. Or maybe an oddball predator. Maybe both. Hogarth waved and called at the man but he kept on walking.
"Excuse me, sir. I'd just like a word…"
The little man feigned deafness, so Hogarth upped his pace and reached him as he was about to set foot through the door. Just as he was about to follow the little man inside, Freddie Halstead stepped out with one of the volunteers, the guy who usually manned the reception while dressed up like a Victorian, replete with bushy sideburns and a waistcoat. The place was nothing if not colourful. Both Halstead and his volunteer glanced at Hogarth and gave a nod. From the sound of it, they were still talking about the memorial service.
"… as well as it could have done, really…"
Halstead seemed tense and busy. His forehead looked tight and his eyes seemed to look in three directions at once. In a place like this, working with people like these, he must have needed to have eyes in the back of his head. Hogarth banked the observation and smiled at the odd little man who was still trying to get away.
"Can I have a word, sir?"

"Why? What have I done?" said the man with a strange intonation. It wasn't an accent, as such, just a way of speaking. He was definitely one of the soft ones.

"Nothing, I'm sure," said Hogarth. "It's a word, that's all."

Hogarth led the man back to the relative privacy of the side fence overlooking the car park fifteen feet below. Nearby, Freddie Halstead was listening as the Victorian-styled volunteer chewed his ear and smoked a roll-up. Hogarth turned his attention to his own little man who had bright eyes and a puffy grey beard. There were flecks of egg mayonnaise and sandwich crumbs trapped between the hairs. His tongue hung loose, framed by an open mouth.

"Do you remember the volunteer Helen Brimelow, Mr...?"

"Pardon?" said the man.

Hogarth winced and started again. He was pretty sure Pardon wasn't the man's name.

Over in the square yard, Suitcase was still laughing at his expense.

The parents by the playground were outright gossips. More than a few of them disliked the food bank being so close to their tower blocks. Palmer sympathised. The Refuge Food Bank had occupied the community centre for as long as she'd been in the force. Eleven years and more. She had seen Freddie Halstead's face in the paper a few times, alongside the other managers, making their pleas for new food donations and promoting the odd community event to keep the locals on side. Fun days with bouncy castles. Community barbeques. But it wasn't enough for the likes of people like this. Palmer doubted free gold bullion and tickets to Barbados would have been enough to keep them happy. The loudest of the bunch was a mum who had her hair pulled into a tight ponytail, giving her face the classic *Croydon facelift* look. Her eyes were angry and her manner brusque. The child in her buggy seemed just like his mother. The kid's face was puce and he was screaming but she was too busy complaining to notice.

"That's one more thing they've done for us – now they're bringing in killers as well as junkies and drug dealers. I thought the council were going to get rid of the place years ago, but look at it, it's still here, along with all those bloody wasters, bold as brass."

The young woman drew nods and supportive comments from her group.

"It ain't right," said one of them, a man with a big dog straining on the leash by his knees. "They should get shut down. It's disgusting."

"They're not all bad," said Palmer. "We were there yesterday. They did a service for Helen Brimelow."

"The dead girl," snapped the woman with the ponytail. "Least they could do, I reckon – seeing as they're the ones who got her killed in the first place."

PCSO Ecrin Kaplan winced at the comment, making a small circle of her mouth. No matter what face she made, the olive-skinned young woman always seemed to look stunning.

"What?" said the ponytailed woman.

"The food bank people are not the ones who got her killed," said Kaplan. "They're here to help people. If you needed food, they'd help you, too, you know," said Kaplan. Palmer gave her a look, warning her not to say things she didn't know to be true.

"At least… we don't believe they're involved," said Kaplan, correcting herself. "But it's highly unlikely," she added.

"Always the family that did it, so they say," said the man with the dog, with a knowing tone. "Have you spoken to the dead girl's father? He only lives across the street, you know? I've seen him. Fella's in bits. Doesn't mean he didn't do it though, eh?"

Palmer pursed her lips and exchanged a glance with Kaplan. She wondered how Hogarth was getting on across the other side. She caught a glimpse of him leaning on the blue side railings, talking to a podgy, bearded little man who could have looked at home in a Tolkien story. He's doing as well as I am, she thought. Clutching at straws…

"At this stage, we've spoken to everyone we can," said Palmer. "But there's a chance we've missed a key witness along the way, which is why we're talking to residents here today."

"Which means they haven't got a clue," said the girl with the ponytail. The others were not going to be rude in public, but Palmer saw the same belief was written on their faces. The way things were going, Palmer couldn't help but agree.

"We've got plenty of clues," Palmer found herself saying, "Our current work is about connecting them to the right people."

The gang looked pleased that they had managed to prise a new nugget of gossip from Palmer. Palmer was less pleased, and Ecrin Kaplan saw it on her face. They both knew her words were close to fabrication. She couldn't help it. She didn't want that trappy cow getting the last word.

"Shall I go and ask those kids over there, DS Palmer?" said Kaplan, nodding her cap at a group of teens exiting the nearest block. It was a gang of four, two boys and two girls decked out in dark hoodies and baseball caps, hands shoved deep in their pockets, mischievous smiles and attitude written across their faces.

"Worth a go," said Palmer. "Catch them before they leave the estate. And stay around. I might be in need of your services again, Ecrin."

PCSO Kaplan glanced at the mouthy residents around Palmer and gave a nod of sympathy.

"Of course. I'll be back in two."

Palmer watched Kaplan march away around the tiny playground. Now she was jealous. Lately, the workdays had been slow-going and desperate affairs, poring over clues and hints of evidence already evaluated and dismissed, chasing up pathology for any further word, hoping for last-second DNA evidence from the killer's semen, or blood. None had come in. And every day the case seemed to become a little bit drier, a little more abstract. Already, Helen Brimelow felt like a cold case in the making. She knew it was eating Hogarth from the inside. If it wasn't for the hindrance of her niece at home, Palmer wondered if the girl's murder might have hit her just the same.

"Well? What do you wanna know?" said the ringleader girl, bringing Palmer back to the present. One of the tower blocks loomed high above, casting a long shadow over all of them. Palmer gazed up and wondered if any of those flats harboured their killer.

"Did any of you personally know the girl?" said Palmer.

"No," said the ponytailed girl.

"What about the rest of you?" she asked again.

"No," repeated the woman, speaking for them all. "If we knew, we would have told you, right?"

Palmer took in a sharp breath.

"If you don't mind, madam, I'd like to hear the answer from them."

Each one shook their head or said No.
"Told you, didn't I?" said the woman, adding a tut before she shook her head.
"I *saw* her, though," said the man with the dog.
Palmer's eyes flicked toward the man's face and locked on.
"Yes," said Palmer.
"Pretty little thing. Hard to miss, compared with the others."
"Careful, Roger. You'll end up making yourself sound like their man," said one of the others.
"Yeah," chuckled another. "If they can't find the killer, they'll soon fit someone up for it."
Palmer didn't bite.
"You were saying?"
"She was eye-catching, that's all," said the man with a shrug. Pretty, but mostly you noticed her because she was always so well dressed. Compared to the rest of them, I mean. In a place like this, she had the X-factor."
"You think the way she dressed brought the wrong kind of attention?" said Palmer. She remembered the naked body from the beach hut. The long gouging wound from throat down to her abdomen. The torn and bloodied clothes dumped in the corner of the hut. None of those clothes were expensive labels. They were all high street brands. But the colours had all matched, carefully selected. Yes, the girl did have style. Unusual, in a way. Most of the young Christians she'd ever met were geeky, gawkish, and had little clue about fashion or style. Helen Brimelow was young and Christian and maybe she had bordered on the geeky, but she had fashion sense as well as a kind heart.
The man shook his head.
"She wasn't tarty. Not in the least. She just looked... classy."
Palmer nodded. "Did you ever see her getting any unwanted attention?"

"I wouldn't know," he said firmly. "I don't set foot in that place. Haven't done for years at any rate." He indicated the food bank.

"Did you ever see anyone gawping at her when she was outside the place?" she asked.

"Oh, there are always people looking at young girls. You've got what, about two hundred flats around here. Nearly three. Then there's all the dossers and junkies over there. It would have been a miracle if she wasn't getting ogled day in, day out."

Palmer narrowed her eyes.

"But you didn't see it yourself?"

The man shook his head. His dog looked up at him as if he was listening. But there was a certain look in the eye of the woman with the big mouth and the screaming baby. A glint of mischief. The promise of trouble. Or something else. What did she know?

"What is it?" asked Palmer.

At first the woman bit her lip, but then she couldn't resist. She started with a shake of the head.

"I don't like to speak ill of the dead, but these Bible-bashing creeps think they're invincible, don't they?"

"Go on," said Palmer, locking eyes with the girl.

"Let's just say I don't think she was intimidated by talking to people on the wrong side of the tracks."

"We know she wasn't," said Palmer. "She worked in the food bank. She served them food and prayed for some of them on a regular basis."

"Hands-on healing, right?" said the girl. "I heard she did some of that outside of those four walls."

"What do you mean?" said Palmer.

The girl bit her lip again and looked around at her companions for their reactions. Palmer gave her a hard look.
"I need your name. What is it, please?"
The question made the ponytailed girl meet Palmer's eye. Palmer watched her swallow.
"But I'm not involved," she said, turning defensive. "I'm not even a witness."
"Maybe not, but you are claiming to know something about the murder victim."
"My name is Gardener. Melissa Gardener. But I don't need no trouble."
Palmer committed the name to memory.
"Whatever you think you saw – I need you to spell it out."
The girl puffed her cheeks and looked at her baby for the first time in several minutes. He was still crying.
"I saw her talking to some of them down by the bakery there on the corner. And out by the Co-op."
Palmer got the local geography right in her mind and gave a nod. The old bakery was just a hundred yards away, in plain sight. The Co-op supermarket was a block away.
"Who was she talking to?"
"I dunno. Could have been anyone. But like Roger here says, she was the one you noticed. Always done up to the nines, like she thought she was something special. That's what did for her in the end though, wasn't it?"
Palmer thought she detected a hint of smug satisfaction in the young woman's voice. As if justice had been done – Helen Brimelow had been struck down for breaking the local dress code of leggings, jeans, and tracksuit bottoms.
"Melissa, I'll need you to think back, to try and remember who she was with."
"It could have been anyone, like I said."

Palmer shook her head. "I'm afraid that's not good enough—"
Before Palmer could finish her words, she heard her name being called across the playground.
"DS Palmer!" Palmer and the group with her turned their heads to see Kaplan approaching in a hurry.
"Ecrin?" said Palmer.
"Can I have a word, please?"
Palmer nodded and left the group with a nod, her eyes landing last on Melissa Gardener before she walked away. Kaplan waited for her by the distant corner of the platform, almost within touching distance of the nearest tower block.
"What is it?" said Palmer, keeping her voice down.
Kaplan made sure to keep her voice even lower.
"Those youths. One of them said he knew Helen Brimelow. The others made fun of him, saying he had a crush on her. The lad, his name is Samuel George – he didn't deny it. Then the others said something of note. They said George never had a chance because Helen only liked to slum it with the older men."
Palmer frowned. "You pulled them up on that, I hope, made them clarify…?"
"Yeah. They didn't want to, but one of the young women spilt the rest before they went off."
"The rest?" said Palmer.
Palmer nodded. "This girl, called Nevie Smith, she said Helen was friends with one or two of the food bank users who live in this block."
She nodded at the tower block behind them.

"Do you think the story's genuine or malicious? It seems some women were jealous of Helen because of the way she dressed."

Kaplan nodded. "She was stylish, wasn't she? They said the same. But no, I don't think this was malicious. The girl wouldn't give me any names – her boyfriend warned her off – but she said she knew who the men were. One especially."

Palmer shook her head. "That can't be right. From what we heard, Helen Brimelow had too much sense for that. She was too straight-laced to take those kinds of risks."

"Maybe we don't know the girl as well as we thought we did…" ventured Kaplan.

"If that's true, then no one did. Good work, Ecrin," said Palmer. She clapped a hand on the girl's shoulder. "We'll need their names and numbers right away."

"No problem," said Kaplan. "It's all here."

Palmer nodded.

"Then I'll let you go and break the happy news to DI Hogarth," said Palmer, nodding across the way.

"He looks like he needs saving, doesn't he?"

"He's clearly not as good as you at the community work," said Palmer.

"No surprise there," said Kaplan.

Palmer watched the young woman set off before she turned back to her small audience standing at the corner of the playground. Melissa Gardner gave Palmer a severe look. But with a fresh lead in hand, Palmer had the wind in her sails, and she had every intention of squeezing the unpleasant woman for every drop of information she could get.

Eight

If sainthoods had been given for work ethic and heart, food bank manager Gordon would have been right up there with Mother Teresa. Gordon was another of the three men who led the Refuge and managed the staff and volunteers, and deep down, of the three, Freddie Halstead knew Gordon was the best. He was a workaholic and he did it all for the Lord. Beyond Gordon there was Zack. Zack was the figurehead and founder of the place, the one who had made it all possible. No one could match Zack when he was on form. The man was like a revivalist preacher, able to inspire, motivate, and bring something special from the great beyond to get everyone going. But his specialist skills came at a price. He burned like a Roman candle, but once he was done, he needed plenty of rest to restore his reserves. Hence his latest sabbatical. These days the show was left to Gordon and Freddie.

Freddie mostly liked his part of the show. He worked like a ping-pong ball, bouncing between the walls of the building, meeting and greeting, ensuring all the volunteers felt appreciated, providing a word of encouragement where it was needed, speaking to the workers from the various agencies who used the place as a venue to help the folks in need. Freddie's official job title was community outreach worker, but it encompassed much more. A little preaching. A lot of paperwork. Some basic management and a lot of people work. It had all been fun, especially at the start. But lately, Freddie Halstead had felt himself gliding. The inner fire the Christians spoke of… the spark… sometimes he wondered if his burned as brightly as it had at the start.

These days, he felt like a passenger. Someone on the back of the bus, watching it all happen. With Ollie to think of, he was far less than that.

Today the free café was extremely busy. The place was a buzz of banter, laughter, conversation, and more than a hint of unwashed body odour. Near on a hundred guests occupied every chair, stood in every free space, and ate from every plate. Freddie flew between them, smiling and nodding, going about his work even as his mind drifted elsewhere. But he soon found his smile wearing thin. It was almost time, but he had other things to consider beside himself.

Freddie walked out into the hallway, opened the side cupboard door and walked in and locked it behind him. Surrounded by stacks of coffee tins, nappies and supplies for Christmas, he took a deep breath and inspected his mobile. Nothing. He thought of calling the NHS team to see if Ollie had made his group session, but a moment's thought of how many calls he would have to make brought a shake of his head. Ollie knew he was due there today. Freddie wondered if he'd gone. He'd said he didn't like it there lately. The people were getting on his nerves. Typical. Freddie remembered the cat incident and winced with almost physical discomfort. He wondered how long the cat thing had been going on. Was it down to neglect on his part? Had he been too busy? Nature or nurture… if it was the latter then Freddie expected he would be to blame. Their mother certainly hadn't played any role in it. She hadn't played a role in anything. There was a loud knocking at the door.

"Freddie? You in there?"

It was Gordon, which meant there was a problem. Freddie opened the door and looked at him.

"You okay?" said Gordon, looking him deep in the eye.

"I... I..."

"It's okay," said Gordon. The big man's eyes softened and he put a hand on Freddie's shoulder. "I'll pray for you."

"No," said Freddie, a little too quickly. "It's busy. What's the problem?"

"Nutty Nell is looking for you out there."

"Damn," said Freddie. "Anyone but her today." Gordon offered a weak smile as compensation for the news. Nutty Nell was one of their most demanding service users. Freddie had indulged her neediness for so long, he wasn't able to think of a clear way out. But he couldn't face the woman's blathering, not today. He dragged a hand down his face and looked at Gordon.

"Can you ask her to wait?"

"Wait? How long? A week, a month or a year?" Gordon chuckled. Freddie didn't.

"Five, maybe ten minutes. I need some air."

"Sure," said Gordon. "No problem."

Freddie nodded his thanks at the big man then slid past him into the hallway. He threaded through the malingerers to reach the world outside. He saw the police detectives had already gone. Good. They would be one less burden he had to think about. There was no bringing Helen back and all the police would do was agitate the punters. And agitated punters meant problems inside the building. He walked along throwing the odd wave at a few of the smokers and swapping the required banter with whoever wanted to trade words, but Freddie made sure he walked alone. He reached the distant corner of the first-floor platform and took the curling slope until the food bank building was almost hidden from view. He kept walking, passing alongside a tower block, heading for the triangle of redundant garages behind it. Then he typed another text on his phone screen and pulled one of his guilty secrets from his back pocket. A ten pack of cigarettes. Gordon must have known, but he didn't say anything. He lit one and waited and looked around the rough neighbourhood. But rough as it was, this little spot was a quiet concrete oasis. His oasis. And now the text had been sent, all he could do was wait. It wouldn't be long before his comfort arrived.

Palmer's niece had been walking too. She'd done a mile plus already, her heels clacking along the steady gradient of Victoria Avenue as she passed the council offices and the police station where her aunt worked, squirming as she hoped her aunt wouldn't see. At the courthouse, she was ogled and wolf-whistled by a couple of smoking lads in tracksuits. They were all gelled hair, scarred faces, and too much aggression. Aaliyah was young, but she was smart enough. Boys outside a courthouse were not to be encouraged. Her phone buzzed as she reached the busy corner junction by Southend Victoria train station. She could have got a train to London. She hadn't done that in a while, but no, not today. Because something else had already piqued her interest. A taste of life she hadn't seen before. The Refuge. It was colourful beyond words, exciting, and dangerous all at the same time. Living in the neat, tree-lined suburbs of Rayleigh, a mostly well-to-do safe kind of place, Aaliyah had never known such wonderful chaos thrived just six miles down the road. She had to go back. No matter what her aunt said, it was a done deal. Aaliyah stopped outside the red-brick train station, not far from the statue of the kissing couple. There was a fresh message on her phone screen. It was the second she'd received that morning. She decided to ignore it, just like the last.

What are you doing? Are you still at home? Let me know. I'm supposed to be responsible for you.

The girl rolled her eyes and tutted. She was about to put the phone away in her pocket but thought better of it. She bit her lip as she composed a message in her head. As soon as she had something to say, she began to prod the screen.

I'm fine. I'm looking at a couple of job sites, then going out for a few bits. I'll get the milk, too. Now stop worrying x

The girl already knew that nothing was going to stop Sue worrying, but the reply might buy her a few hours without another bout of hassling messages. She put the phone away and turned the corner onto the busy concrete world of Queensway, a dual carriageway snarled up with traffic. There they were, dead ahead – the three tower blocks, beige and cream, with their fourth lonely sister block across the wide street. Her destination lay between the three blocks. Another world of rainbow colours, infinite possibilities, and adventure. A place where things happened. Despite what she'd seen with her own eyes, and all Palmer had told her about the place, she couldn't keep away. She didn't want to. With a burst of excitement, the girl upped her pace, hoping the food bank might still be open by the time she arrived. Two minutes later, she passed the triangular tip of the estate grounds – a triangle of high iron fences guarding a small world of bricks, concrete, weeds, and unwanted trash discarded at the margins. A rotting, sodden mattress. A broken-down fridge, door wide open, inside grey with mould and dirt. Then the sound of a voice nearby made her slow down. She narrowed her eyes and tightened her temples as she listened. It was a voice she recognised, but it took her a moment to place. As soon as she did, she felt a new burst of energy, and a hint of nerves. What was *he* doing out *here?* Aaliyah swallowed, swept her tinted hair back, straightened her shoulders and started to walk on, hoping the man would notice her as she passed by. But as soon as she took two steps past the edge of the brown brick garages on the other side of the fence, she changed her mind and stepped back. Yes, it was him. The man with the cool beard and slicked hair – the man with the tattoos who ran the food bank. He was so cool. As much as the food bank had been her destination, the man had always been part of her aim.

Freddie Halstead lit a second cigarette. His company had arrived a little late, so Gordon would have to run the show on his own for a little longer yet. He knew the big man wouldn't mind. He always seemed content no matter what life – or the food bank – threw at him. Besides, feeling like this, Freddie reckoned he didn't have any choice. There were things he needed to say, things he hoped to do before he could face the rest of the day.
Dave Johnson was one of the latest volunteers who had drifted away from the place. Drifting away happened. It was a fact of life. In a place like the Refuge, volunteers were prone to burn out just as much as the staff. More so, in a way. And Dave had burnt out a few times already. His teaching career had taken its toll on him. The Refuge must have seemed like fun for a while, a place to put his faith into practice. Until it wasn't anymore. Then there was his

daughter, Sharon. Sweet blonde Sharon, with her twinkling blue eyes; a woman full of compassion and heart, but who could only last in the place for a few weeks at a time. Yet, she still kept coming back… But what happened to Helen had changed everything, and he doubted she'd be back this time. Freddie had always found it impossible to say he missed her. Instead, he always told her that the place missed her. The team missed her. The service users. Anyone and everyone but him.

"You know I appreciate you coming," said Halstead. Just around the corner stood Aaliyah, on the other side of the fence, listening.

"Yes," said the smaller, older man. "It's good to see you."

"Yes, it is," said Sharon. "I only wish it had been in much better circumstances."

"You know what the place was like," said Freddie. "There was always some tragedy around the corner. Some worse than others. It's the nature of the beast."

"But a tragedy like this…?"

Aaliyah glanced around the corner of the ramshackle brick sheds and garages to see Halstead nodding before he blew a cloud of smoke into the air.

"The Refuge doesn't need the controversy, does it?" said the older man. "Plenty of people have always had it in for the place."

Halstead shrugged. "Because it's church-based. The church is an anathema to some people. It's like a swear word. People's minds are clouded with sin. It's the way of the world these days."

"You're doing good work here, Freddie. Don't ever doubt that," said the older man. He put a hand on Halstead's shoulder.

"I try not to, Dave. But sometimes, the work isn't enough, is it? Not in the middle of all the horror that goes on around us."

"Stay strong, Freddie," said the woman, in a honeyed voice. Aaliyah watched as the woman with the blonde hair laid a supportive hand on Freddie's tattooed arm and squeezed. She watched the two exchange a glance. There was something between them, barely perceptible, but definitely there. A tinge of jealousy prodded at Aaliyah's chest.

"He is strong, aren't you Freddie?" said the older man. "He just needs to remember where his strength comes from, that's all."

Halstead laughed and the man and woman moved a little way past him, as if ready to leave.

"It's good to see you, Freddie," said the man. "But I've got to get going. Got an appointment at the doctor's surgery down there in ten minutes."

"Of course. Take care of yourself, Dave. God bless."

He smiled at them as they were about to drift away. Aaliyah watched his face flicker as if caught in a moment of indecision. Then she watched him call out.

"Sharon, mind if I have a word?"

The blonde and her father both looked back. The father gave his daughter a look. "It's fine. See you in there."

The woman nodded. They both waited quietly as the older man walked away. Aaliyah stayed watching as the man called Dave walked through the open gate. Aaliyah realised the man would pass her on his way to the doctor's surgery so hastily pulled her phone from her pocket, moved a few steps away from her hiding place, and put her phone to her ear.

The man soon passed her without so much as a glance and once he was gone, Aaliyah lowered her phone and stepped back to the fence. She quickly tuned her ears to the conversation on the other side.

"You seem stressed, Freddie," said the woman softly.

"It's not just Helen Brimelow, it's my brother too. He's really off lately."

"Still causing you problems?"

Halstead nodded.

"But I'd guess Helen's death makes it all worse."

"It makes everything worse."

The blonde nodded and sighed. "How can I help?"

"It'd be nice to see you back up there sometime."

"Not for a while. Maybe when they've caught this sicko, I'll think about it…"

"I understand," said Halstead.

There was a pause before Halstead continued.

"The police are still on this one."

"They have to be."

"But I didn't realise they'd target us like this."

"Us?" said the woman.

"I meant the Refuge. The food bank. We're the good guys, after all. Helen was one of us."

"But the service users. The guests. You don't know about them. It could be one of them that did it. The police are doing their job."

"They'll talk to you soon enough. You and your father. You both knew Helen."

Silence. Aaliyah looked and saw them exchange a meaningful glance. Yes, there was something between them.

"When they talk to you make sure they understand we're not the villains here."
"Of course you're not."
"Then they should be looking elsewhere. Out there in the town."
"They're doing their job, Freddie," she said, her voice silken. "It's only natural that they'd look here—"
Aaliyah edged around the corner to watch Halstead and the blonde woman looking at each other. Halstead's chiselled face seemed to be imparting some instruction. The woman nodded her head.
"I'll remind them to let you get on with the good work. Not that they'd listen to us."
"Appreciate it, Sharon. It's good to see you're on our side."
"Why wouldn't I be?" said the young woman.
"Because… I don't know."
The silence lasted a second before she squeezed Halstead's arm and laid a faint kiss on his cheek.
"Take it easy, Freddie. I'll see you when the dust has settled."
"Fine. Go then," he said, as she turned away.
The blonde woman turned and looked back at him.
"Sorry, my dad's expecting me to go with him. He's been ill lately…"
"It's okay, Sharon. He's keeping an eye on you, like a father should."
Freddie looked away. He took a last drag of his cigarette before flicking his fag end into the gutter. Aaliyah's eyes studied the changing contours of the man's muscles as his arm flexed. He dragged a hand back across his slicked dark hair.
"You okay?" said the blonde.
"I don't know. I can't seem to tell anymore."

The blonde pursed her lips and looked at him once more and nodded a goodbye before she turned and walked away. If there had been something between them Aaliyah sensed it must have already cooled. She watched Halstead as he shook his head and looked up to the sky. Sharon rounded the fence and came towards her. Aaliyah studied her phone screen and pretended to thumb a text, but she sensed the woman frowning at her as she passed. Aaliyah ignored her until she was long gone. As she put her phone away, a faint smile crept across her face. Yes, the man was single, and if not single, he certainly seemed available. She suddenly sensed the adventure she planned had the potential to get even better than she'd imagined. Aaliyah shook her head. So was he a priest or a player? Aaliyah wasn't quite sure which option she preferred, but studying those tattoos, her mind was changing fast…

Nine

At a stroke, Hogarth decided to break with established procedure to invite Kaplan into the interview room with them. But then procedure was like any rule. It was useful when it helped, to be disregarded when it didn't. PCSO Kaplan was showing a lot of promise. Hogarth knew it was bound to irk the likes of PC Dawson that his ambitious girlfriend, Bec Rawlins, was being passed over in the promotion of PCSO to constable proper, but what Hogarth had in mind was more than promotion in uniform. If Melford could be persuaded, he saw the girl being fast-tracked to fill the shoes DC Simmons had left behind. Palmer had already taken her seat. Hogarth leaned back in his chair and looked at the door as it finally opened. Kaplan stood at the door, a coy smile on her olive-skinned face. Hogarth gave her a nod and she walked into IR1, shutting the door behind her. "Take a seat if you like," said Hogarth.
"I'll be fine here thanks, sir," said Kaplan, moving towards the back wall.
"Suit yourself," he said.
"What's all this?" said the nervous young man seated in front of them. Hogarth turned his attention to the guy on the other side of the scratched-up table. Hogarth's smile faded, and a cutting spark returned to his narrow eyes.
"It's called an interview," said Hogarth.
The young man looked at each of them in turn.
"You arresting me then?"
"I doubt it," said Hogarth. "Unless you prove obstructive… or have something you'd like to confess?"

The young man swallowed and shook his head firmly.
"Do I need a lawyer?"
"If you were in America maybe. We call them solicitors. Why? Is there was something you were worried about?"
The young man shook his head again and flicked his eyes down to the table. He traced his fingertips over the etchings, swear words, and insults of suspects past.
"I wouldn't do that if I were you," said Hogarth. "This place only gets a clean now and then. But those deep scratches," Hogarth screwed up his face and shook his head, "I doubt the Dettol reaches them. Not very hygienic."
The young man withdrew his hand.
Palmer cleared her throat and leaned forward to attract the young man's attention.
"Your name is Samuel George. You live at twenty-six Haycock Tower. And you're eighteen years old? Is that right?"
Samuel nodded. "Yeah. And I already told the woman officer over there all I know. I don't see why I should be brought in here."
"To help us with our enquiries, Sam," said Palmer.
"Stop being so bloody defensive," said Hogarth, "and you'll be out of here in two shakes of a lamb's tail."
"I've already said everything I could."
"Everything you *could*," said Hogarth. "But it's the word *could* that bothers me. It suggests there might be more which, for some reason, you feel unable to share. Why might that be, I wonder?"
"No… You're wrong," said Sam.
"All you need to do is answer our questions, Sam," said Palmer, "then you'll be on your way."

There was a moment's silence while the young man looked at each of the faces ranged around the room, evaluating his position. He shifted in his seat and clasped his hands together.

"What do you want to know?"

"Helen Brimelow. We're told you know who she was," said Palmer. "We've also been told that you happened to have seen her spending time with certain people around the Queensway Estate. Certain people who may not have been her type, if you know what I mean."

"Everyone knows who she was," said George, with a shrug. "Because she was killed. They say the crazy bastard gutted her like a fish."

Hogarth's lip curled, but he swiftly brought himself to order. A raw nerve had been struck, nothing more. No malice was intended. The boy was young enough to still be excitable about the grimmest of events.

"You knew her," said Palmer. "You also knew she was hanging around with people from the tower blocks. All we need to know is who, when, and why." George tutted and shook his head.

"Come on, man, it's got to be someone from the blocks, now has it? We always get a bad rep."

"No one says that. Yet," said Hogarth.

"Anyway, what do you think I am? The dead girl's diary?"

"No," said Palmer. "But something *is* bothering you, isn't it? Because the more we ask the more awkward you become."

"Why is this so difficult, Samuel?" said Hogarth. "Don't you want to help us find the killer?"

"If I could help, I would have told you at the start."

"Would you?" said Hogarth. "Answer our questions. They're simple enough."

"I'm telling you, you're barking up the wrong tree."

"Maybe," said Hogarth. "But that's our prerogative. Perhaps you do need a solicitor, after all, Samuel. Because it seems to me there is something you'd like to hide. Is that the case, young man?"

"Of course not."

"Then why be so evasive?"

"Sam," said Palmer. "We know you saw Helen Brimelow with certain individuals. You've already told PSCO Kaplan that much. All we ask is that you go one stage further and tell us who they were."

"Certain individuals," said the boy with a quiet sigh. He shook his head.

The young man looked at Kaplan then Palmer. She watched as his face turned pale, then he shook his head.

"Sam, you're not helping yourself here," said Palmer.

"That's 'cause it's not safe!" spat the boy, suddenly looking up from his hands.

"Why not?!" replied Hogarth.

"Because the estate isn't safe, man. Get with it! It ain't safe for nobody. But especially not for grasses and people who snitch to the police. You can get shivved for that, man. I can't do it. You shouldn't even be asking."

"Asking you to help us find a killer?" said Hogarth. "Is it him you're protecting, Sam? The killer?"

Palmer eyed Hogarth, but he ignored her. He was exploiting the young man's naivety for all it was worth and scaring him half to death in the process.

"I had nothing to do with what happened to that girl. It was sick. Everyone knows that. Despicable. Man, I used to chat with her sometimes myself. Just say hello, and everything—"

"Then just tell us the truth!" said Hogarth, banging his hand on the table. "You knew her. You chatted to her... Did she deserve to die?"

The question seemed to wrongfoot the boy. He opened his mouth and shook his head.

"Then help us find her killer. Tell us who she met with so we can rule them in or out. That's the limit of what we want from you. Tell us and you're in the clear."

The young man fell silent. Hogarth leaned back and folded his arms. When Palmer glanced his way, he didn't look at her but instead gave the subtlest of nods. The baton had been passed. She took a breath and leaned into the fray. Her voice was soft and subtle, full of empathy.

"Even if this is hard, you have to tell us. You see that, don't you?"

She let the silence linger, the truth settle in. Samuel George opened his mouth.

"She was a sweet girl. Sincere... She was a looker too... but I think she had a problem. She seemed to like the bad boys."

"Bad boys?" said Palmer.

George nodded.

"How many were there?" asked Palmer.

"She chatted to a few, but there was only one she was close with. I think she thought she could help him because she was a God-botherer. She wanted to fix them all, didn't she?"

"Who was it, Sam??" said Palmer.

"I saw her chatting to Jason Compton. Nickname Compo."

Palmer made a note, as did Kaplan behind her. They watched the young man take another sharp breath. He started to struggle.

"But it wasn't him. She wasn't sleeping with him."

"What?" Palmer and Hogarth's eyes flickered with surprise.

"She had a fling with one of them. I know she did. I saw them kissing. That's when I knew for sure…"
"You said she had a fling?" said Hogarth, narrowing his eyes.
"Yeah. She was a good little Christian girl except when it came to…" George's words trailed away before he continued. "You can't let him know this came from me. You do, I'm as good as dead."
"Spit it out," said Hogarth.
The boy looked him in the eye. Hogarth slapped the table again.
"Spit it out!"
Samuel covered his face, closed his eyes, shook his head.
"Kevin Robbins," he announced, forcing the words out. "She was seeing Kevin Robbins. They call him Razor Robbins, but then you people probably know that."
Hogarth crumpled his chin and shook his head.
"Come on!" said the young man. "Because he slices people up. He does it so that people don't mess with him. Now look what you've made me do!"
"I wouldn't worry if I were you," said Hogarth, rising to his feet. "If old Razor was involved in Helen's murder, he won't be seeing any razors for a very long time. Tell us where we can find this man and you're free to go."
George had turned pale, his eyes inward.
"That name mean anything to you, Kaplan?" said Hogarth, turning to gauge the PCSO's reaction.
"I've heard the name, sir. Seen him about too. Thin, dark hair, surly. Bowl-style brown hair. Very unapproachable. Known to everyone on the beat as potentially violent."
Hogarth nodded and rubbed his chin.

"Now, I really want to pay the man a visit," said Hogarth. Beneath the DI's grim exterior, Palmer knew he was close to smiling.

"That was good what you did with Kaplan, in there," said Palmer. "Though it'll raise a few eyebrows with the others."
"Sod the others," said Hogarth as he opened the door of his unmarked Vauxhall Insignia.
He'd had the car a few years, and the wear and tear was beginning to show. One of the kids in his street had worked out he was a policeman and given it a keying along one side. He knew there was little point asking for the police to pay for the repair, and Hogarth was damned if he was going to subsidise it, so he'd applied some T-cut that came in a lipstick-shaped tube. The lipstick job worked as well as it could but in some lights, the thick line was still visible. He stared at the disguised key line before he got in. Hogarth knew himself to be a vain and finicky man. Such things bothered him. Palmer knew better than to mention it.
Hogarth turned on the ignition and began to reverse out of his space in the police compound car park.
Hogarth glanced at Palmer as he checked the mirrors.
"You'd want her on the team then?" said Palmer, refusing to play along with Hogarth's feigned ignorance. "Ecrin, I mean."
Hogarth shrugged. "I'd rather have her than any of those turds from Basildon. Faye Gordon would probably tell them stories on us. We don't need an enemy in the camp."
"You know Ecrin's at least six months away from qualifying? Then you'd have to get her approved by Melford to make DC."

"She won't rock the boat, Sue. There's value in that. And she'll bring more than she takes. We saw that already once today."

Palmer nodded as the big electric gate slid open to let them out of the compound car park.

"You're right. But Bec Rawlins will have good reason to be pissed off. She's been hankering after promotion for years."

"Not my department, Sue. Besides, who said working in the police was ever fair? Certainly not me. My career is living proof of that, otherwise, I wouldn't have ended up with Melford on my back."

Palmer winced. "You have given him reason – at times."

"Thanks for the vote of support! Don't go sharing that opinion with Kaplan before she starts."

Palmer waited for the moment to pass before she spoke again.

"How are you going to make it work until then?"

Hogarth sighed.

"We'll lean on her here and there. Beg and borrow her from the Neighbourhood Team when we can. If they see her already effectively doing the job, it might force their hand."

"Neighbourhood won't like it either."

"I can do the job, Sue, or I can do the office politics. I'll stick with the job."

"So long as it's done your way."

"Too right. But you saw her, the girl's keen, and who knows, it might even help her get over Simmons."

PCSO Ecrin Kaplan had been living with Simmons when he gave in and slept with the notorious local hack, Alice Perry. Until the fling, theirs had looked a solid relationship but between Simmons and Alice Perry, all that had been left was a smoking crater. Even so, Kaplan had rarely complained. She'd moved back in with her family, got her head down, and got on with the job – working harder than ever to seek promotion. It was the kind of stoic grit Hogarth had always admired.

Palmer was silent.

"What's the matter with you?" said Hogarth. "I thought you'd be pleased. One up for women's lib and all that."

"This has nothing to do with women's lib."

"So you're happy, are you? Because you don't bloody seem it."

"I'm happy for her, yes. But we'd best not wear her out before she joins the team. It might backfire on her."

"Then we'll be careful. I don't want a stranger foisted on us if I can help it."

Palmer sucked in a deep breath.

"And you know why I'll be careful, Sue?"

She looked at him.

"Because I've got you watching me." He smiled, but Palmer wasn't buying it.

"Come on," she replied. "Melford might have asked me to report on you, but I'm not going to do it. You know that."

"Not unless I do something really dicey, eh?"

Palmer puffed out her cheeks.

"What is it with you today?" he said.

"The interview," she admitted. "The way you pushed Samuel George. I thought it was a little extreme at times."

Hogarth kept his eyes on the road. Palmer glanced across and watched his nostrils flare as he chewed over her words. A moment later he looked back.

"We need a result. You know how bad we need it. We're two weeks in and counting, and I can feel the brass passing the buck already. It'll land on us."

"Will it?" said Palmer.

Hogarth nodded. "That's why Melford's chasing us up. He's under pressure, and now so are we. If we don't get something soon, it'll only get worse."

"This could be it. George gave us something new, didn't he?"

"Let's hope so… You know, now that poor Helen Brimelow doesn't seem so saintly, I want that killer even more. That girl might have been playing with fire, but she didn't deserve to get burned like that."

Palmer nodded, but he saw the strained look on her face.

"Let's face it," said Hogarth. "I'm not the reason you're irritated. This is about your situation with Little Madame Pompidou."

"Now you're sounding old."

"Getting older every day, Sue. But don't you get all haughty with me. I can see straight through that bad mood. It's the niece, isn't it? What's her name? Kum-by-yah?"

Palmer rolled her eyes. "You know her name."

"Bit of a mouthful though. It doesn't suit her, either. She looks more like a Stacey or a Danielle to me."

Palmer smiled. "My sister had some affectations. Her daughter's name was one of them. Sadly, motherhood didn't quite suit any of them."

"Doesn't suit you either, though, does it?"

Palmer pursed her lips. "I suppose I've lived a fair old time without any kind of company."

"And she's not really the kind of company you need, is she?"

Palmer cleared her throat and turned away to stare out of the passenger window. Their conversation had ventured into uncomfortable territory, and Palmer had no intention of going any further. She kept her eyes on the street until she felt the heat in her cheeks start to recede. Hogarth glanced at her averted profile. Women had always been a mystery to him. But he knew one thing for sure… Palmer seemed more irritated than ever.

Kevin Robbins, nicknamed Razor, lived at eighty-six Haycock Tower. His flat was in the heady heights of the building, which meant a longer ride in the urine-scented lift than either of them would have liked, but the climb up the stairs would have been even more intolerable, and the smells probably worse. When they arrived, they found the tenth floor ripe with all kinds of other fragrances. Greasy fried food, old tobacco smoke, pets, and a hint of skunk.
"Any bets as to whose flat the skunk smoke is coming from?" said Hogarth.
"Up here, it could be any or all of them. Some of the older people here don't seem to know better than the younger ones."
Hogarth fixed his eyes on the chipped royal blue door of number eighty-six.
"I know which door my money's on."
Hogarth thumbed the doorbell, but it was silent. The battery had probably died years ago and never been replaced. They could have let the man know they were coming by using the external intercom, but if they had done so, Robbins would have almost certainly flown the coop before they reached his door. Murderer or not, Robbins had a rep. There were probably a half dozen crimes he was worried about getting collared for.
Hogarth shook his head and banged the fleshy heel of his fist against the door.

"Robbins. Open up. It's the police."

"Not sure that's going to help us," said Palmer.

Hogarth looked her in the eye. "He's opening up whether he likes it or not."

Hogarth banged the door again. Still no answer.

"He might have left for the day?" said Palmer. "Once his sort leave the house, that's it until the early hours."

"Could be," said Hogarth but Palmer saw he wasn't convinced. Her brow dipped low over her eyes, and she slid her mobile phone from her pocket and stole a glance. Aaliyah still hadn't replied.

"I'd give up on that if I were you," said Hogarth, without looking around. Palmer was surprised he'd noticed her sleight of hand. He hammered the door a third time before he looked around.

"I've met a few girls like your niece in my time. Even dated one or two of them, back in the day. It's no good ever trying to make them bend to your will. They'll only ever snap back in your face then do whatever the hell they like anyway."

"Thanks for the parenting advice. I never knew you were such an expert."

"I'm not, and neither are you. But trust me on this one. Stop pushing and she'll start acting better. Think of it as a version of treat 'em mean, keep 'em keen."

Palmer rolled her eyes and looked at the door, directing Hogarth's attention back to the job at hand.

"Are we going to waste any more time here or shall we see if he's down at the food bank?"

"He wasn't down there before," said Hogarth. "One of those idiots in the concrete square would have let slip if he was. None of them can keep a secret for want of gossip when they've got drink inside 'em."

"We could try Warrior Square then?"

"Or the crack dens or doss houses. But I'm really not in the mood to go chasing another waster with Melford pushing for a result."

Palmer took the comment as another barb and pursed her lips, but Hogarth's voice trailed off. His tone was so neutral she held her tongue. Hogarth narrowed his eyes. Something about the unpleasant fug in the draughty hallway had bothered him. It was more than full dustbins, smoke and pets… His mouth flattened and he groaned as he dropped to his haunches. He flipped the letterbox of eighty-six open and peered into the dingy darkness within, but the odour within made him snap the letter box shut and flinch away, holding his breath.

"Crikey O'Riley…" he said. He pulled away and looked up at Palmer.

The moody look on her face softened by a degree or two. "What is it?"

Hogarth dragged himself to his feet and grimaced.

"We're going in," he said, his voice firm.

"What do you mean, we've got no cause—"

But Hogarth had already pulled back past her. He fixed his eyes on the door, before lunging and slamming the heel of one tan brogue hard against the lock. The door crunched in the frame, and the resulting thud echoed all around the lobby, sounding as if the impact had been twenty times worse. But the door held. Hogarth bared his teeth and drew back for another go.

"What—"

"Either Robbins has been living in his own filth, Palmer, or something else is causing that stench in there."

Hogarth pulled back and again slammed his boot hard and directly onto the face of the lock. The crunch of splitting wood was loud as a thunder crack. The door flew open into a dingy brown darkness. A faint rectangle of light came from around the edges of the front room curtains at the end of the hall, dead ahead. But what hit both of them was the stench; it came at them like a wall, pungent, thick, and enough to make Palmer turn away. One of the nearby flat doors opened by a few degrees. A mature woman looked out through the narrow gap, the chain still on the door.
"Whatever is going on out here?" she said.
"Police business," said Palmer. "Please go in and close the door."
The woman's eyes flared, but she nodded at once and did as she was told.
Hogarth stepped into the narrow hallway of the flat, resolving to breathe through his mouth, and as little as he possibly could. The air seemed rotten.
He marched into the flat, flicking on lights as he went, searching for the switches with the backs of his hands so he didn't risk catching something. The kitchenette was a bombsite. But he stopped in the doorway, recognising certain items as soon as he saw them. Palmer joined his side and nodded. She saw the discoloured tablespoon, and the small white plastic bottle, lid off, left beside a small, upturned cup and an electric camping stove.
"Spoon. Bicarb…" said Palmer.
"Citric Acid over there too," said Hogarth.
"Robbins is a heroin junkie," said Palmer. "Looks like his cooker wasn't working though. That would explain the camping stove."

"And the smell…" said Hogarth, pushing on down the corridor, "should be explained by this." He flicked on the living room light and watched as the room came into sharp relief. There, in a dated cream leather recliner, was a man with a hard, weary face and a bowl cut of dark hair. His eyes were half open. There were lines all over his forehead and a week's worth of stubble over his chin. His head lay to one side, his eyes glazed but bone dry and far away.

"He's been dead for days," said Hogarth. "I'd say at least a week by the smell of him."

Hogarth marched past the prone body and peeled the curtains back to let in the light. Even the curtains felt damp and greasy to the touch. He opened the windows as wide as he could, as many as he could find. The fresh cold air rushed in and he took a lungful and looked out at the vista of the distant estuary for a moment's respite. Then he turned back and got to work.

"Another dead end," said Palmer, with a frustrated sigh. "Do you think it was suicide?"

Hogarth walked around the chair to face the dead man's body. He took a good look. His hair and clothes dated him as something of an Oasis fan. But even for a dead man, Hogarth thought Robbins had aged well. He couldn't help thinking he was almost the same age as Robbins… the possibility that the dead man might have looked better than him even when dead passed through his mind. A bitter smile tried to bother Hogarth's lips but failed.

"Suicide at the loss of his girlfriend?" said Hogarth. "Or suicide because he was guilty of her murder?"

"It's possible, isn't it?" said Palmer.

Hogarth stroked his jutting chin and stared at the corpse. "Possible, but not likely. Not for a man like him. A junkie his age will have seen a fair few friends die in his time. Look at him. How he lived. Drugs turn people like him into cold-hearted survivalists. Opportunists, too. It's a dog eat dog world, being a junkie. You've seen it. Down there by the food bank, most of those people couldn't give a rat's arse about anyone but themselves. Granted, it's good that the Refuge is trying to do something, but…"

"They're all a lost cause then?" said Palmer. "No. I don't think so. Not all of them. And Helen Brimelow must have seen something in him."

Hogarth's eyes sparked at her. He scratched his temple. "There might be hope for some of them. But this one looks like the other kind to me."

Hogarth toed the detritus on the dirty carpet by the man's feet. A full ashtray, an open tobacco pouch, an empty beer can and a butterfly knife, left open, blade half hidden by the chair.

"That's a weapon," said Hogarth. "We already know that Robbins here was no angel."

"Then why did Helen Brimelow go for him?"

Hogarth ran his eyes over the man's narrow face, tidy hair and orderly clothes.

"Nice bit of rough? Because he still had his looks, maybe. Because he was a charmer. Because she romanticised the bloody lot of them, who knows? Some young people think of drugs as glamorous. I blame it on the movies and music. They see the world through different eyes to us."

"But we were into all that when we were young, weren't we?"

By way of an answer, Hogarth crumpled his chin.

"Is he a suspect?"

"Wouldn't that be neat and tidy, but no, I don't think so…"

"Why not?" said Palmer, frowning.

"It's not suicide, is it? Where's the note? I can't see it. And there's nothing of the girl anywhere in sight. No photograph. No newspaper clipping about her murder. Nothing. No. This here was Robbins kicking back, getting his kicks for the day. He wasn't pining for Helen Brimelow when this happened."

"Perhaps he felt guilty for what he'd done?"

Hogarth shook his head. He eyed the man's arm, and carefully pulled back his sleeve without touching the dead man's skin. He ran his eyes over the dead man's clean, pale grey forearm. He saw a few scars and pockmarks, the injuries left behind by a decade and more of drug use. But there were far fewer scars than he'd expected. He looked at the empty syringe down by the side of the chair.

"Guilty? I doubt this man ever knew the meaning of the word. But," said Hogarth, changing tone as he looked back at Palmer, "we can't rule it out."

Palmer nodded.

"Because…" said Hogarth.

"Because?" said Palmer.

"Because looking at his arm, Kevin Robbins wasn't as much of a junkie as I suspected. He was forty-four, and he's got arms cleaner than plenty of twenty-five-year-old junkies I've seen."

"Then he wasn't an addict?"

"Oh, I'd say he was. Just not your hardcore type."

"I don't get it," said Palmer. "What do you make of this, if it wasn't suicide?"

Hogarth caught Palmer's frustrated tone and raised a hand. "Hey. I'm not ruling it out, but I'd say this looks more like a classic OD to me – too much of a good thing rather than a remorse suicide or a grief-stricken lover."

Unable to see what Hogarth was seeing, Palmer shook her head in frustration. Hogarth was being obstinate again. The hangover was keeping him from seeing clearly.

"Have you considered that you might be wrong on this?"

"I considered it," said Hogarth. "But look. He's in good nick for a junkie. That doesn't make it work."

"It makes more sense if he topped himself over Helen Brimelow," said Palmer.

"It makes it *convenient*," said Hogarth. "But I don't like convenient. Not after two weeks of nothing then a free lunch like this. That would make even less sense. Look around. See if you can find whatever gear he stuck in that needle. I want it analysed."

"It's bound to be heroin," said Palmer.

"Without a doubt, but there's more to this than meets the eye."

"You still think it's suspicious?"

"I think it's all suspicious, Sue. But I'll tell you one thing I know for certain. Even if you're right and Robbins here topped himself because of Helen Brimelow, there's no way a man like this would have been smart enough to keep us at bay for a whole two weeks – not if he was the one who killed her."

Seeing the weary look on Hogarth's face and the darkness around his eyes, Palmer made no comment. She felt far less certain of Hogarth's present powers than she had before. Hogarth grimaced at the lack of response then took a breath and turned back to the kitchen in the hunt for the drugs.

"Call it in. One of us is right. The quicker we know which, the better it'll be."

Palmer made the call to notify their colleagues. Because of their doubts, eighty-six Haycock would be treated as a crime scene.

When she was done with the call, Hogarth emerged from the kitchen. From the look in his eyes, she knew he had found something.

"What is it?"

"A wrap, left open in the cutlery drawer. The drawer was open. Unusual, that. The wrap was jam-packed full of good, pure, pale brown powder too, and the wrap had been left open. Must have cost him a fortune. Which gives us another question. How does a man like him afford gear of that quality, and in that amount?"

"I suppose you've got a theory," said Palmer, unwilling to play the foil to Hogarth's rhetorical games.

"Not yet, no. But it makes me wonder…"

"You can't be putting his OD down to a coincidence, surely? Brimelow dies, then her lover dies a week later for no clear reason… because that's what it sounds like you're saying."

"Not coincidence. But I'm not putting it down to grief or guilt either. I don't like coincidences, and I don't like things too neat."

"It's not neat. You can't call this neat. But it might be logical."

"Logical?" said Hogarth. "Yes, it might be that. And now, our job's to find out where the logic comes in."

Palmer relented with a weary nod.

Through the open windows they heard the first faint sirens burst into life as they left the police station car park across town.

Ten

When evening came, Palmer was pleasantly surprised to find her niece at home. After Hogarth's mansplaining about how to handle a teenager, Palmer had resigned herself to the fact her niece wasn't going to obey her in any way. The result was she hadn't bothered with chasing her up for a whole afternoon. So when Palmer walked into the hallway of her flat, she wondered if she might have accidentally applied Hogarth's advice. Perhaps he was onto something because she was met by the comforting sound of television canned laughter and applause, and the smell of a fragrant hot dinner. It was probably a microwave meal, and there was always a strong chance that Aaliyah had prepared the meal for herself, but after the grim sights and sounds of Kevin Robbins' apartment of death, her own small home felt like a place of beauty, warmth, and comfort. Palmer walked into the living room, arms folded, ready for anything. She found Aaliyah sprawled on the sofa, smiling. There was a tray on the coffee table which was adorned with a bottle of white wine, the bottle suitably cold-misted, accompanied by a bowl of fat juicy olives and a bowl of crisps. Aaliyah twisted a lock of hair around her fingers and smiled an unreadable smile. Palmer glanced at the television. There was a quiz show on the box. *Pointless.* It was a show neither of them had ever watched by choice. Palmer tossed her handbag down to the armchair and put her hands on her hips.
"So, what's all this in aid of?" she said with a smile.
"Nothing," said Aaliyah, eyeing the TV screen. The flickering glow filled her face and showed traces of some

well-applied make-up. The girl was good with the slap in a way Palmer had never been. Neither had her sister, come to think of it.

"I suppose I got an insight into your job," said the girl. "That's all. I guess it must be quite tough out there, dealing with all those ruffians and criminals."

"It can be," said Palmer in a guarded tone. She felt the tense suspicion in her body and decided she was being unfair. She had brought her work mindset home again. Didn't her niece deserve the benefit of the doubt? She was barely more than a child, after all. "But you get used to it, after a while."

"Do you?" said Aaliyah, her eyes glinting with the television light.

"Sort of," said Palmer. "But there are a few things you never get used to."

"Like what?" said the girl, turning to face Palmer as she sat down in the big armchair.

"Like dead bodies. Putrefying flesh…"

Aaliyah made a face. "Eurggh."

"But we don't need to go there, do we?" said Palmer.

"You can talk if that's what you need," said the girl, sounding uncertain.

"No. You didn't move here to become my counsellor, did you? How was your day? I tried to contact you. A few times, actually."

"Sorry. I just didn't feel like replying. I'm not used to people calling me all the time. Or text. Mum never kept tabs on me like you do. I've got used to my freedom."

"I'm not trying to cramp your style, Ali. I'm just trying to give you a couple of boundaries. To help you. We all need them, you know?"

The girl looked at her, silently, doubts written all over her face.

"Seriously," said Palmer. "You're not even eighteen, yet, after all."
The girl rolled her eyes. "It's so close I might as well be."
"Not in the eyes of the law, you're not. You can have your freedom, Aaliyah – but with some helpful rules."
The girl made a face.
"And, seeing as you're living under my roof…"
The girl sighed, and Palmer reclined in her seat. She changed tack. "Now what's all this in aid of?"
"I made you some dinner. That's all. Thought you might like it. And a glass of wine never goes amiss, does it?"
Palmer eyed the wine. It did look rather tempting.
"It'll be the first time you've cooked since you've been here."
"So?" said the girl.
Palmer shook her head once then said nothing.
"You're all cop, aren't you?" said the girl. "I was just trying to do something nice. I might have even been trying to say sorry… for being such a bother to you."
"You're not a bother…"
The girl met her aunt's eyes accusingly and Palmer stopped talking. There was a moment's silence between them.
"There's moussaka in the oven. It's still hot. Shall I dish it up for you?"
Palmer looked at the girl's face and tried to read through the make-up, looking into her eyes in the changing light from the TV screen.
"That would be nice," Palmer eventually replied. The girl got up from the sofa, walked out into the hallway and disappeared into the brightly lit kitchen.
The bang and clatter of open and shutting doors filled the air and two minutes later, her niece reappeared carrying a tray

with a plate of steaming moussaka, a green leaf salad, and an empty wine glass. She handed it to Palmer, keenly looking for a response. Palmer forced a smile.

"Thanks," she said.

"Can I pour you some wine?"

"Yes, thanks. Just a little."

The girl unscrewed the bottle and poured the glass until it was almost full. "That's enough."

"Relax," said the girl. "You never relax, do you?"

"Rarely, it's true… But I can't help but be surprised. Your mum never mentioned that you cooked."

"Don't get excited, Sue. All of this came out of a packet."

"It's nice, all the same. Aren't you going to have some?"

"I'll have a bit after you. You should have the lion's share, seeing as you work all day…"

Palmer gave a nod and started to eat. She felt the girl watching her as she cut a piece of moussaka and put it into her mouth. She made an appreciative noise. It tasted well enough, but the questions in her mind were distracting from the meal. When the plate was two-thirds empty, and the crunchy lettuce had been left untouched, she put the tray aside and tapped her stomach.

"Delicious. That was plenty, thanks."

"Good," said her niece. "Now drink your wine and chill out."

Palmer rolled her tongue around the back of her teeth, probing a loose strand of lamb. She picked up her glass and took a sip. Her eyes lingered on Aaliyah's face as she drank.

"What are you up to?"

"Up to?"

"All this fuss, for me. What's it all about?"

"Nothing," said the girl. But she looked away, and Palmer saw there was something.

She waited a moment and took another sip.

"Think of it as a thank you," she said.

Palmer sipped again, but carefully now. Something was coming, she felt it in the air. A request. A shock piece of news. A new boyfriend… No, that would have been the worst news. Her sister would have never forgiven her for letting it happen – as if she would have had any choice in the matter. Palmer looked blankly at the TV screen and waited. Two more minutes passed. The girl looked at her, and Palmer met her eye.

"Freedom with some guidelines – that sounds okay – I guess," said the girl.

Palmer braced herself.

"But those rules could be flexible, for different situations, and different kinds of purposes, couldn't they?"

"Not usually," said Palmer. "In police work, you either have a rule or you don't. Shades of grey never work, not in my experience."

"But this isn't police work. This is just us, right?"

"Where are you going with this, Aaliyah?"

"Nowhere. Just theorising, that's all."

Theorising. As if she needed any more of that. Or anyone else suggesting they knew better than her. Getting patronised by a seventeen-year-old was galling.

"Theorising," said Palmer.

"Yeah. Don't panic. I wasn't about to push those boundaries or anything!" she said, with an affected laugh. Immediately, Palmer knew she meant the opposite. Palmer nodded and narrowed her eyes.

"Just nipping to the loo," said Palmer, setting her glass aside and standing up. She felt the girl's eyes on her back as she

left the living room. As soon as she was in the hallway, Palmer shook her head. She looked left into the kitchen and saw the girl's little clutch bag on the kitchen counter. But looking at the coat hooks near the bathroom door, she changed her mind. There was the girl's coat, the purple jacket she usually wore, hanging from the hook. Palmer grabbed it and took it with her into the bathroom. She locked the door and sat down on the closed toilet lid then started a systematic search of the coat pockets, not knowing what she was looking for. A scribbled phone number? A condom, maybe? A bag of pills, at worst. But there was nothing so incriminating. Last of all, she tried the inside pocket and found a folded slip of paper. Gotcha… Palmer unfolded the paper, half expecting to see a profane or pornographic note from a male suitor, but what she found took her by surprise. Her mouth dropped open as she scanned the printed text and the photograph below it.
Reach Out!
Free Talk and Dinner, the Refuge Food Bank, 8 pm.
The photograph showed a thin bald man with a smile so wide and bright Palmer might have thought he was on something, but he was a Christian. The flyer said the speaker was fresh back from working as a missionary in Africa. Missionary to Africa? Did they still do that kind of thing? It seemed they did. She looked at the flyer and saw the talk was booked for that very evening. Hardly Aaliyah's kind of thing, was it? But Helen Brimelow had once been lured in to help. Palmer frowned. What had Helen Brimelow been lured by, exactly? The promise of salvation and of spreading the good news? Or by the mysterious strangers that darkened the food bank's doors three days a week. She was being unfair, of course. Helen had been a saint, and had done a lot of good work, but try as she might, Palmer was having a hard time

seeing her niece as any kind of saint in the making. Armed with her suspicions, Palmer stood up from the toilet, flushed it, and slipped the note back in the jacket pocket. She opened the door, glanced to the open living room, saw it was safe, and put the purple jacket back on its hook. Palmer walked back into the living room, smiling, sweeping her fringe from her eyes as if nothing was wrong. She sat down and made a show of picking up her wine glass.

Her niece smiled and looked at the glass.

"So," said Palmer. "What did you make of that place the other day? The food bank?"

"What?" said Aaliyah.

"The Refuge food bank," said Palmer, sipping her wine. "What did you make of it?"

"Oh. That place. Yeah, I thought it was interesting. Very colourful."

"Colourful? You can say that again."

"You know, the volunteers, the guests… the murals on the walls… the songs they sang, I found it all kind of… intriguing."

"I'll bet it was," said Palmer. She put the wine glass to her lips again, made to sip, but this time she didn't drink. She waited.

"Intriguing…?" said Palmer.

"Yeah. Like, maybe it would be good for me to see what they're on about. All this Christian stuff. I've never really thought much about it before."

"Thought about God, you mean?"

"Maybe. About all kinds of things."

Palmer nodded.

"In fact… seeing as we've just been talking about my freedom, and seeing as the place is pretty much just a church, I was thinking… There's a service there tonight. A talk. I was thinking I might go along."

"Go to the Refuge? Tonight?"

"Yes," said the girl, with an emphatic nod. "Tonight. They're serving a dinner. I could go there. I could help them. You said you wanted me to do something, didn't you? And it is a church, after all…"

"I really don't think that's the kind of place your mother would want you—"

"I don't give a shit what my mum wants! She doesn't give a shit about me, does she? That's why she's chucked me over to you."

"Then maybe I care, Aaliyah."

"And maybe you do. But this is exactly the kind of freedom I need. It's a church, Sue. I'll be fine."

Palmer frowned.

"It's a church," said the girl. "If you say no to that, where would you say yes to?"

Palmer puffed her cheeks. The girl smiled.

"Don't worry. Honest. I'll be back by ten."

"Ten?"

"Yeah. I promise. You won't have to worry."

"Oh, I won't worry," said Palmer.

"Why not?" said Aliyah.

"Because I'm coming with you."

"What? But you can't even drive. You've been drinking. And you're tired. You've been working all day."

Palmer smiled. "Don't worry. I'm still well within the legal limit. I made sure of it. Just in case."

"What about my freedom?!" said the girl.

"You're seventeen years old, and those men were looking at you the way lions look at fresh meat. I'm coming with you, end of story."
"You can be real drag, Sue."
"You're welcome," she said, standing up again. "Now, don't you dare try and run out while I'm getting changed or there'll be hell to pay."
"Bit ironic, don't you think?" said the girl.
"What's ironic?" said Palmer, raising an eyebrow.
"I want to go to church, so you're threatening me with hell?"
Palmer shook her head and walked away. *Teenagers!*

Thankfully, the wine hadn't done much. Palmer had been careful to drink only a few sips. But the moussaka felt heavy in her stomach, weighing her down, making the waist of her skirt uncomfortably tight. The food had made her tired too, but there was no way she could let her niece off the leash near the Refuge – especially at night. Palmer parked up in a space right beside the gate of the estate, out on Coleman Street. If she had owned any other type of car, she might have worried about it there. As it was, she still had the same old Corsa with the dent in the bonnet that she'd put up with for years.
"You shouldn't have come tonight, you know that?" said Aaliyah.
Palmer pulled up the handbrake and switched off the engine. They sat in the small dark car, faces dim and grey. Brassy yellow lights were on in the windows of the Refuge. A couple of small groups of the usual type lingered near the front door, smoking and drinking.

Aaliyah seemed nervous. Excited, too.

"Why not?" said Palmer. "What did you have in mind?"

"I wanted to scope the place out, you know. See what it was like. I thought I might even volunteer if I liked the place."

"That's really not a good idea, Aaliyah."

"The psycho you're looking for is hardly likely to hit the place twice, is he? He'd be caught in a heartbeat. Besides, the girl only volunteered there. Doesn't mean that's where he found her."

"Killers aren't always logical. They can be impulsive, irrational, run by their urges. He could be watching everyone up there, even now."

Palmer experienced a brief flashback to the pale bloodless body in the beach hut... a sickening vision of the cold gaping wound.

"It's cute that you want to look after me, Sue. But please don't push it too far. I'm a grown-up, now."

Before Palmer could reply, the girl opened the car door and slammed it shut behind her. Palmer sucked in a breath and set off after her. The girl kept a good pace, keeping ten then twenty feet ahead of her all the way up towards the dark exterior of the Refuge. Looking ahead of her, Palmer was glad that she saw mostly Hogarth's 'soft types' in the waiting groups. But the predators would still be around. And the chancers, such as Suitcase, too. Maybe they were already inside.

"The evening just got a lot more interesting," said one of the motley crew to his friends, adding a crude and wheezy laugh.

"Oi, cheeky!" said Aaliyah, smiling. She left the smokers and turned directly to the white uPVC door which was set into the wall covered in detailed and colourful murals. The murals were unreadable in the evening light, just a mess of swirls and strange faces. Aaliyah had plunged the door handle and walked into the bright interior before Palmer caught up with her. When she arrived, the door was gently banged in her face. Another crude laugh sounded behind her. Palmer turned around and shot a hard stare worthy of Hogarth. "You lot can shut your mouths," she said.

"*Ooh-ooh!* Think she needs some prayer," said another, laughing.

Palmer went inside. Unlike during the daytime food bank hours, the front reception desk was unmanned, and the place felt strangely empty. Palmer sensed movement and people further inside the building, but the place felt different. She heard soft rock music being played over the speakers in the main room. As she walked down the corridor, she realised the songs were about God, Jesus and the cross. Palmer had never felt called to religion. The words and concepts had always grated with her in some way she couldn't quite explain. In the same way, the song lyrics made her feel awkward and out of place. Palmer looked through the netted glass of the fire door into the main hall and saw the central hall had been set out much the same as for the memorial service – rows of leather seats set up like pews, side by side. A few of the wooden café tables had been set up at the back – ready for the promised evening dinners to be served after the talk. But from the look of the many empty seats, it was going to be a quiet night. Palmer counted thirteen guests and two hosts. One of the hosts was the man from the photograph on the flyer – the missionary come home. The other was the hipster food bank manager and community man, Freddie Halstead. Halstead seemed busy, toying with a projector that was beaming light and images onto the back wall, while the missionary man noticed Palmer through the glass and beckoned her inside. Palmer's heart sank. Her eyes drifted across the room to see Aaliyah already in animated conversation with one of the male volunteers who was setting up the heated serving bain-maries at the back counter. The volunteer was dressed no better than the people outside – baggy jeans, slouchy cardigan, and a baseball cap. He looked twice Aaliyah's age at least. Palmer's brow dipped low over her eyes. Why did the girl always want to invite trouble?

She strode through the door and made a beeline towards them, already appraising the volunteer with the baseball cap. He looked a little odd, she decided, but was he a killer? No way to tell until she got his name and ran a check; all the same she didn't think she'd seen him before...

"Good evening!" said a voice by her shoulder. The smell of an older man's aftershave filled her nostrils – all pine needles, citrus, and woodland. Palmer turned to see the missionary close by, offering her a hand to shake. His smile was wide, his teeth shiny, his eyes almost maniacal in their eagerness to greet her. Palmer told herself to run his name through the system in the morning.

"I'm Dennis Corby. Corby like the trouser press," he said, as if it were a joke. Palmer's lips wrinkled. She didn't manage a smile.

"I'm speaking tonight."

"Yes, I recognise you from the flyer."

"You do?" said the man, almost sounding surprised. "Wonderful."

Palmer heard Aaliyah's distinctive laugh from the other side of the room. The volunteer with her joined in the laughter. Palmer shot a look at them and saw Aaliyah laying a hand on the man's arm. Either she was too keen to fit in, or the man was making an impression. Palmer's mood took a turn for the worse.

"Are you a believer, or a seeker?"

"Sorry?" said Palmer. She met the man's eyes but her thoughts were elsewhere.

"A believer or a seeker?" he repeated. This time Corby must have noticed the glint of anger in Palmer's eyes because his smile wavered.

"That must put me in the seeker category," said Palmer. She nodded towards Aaliyah. "But I've found what I'm looking for. I'm here to keep that one safe. Hope the talk goes well."

"You never know," he replied. "I have a feeling my words could be for you as much as anyone else here tonight. The Lord brought you here for a reason, after all."

"I'm sure," said Palmer. "What was your name again?"

"Dennis—"

"Oh yes. Corby. Like the trouser press. Excuse me, Dennis."

The man nodded as Palmer made off to the back of the room. She saw the dishevelled volunteer leaning close to whisper something at Aaliyah. Whatever he had said made Aaliyah laugh out loud, but she covered her mouth and regained her composure just in time to see her aunt arrive at her side.

"I didn't know you knew anyone in here," said Palmer.

"I don't," said her niece, the smile sliding away from her face.

"Then you two have made friends pretty quickly."

"We've only just met, haven't we, Josh?"

The man looked at Palmer and nodded. The long, straggly brown hair coming out of the back of his cap made him seem young, but he had strange and serious eyes, and the lines on his face dated him at around forty or thereabouts.

"Josh," said Palmer. She offered a hand. "I've been around the food bank so many times lately I thought I must know everyone here by now."

Josh nodded and adjusted the peak of his cap. From the lack of light in his eyes and his flat line of a mouth, Palmer wondered whether he was either socially or mentally challenged. There seemed something off, but she couldn't place it.

"Oh, I don't come here often," he said. The man was well spoken, nothing like what Palmer had expected.

"No?" said Palmer.

"No, I usually volunteer at the church on Sundays. But as tonight is a church night, not a food bank night, I thought I'd come to help."

"You're from the church?"

The man nodded. "Yes. I'm a regular there."

Palmer's mouth twitched.

"What's your surname, Josh?"

"Sue!" said her niece. "Josh is just a volunteer." Palmer ignored her.

Josh scratched the back of his head.

"Burdon. Why do you ask?"

"Habit, I'm afraid. I'm a police officer."

Aaliyah shook her head. "She's also my aunt, but sometimes it feels like she's more like my jailor."

"Now, now," said Josh, without a trace of a smile. "I'm sure she's looking after you. Something to do with that appalling murder, I take it."

Palmer looked deep into the man's dark eyes. They were unreadable.

"Not really, I'm here for my niece. It pays to be careful."

"It does, indeed. You can't be too careful these days, can you?" he said. A fraction of a smile broke across his face before he seemed to become serious again. Palmer's eyes narrowed, but she tried to hide it.

"Maybe we should go and take a seat. Find out what this evening's talk is about," said Palmer.

"Good idea. Why don't you go and pick us some good seats? I'll be along in a minute or two," said Aaliyah, with a cocky smile. Palmer arched an eyebrow and walked away. For the time being, she didn't mind leaving the girl where she was. Palmer picked her way between the chairs, heading for the trouser-press preacher. As soon as Corby saw her, he clasped his hands together and smiled.

"That man over there, the one preparing the food," said Palmer quietly. She nodded back across her shoulder. "Josh."

"Yes?" said the man.

"He helps at the church?"

"Yes, I believe so."

"Do you know anything about him? What he does there? Who he hangs around with? He strikes me as a little... different."

Corby opened his mouth and the lines of his forehead concertinaed high over his face. He looked around, struggling to answer.

"I'm sorry, I don't think I can help you there. I'm just a guest of the church here. I don't know much about the people here."

The hipster Halstead looked up from the projector. He frowned as he ran his eyes between the Palmer and Corby. He smiled. It was a dutiful smile, warm and friendly. It looked natural enough, but Palmer surmised it wasn't. In his job, it was probably the product of a lot of practice.

Halstead moved across the room and threaded his hands into his pockets.

"You're from the investigation into Helen's…"

"Murder," said Palmer. "That's right."

"Yeah. I still find it difficult to say the word. I know it's true all the same, but you know… it's still horrible to say it."

Palmer nodded. "Murder is the harshest of words, but it still doesn't do justice to the crime it describes."

"Quite so," said Corby, with a solemn nod.

"You were asking about Josh?" said Halstead.

"That's right. My niece seems to have hit it off with him right away…"

"Your niece? She's pretty talkative. She was here before, wasn't she?"

Palmer hesitated, before making a grudging admission. "Yes. She seems to have taken a shine to the place."

Halstead grinned. "That happens a lot here. And we know why, don't we, Dennis?"

"Indeed, we do. The good Lord moves people as he sees fit. He calls them to his presence."

In other circumstances, Palmer might have rolled her eyes. If Hogarth had been present, she was sure he would have said something sharp, but Palmer was too polite for that, and there was *something* about the place. She glanced across the hall to see her niece helping Josh to plug the electric bain-maries into the sockets and stack the plates.

"She seems like she's got a big heart," said Corby.

"Matches her head," said Palmer. "What can you tell me about Josh over there?"

Halstead shook his head slowly.

"Josh? He's really not your man."

Palmer pursed her lips. "In the seventies, the police interviewed the Yorkshire Ripper more than once before they finally nicked him. They thought they had the wrong man. He killed several more people in between those interviews. We can't rule anybody out."

"I understand what you're saying," said Halstead. "But Josh is different."

"I gathered he's different. A little stiff, even. Strikes me as odd, and yet somehow he's making my niece laugh."

"He's got a very dry wit," said Halstead. "In fact, he's got a very good sense of humour for a man with Asperger's. He's come a long way through volunteering."

"Asperger's?"

Halstead nodded. "These days he'll meet your eye, but a few years back he couldn't even manage that."

"Did he know Helen Brimelow?"

"Their paths may have crossed, but I never noticed them together. Helen went to the main church because of what we do here. Josh was already there. He's been going there for years. They were different in so many ways. The church is a very busy place on a Sunday – there's too many people to get to know each other well."

Palmer nodded, but she didn't look convinced and Halstead saw it.

"It won't be him, honestly. I've dealt with a lot of people with mental health issues and social behavioural things going on."

"In your work, I take it?" said Palmer.

"Yes, in my work as well. But Josh hasn't got it in him. He's as gentle as they come."

"In your work *as well?*" said Palmer.

Halstead nodded.

"My brother has special needs. A whole range of them. I don't even think they've all been properly diagnosed. They seem to find another definition for him every year or so."

"I see."

Halstead made a point of looking at the big clock on the side wall. It was ten minutes past the hour.

"Doesn't look like we're going to get many in tonight. Right, Dennis. I think we'd best make a start. Josh won't be happy if that food goes dry…"

Halstead smirked for Palmer's benefit and clapped his hands.

"Mr Halstead," she said.

"Yes."

"Just one thing. Did you ever see Helen getting friendly with anybody from the tower blocks?"

Halstead frowned and studied Palmer's face.

"A service user, you mean?"

Palmer nodded, then shrugged. "Either one of your regulars, or someone you would have seen on the estate."

She watched Halstead as he considered the question. He looked away in thought. When he looked up he shook his head. "No. Helen knew mixing with people on the estate wasn't recommended. It's against our code of conduct here – it's for volunteer safety, you understand."

"I understand," said Palmer.

"Why? What happened, Inspector?"

"Detective Sergeant," she corrected. "I'm not at liberty to say, Mr Halstead."

Halstead nodded. "I see. What a mess this is," he said.

"Don't you ever have any downtime, Detective Sergeant?"

Palmer wrinkled her brow. "Why do you ask?"

Halstead nodded at the clock again. "Your working hours are beginning to look as bad as ours."

Palmer tried for a smile. "No. They're much worse, believe me. Right, I'd best go and drag my niece away from your volunteer."

Halstead smiled and moved to the front of the hall. As he started the announcements and introductions, Palmer took her seat with Aaliyah at her side. Behind them, Josh continued setting up the food serving area.

"You're like a girl on a mission here tonight," whispered Palmer.

"You're one to talk," the girl replied. "Is everyone in here one of your suspects?"

Palmer glanced up as the hall door opened, and three heavy-set figures with tired, boozy eyes and stubbly faces shambled in. One of them was Suitcase, large and stumbling. The other two were vaguely familiar, and no less threatening for it.

"Pretty much," said Palmer, eyeing the three men. She saw the glint appear in the big men's eyes one by one as they landed on Aaliyah's well-styled hair. Suitcase elbowed one of his fellow miscreants and whispered as they took a seat. Palmer glowered at them, but they refused to meet her eye. As for her niece, her eyes were already elsewhere. Facing front, Aaliyah's eyes were glued to Freddie Halstead's tattooed, muscular physique as he spoke. Before the end of his introductions, the girl had locked onto his eyes. Halstead looked back and received the full force of their suggestive gleam. For a moment, he fumbled his words but recovered enough for most not to notice. Aaliyah smouldered at him from the thin crowd. If anyone had paid close enough attention, they might have seen the slightest wrinkle of a smile on Halstead's face and a hint of colour about his cheeks. Halstead's eyes returned to Aaliyah's one last time before he took his seat and led the applause for Dennis Corby. As Palmer pinpointed the seats of the three risky men behind her, her niece smiled, pleased as punch. He had noticed her. And he had noticed her in exactly the way she'd hoped.

Eleven

Hogarth reached for the bottle on the mantelpiece. The way he was going it would be empty by tomorrow night. Christmas had come early, it seemed. Some joke that was. There had been no presents, no leads, no joy of any kind. Not unless he counted his nights with Andi. She was a fine woman, plenty enough to keep him warm at night and more besides, but from her no-show, Hogarth reckoned he had blown it. The late-night visit to David Brimelow had been irritating enough as it was – and now he was going to pay for it in more ways than one. Still, it wasn't just Brimelow's fault. His mind had been wandering for days now and his sudden taste for evening walks had been driving the woman up the wall. In short, it seemed he had been doing everything he could to get rid of her – without even realising it.
"Is that what you want?" he grumbled to himself as he looked at his whisky bottle. "To turn yourself into a total lonely old loser?"
He curled his lip and set his jaw. "Self-pity doesn't suit you either, Joe. You made this bloody bed, so now you lie in it."
He looked up and saw his reflection in the mirror above the fireplace. He looked achingly tired, but the fire in his eyes burned brightly. Sleep wouldn't come easy again tonight. He wondered if another measure or two would fix matters. Trouble was, he'd be even worse the next day. He knew Palmer had already noticed his drinking and didn't want a

meddlesome PC like Orton adding his gossip into the mix. The DCI would soon be back on his case.

"Back to the late-night walkies for you then," he muttered. "But not without a last little tot." He added the smallest dash of malt to his tumbler and planted the bottle back on the mantel. He sucked the liquor between his teeth, letting it scald and numb his tongue before he swallowed it with bitter relish. If he was going out again, he needed to let Andi know. There was no real chance of her showing up at this time of night, but if she did, and the house was empty he knew she would leave again. The truth was he missed her company. She was from a different station, a different beat. Safe, almost. It was nearly as good as having a missus who had nothing to do with the job. Almost.

He dialled her number and waited for her to answer. The answering service kicked in.

"Andi, this is Joe. Just calling to see if you're okay. To apologise too, if I should. I see you've left your stuff. Hope that means I'll see you again."

They were the softest words he could manage. They felt stumbling, awkward and insufficient. He hoped it would be enough. Was it love? Hardly. Love was a rose-hued sentiment, flowers and ribbons, a marketing idea he rarely entertained these days, though he may have been there once. Perhaps twice. It was hard to be sure about such things. He finished his whisky, put on his overcoat, and grabbed his keys. The brook was calling. He hoped it would clear his mind of the torturous images, and the unanswerable questions. Now he had two dead bodies to pick over. It turned out that Kevin Robbins was well known by the longest-serving officers at the nick. For twenty years the man had been collecting offences for violence, theft, robbery and extortion of all kinds – and yet somehow he had avoided a lengthy sentence. There had been far fewer offences lately, but no one would miss him. The man's death had done the town a favour. But still, Hogarth found himself like a child trying to ram a square block into a round hole. Each time, no matter how much force of will he used, the Robbins piece just wouldn't fit the Brimelow murder. Especially the nature of the man's death. It was odd. A clean-looking heroin user? A junkie who dies of an overdose within a fortnight of his secret girlfriend? It was impossible to say if they were still lovers by then, or whether their affair had just been a fling. Impossible to say much at all until the forensics were in, and Ed Quentin's final pathology report was complete. But from the outside looking in, Hogarth couldn't believe the man's death was suicide. The overdose still bothered him. But why? It gnawed at him, a question he couldn't answer.

Robbins' dead eyes came to his mind as he closed the front door and strode down the street towards Fairfax Drive. He pushed the images from his mind, and looked up, hunting for the moon, but a blanket of grey cloud had hidden it from view.

He passed along the side road which took him across the first part of the brook then paused and looked down into the tree-lined concrete cutting. In parts, the brook was no more than a ditch, but it was as close to a river as he could get at this end of town. The trickle of the invisible water was soothing in a way he couldn't explain. But he needed more than this concrete cutting. He needed to walk along by the brook, hoping the darkness and the sound of water would ease his mind further still.

He turned left and past the wide towers of Southend hospital. When he reached the far end of the hospital

grounds, he turned left again to rejoin the brook and loop back home. By now the moon had broken through the clouds and cast a silver light down over the concrete banks. It looked more natural here, more riverlike. He watched the gentle rush glinting in the light, and then he set off, to follow the flow as far as the town would let him. As he walked, Hogarth heard a rustling sound. He stopped and noticed one of the hedges on his left shaking. There was a sound of scraping, like paper on paper. Hogarth didn't want his stroll disturbed, so he decided to keep his footsteps light and push past whatever was in the hedge. But just as he passed the shaking hedge, the short, messy little figure of Gerald Gilmot stepped out like a freak from a horror film. Hogarth felt his heart lurch but refused to show it in his face. Gilmot was grey faced in the moonlight, eyes pinpricked with its light.
"Evening, Gerald," said Hogarth, making to pass him by, but the little man shuffled to block his way.
"Inspector. You stink of booze again. You're no better than that the rest of us, are you?"
Hogarth frowned. "Never said I was better than anyone, Gerald. Not even you."
Gilmot grinned at him, souring the air with his awful breath. "You've got a guilty conscience, haven't you?"
"Change the record, Gerald. It's getting dull."
"I'm right though, aren't I? You know, you remind me of my old man. He was the same. He used to drink, then he beat us because he felt bad about it. So he drank some more. Vicious circle, happened for years, right up to the time I gave it back to him."
"Nice little tale. Is that supposed to mean something, Gerald?" said Hogarth, meeting the man's eyes.
Gilmot shrank back. "No. Just an observation. Drunks are like rats in traps."

"Very sage, Gilmot. I suppose that makes you a free spirit."

"Freer than some."

"Nice to hear. Now, if observing is what you do best, I'd shut your mouth and stick with that. All the verbiage is way too much." Hogarth stepped onto the verge to get past the smaller man.

"I'm right though, aren't I? You're an ogre with a guilty conscience."

"Don't be absurd. I didn't kill that girl. I'd like to get my hands on the one who did."

Gilmot nodded. "Maybe. But you've done something bad, haven't you?"

"That's right. Right now I'm having bad thoughts about you, Gerald. About what I'm going to do to you unless you shut up and leave me alone."

Hogarth stepped past him but looked back. "By the way, if I'm an ogre, you must be a troll. They hang around waterways, blocking people's way, don't they? Another tale for you, Gerald. Look it up."

Hogarth left the little man standing in the middle of the dark path, staring after him.

"Bastard."

Hogarth heard the word but gave no reply. Gilmot was no more than a pest. Not even worthy of swatting. But he was right about Hogarth having done wrong. He had failed Andi, failed his team when DC Simmons lost his way, and he had failed the only woman he came close to loving. Yes, had done a lot of things wrong. But he was determined that letting Helen Brimelow's killer run loose on the streets wasn't going to be one of them. It was no good. Sleep wasn't coming anytime soon. Gerald Gilmot had put paid to that.

But talking of rats in traps had brought a certain face to mind. With his fire fully stoked, Hogarth had one more bad thing to do before he could call it a night. Bad, necessary, and utterly impossible to resist…

A light was on at Simon Drawton's house. Hogarth moved to the front door and peered through the darkened glass. It was empty. The rooms further on were pitch black. But it was too early for Drawton to be sleeping. Hogarth had studied the man for a long time and knew his habits well enough. He stayed up late and got up early for his home-based work. Hogarth knew there had to be something indecent and incriminating on those machines of his but as the case against him had never taken off, they had never been given permission to confiscate his technology. It could have been a game-changer, but Drawton had been protected by his clique. It was a hateful episode, and Hogarth still couldn't let it go.
The light from the front room escaped around the edges of the curtains but Hogarth was suspicious. He moved to the big bay window, looking left and right to ensure he hadn't been seen by anyone in the manse, or in the big house next door. He pushed himself up on the concrete sill until he was high enough to press his knees on it. Thankfully, the lane where Drawton lived was almost permanently quiet. Hogarth stretched out his body, meerkat-like, peering through the gap at the top of the curtains. He peered inside and saw the front room was empty. He slid back from the window ledge, scuffing his knees and muttering a swear word under his breath. He took out his mobile phone. He had kept Drawton's number with the firm intention of hounding the man to his grave, but since Melford had started breathing down his neck, he had managed to hold himself in check.

Just. He selected Drawton's number and hit the call button. A phone rang and echoed inside the house. As expected, no one answered. Hogarth grinned to himself.

"Where are you, Drawton? *Who's next...?*"

Hogarth slipped the phone away and looked at the house. Wherever the scumbag was, he would be up to no good. A creature of habit like him only broke with routine when they were compelled to do so. When they felt *the urge...* Hogarth felt an urge of his own. He walked to the corner of the house and eyed the narrow gap at the side of the building. It was blocked, and far too narrow to walk down, but the big house on the right was always empty. Maybe a buy-to-let. Maybe the owner worked abroad. Either way, Hogarth was glad of it. He entered the neighbouring front garden and headed directly for the side gate. He tried it and found it shut firm. But there was no padlock. He slid the bolt and walked into the dark gap closing the gate behind him. He was a bad man. Gerald Gilmot had him to a tee. In the back garden, he looked at the fence. It was strong and sturdy. There was a set of two flowery wrought iron chairs around a small white table. Hogarth hefted one of them in his hand and dumped it on the muddy border. Its legs bit into the soil as he climbed onto the seat. He swung one awkward leg over the fence, then dragged the other over before he found himself flailing with nowhere to go but down. He let go and dropped down to the mud with a bone-shaking impact, felt mostly in his shoulder and hip. Hogarth grunted in pain and looked up at the rear of Drawton's big house. It was pitch black, all of it. Hogarth dusted himself down and went to the back door. It was old but in good order. Wooden, and not double glazed. He almost dismissed the door, expecting it to be locked as a matter of course, but tried it anyway. Hogarth smiled a broad smile as the door opened with ease. Either the lack of a side entrance had left Drawton complacent or there had been more pressing matters on his mind. Hogarth walked inside and closed the door behind him. He was in the big kitchen. He remembered the posh coffee and fighting temptation with the kettle. He pushed on.

Whatever Hogarth was looking for, he knew there would be a place for it. It would have a home, and that home might be obvious. For though Simon Drawton certainly had some dark secrets, no one had ever come close to unearthing them before, and because of his contacts, the man probably believed no one ever would. Hogarth bared his teeth. He set off up the wide, polished wooden staircase. He had the feeling he was getting somewhere. It felt good. If there was a connection between Drawton and Helen Brimelow's murder, Hogarth suspected this was the closest he would get before the wagons circled once again. If there was something to be had, he would have it tonight, or not at all.

Hogarth roamed the upper rooms in the dark. Rooms which Helen might have seen before she died. He flicked on the lights of the front rooms, looked inside and dismissed each in turn. The first was a bedroom – Drawton's own. It smelt of manly aftershaves, sandalwoods and leather. Everything in the room was meticulously tidy. There was no sign of the bed or his home being shared with a lover or any other human being. He flicked the light off and went into a smaller bedroom. There was a single bed, untouched, sheets folded tight and neat as if the bed had been ironed that way. He switched the light off. The bed was for show, the room unused. Hogarth walked to the back of the top floor. The room dead ahead was a bathroom. To satisfy his curiosity he pulled the string light switch and opened the mirrored medicine cabinet. He found a classic steel safety razor, shaving cream in a tin, and a matching brush. There was a brush, a comb, Germolene, and even a pack of Durex nestled amongst the painkillers and Piriton.

"Protection, Drawton? As if you'd get the chance."

But he remembered. Helen Brimelow had almost certainly been raped before her death. No semen had been found, and there had been traces of latex, spermicide and lubricants consistent with the use of a condom.

"You only use the condoms to hide the evidence, don't you?" he muttered. He closed the cabinet to find his own vicious face glaring back at him. Hogarth left the room, switched off the light and made his way to his last port of call. The back room. The one with the desks and the self-important monitors, set up as if Drawton imagined he was in control of the whole world. Powerful, entitled, protected. But he wasn't insulated from everything. Not from a wildcard like Hogarth. Perhaps that was his only weakness.

Hogarth glanced around the room. It was too big for the desk. There was too much space to feel comfortable. The desk sat beside a small steel filing cabinet. There was a box file on the top and a meshed metal in-tray beside the screens. Hogarth knew he was no techie. He had no chance of getting past the passwords of the computers. Instead, he had to bank on the fact that Drawton was even older than he was. A man of the old ways. With his mock Etonian style and bearing, it wasn't hard to imagine. Hogarth turned the key in the top corner of the filing cabinet, opened the top drawer, and found endless hanging files with details of financial trades on them. The documents were typed, intricate, dead, dull. If they held anything of use, he wasn't going to be the man to find it. He shut the drawer. The contents of the second drawer were exactly like the first. He pulled a few random files apart and inspected them. These trades were older, each sheet a few years old. Big sums had been paid out. Large profits made; in some cases, more than two years of Hogarth's salary had been made in a single transaction. He snorted and returned the files becoming aware of the time. He needed to be away before Drawton returned from whatever seedy endeavour he was engaged in. If not, another meeting with Melford loomed, suspension the most likely result.

Out of desperation, Hogarth looked at the in-tray, the pending tray, and everything in between. He looked under the mouse mat, and beneath the small mock-Persian rug behind the office chair, but found nothing. Nothing at all. He lifted the computer monitors, tilting each one back to reveal the empty spaces beneath. This man wasn't innocent, so where were his secrets? Hogarth started for the door, aiming to double-check the other rooms. But then he took one more look at the metal filing cabinet. He walked directly to it, opening the top drawer. This time, Hogarth delved a hand between the hanging files into the belly of the drawer beneath. He parted the files and looked inside. He saw nothing. Just the black metal skin of the drawer itself. He opened the next drawer and repeated the process. Dragging his fingers across the bottom, he disturbed something smooth and cold. He pulled it free. It was a pen. A nice one, too. It had a green and black marble effect along its surface. Hogarth discarded the pen and pulled the hanging files wide apart. White paper shone back at him, and he saw there were notes on the sheets – both typed and handwritten. Hogarth retrieved what he could. The pen, and a thin stack of neat white papers. He laid them all on the desk and sat down in

Drawton's chair, briefly steepling his fingers as he looked at his findings. The first sheet was a copy of a letter of complaint – a complaint about him. It had been sent to none other than James Hartigan MP, the man he hated with a vengeance. The letter was a month old. Hogarth's jaw tightened, but he scanned it quickly because this was not the meat he was looking for. *Disrespectful, unlawful, roguish, dishevelled, aggressive, and oozing hate and violence* were just some of the phrases Drawton had used to describe him. Hogarth baulked at none of them, apart from being dishevelled, even though he knew it was true. The job had worn down his attire as much as his attitude. The second sheet was a copy of a similar complaint directed at the chief constable of the force Essex wide.

"Just another one of your bum chums, Drawton?" Hogarth didn't bother to read it. He set another few complaints with the others. The next batch of papers seemed far more interesting but he found no smoking gun. No photographs of the abuses the man had gotten away with, no confessions, nothing of that ilk. But there were handwritten notes – all on good quality paper – all neatly written, a paragraph for each entry, and a matching date. The dates were regularly spaced apart, a week at a time. Hogarth frowned and looked beneath the notes, still hunting for something on Helen Brimelow, but without success. He returned to the notes on the fancy paper, and started to read the single paragraph entries written in Drawton's hand:

> They call it therapy, but I only go for my own amusement – and because it proves I am willing to deal with my supposed 'ill habits'. The facilitator of

> this group is supposed to be a qualified
> psychotherapist – his assistant, a counsellor by trade.
> But they seem no more skilled than I am in the arts of
> the human mind. It's a procedural and therapeutic
> waste of time, the whole thing. But there are some
> minor good points which keep me entertained. A few
> of the other group members are interesting.

Interesting... by interesting, Hogarth assumed the man meant sexually interesting. He narrowed his eyes and flicked on through the notes. At one point, Drawton mentioned someone who was often silent, someone who blurted out that he wanted to hurt people. The counsellor asked who and why. The unspecified person said because they deserved it. Who deserves it? The answer: All of them.
"A support group for psychopaths," muttered Hogarth. "Of course you'd be amongst them, Drawton."
He flicked the pages and read on, searching for mention of names. Female names. Dates of declared urges which might correspond to the date of the murder. Hogarth searched every self-obsessed, mocking page until he finally closed the pack of notes more unsatisfied than ever.
"Where is it, you bastard? Where have you hidden the proof?"
He slammed the notes down on the desk, face down, and put his head into his hands. He knitted his eyes shut and took a restorative breath. When he opened them again, about to return everything to its place, his eyes landed on the neat, even hand on the back of the last sheet. And there, Hogarth saw a name he recognised.

> Young Halstead is awkward in the extreme. I had
> assumed the boy had some kind of mental deficiency

from the way in which he studiously avoids conversation, almost all eye contact, and even polite questioning. Yet every now and then he says something so direct, so earnest, so against the run of play, that I simply can't help but laugh out loud. Maybe the reason this young man is so silent is because he has no need of this so-called therapy any more than I do. I think he sees the world clearly – more clearly than most.

"Halstead?" said Hogarth, frowning.
He flicked the pages back another week.
Today Oliver made a comment about everybody hiding their innermost desires. He suggested, blithely, that even the counsellor was pretending to be someone he wasn't in order to keep his job – an image kept for public consumption. I regarded this as both astute and honest, and it fascinates me that such sharp wisdom could come from someone who seems to operate in the world as an idiot. He sees beneath the skin of things, as I do. I think I like this Oliver. I wonder what a boy as bold as him could do, given time. In fact, the more I hear him speak, the more I wonder. I wonder where his insights come from. What drives them? And most interesting of all, where they are going, because as much as I know they have come from somewhere, I feel they have a destination too. I know it. Have I met a kindred spirit, in the shape of a socially defective man-child? I fear the answer to that question. What does it say about me?
"It says everything, Drawton. Absolutely everything," Hogarth replied.

Hogarth put the papers and the pen back in order, along with the copied complaints, and laid them beneath the hanging files in the bottom drawer. He closed the drawer, turned the key in the lock, and adjusted the monitors, making everything as it was.

"If you like writing notes like that... then there must be more somewhere..."

Hogarth set the chair back behind the desk and looked around the room. But as he looked he heard the sound of movement outside. Footsteps echoing as they scraped close to the house. He frowned and glanced at the desk clock. It was late. Late enough to get caught in the act. He switched off the light and left the room. Downstairs, the footsteps were getting close. He descended the stairs quietly, and as fast as he could. A thin shape was emerging from the darkness, becoming clearer as it approached the bevelled glass of the wide front door. Hogarth backed away to the kitchen. Drawton was home. His job was back on the line. Hogarth listened to the jangling of keys and made a darting move for the back door. This time, its master home, the back door tried to resist him, the wood sticking against the frame, but Hogarth barged it open and stepped out into the blackness. Inside, the front door slammed and the hallway light came on. Hogarth closed the backdoor gently and stepped into the dark garden. He moved to the fence, which looked impossibly high to climb without a chair, but there was nothing to help him. He glanced at the corner of the house and decided it was close enough. Hogarth pressed his shoe heel against the bricks and pushed up as high and hard as he could. His legs burned, as did his arm and chest, as he tried to pull himself up over the fence. He groaned with the effort but just managed to haul his body over the top as the kitchen light flicked on, bathing the garden with yellow light.

Legs flailing behind him, Hogarth threw himself over, gritted his teeth, and slammed down into a winded, aching heap on the mulch below. He stood up, brushed the soil and damp leaves from his jacket, and grumbled to himself until he was merely wet and cold but not quite so filthy. Time for home. One more whisky then bed. Hogarth didn't yet know the value of what he'd seen, but he knew it meant something. Hogarth limped back to his car and straightened out his back. His spine cracked in protest. He got into his car and drove home for one more dram. Maybe two.

Twelve

The church talk lasted exactly thirty-seven minutes – at least twenty-seven minutes too long by Palmer's reckoning and judging from the tutting, and irritated faces amongst the gathering, she wasn't the only one to think so.

None of the guests accepted the offer of prayer given by the old preacher at the front. Dennis Corby had looked upset, and Palmer almost pitied him – though not enough to accept an invitation to the front when he offered a prayer her way. But as Palmer gave a polite shake of the head, her niece bolted up out of her chair and raised her hand.

"I'd like a prayer," she said. Palmer looked up at her. The shot of courage which had made her niece stand up seemed to have suddenly deserted her. She was red faced and nervous, and looked more like a schoolgirl than ever, despite the make-up, clothes, and hair.

"Excellent, excellent," said the older man, before he added. "I'll pray for you at the end."

"I can help with that if you like!" called one of the big men at the back, guffawing as he spoke.

Corby ignored the comment with the practised ease of a church pastor. Halstead shook his head at the man in the crowd.

When Aaliyah sat down, Palmer leaned across to whisper, but the girl beat her to it.

"Alright, alright, no need to make me feel any more embarrassed."

"No. You did that by yourself. It's nine o'clock, by the way, and I've got work in the morning."

"I thought you were working now," said Aaliyah coldly. "Besides, I want to eat with them. You're here now, you'll have to wait."

"What about that moussaka?"

"That's all yours."

"What's all this about, Ali?"

"I'm curious, that's all," she said.

"So am I," said Palmer. "Mainly about you." But Palmer wasn't just curious about her niece's motives. She was interested in all of them. The guests. The service users. The residents. She felt they'd only barely scratched the surface of these people, but there were hundreds of them, thousands even. Someone must have seen what had happened between Kevin Robbins and Helen… some of them might have been friendly enough to see their relationship at close hand. But where to begin? There was so much work to be done, yet their team was smaller than ever. On top of that, she had her niece to deal with. Palmer watched as Aaliyah went up to the front of the hall. As Halstead packed away the projector and rolled away the screen, Corby hovered a hand over her niece's head. Palmer watched intently, making sure no funny business was about to happen. The old man closed his eyes and spoke a fervent prayer. When he was done, he patted Aaliyah's arm, smiled, and sent her on her way. Aaliyah paused by the projector desk, and Palmer watched her exchange pleasantries with Halstead before he returned to packing away the equipment and chairs. There was something in the way Halstead and Aaliyah had looked at one another… a warmth between them. Attraction?

Rapport? Who knew? If it had lasted any longer than a few seconds, Palmer might have been bothered, but Halstead was a busy man. Chance meetings probably happened all the time. But that still didn't mean Aaliyah wasn't flirting with him.

"Nice prayer, was it?" said Palmer as the girl returned. Her niece blushed and then glowered.

"We'll eat then we can go," she replied.

"Get what you came for, did you?" said Palmer.

Aaliyah didn't say a word. Palmer had the feeling she didn't know the answer to the question and let it go. She knew her job as chaperone wasn't finished yet. The dinner queue jostle was likely to pose some more problems, particularly if the previous sandwich queue was anything to go by. Palmer joined the food queue beside her niece and stayed close. The offering smelled good. Chilli con carne served over jacket potatoes. Cheap, but healthy fare and filling too. She was almost tempted to have another bite to eat but the waistband of her skirt warned her not to. Aaliyah opted for chilli with a dollop of crème fraiche – always looking after her waistline, always thinking of her looks – then she took the table in the middle of the hall. A statement, Palmer decided. Look at me, why don't you? Or was it a mark of the girl's innocence? Her naivety? She didn't seem to realise that as much as these people seemed kind and friendly, each and every one of them might have been a threat in some way. The girl ate quietly, as if soaking up the unusual atmosphere. Palmer looked around and studied faces and behaviour. Every visit was a new opportunity. Before the girl's meal was half done, Suitcase sat down beside Palmer, diagonally opposite her niece, his drooping eyes making his interest all too clear.

"So, you like it in here, do you?" he said. His eyes were bleary, his pink face sweaty. He smelt of extra strong beer, sweat, chilli and beef. Aaliyah finished chewing before she answered. Her eyes were filled with a smile.

"What's it to you?" said Palmer.

"It's a free country, ma'am. Especially in here. It's not your jurisdiction. It's the good Lord's. I'm chatting with the young lady here, that's all."

Aaliyah swallowed.

"Yeah. I like it," she said.

"Thinking of volunteering, are you? They could do with some new blood in here. Pardon the phrase. Just after what happened to that girl, all the women in here seem to have been scared off. A few of the other volunteers haven't come back since."

"I heard that," said Aaliyah. "I'm not scared." Palmer shot her a look.

"Those were the smart ones," said Palmer.

"Fortune favours the brave," said Aaliyah, eyes gleaming.

"Don't be silly. That's just a dumb line from a movie. That's not real life."

"I don't want real life. Not if it's all bloody boring."

Suitcase laughed out loud. "That told you, didn't it?"

Palmer gave the unpleasant man a glare but he kept on smiling.

"She sounds ideal for this place, absolutely ideal. A pretty girl with some chutzpah to get the place back on its feet."

"She's not volunteering," said Palmer.

"Aren't I?" said Aaliyah.

"It's out of the question," said Palmer. "There's a murder investigation going on."

"Your investigation, not mine. Your job. You want me to do something worthwhile, don't you?"

Palmer struggled for words.

"Maybe this is it," said the girl. She stood up before Palmer could reply, lifted her finished plate and turned away. "I'm going to get a cuppa. You want one?"

Palmer shook her head and turned back to face Suitcase. She leaned a degree closer to the man's sweaty, stinking face.

"Before you get any ideas, be warned. You mess with her and you'll be in very serious trouble with me."

"Alright, aunty, keep your hair on."

"I mean it, Suitcase. Tell your friends."

"You can bet I will," he replied. "We'll have a good old belly laugh about you tonight." The big man started to heave himself out of his seat.

"Wait a minute," said Palmer.

"Why? Miss me already?"

Palmer didn't deign to respond. "Kevin Robbins. Razor Robbins. Did you know him?"

Suitcase frowned and rubbed a hand over his jaw. "Everyone knew that tosspot. He OD'd, didn't he? And before you start, that had nothing to do with me."

"Why would it?"

"Only because you people always try and fit me up for something. I came here to chill out tonight, not for an interrogation by the SS."

"We're having a chat, that's all."

"Yeah. What about?" said Suitcase, looking increasingly uncomfortable.

"About Kevin Robbins. And Helen Brimelow. You always act like you're the man at the centre, all the spokes of the wheel lead back to you, don't they?"

"Now and then," he replied.

"So, come on then…"

"What?"

"I want to hear what you know about Robbins and Helen. And I want to know everything you know too."

Suitcase sighed out loud.

"Don't worry," said Palmer. "When you're finished you can get your dinner…"

"If there's any left," he groaned.

"Better start now then, eh?"

As Suitcase sat down in front of her, a girl in the food queue glanced back at them. She shared her gaze between Suitcase and Palmer. Palmer looked back. The girl was in her late twenties, blonde hair tied back, pretty but hard faced, and wearing too much pink eyeshadow. To match her pink tracksuit top. As soon as she saw Palmer looking at her, the girl's face hardened further still and she turned away. Palmer noted the look but didn't think much of it. The food bank was always full of difficult people with sharp edges and spiky personalities. Maybe she was dating Suitcase and wanted him to eat with her. But looking at Suitcase, Palmer decided that was unlikely. She was far too pretty for him. The big old drunk was hardly a catch.

"Come on then," said Suitcase, sniffing. "Let's get this over with."

Oh, yes. Her aunt was back on the job, alright. Aaliyah could see Palmer's manner had changed. She had turned back into the bulldog she had seen before. Eyes sharp, leaning forward like a predator waiting to take a bite. Credit to her, the big ugly man at the table seemed intimidated. And now they were talking, and her aunt seemed totally absorbed. Good job. It meant Aaliyah was finally free to pursue her main interest. But to get away with it, she would need to be fast.

While most of the guests had their heads buried in their dinner plates – a mix of obviously homeless people and other scruffy locals - Aaliyah watched the speaker Dennis shake hands with Freddie Halstead before Corby hung a satchel on his arm and got on his way. The old man waved at her, a big black leather Bible tucked under his other arm, before he walked out of the hall and down the corridor towards the exit. Halstead was packing up too. Aaliyah watched as he zipped the projector and laptop into their respective bags and piled them up on a seat by the door. When the packing was done, Aaliyah saw her chance. She stole a glance back at her aunt. Palmer was still busy with the big man, who looked increasingly pained as he spoke. Aaliyah darted across the hall.

"Leaving your own party?" said the girl. "That's a little bit rude, isn't it?"

Freddie Halstead looked up. When he saw Aaliyah standing beside him, eyes sparkling at him, he did a double-take and smiled back.

"I'm not leaving. I'm just packing my car."

"So you can make a quick exit when all this is done?"

"That obvious, am I?"

Aaliyah nodded. "'Fraid so."

"I've got an early start in the morning."

"Not the first time I've heard that line tonight,"

"No. Probably not," said Halstead, glancing towards Palmer. "Besides," he added. "I've got someone at home who needs me."

Aaliyah's face wavered. Freddie smiled, sensing her thoughts. "Oh, not like that. It's my brother. You met him the other day, I think."

"He lives with you?"

"Yeah. He needs me. He thinks he doesn't but… well, that's natural isn't it?"

Halstead began to pick up the bags and boxes, loading them against his chest.

"Here. Let me help you with those," said Aaliyah, nodding at the pile.

"You sure?" he said.

"Why not? We can chat on the way out."

Halstead nodded. His lips twitched with a smile, but he held it back.

They left the main hall and walked out into the corridor to find a young man with a pale face heading directly towards them. Halstead slowed down at her side. It took Aaliyah a moment to place the newcomer, but when Halstead greeted the man, she realised.

"Ollie," said Halstead. "What are you doing here?"

"You didn't invite me, but I thought you might need some help," he said. The younger man looked off – serious, and sweaty, and stressed. His eyes darted around but didn't meet her gaze.

"If I'd needed help, I would have asked."

"Then why didn't you? What have I done?"

Freddie Halstead shot Aaliyah a look. The younger man saw it but said nothing.

"Look, Ollie. Just go into the hall and wait for me. Get yourself a plate of food if you like. It's good stuff tonight."

The young man gave them a quick sullen look before he relented with a nod. He stepped aside to let them pass. But instead of going into the noisy hall, he lingered by the door, turning to watch his brother and the girl slink away with their excuse of boxes and equipment. He knew they were already chatting under their breath, probably about him. He looked at the girl's back. Her long-tinted hair, her shapely lithe figure. Yeah, it made sense why Freddie hadn't invited him tonight. But it was good he'd come. At least he knew where he stood in Freddie's list of priorities. And where he stood was the same as ever – on the outside, looking in – not wanting to be left out in the cold, but equally hating the glare of the spotlight. Ollie put his hand on the hall door and considered his options. Without even noticing, he started to grind his teeth while he took the time to make his decision.

Freddie balanced the black equipment bags in one arm while he pressed the key fob button with the other. The indicator lights of his hatchback flashed and the locks whirred. He opened the boot and put the black bags into the tidy boot space.
"In there, thanks. Great. Thanks for your help. Your name's Aaliyah, right? Like the R 'n' B singer."
"You've got a very good memory," she said.
"Hard to forget a name like that. And I never forget a pretty face."
She looked at him, her glinting eyes flicking between his.
"Sorry. I probably shouldn't have said that. Old habits die hard. I don't know you well enough."
"No, it's fine," she said. "It was cheesy, but I liked it."
Halstead nodded. "I saw you with Josh earlier. You two were getting on like a house on fire. Not many people get much traction with him. I think you'd fit in pretty well here."
"Thanks. I think I would too."
They looked at one another and Freddie narrowed his eyes.
"What is it?" he asked. "You look like you've got something on your mind."

"Well spotted," said Aaliyah, smiling. She pulled her hair from her face. "Actually, I don't know if I should even say this, but…"

"But?" said Freddie. He raised an eyebrow.

"I kind of saw you earlier today."

"Kind of saw me?" he said, laughing. "What does that even mean?"

"It means that I think you were having some kind of meeting with some old friends. Volunteers."

Halstead frowned in thought, then nodded. "This afternoon? Where? I didn't see you in the building…" The penny dropped. "You mean out over there, in the bit beyond the tower block?"

Aaliyah nodded.

"Funny. I didn't see you," he replied.

"You looked busy."

Another silence.

"I kind of had the feeling that…"

"Go on," said Halstead, his eyes shining under the street lamps of the estate. "Say what's on your mind."

"That you knew that blonde girl. That you might have known her really, really well."

"Sharon? Yeah… Of course, I know her. Sharon was a great volunteer. A proper soldier. This thing with poor Helen has put her off—"

Aaliyah interrupted him. "It kind of felt to me… that you were, well… flirting with each other. Like there was some sort of history between you."

"You've got a vivid imagination, young lady."

Aaliyah shook her head. "Not really. It's just the way you were together."

"What's this about?" said Freddie, frowning. "I've never had a relationship with Sharon."

"But you seemed so *friendly,*" she replied. There was something in the way she said the word – it was clear she meant more than friends.

"I'm not sure we know each other well enough to be talking like this," he said.

Aaliyah shrugged and kept her smile in place.

"I'm not allowed to do anything like that. I work for the church, Aaliyah, and I take that seriously. It's against the rules of my job."

Aaliyah nodded slowly. They looked at one another. "Must be very difficult for you, having feelings for people. That's only natural. But you being a man of the cloth and all, I don't suppose you can do anything about them, can you?"

Aaliyah offered a smile which was supposed to be innocent but Halstead looked into her eyes, a hesitant smile flickering on his face. He'd been around the food bank outreach for a long while now. Years, in fact. He'd seen more than a few smiles, met more than a few types of girl along the way. His job didn't provide much in the way of career skills, but the one thing it did teach him was people. He saw straight through her innocence. He felt he could see right down into the very core of the girl, and what she was all about, and what her words were really asking.

"I take it seriously, but they don't own me, Aaliyah. No one does."

"Interesting," said the girl, nodding to herself, a smile still etched on her face. As she looked away, Halstead looked up to the first-floor platform where a few of the malingerers were already smoking after their dinners, leaning on the railing. None of them seemed to be paying any attention to them. But when Halstead's eyes raked across the side of the

food bank, he saw a familiar face silhouetted against one of the hall's main windows and recognised the shape of his brother's head the moment he saw it. A cold, twisting feeling knotted his stomach.
"I think I'd like to volunteer," said the girl suddenly.
"Would you now?" said Halstead. This time, he studied the glint in her eye. Aaliyah studied the gleam in his. "I'm not sure we need anyone quite as sharp as you on the team."
"Don't worry. I can keep a secret…"
Halstead nodded. The girl folded her arms and they headed back for the curling slope that led back up to the first floor and the food bank.

If Suitcase knew something worth having, then he hadn't shared it. After a five-minute grilling, a big drunk lug like him should have cracked. Suitcase knew Robbins, yes. He knew him as in the fact they had been enemies on the estate. Rivals. Scallywags who had put one over the other many times across the years, and as a result they had become sworn enemies. Suitcase hadn't wanted to give Robbins the credit of scoring a pretty girl like young Helen Brimelow. But when it came to the subject of Robbins' overdose, the tone of the conversation had changed.
"Killed himself because he was pining for her?" Suitcase shook his head. "Nah. I can't see that. Not that bastard. Not for a minute. Old Razor was a nasty piece of work. We hated each other's guts, like I told you. And he was as hard as nails. He would have robbed his own granny so he could buy some brown. In fact, he probably did."

"Fine. He was a louse. But I don't see what that's got to do with the man taking an overdose," said Palmer, sticking to her guns.

"Then you're not listening, are you?" said Suitcase. "He was a scumbag, a poser, and all he loved was himself. There was no way he topped himself because of that girl dying. I saw him what, a week ago? If he was gonna top himself over her, he would have done it the moment it happened, am I right?"

"Not necessarily…" said Palmer.

"You know I'm right. He would have done it there and then. That's what happened when that TV presenter bird topped herself, remember? She went, then her geezer went next, just a day or so later. Like dominoes. It's what lovebirds do. Razor wasn't the type, believe me."

"Then if he didn't kill himself and he didn't OD, what happened to them?"

"That's your department, innit?"

Palmer gave him a look.

"My dinner's getting cold," he mumbled.

"They'll keep it warm for you," said Palmer.

"Look. Maybe Razor was shagging that girl…"

"Was he or wasn't he?" said Palmer.

Suitcase tilted his big head left and right. "Look. He might have been. I saw them talking once. They looked pretty close. I thought it was odd."

Palmer nodded to herself. Suitcase had likely been jealous – he didn't want to admit his adversary had beaten him to a pretty girl, even after his death.

"Tell me more," said Palmer.

"That's all I can say. It's a maybe. A probably, even. But look. He wouldn't have done that to himself. He loved himself far too much for that. He went through a lot of birds, believe me, and after he binned them, there was never any tears. He wasn't like that. He wasn't a kind man."

"But maybe he was like that," said Palmer. "In private. There must have been a reason Helen went for him."

"Course there was. For her, Razor was a bit of rough. You know it yourself, that girl of yours is no different. These little girls are like moths to a flame when they get in this place. Believe me. It's inevitable."

Palmer frowned. "Don't bank on it."

Suitcase chuckled. "You know I'm right." The big man shunted back in his chair, wiped his sweating brow with his hand and looked at his shiny wet fingers.

"But the biggest reason that man wouldn't have OD'd is this. He was a leisure-time junkie. A part-timer. A few-times-a-week man. Thought he was better than everyone else because of that. Thought he wasn't an addict, didn't he? Kept putting that idea around, like he was special."

"Was it true?" said Palmer.

Suitcase nodded. "Special? No. Sod that. He weren't special. But he looked cleaner than a lot of other junkies, yeah. So I guess he had it under control."

"But?"

"No buts. I don't get how or why he kicked the bucket like he did, but I'm not sorry that he's gone. I hated his guts, and he hated mine. This estate will be better off without him, believe me."

Palmer shook her head and looked around the hall for her niece. Aaliyah was nowhere to be seen. Suitcase smiled as he followed her eyes.

"Are we done yet?" he said, splaying his big arms out at his sides. But Palmer didn't answer. Her eyes raked across the small groups of swarthy men and badly dressed women – the ones sitting at the tables, the ones standing around, the ones blocking her view. She watched as Josh, the cap-wearing volunteer dragged the unused chairs to the side walls, packing up as the guests finished their meals.

"Yeah, we're done," said Suitcase, with a wheezy laugh. "Don't worry," he added, as he turned away. He raised a hand in a goodbye wave, his fingers barely poking out from the sleeves of his jacket. "The girl will be fine. Probably."

Palmer stood up, in a near fit of panic. She moved to the front of the hall where Corby had given his talk. He was gone. Halstead was gone too. But Palmer saw there was a young man sitting on one of the couches beneath the high rectangular windows. He was bouncing his knees, biting his nails. When Palmer stopped before him, the young man looked up and she realised who it was.

"You're Freddie's brother."

The young man's eyes stayed dark and distant.

"Where is Freddie? Shouldn't he be manning the building?"

"You should ask him," said the young man.

Palmer looked around. She swallowed as a jab of panic reached her throat.

"My niece. Dark hair, purple tint. Young girl. Have you seen her?"

The boy was unresponsive.

"You spoke to her the other day," said Palmer.

The man looked up.

"The pretty one. The one with the nice hair and happy face."

Palmer swallowed again. She didn't like the way he'd said that. Didn't like the sharpness in his quick, flitting eyes. Suitcase's disturbing words swam around her mind, filling her with unease. Every man in the place was a potential threat. Everyone a potential murderer. When the young

Halstead saw the look on Palmer's face, he stopped biting his fingers and pointed towards the door.

"There she is. Now, doesn't she look happy?"

Palmer snapped around to see her niece smiling and circulating with the guests as if she was one of the established faces among the crowd. She was working it like a natural, like the host of a party. She noticed Freddie Halstead in the kitchen, behind the hatch, fussing with the electrics, talking to a guest as he sipped a hot cuppa.

Without another word, Palmer left the young Halstead in his seat and marched over to her niece. Aaliyah was chatting with a large, old man and woman. Each one had an oversized stomach. They seemed genial, like two Buddhas gazing up at her niece as she spoke.

"That's enough, Aaliyah. We're going."

The girl looked at her, aggrieved. "What?"

"You've had your fun, so now we're going. Grab your stuff. We're off."

But Aaliyah barely moved. Palmer grabbed her coat from the back of a chair and stuffed it into the girl's arms.

"Time to go," she said to the rotund couple, nodding as she steered Aaliyah towards the door.

The girl kept her voice down as he complained.

"You shouldn't have come here, Sue. You're ruining everything."

"You shouldn't have come either – for some very obvious reasons I shouldn't have to explain."

As they walked along the corridor, Freddie Halstead appeared framed in the doorway of the kitchen. As Aaliyah looked back across her shoulder, Halstead looked down the hallway and met her eyes. He smiled and nodded back.

Palmer tried to read the look in her niece's eyes, but when she looked back, all she saw was Halstead busily loading cutlery into a drawer. The communication had passed her by. Palmer steered Aaliyah towards the door and out into the darkness.

"What reasons?" snapped Aaliyah.

"Two words!" said Palmer. Her loud voice echoed between the tower blocks on all sides. She lowered her voice. "Murder Investigation!"

"Oh please. One girl died, out of *how many?*"

Palmer shook her head in disbelief and started walking. She slowed until she heard her niece following her. Finally, the girl reached her side. Aaliyah was wearing a quiet, smug smile on her face.

"I hope you enjoyed yourself in there," spat Palmer. "Because that'll be the last time."

The girl knew better than to answer back, but her face spoke volumes. Trouble was Palmer knew there was little she could do to stop her niece returning. The girl was beyond her control. There was one thing she could do – send her back to her mother. Six miles away in a whole other town, a middle-class town, where she would be safe. But that would have been admitting failure, not just to herself, but to her sister as well. Losing face to her moody sister was out of the question. And worse, the girl would have been discarded by yet another of her family members. She just couldn't do it. She couldn't send her back. As they walked down the curving slope, Palmer stopped in her tracks.

"Just promise me something. Promise me *one* thing!"

"What?" said Aaliyah.

"That you won't come back here. I mean it. This place is off limits."

The girl looked in her aunt's eyes and shrugged. It took her a moment to answer.

"Sure, if that's what it takes."

Palmer gave a curt nod, examined the girl's eyes then led the way down the slope. Her niece followed a few feet behind. She looked back at the community centre building, hoping to see the warm dark eyes of Freddie Halstead, watching from the window. Instead, she saw his brother, standing behind the glass. Something about his look bothered her, but he was Freddie's brother. Soon, she hoped, she would know him too. Who knew the future? Perhaps by being close with Freddie, they might even become friends. Making sure her aunt wasn't watching, Aaliyah waved at him. But the man didn't wave back. He just stood at the glass and stared.

By the time they reached solid ground, Aaliyah had resolved to thaw her aunt's bad mood. The girl had achieved what she'd come for. She didn't want her aunt to spoil it. She slid an arm around Palmer's waist and pressed in for a sisterly side-hug. Palmer gave her a cynical look, but it lasted no more than a few seconds.

"I'm only trying to keep you safe, you know," said Palmer.

"I know. I just wish you wouldn't be so heavy about it. You're not thinking of sending me back to mum's are you?"

"No," lied Palmer, without skipping a beat. "But you won't go back up there, will you?"

"No," said Aaliyah, just as fast and just as firm.

As they climbed into Palmer's car, a second silhouette appeared at the window on the first floor. Aaliyah spotted them and paused as she ducked down into the car. She raised her hand and waved at Freddie and Ollie before she got in. She closed the door and pulled her seatbelt tight.

"You've suddenly got a face like a Cheshire cat," said Palmer, as she started the engine.

"No law against being happy, is there?"

"Given time," said Palmer. "Given time."

Thirteen

Halstead drove home and thought of his meeting with the girl in the car park. He wondered about her eavesdropping on his meeting with Sharon and her father... Why would she have done such a thing? Someone with intuition like hers could have destroyed his job. His career, if it could ever be called such a thing. In his job, hooking up with women was forbidden and once tainted by the rumour of crossing the line, having affairs with church-going women, a church worker like him might never work again. Sharon wasn't married. She was available, and he knew there was something between them. But she was off limits. The job made everything so hard. But part of it was the church-going women themselves. They knew he was off limits too, which meant they were content to play their part in the tension of an unconsummated love affair. Some of them became co-conspirators. He'd kissed Sharon once at the Christmas party. A drunken snog after too many Courvoisiers and a fumble in the office, but that was as far as it went. Hands went delving, lips searching, but never beyond the point of clothes-on passion, a stolen moment in the office. After that, there had been feelings and a subtext between their every encounter. They fancied one another, absolutely, but it was never to be. Sometimes he felt as if he was straining at the leash when they met, and at other times he found himself enjoying the sexual tension that went with the job. But someone second-guessing him, seeing deeper into his sexual nature as the young girl had... that was alarming. Intriguing too. The young girl was a looker, and by hell, she knew it. She was dangerous. If she proposed to tell someone what she had guessed about him and Sharon, then there was a good chance of a reprimand, or worse. Freddie shook his head as he drove. He reassured himself and smiled. He was worrying about nothing. After what she'd said by the car, he doubted that outing him as a red-blooded male was exactly what she was interested in. He suspected she wanted to know that red-blooded male herself. Up close and personal. Don't mind if I do, thought Freddie. But he was kidding himself. There were too many possible complications. Too many danger signs, like her police detective aunt. But she looked old enough to be legal. She wanted to volunteer. Though chances were that she too might become another off-limits love interest designed to frustrate him. The job was cruel like that, and yet it was exciting. *I can keep a secret;* her words. What if he suggested she didn't volunteer... at least, not at the Refuge centre? He wondered if it would work, thinking of all the possible ways he could facilitate it, but before long, his mind was trading in pure fantasy. Yes, the girl looked delicious, and she had more or less invited him to think about her as an option. But Halstead knew a walking scandal when he saw one. She was a cop's niece... they were in the middle of Helen's murder investigation... if he gave in, the church would once again end up in the dock. If he did what he wanted to do, where would it end? There were plenty of people who wanted to destroy the food bank – even people on the council. There was no way he could allow himself to be the cause. He loved the place. Loved the work. But he was still achingly human. It was a mess. Lately, he felt as if life had set out to constrict him, like a boa coiling ever tighter around his throat. The church life had been full of promise. He'd abandoned the nine to five in pursuit of a better way. But the job was all consuming. These days it barely gave him the time he needed to stop Ollie from sliding into deep trouble, let alone the chance of a sex life. These days it gave him nothing, and it took all he had – and as the Good Book decreed – he should have been happy about it. But he wasn't. His happiness was flagging. Maybe the girl had been sent as a test. Ollie had certainly been testing lately. *Yet another test? Really?*

"You're thinking about that girl, aren't you?" said Ollie, sitting in the car at his side.

"What?" said Halstead, looking around.

"I saw you and her. Not bad. She has a body like a fashion model. But the brain isn't up to much."

"Come on. You don't know her, Ollie!"

His brother offered something like a thin smile. It didn't reach his eyes.

"And you do? You've barely met her and already you're defending her."

"I'm not… and no, I wasn't thinking about her."

"Liar," said his brother quietly.

"Ollie, stop it."

"Isn't lying one of those ten commandments of yours?"

"Ollie."

"You'll go to hell if it is."

"People do a lot of things that seem wrong," said Freddie. "I don't think all of them go to hell."

"So now you're inventing your own commandments? Nice work, Freddie. You should start the church of Fred. The Bible according to Fred."

"And what Bible do you follow, Ollie?"

"None. I never said I did. That was your thing. It gave you a way out of the things you didn't like. I never needed that."
"You sound like a smart-arse. An ungrateful smart-arse. What have you been doing today while I was out? It better not have been anything to do with those cats."
His brother looked at him. They shared a glance. Ollie's eyes were cold and mocking.
"You would have known what I was doing if you'd taken me to work with you tonight. I'd have been safe. So would the cats. But then, maybe, I'd have cramped your style."
Freddie shook his head.
"I try, Ollie. God knows I try."
His brother laughed.
Freddie's mind drifted between Sharon's blonde hair and sparkling blue eyes and Aaliyah's mischievous smile and sparkle. If the media glare hadn't been so intense, maybe, just maybe he would have risked something. To be wanted, and to kiss someone he wanted… it sounded like bliss. The feeling welled up in him like an unspent charge. It was strong enough to make him feel transparent and self-conscious. If the girl could see how he had felt about Sharon, maybe Ollie could see what he felt about Aaliyah. It wasn't a pleasant sensation.
"Anyway, what did you get up to today, Ollie?" he repeated, pulling his mind away from the sordid cul-de-sac where it was leading him.
"No need to worry," his brother replied, as they turned the corner of their street.
"The cats are fine."
Halstead parked up and Ollie got out of the car, slamming the door. Freddie sighed and took a breath. He got out of the car slowly and looked up at the big old church across the street. Wherever he went, the church seemed to follow him.

The old stone building belonged to another denomination. Methodist. Years back the place had been modernised, a glass atrium built at the front, while half the back areas had been sold off as apartments to the city-boy commuters. He locked his car and walked around to his boot to retrieve the equipment from Corby's evening talk. As Freddie opened the boot he heard a scuff of movement on the other side of the street.

"Ollie, if that's you, stop messing about there and give me a hand…"

"It's not Ollie," said a prim voice.

Halstead's eyes widened in surprise. He dropped the black bags back into the boot and stood up. His heart lurched into overdrive as he looked up to see a thin man edged in silver light coming towards him across the street from the church. When he got close, the nearest street lamps washed the stranger's face in yellow light. The man had a face which looked about to break into a smile at any moment but didn't. He had school-boyish hair, combed and set with an old-fashioned parting. Halstead guessed he was in his fifties. He wore glasses, a waxed jacket, and two-tone moccasins. Halstead knew plenty of people from church circles – people who came from all over town, and the man looked the type. There was more than a chance he might have met the strange man before. Accordingly, he offered a smile.

"Sorry, I thought you were someone else."

Halstead looked around and saw his brother had already gone in.

"You're Freddie Halstead, aren't you?" said the man. He was well spoken, prim and tidy. After a good look, Freddie was certain the man reminded him of someone. Not someone he knew maybe, but someone in parliament, perhaps.

"That's me," said Freddie. Trying to put himself at ease, he slid his hands into his jeans pockets. "I don't think I know you."

The man finally smiled.

"No, maybe not. But I'm a church-goer, too. I attend Avenue Baptist mostly, the one up the road there."

"I know Avenue. A good church. Good outreach programme too."

The man nodded and looked at Freddie's eyes, deep and clear.

"So, you live with your brother, do you?"

Freddie frowned. "He's got special needs. I look after him."

"Very noble."

"It's not noble at all. It's necessary," said Freddie. "Someone has to do it."

"Humble as well, I see."

Halstead shifted on his feet. "I'm sorry. It's late, I'd better go in... how did you recognise me, anyway?"

The man smiled wider. "You're an outreach worker. I've seen your face in The Record every time you do one of those food appeals or community street parties. I take an interest in such things."

Halstead's frown stayed in place, but he offered a nod.

"Then, of course, there was the murder."

Halstead stiffened.

"The murder? You mean Helen? Why would you mention that?"

"It's the only murder I can think of lately."

The men looked at one another.

"Dreadful business, the loss of one so young," said the man. "So innocent. So full of enthusiasm for doing good works.

All that life ahead of her – torn out of her hands when someone took her life."
"It was awful. Yes."
The man's eyes gleamed at his. "I'm sure it was. Have you any idea who might have done it?"
Halstead turned away and slammed his boot. "Sorry. But if I did, I'd have told the police, I wouldn't be standing around here discussing it with strangers. Not even church-going ones."
"Point taken," said the well-spoken man.
Halstead turned to face the man. He was about to turn and walk away, but he changed his mind and looked back.
"How did you know I lived here? It would have been better to see me at the food bank – or the office."
"It might have been easier. But not better, certainly not for you or your brother. As for how I found you… well, personal addresses aren't so hard to track down these days."
Freddie narrowed his eyes.
"And the notices on your church website said your service was finishing late. A little guesswork and then a moonlit walk and here we are."
Freddie Halstead narrowed his eyes. His jaw tensed. "I'm beginning to think I should call the police about this little conversation."
"Maybe you should," said the stranger. "Or maybe I should. After all, I happen to know them quite well these days."
"Don't bother," said Freddie. "I'll call them myself." He locked his car with the fob and turned for the gate between the overgrown hedges outside his house.
"It was a sexual crime, of course."
Freddie turned around, stopping between the hedges.

"Sexual?"

"The crime. The murder. Nasty, but obvious and crude. You must see that yourself. From what I hear, the murderer slashed a merciless line down through her body, from throat to abdomen. It's disgustingly obvious what drove him to do it."

A silence followed while both men looked each other in the eye.

"I'm not sure I want to hear any more of this," said Freddie.

"Probably not. But here we are. It was a murder borne of lust, Mr Halstead. Sickening, depraved lust. I don't think the culprit was able to control himself."

"Don't think?" said Halstead. "Maybe you know something about it?"

The stranger smiled.

"I find myself a bit of an expert where things like this are concerned."

"Things?" said Halstead.

"Life... death... burdens, and affairs of the heart. It's all so complicated, isn't it? And it always rises to the surface. There's no place else for these things to go."

"That's enough. You're beginning to disturb me," said Freddie.

"I dare say I am, Mr Halstead. But you never know. Maybe our little chat might help you think of something – something to help the police in finding this killer."

"I'll call them," said Freddie. "And when I do, I'll be telling them about you."

"Of course," said the man. He smiled at Halstead and turned to leave. "Goodnight, Mr Halstead. Keep up all the good work. And er, best wishes with everything else."

Halstead stepped through the gate and watched as the thin man walked away. He heard the man's fading footsteps long after the man was gone from sight. Freddie shook his head. The Lord always had a way of catching up with him. Today he had received a shot across his bows more than once. First from Sharon, then the new girl, and now a total stranger. This one rocked him most of all. It seemed eyes were on him and his brother, and not all of them were friendly.

"What's the matter?" Freddie jumped. He turned around to see his brother walking back along the dark path from the door of their house. Ollie's face was in shadow, but Freddie felt his hard eyes.

"There was someone here just now. Did you see him?"

"No," said Ollie. "I thought you'd gone out and left me again."

"As if I'd do that," said Freddie. He walked up the path, putting on a smile for his brother. As he reached his brother's side, he hefted his bags into one arm and tried to muss up Ollie's hair, but his brother dodged him. They walked up the stairs and Freddie locked them into the flat, flicked the snib and slid the chain. When they were secure, he cut two sandwiches and made a glass of milk. He put the food in front of the PlayStation where Ollie was already playing hard. On the screen, a barbarian with an axe was busy hacking down an army of aggressive green orcs. Ollie's eyes were glued to the screen. His lips opened and closed wordlessly.

"I'll be back in a minute or two, okay?" said Halstead. Ollie nodded. That was all the response he got.

Sharon's face came to mind first of all. Her sparkling blue eyes, baby pink lips. Warm and tender. Next were the shining, flirtatious eyes of the new girl standing beside him by his car, inviting him to break every taboo, because she saw he was tempted. It was all seen. Everything. It seemed it was all known. His every thought seemed to have real-world consequences. But the man outside had bothered him most of all. A man sent by God to act as his conscience? To end his sinning ways? Or a despicable creature from the other place? Or perhaps, no one at all… just another town weirdo getting his kicks the only way he knew how. But Freddie Halstead was troubled. Life was sending him a message. His problems were crowding out everything good in his life. He was teetering on the edge of a precipice and he didn't want to fall. Not yet. The stranger would have to be dealt with head on. There was no way around it. But he didn't want to think about that yet. He needed to stop thinking. To stop the pressure.

He walked into his bedroom and shut the door then slid the heavy white chest of drawers across his door. He thought of reading his old favourites but decided he needed something special after a day like this. A reminder of how it had come to this. He dumped himself on top of the duvet, lay down, and for a time he looked up at the ceiling, simply breathing. After a while, he knitted his eyes shut, then dipped his hand under his bed. He pulled out the old round tin he'd had for years, the tin which used to contain Christmas chocolates. He took off the lid and dug his hand beneath his passport, his emergency cash, and the barely used hip flask. There. He pulled out his folded porn magazine and dumped it on the duvet. He leafed through the pages quickly, barely bothering to look at the naked women as he flicked by. As soon as he found what he was looking for, he stopped turning the pages. There, folded in half, was an innocuous-looking piece of paper. He opened it up, flattened it, and picked up the two photographs which lay inside the folded note. He took the photographs and looked at them in turn. One was nice, but the other image was truly special. It was the selfie Helen had taken for him back at the beginning, when things had seemed so promising. She'd been brave and sent it to him after the first brief frisson between them. The almost kiss. Brave didn't do it justice. The sweet, church-going girl had surprised him with her photo message, and when he'd opened it, he'd taken a sharp breath. She was naked and the first time he saw it, Freddie had been unable to believe it. The image showed the same sweet church girl he'd seen most Sundays, the same girl who volunteered to serve sandwiches to the homeless, who prayed devoutly at all the meetings, but the eyes of the girl in the photograph lured him in, making him promises, hinting at secrets only he would be told. It was a different girl, and the very same. His eyes scrolled down her naked body, while her image peered at him from over the rim of her spectacles. He swallowed, feeling guilty and sinful. He put the photograph down on the bed and picked up the folded note beside it. It was a self-written transcript of their one salacious phone call. Because it had been so good, he'd wanted to remember it. So he'd written it down as soon as the call had ended, remembering the smooth sound of her voice as he wrote. The phone call had been shocking and wonderful. All that passion, all that yearning. He nodded to himself and knitted his eyes shut. And in his head, he saw another image. A new image, as clear and sharp as a photograph, permanently frozen in his mind. The new image was a souveni - after all the yearning had come to nought - an image of beautiful Helen Brimelow splayed across the sand-strewn, wooden floor of a cold and empty beach hut, her head propped in one corner, her naked body torn open. The image in his head was so crisp, so clear, it felt as if he was still there, the salt air stinging his face, the blood turning cold on his hands. Tears spilled from his tight-shut eyes, and Freddie Halstead wiped each one away as quickly as they fell. There could be no tears anymore. There could be no memory. All of it had to fade from existence. The world was beginning to close in, to steal what little freedom remained in his life. Yes, his secret life would have to fade from existence. But not yet. Not until he had tried one last time to get what was owing. One last chance to taste pleasure before it was stolen for good. Thankfully, that chance was waiting for him. The girl had sent him a text message. She was keen. It wasn't that hard to find his mobile number, if you wanted to. Over the last few years, he'd published his mobile number freely, using it as a contact point for community events. A few had made their way onto the internet, just a quick Google search away from whoever wanted to find him. Maybe that was how the stranger outside had started off… Halstead read the girl's text message through teary eyes.

Freddie, is this your number? I had fun chatting with you tonight. Can we do it again soon? Call me whenever you like. Aaliyah xx

Freddie thought of the stranger and his insinuations. Trouble was coming. It felt inevitable. But maybe there was one more chance for him yet. One more, and then Freddie Halstead knew it had to come to an end.

Fourteen

"Where did this lead come from?" said Palmer.
"It's not a lead. It's a speculative visit, that's all," said Hogarth. He looked across at Palmer from behind the steering wheel of his Insignia. Hogarth's eyes looked narrow and tight. He'd arranged by text to pick Palmer up from her home on the way. She knew he wanted to escape another order into DCI Melford's office as much as anything else. The daily updates were a burden to them both, and from the look of Hogarth, he wasn't in the best place to be dealing with them. Melford would ask her for the update, nonetheless. She wondered what she might tell him this time. Hogarth was a good copper. Hard and spiky to deal with certainly, and a ruthless, blunt instrument when he was in a bad mood, but he was a good man and he got more results than he was credited for. She shouldn't have had to cover for him but Palmer knew some of his whims had brought them success in the past. She needed to be patient with him. So long as a result was coming, she would continue to tell Melford whatever he needed to keep him at bay.
"Speculative?" she asked. "Where did the speculation come from?"
"Same place as it always does," said Hogarth, tapping his temple. "The old noggin."
"Hope it's not unfounded speculation. We can't afford any more rabbit holes," said Palmer.
"Don't I know it. No, this one might help us. I did some extra digging last night, and I found something interesting."

Palmer waited and Hogarth glanced at her.

"Freddie Halstead's brother. He volunteers at the food bank."

"Yeah. He was one of the eighty names on the list the church gave us. I met him the other day. Very different to his brother. Got some kind of mental health condition."

"Yeah. That's what Drawton liked about him."

"Drawton?" said Palmer, frowning. "You didn't, did you? Not again!"

"Don't get your knickers in a twist. It's not as if I even saw him. I just took a little look around his gaff, on the off-chance he left some evidence lying around."

"You mean you broke into his house?"

"No. Nothing got broken. I was like a ghost. In and out, just like that."

As Hogarth recalled his narrow escape over the garden fence, his midriff, back and shoulder ached in unison. He reminded himself to buy some painkillers.

Palmer's silence bothered him. He saw a troubled look on her face.

"Hold on, Sue. You're not thinking of reporting me to the headmaster? I did it for the case. We've been working with scraps the whole time. Pathology on Robbins will tell us he OD'd. We know that's what they'll say. But that doesn't give us diddly squat. We still don't know what happened between him and Helen Brimelow, and there's no evidence that he killed her."

"If you went into Drawton's house, then you must either think he's still the culprit or—"

"Or I'm looking for evidence about the sexual assaults on those girls. Yes. If I found something on either one, it would have been a win."

"Do you seriously think he killed Helen? We know about his involvement in those assaults but there's less than nothing to link him to Helen Brimelow."

"She was the right age, the right type for him. Helen Brimelow's a close match."

"He didn't kill the others. They walked away."

"Probably after a nice pay-off in return for staying silent."

"But Helen was cut apart. There's no comparison."

Hogarth snorted. "I thought he might be getting worse. It happens. Perverts get thirsty. Their MOs can change."

"Not often. But you didn't find anything?"

"Nothing concrete. Nothing on Drawton, at least. I should have known he was too bloody good at clearing away his tracks. Well? Are you going to tell Melford or not?"

"Of course not."

Hogarth looked at her. Palmer met his eye.

"If I did that, you'd be out. And the team would be finished."

The look in Hogarth's eye expressed his thanks.

"I'm trying to solve the case, that's all I'm about. And if we keep pushing, and if we don't let anything get in the way of that result, then we'll find this killer and we'll put them away."

Palmer nodded. "If Drawton had found you, it wouldn't matter either way. You'd have been out."

Hogarth offered a hint of a grin. "But he didn't find me, did he?"

"What did you get?"

"I found some odd little *dear diary* pieces Drawton keeps hidden in his filing cabinet. They weren't nearly as interesting as I'd hoped, but still… They revealed he goes to an NHS psychiatric group therapy session. I bet he had to agree to attend as part of his pact with the slimeballs who got him off. From a letter I saw, it seems he's in with the chief constable. Maybe the chief forced him to attend. Either way, it's clear that Drawton is a reluctant participant."

"Where does Halstead's brother come in?" said Palmer, but her mind was drifting even as she asked the question. Ollie Halstead, the strange young man with the awkward bearing, and the cold, almost contemptuous way he'd spoken to her at the Refuge. She began to wonder. Hogarth looked at her and saw her thinking. He narrowed his eyes.

"Drawton's notes said Halstead's brother was in attendance at these meetings. He gave the impression that Ollie Halstead said some very dark things during the sessions – things that got a rise out of Drawton. Drawton seems to have taken a keen interest in Ollie Halstead since then and I've been wondering if Drawton has taken the boy under his wing. An unpleasant thought but—"

"But it's possible. Hmmm. I see. Ollie Halstead is not a boy, you know. He acts like it, looks like one, but if Fred Halstead is about forty, the brother is likely in his thirties at least. I saw him last night. He's certainly a cold fish. I'd put it down to him being on the spectrum—"

"Spectrum?"

"Asperger's, autism, that spectrum. But if he's attending a group like that – a group with Drawton – maybe he's worse than I thought."

"You saw him last night? I wasn't the only one grafting after hours, was I?"

Palmer rolled her eyes.

"My niece has taken a shine to the food bank. She dragged me down there for a church meeting."

"Oh? You're going to convert?"

"Not any time soon. But judging from Aaliyah's enthusiasm, you'd think she was interested."

"Seriously. No, I can't see that? She's into the adventure of the place. The excitement of being around all that street life. Either that or she's seen something you haven't."

"I watched her all night. Believe me, she had no chance to get up to anything. Although I took my eyes off her for five minutes while talking to Suitcase."

"Suitcase? My, my, you did have all the fun."

"I asked him about Kevin Robbins. Suitcase was with you on this one. He said Robbins wouldn't have taken his life over a girl – over *any* girl. He said the man was self-centred through and through. He also said it was incredibly unlikely that Robbins died of an overdose. Robbins was proud of being an in-control drug user. He was a long-term dabbler, proud of being better than the rest of them. Suitcase hated him for it."

"I bet he did. So, Robbins remains a mystery then. It's the timing which gets me. If he'd died at any other time, a few weeks after Helen, a few months, you'd say the deaths weren't linked. But he's dead inside a week of his girlfriend's murder… There's a link, but we're not seeing it."

Palmer nodded. "That's why I asked. It didn't get us any further, but at least it confirmed a few things. Where are we going, anyway?"

"The therapy sessions are held in one of those old solicitor-type offices in Clarence Road. It's a therapy company, probably milking the NHS budget for all its worth. I called ahead. The counsellor, Hamish Thompson, will be in at nine."

"Is he expecting us?"

Hogarth shook his head. "No. I prefer the answers they give when we catch them unawares. It's always more honest, and if not, I can see they're lying."

"Why would these people lie?"

"I don't know," said Hogarth. He looked at her with a glint in his eye. "But people do, don't they?"

Hamish Thompson had the flame-red hair of a true Celtic Scotsman, but when he opened his mouth his accent let him down. His hair was curly, his pink face was freckled, but he was a small, smiley, yet nervous looking man. He greeted them in the waiting room. He was dressed down to the point of wearing a plain T-shirt beneath a cardigan with the added affectation of a scarf around his neck. Hogarth's first impression of Hamish Thompson took an instant turn for the worse.

"Good morning. I'm Hamish. I'm not sure why you're here," he said, flicking his gaze to the receptionist who had called him from his office, "but I'd be glad to help you if I can."

"It's about one of your group therapy sessions," said Hogarth. "You host a meeting here with another professional. A psychologist or psychiatrist. The meeting includes a man called Simon Drawton and another called Oliver Halstead."

The man looked again at his receptionist. Hogarth followed his gaze. After a moment, he worked it out. The man was aware of company rules. Breaking them wouldn't go unnoticed by the receptionist. Hogarth sympathised. He gave a nod of understanding.

"Just a general understanding of the group setting might be enough, Mr Thompson."

"A general understanding about two very specific names? I'm not sure I can help you. Data protection, client confidentiality. You must know how it is."
"Of course. I don't expect you to divulge anything too much. But seeing as this is part of a murder investigation, we'd have to come back in a day or so with the authority we need. But that would only cost us valuable time."
Thompson offered a smile which looked more pained than pleased.
"I get the picture. That poor, poor girl they found in the beach hut. It was awful what happened to her."
"Yes, it was," said Hogarth.
The man nodded and ushered them out of the empty waiting room. Hogarth noted that he didn't look at the receptionist this time. The woman dipped her head and got back to whatever she was doing behind her screen.

Thompson's office was a small, bright affair with coloured lever-arch files neatly shelved and the odd brightly coloured object thrown in to lighten the place for a sense of 'fun' which didn't achieve its aim. Thompson sat down behind his empty desk and offered them each a chair. They took one, and Thompson pointed to the water cooler behind their backs.
"Help yourself."
"No thanks," said Hogarth. Palmer shook her head. "This therapy group. What is it about? Why are those two in it?"
"It does what it says on the tin, Inspector. Group Therapy. They talk, we listen, they reflect on what they are saying, and we support them in the process of coming to understand themselves; their problems, their triggers, their emotions."

"Bit of a mixed bag though. A stiff, upper-class pervert who chases young girls for fun, and a man with Ollie Halstead's obvious challenges. They're very different people."

Thompson offered a pursed-lipped smile.

"Not as different as you might imagine. And I really don't think I can get into Mr Drawton's reasons for being here."

"No, but you knew who I was talking about, didn't you?" said Hogarth.

"As for Ollie, not all his challenges are as obvious as his main condition."

"His Asperger's?" said Palmer.

"As you say," said Thompson carefully.

"Okay, then. These secondary conditions, whatever they are…" said Hogarth, fishing.

"I can't say what they are. It remains confidential."

"But if I allude to them, you could tell me if I was wrong, maybe?" said Hogarth.

Thompson looked flummoxed, but Hogarth pressed on.

"From what you've said, I might assume they have something in common," said Hogarth, staring into Thompson's eyes. "I know that Ollie makes the odd, shocking and sinister remark when he's in your sessions. Remarks which sometimes challenge your authority. Remarks which Mr Drawton finds amusing, or perhaps, inspiring."

"How would you know about any of that?" said Thompson.

"Part of the investigation, Mr Thompson. All you need do is confirm what we've already been told, that's all. An indication would suffice."

Thompson stayed still as if he sensed a trap.

"Simon Drawton was involved in allegations of sexually abusing young girls. He's a very dark man, Mr Thompson. I know Ollie Halstead fascinates him, and because of that,

Ollie Halstead now fascinates me. Drawton thinks they are kindred spirits. That's a concern for me, because, if I'm right, young Mr Halstead could be an even more intense character than Drawton. You see what I'm saying here, Mr Thompson? You may not know who or what you're dealing with. Or perhaps you do…?"
The man paled.
"Of course not. You're suggesting Ollie or Simon could have been involved in something awful. If that's true, you'd best speak to my superiors. I work at the coal face, Inspector. We're helping these people as best we can. We have access to what's in their clinical files, but we don't know what they do in their private lives, the things the clinicians don't see. Ollie has very complex needs. That's the limit of it."
"Is he a killer, Mr Thompson?"
Palmer blanched and shifted in her chair. It took Thompson a long moment to respond.
"You're asking for a professional opinion? I can't give you one. I'm sorry. That's well above my paygrade."
"Then what can you tell us, Mr Thompson? Remember, a girl is dead, and there could yet be others."
"This isn't fair. I should ask you to leave and contact my superior."
"We'll do that," said Hogarth. "But first, tell us. Do you think these men are kindred spirits?"
"I see them for an hour and a half once a week. We're just one of the NHS centres where Ollie receives help. You need to speak to his dedicated support team."
Hogarth's eyes probed the man, unrelenting. "You said these things may not be written down in black and white. I'm here now, asking you."

"Kindred spirits," said Palmer. The man was only too glad to look away from Hogarth to meet Palmer's eye.

"It's not a medical term, is it?" said Palmer. "You'd be committing to nothing by saying either way."

Thompson hesitated. "Simon does.... seem to find Ollie *amusing*, yes. But to me, it seems rather a one-way street. Drawton is more interested in Ollie than Ollie is in him. You already know one of Ollie's main conditions. He's not prone to making friends. He's not interested in any of that. Frankly, he's very hard work and he doesn't want to be here."

"No. I bet Drawton doesn't either. He probably likes how Ollie Halstead tells it like it is."

"Probably so," said Thompson. "Look. I don't think I can tell you any more. We'll have to end this here."

Thompson got up from his desk and looked at the door. Palmer mirrored the man's moves, while Hogarth remained in his seat until the last possible moment; a form of protest, but not exactly a strong one.

"Sorry," said Thompson.

"Don't be sorry, Mr Thompson," said Hogarth. "We'll be back when we need more."

Thomson winced at the comment.

Palmer offered him something approaching a smile. "Just one last thing before we go, then," she said. Thompson gave a wary nod.

"You wouldn't describe them as friends?"

"Ollie and Simon? I said before, Ollie isn't interested in friends. He finds people untrustworthy. Annoying. Distasteful. They're not interesting to him, they get in the way."

Hogarth and Palmer exchanged a glance.

"In the way of what?" said Palmer.

"Of what he wants to do," said Thompson.

"And what does he want to do?" said Palmer.
"I can't divulge any more. But let's just say he's a man driven by his id."
"By his id," said Hogarth. "You mean his sexual and aggressive urges?"
Thompson blushed. "Your words, not mine."
Hogarth grinned. "Then he's got more in common with Drawton than I thought. No wonder he thinks they're kindred spirits. Is there any chance Drawton might be able to talk him around, get chummy with him, or influence him?"
Thompson walked to the door and opened it wide.
"I wouldn't have thought so. Read up on Asperger's, Inspector. That might tell you more than I can now."
"I know a little about the id, Mr Thompson. Not much, but enough to be dangerous," said Hogarth. "Men driven by their id might make a temporary alliance if it gets them closer to what they need."
"With the id there's no thinking involved, Inspector. The id goes with its instincts, follows its urges. That's how it works."
"Absolutely," said Hogarth, looking pleased. "Thanks, Mr Thompson, you've been a great help."
Hogarth's satisfied expression made Thompson look upset. He held the door open for them until they walked out. Hogarth offered the man a hand and Thompson took it limply.
"We'll be in touch," Hogarth said.
"Next time call head office." Thompson withdrew and closed the door on them. Palmer gave Hogarth a look.

"Do you think you pushed too hard? He could have proved useful later."

"And he will, when we've charged someone. Think – we've only come as far as we have now because we pushed that man. We're getting closer. If not for that, we'd still be pondering Kevin Robbins."

"Robbins is still an issue," said Palmer.

"Yes, he is. But we're scenting something new. You said it yourself, Ollie Halstead is a weirdo. Maybe his brother, Freddie, makes him volunteer to keep him busy. To keep him out of trouble."

"If that's true, it's hardly a good idea. The place is full of all kinds of temptation."

As they walked out of the office, Palmer's mind had turned to her niece. She needed to speak to the girl, to warn her to stick to her promise. As Hogarth got into the driver's seat and buckled up, Palmer looked out of the window and put her phone to her ear. Aaliyah's phone rang a long time but no answer came.

Hogarth turned the key in the ignition and the engine growled into life.

"All the chasing in the world isn't going to keep that girl from doing whatever she wants to do. She's seventeen. You're not her mother. You have to let it go."

"Easy for you to say, her mother will hold me responsible. And as for letting it go, you're hardly one to talk."

"Meaning?"

"You know who I mean. Drawton."

"You're changing the subject, Sue." Hogarth pulled out onto the street and drove away from the centre of town.

"And so are you," she said. "If there's a chance that Ollie Halstead is the killer, I have to keep her away from there."

Hogarth wrinkled his nose, pausing before he replied.

"There's a chance. But I don't think Ollie's the type of boy your niece would be interested in. That's not the kind of danger she's after. I think you have to worry about her and Freddie Halstead."

Palmer noted Hogarth's tone. Something had been left unsaid. She gave him a look until he spat it out.

"But… Drawton's a different kettle of fish. If Drawton has been grooming the lad, coaching him, then he could be a threat. Drawton seems to be able to persuade anyone to do anything."

Palmer swallowed and took a moment before she spoke.

"Do you think all this talk of Drawton might be clouding the current case?"

"You think? Then how come he's gotten close to a man we see as another potential killer? Coincidences, Palmer. We've never liked them, have we?"

Hogarth had a point. Perhaps there was a chance the DI had been right all along. Maybe Drawton was involved. Either way, Palmer knew she had to keep her niece away from the food bank, no matter what.

"Do you mind if we drive by my place? I need to pick up my car," said Palmer.

"You want to check up on your niece."

"Am I that obvious?"

"Pretty much," said Hogarth. "But don't worry. When it comes to dealing with you, I get the feeling you see through me the same. Fine. Let's go."

After Hogarth dropped her off, Palmer was left peering up at the thick grey net curtains of her upstairs flat. She saw no movement. Palmer hoped it was a good sign. It was still relatively early. The girl was probably still in bed.

Palmer unlocked the outer door, picked up the slew of unwanted post dumped on the porch mat, then opened the door to her flat. As soon as she was inside, she looked up and called Aaliyah's name up the staircase. There was no reply.

"Ali?" she called. Now there was a hint of worry in her voice. She closed the door and tramped up the stairs, building up a manufactured fit of irritation with which to rebuke her niece for sleeping in. All the while, she had a nagging feeling…

Palmer walked up to the attic – the white-painted loft room which had been hastily tidied and into a bedroom for her niece. Her futon bed was unmade and empty. The girl's fashion and music magazines were cast around the floor, pages left wide open. There was a small artillery of make-up and lipstick tubes, along with several lippy-smeared tissues on the floor, and a discarded mirror. Palmer hadn't been up here for days. There was no telling when the items were used. But she didn't like it and not because of the mess.

"Damn it, Aaliyah. Where the hell are you?"

Palmer opened the Velux window to drag in some fresh air before she dialled her niece's number from her mobile's frequent calls list. She let it ring a good long time before it went to voicemail.

"Call me," she snapped and ended the call.

She narrowed her eyes and looked around the painted floorboards. There, by the bed, she spied something else. A piece of paper, a flyer, with a coloured logo which she recognised. Palmer bent down to retrieve it. Yes, she knew it. It was the stylised logo of the Refuge food bank, the words written beside a cartoon hand offering a cartoon heart to another hand. The words were italicised and green, just like those on the wall of the building and on the evening talk flyer.

"What is it with you and that place?" she muttered. Whatever it was, it had to be stamped out, and fast. Palmer knew what she had to do. Hogarth would understand. The case was already at an impasse. It could wait another hour or so, or maybe, if John Dickens' crime scene mob were still combing through Kevin Robbins' apartment, she could kill two birds with one stone and ask for an update from the horse's mouth. Palmer dropped the food bank flyer to the floor, and toed it back towards Aaliyah's messy bed, then she set off, clattering down the white-painted steps in a hurry.

Fifteen

By half past ten, the next opening session for the Refuge food bank was a mere half hour away. Already a queue stretched from the front door to the platform's side railing thirty feet away. Palmer eyed the queue as she shut the door of her Corsa. The place never seemed to stop. She was beginning to feel overwhelmed by the pressure of the case, worries about Hogarth losing focus, and now her niece. Her chest felt tight. She took a deep breath and looked around the ground floor car park of the estate. A battered white Transit van stood at the foot of the curling slope which led up to the first-floor platform. The van's back doors were open, and several hefty blokes of various ages were pulling out green crates and loading them into roll-cage trolleys. From the look of the men's faces, the crates looked heavy. When the last crate was loaded and the trolley full, two of the men started to haul and push the cumbersome beast up the steep slope, one pulling, one pushing. Another empty cage was waiting to replace the departed one and was immediately shifted into position behind the van. Palmer pursed her lips and made a wary approach. The older of the men by the van saw her coming. He was at least six feet tall, probably more, and wide with it. He was the one doing the unloading, passing the big crates to the others to load onto the trolleys. He was a large man, unshaven, the kind who looked like he could have punched holes through walls but the genial smile that appeared on his face as Palmer came near, suggested he wasn't as tough as he looked. Or at least not on work time.

"Can I help you?" he said, stepping out from between the van doors and the trolley. He was wearing fingerless woollen gloves and a sturdy black sports jacket that had seen better days.

"You work at the food bank?" she said.

"Yes." He nodded, his smile still in place. "I'm one of the managers. My name's Gordon. If this is anything to do with funding, admin or donations you'll need to speak to Freddie Halstead. Our main manager is on sabbatical."

"Sabbatical? What? Like a college professor?"

The big man chuckled.

"It happens in churches sometimes too. This is a church project. You did know that, didn't you?" Mentioning the word church had brought a glint to his eye. Palmer deduced that he was a believer.

"So I heard," she said.

"This isn't about funding, is it?"

"How long's your main guy been on sabbatical then?"

"Oh, a couple of months. It's nothing, really. He's a good man, but this place can eat you up. It's hard dealing with needy people all the time. You have to take it steady."

"I can imagine. That lot in your faces every day, close up and personal. Then there's all this work to think of. It looks like you're in charge of the food then?"

"Pretty much. You from the council, are you?"

Palmer shook her head. "No. I'm from the police. Detective Sergeant Palmer."

The big man nodded. "Thought you looked familiar. This about Helen or Razor?"

"Actually, this is a little more personal. My niece seems to have taken an interest in your food bank."

Gordon's smile broadened. "A lot of people do. It's a special place. Spiritual. It appeals to something deep inside us." The man patted his chest. "Something not many people can articulate."

For a big lug in fingerless gloves, the man seemed charmingly philosophical. Palmer sensed there was a something of the preacher in him too.

"But my niece isn't old enough to hang around here."

The man rubbed his chin. "Young, eh? Maybe she could volunteer to help when we're closed. We've got rules, you see. But when we're setting up, it's volunteers only, she'd be safe enough then."

"After all the trouble I don't think I want her hanging around here at all."

Gordon nodded. "Yeah. It's a problem. We've lost a few of our lady volunteers already. With Razor going as well, I dare say we'll lose a few more."

"My niece," said Palmer. "She came here last night. I think she might have come back here again this morning. I can't really allow it. Not while the investigation is ongoing."

Gordon looked back at his remaining companion, a man in a hat who was listening as he loaded a trolley.

"Have you seen any new young ladies up there this morning, Alan?"

"I should be so lucky," said a cheeky young voice from beneath a blue beanie.

Palmer arched her eyebrow. The big man saw it and smiled.

"I was up there twenty minutes back," said Gordon. "It was just the usual skeleton crew then. No new team members, or young ladies to speak of."

"Was Ollie Halstead up there?" she asked.

"Ollie?" said the big man, looking puzzled. He scratched his head. "No. Freddie wasn't up there either. He must be over the office at Warrior Square. I suppose him and Ollie could be in later, mind. Why? Is there a problem?"

"So long as my niece isn't in that building, no. Thanks for your help," she said, backing away. "Keep up the good work."

"And you," he said, grinning. "Make sure you find whoever did that to Helen. She was a real treasure."

"Don't worry, we will."

Palmer paused and took a step back towards the man. He read her movements, frowned and put his hands on his hips. "Tell me, can you recall Helen ever getting close with anyone she shouldn't have? One of the service users? A local resident, maybe? Someone like Kevin Robbins, for instance?"

"Razor? No… I always have the girls warned to keep their distance from the service users. She was a smart one too. Helen always listened."

Helen had listened, but it didn't mean she had obeyed. The thought made Palmer narrow her eyes, as she considered her disobedient niece.

"Helen?" said the younger man. The man called Alan put down a green crate and looked at them both, wiping his brow. "I saw Helen talking to Razor once or twice."

"Not in the Refuge, surely?" said Gordon.

"No. Not up there. It was always out on the concrete up there. First time I saw it, I thought he was hassling her. Second time though, it looked like she was hassling him. I thought she was giving him one of those Bible leaflets you people hand out."

"Tracts, you mean?" said Gordon. "Scriptures?"

"Yeah, those," said the volunteer.

"Why didn't you mention it to anyone?" said Gordon.
"I was brand new here back then. I didn't know anyone. It was none of my beeswax, what she did. Besides, that was ages ago, way before they found her down the beach huts."
Gordon sighed and shook his head as if he'd failed in some way. He looked at Palmer.
"Sorry, officer. I honestly didn't know about that."
"It's okay. But that helps. What's your name, sir?"
"Alan. Alan Healy."
"Thank you, Alan. We may need to talk again."
"Sure," said the young man, before plunging back into the van.
"If I find your niece," said the big man, "I'll tell her that you called by."
"Thanks. But it'd be better for both of us if you told her to take a hike," said Palmer.
She waved and walked away, wondering if there was a wedding ring hiding under those gloves. It was just an idle thought, one she pushed away as she looked up at the vast beige and cream obelisk of Haycock tower block looming directly above her. Palmer took a deep breath. An update from the crime scene boys would be no bad thing, especially now they had another witness suggesting Robbins and Brimelow had something going on between them. After a quick check with crime scene, she would circle the food bank once more for one final check on her niece. Just to be sure. Palmer climbed the curving slope and turned left following the short bridge to the entrance for Haycock. There she buzzed number eighty-six for Robbins' flat, and left the buzzer going until one of the SOCOs finally answered.
"Yes?"
"DS Palmer here. Permission to beam aboard."

"You can come up, but I'm afraid there's nothing juicy to be had here."

"Can I be the judge of that?" she said. The SOCO's voice was a young one – possibly Bloom, the easiest to deal with of the whole bunch. The man buzzed her in, and Palmer opened the heavy blue door.

Crime Scene were still hard at it when she entered. A metre square in front of the door had been sectioned off by a cordon of plastic bollards and tape. Palmer ducked under the tape, nudged the battered front door open and John Dickens appeared. She knew the man by his short stocky frame, even before he pulled down his breathing mask and white plastic hood.

"There's nothing here for you yet, DS Palmer."

Palmer nodded at the tape. "The fact you're still here says something."

Dickens lowered his eyes. "It pays to be cautious. Especially, as you've noted, the deceased hardly looks like standard OD material. But we haven't dismissed an overdose. It can happen at any time, to anyone. Every injection these junkies have is like pulling the trigger in a game of Russian roulette."

"He was also a heroin user of twenty years or more, so the man knew what he was doing."

"That's why we're being careful," said Dickens. "And for the Brimelow investigation. It's got to be a fine-tooth comb job, hasn't it? The brass are watching."

"You never do things just to keep people happy, John."

"You know me so well," said Dickens, with a faint smile. "I've got some more possible evidence to look at before we pack up. If what we find can add up with what Ed Quentin finds when he finishes the PM, you'll have your answer. Until then, I'm not going to do anything to keep you happy either, Sue."

"Worth a try, John."

"Hogarth sent you, did he?"

"Not this time," she said.

"Means you're learning all his bad habits," said Dickens. They nodded a goodbye at one another before Dickens shut the door. From the corner of her eye, Palmer saw one of the heavy wood and glass fire doors open. The draught made a sucking noise and brought in a blast of cold air from the stairwell. Palmer looked around to see a young blonde woman standing stock still, holding the door handle on the other side of the glass. Palmer frowned. It took a moment for her to place the woman. She had pink eye shadow and a serious, but coy look in her eyes. The young woman looked from the door of flat eighty-six to Palmer before she turned away and started to move off down the steps. Her quick feet echoed between the concrete walls. Palmer darted for the door and pulled it open. She leaned over the edge of the stairwell and looked down to see the top of the blonde girl's head.

"Stop! I'd like to talk to you. Just a quick word!"

But the girl didn't stop. Palmer made after her, racing down the stairs as fast as she could. She was gaining ground, but three floors on, the girl left the stairwell and turned off onto one of the lower floors.

"No, you don't," said Palmer. She sped up, running down the steps. She followed the woman through the slowly shutting door, to find her fumbling with a key to one of the flat doors. Flat fifty-nine.

"You. You were at the Refuge church dinner last night," she said.

The woman's eyes flicked left and right as if searching for a denial.

Instead, she settled on petulance.

"So?" she said.

"You were watching me, maybe listening too, while I was interviewing the man everyone around here seems to call Suitcase."

"I looked at you. I was just looking around the hall. Big difference. So what?"

"And now I've just seen you looking at the door of Kevin Robbins' flat. Soon as you saw me, you made a run for it. Can you see why I might be interested in that kind of behaviour?"

The young woman's face warped into a scowl as hard as any Palmer had seen. But a moment later it softened back into its usual semi-hardened prettiness. Palmer wasn't fooled. She recognised a crack fiend's scowl when she saw one. Their monstrous come-down rages were notorious.

"I've got nothing to do with what happened to Razor, *alright?*"

"Good," said Palmer. "But I think it might be worth us talking all the same."

"Well, that makes one of us," said the girl. "You'd better come in then, hadn't you?"

The longer she spent in the girl's company, the older she seemed. The blonde was at least in her late twenties or early thirties. It was the pink eyeshadow and baby pink hoodie and pink shoes, which had made Palmer think the woman younger than her years. But beneath the make-up, the lines of ageing were now visible. Even so, she still looked attractive enough. Like Robbins, if she was a drug user, then she hadn't yet fallen all the way down the slippery slope. Palmer saw the photographs of babies on the tiled fireplace and started to change her mind. There was a photograph of an infant in a pink bonnet, and further on a bigger child in a blue baby grow. Palmer took a quick look around the flat and saw plenty of adult mess but none of the detritus – or noise – she would have associated with young children. The drugs had taken their toll at some point, after all. With photos that size, the babies had to be hers.

"Sally-Anne," said the girl, following Palmer's eyes to the photographs. "And that's Donnie. My pride and joy, both of them. Sally-Anne was born five years ago. Donnie two and a half years back. I haven't seen them since. I get to write letters to them, but that's it. What's the point in writing to a baby? The bastards who have them will only throw it all away."

Palmer winced inwardly. She cleared her throat.

"They might save the letters – for when they're both older. People do, you know."

"They won't care, will they? Who knows?" said the girl. "I could be dead by then."

She picked up a packet of cigarettes, lit one up, and put the pack back down.

"Dead?" said Palmer, narrowing her eyes.

"Anything can happen, can't it? And around here it usually does."

Interesting point of view.

"Can I ask your name?" said Palmer.

"Debbie. Debbie Tranter. I'm surprised you needed to ask. I thought the homeless place might have told you already. They seem to think that I'm trouble."

"And are you?" said Palmer. There were a couple of leather armchairs, but they were full of crumpled clothes, and other junk Palmer didn't want to handle. Or think about too closely.

"I'm trouble to those who give me trouble," she said.

"Did you know Kevin Robbins? Or maybe Helen Brimelow?"

The girl raised her cigarette and inspected the glowing embers. She pouted and blew smoke at the ceiling.

"You already know I knew Kevin. That's why you followed me here."

"Not necessarily. There could have been some other reason you were there."

"There isn't. We were friends. I wanted to be nosy, see if I could hear something slip from the front door. I know there are coppers in there."

"Like what?"

"Like if they know what killed him?"

Palmer felt a quickening of her heart. She pursed her lips but kept her composure.

"Do *you* think you know what killed him, Debbie?"

The girl's eyes snapped onto Palmer's face. Her eyes locked on.

"It was an OD, wasn't it?"

"You tell me," said Palmer.

"How am I supposed to know?" said the girl. She studied Palmer as she took another drag of her cigarette.

"You do know something, though, don't you, Debbie?"

"I know Kevin was a selfish prick and was destined to die sooner or later."

Not friends. Lovers, thought Palmer.

"Why do you say that?" she said.

"He was called Razor for a reason. He liked playing the hard man. Liked scaring people. Made him feel big. I saw right through it all of course. It was bullshit. He was a softie, most of the time."

"I heard he was violent," said Palmer.

"Yeah. When he had to be. To keep his rep intact. That's all."

"Tell me about him," said Palmer.

The girl shrugged. "Don't suppose it can hurt, can it? Not now... He was a part time dealer. But not much the last few years. These days he was mostly into buying and selling to top up his benefits."

"Buying and selling what?" said Palmer.

The girl met her eye again.

"Not drugs. Just stolen goods, mostly. He did enough at it to keep himself in good clothes."

Palmer paused before she asked the question.

"Were you close?" she said.

"At times," said Tranter.

"Were you in a relationship with him?"

"I just told you. At times."

"Must have been hard on you."

"He was always hard on me when we fell out. But he wasn't ever violent with me. He was a selfish bastard, but a decent one deep down. He'd dump me off for a month or two at a time, bad mouth me to all and sundry, call me a slag and all that, then a week later, he'd come back and try it on again like nothing had happened. If I was feeling in the mood, I went with it. A few times I told him to go screw himself. There were fireworks then."

"Did his ways make you angry?"

"Of course, they did. We were living together for months at a time, then he tells me to get out because he's got his eye on someone new. Wouldn't you be pissed off?"
Palmer nodded.
The girl prodded the cigarette at her.
"But never enough to kill him, so don't even think about it. I'd hurt someone if I had to defend myself, or my home, or my children, but I'd never kill a man."
She saw the look on Palmer's face and went a stage further.
"And I'd never kill that girl, either, not for any reason, if that's what you're thinking."
Palmer nodded once.
"You believe there is a link between the two deaths then?"
The girl snorted and curled her lip.
"Do me a favour. I know you people aren't always quick off the mark but you generally get there in the end. You've already asked a few people. I know you have. He was shagging her, wasn't he? I even heard them at it once. Like a pair of bloody randy goats. She was barely out of school and he was banging her up in his seedy little cave. Makes me sick. I don't know what a quiet little church mouse like her ever saw in him. Still, it's always the quiet ones…"
Palmer nodded while the woman sucked her cigarette.
"Thanks for being so candid, Debbie. Tell me, did you ever try to confront either of them about their relationship?"
"Kev didn't do relationships. He just liked sex. I'm not sure the little princess realised that until it was too late."
"You think she got upset about it?"
"Yes, of course she did. I heard about it from him, when he was trying to sleaze me back into his bed."
"When was that?"

"Not long before she was found dead in the beach hut. She was after him, not the other way around."

Palmer was thoughtful.

"Listen, not many people around here liked Razor, but that doesn't mean he was a killer. He was a bad boy, yes. An idiot. But no killer."

"You're sure of that, are you?"

"As sure as I am that the girl had a crush on him. She hounded him."

"Hounded him?"

The girl blew another plume of smoke at the yellowed ceiling before she answered.

"Yes," she said.

"Then why did he die?" said Palmer. The question slipped out; she was thinking aloud.

"You mean *how*, don't you?" said the girl.

"If you like," said Palmer quickly.

"I don't know for sure, but Razor was going to get his comeuppance one day. He'd threatened too many people, hurt too many people across the years. Maybe it would happen with a stabbing, or he'd get shot, or get beaten to death. I always suspected the wrong girl would do it. But never an OD. Kev had too much pride to go out like that."

"Yet it looks like an OD," said Palmer.

Debbie Tranter nodded thoughtfully. "Kevin didn't usually have access to any brown like that. That's what gets me."

"What do you mean by that, Debbie?"

The girl bit her lip as if she had let something slip and wanted to retract it.

"What did you mean?" Palmer knew brown was a street term for heroin.

The girl's hard face flashed at her again for a second.

"I mean it would have had to be bloody strong gear to have killed him stone dead. Kev was experienced. He knew what he was doing. That's all. I mean he was seasoned in the ways of heroin."

Palmer narrowed her eyes. "That's not all you meant, though, is it? It almost sounds to me like you've sampled the gear yourself."

The girl put the cigarette in her mouth and bared her arms, laying them out flat, exposing her pale inner elbows.

"Do I look like a junkie to you? My arms are clean."

Palmer stuck to her guns. "All the same, it sounded as if you knew what you were talking about. Maybe you inject between your toes, to keep yourself looking nice."

"I don't like needles, end of story. I'm not a smackhead."

Palmer folded her arms and stared the woman down.

The girl rolled her eyes and shook her head slowly. She took a deep breath and blew it all out. This time when she spoke, she was quieter, less bolshie.

"Maybe… maybe I had a chase of the stuff." A chase. *Smoking.*

"You smoked it?" said Palmer. "You smoked the same stuff that Kevin Robbins used? Where did you get it?"

Tranter bit her lip, as if admitting what she knew was a problem.

When she spoke, the woman didn't answer the question. "Smoking the stuff is never as intense. That's why junkies mainline it. They want it all. They want the highest high, every bit they can get. But man, I was glad I just smoked it. It weighed me off, totally. I mean I almost collapsed. It was a good high, right, but way too intense. It was like it hadn't even been cut right."

Palmer's eyes flicked around the mess-strewn room.
"Who did you get it from?"
The girl shook her head.
"I need to know. This is important, Debbie."
The girl knitted her eyes shut before she blurted a confession.
"I don't know. I didn't buy any. I used some of Kev's."
"When was this?"
"What?" said the girl. By now she was blushing.
"When did you smoke that heroin? When did Kevin give it to you?"
There was a lengthy pause.
"Miss Tranter. If you hold out on me, I'll have you dragged down the station for questioning. So which would you prefer?"
"I didn't do it!"
"So you've said."
"Okay. But just remember that."
The girl stubbed out the cigarette in an overflowing ashtray. Grey ash spilt over the side.
"I used to have a key to his flat, okay? I told him I'd lost it during one of our fallouts. The plan was I'd go and catch him when he was diddling his latest scrubber, catch him in the act, and embarrass him, or whatever. But I never did. I just kept the key. A few days after Kev disappeared, I went up there. I wondered if he'd done a moonlight flit; maybe I wondered if he'd run off after that girl died. I used the key. I went in. And that's when I found him."
"You didn't call it in?"
The girl shook her head. Her eyes misted and she looked away.
"No. I didn't."

"Then what? Your ex was dead in the armchair, so you walked off and took a relaxing hit of heroin from the kitchen...?"

"Not fair! He was dead! I was in shock. I needed something, anything, just to take the edge off. And that's when I took it. I tore some foil from the drawer, took a tiny pinch of gear, and lit it right there on the hob. I went back and cleared up the mess the next day. That's when I realised I'd done something wrong."

"You know this looks pretty bad on you?"

"I couldn't give a shit. I didn't kill him, did I?"

Palmer was yearning for fresh air, but she needed more. "Where did he get this heroin?"

"I don't know. He'd been screwing that church girl right up until she was killed. We weren't really on speaking terms before he died."

Palmer considered what she'd heard. Debbie Tranter was tough, streetwise, and seemed well connected. Connected enough to know the police had interviewed certain people on the estate.

"Where *might* he have got that gear from?"

The girl looked up at the ceiling and took a deep breath. "One of the last days I saw him, not long after they found the girl's body, he came up to me, trying it on again. I was still upset with him, so I gave him the cold shoulder. He told me he'd got something special. A present he wanted to share. I thought he meant a present from the girl. She was dead. So it was pretty weird. Sharing something of hers was the last thing I wanted. I just cut him off and walked away."

"So you think he was talking about the heroin?"

Tranter nodded her head. "Yes. What else could it have been?"

"Who might have given that to him?"

"That's the problem. Who gives away top-grade brown like that? No one. No one at all, not ever."

"Do you know who might have access to heroin of that grade?"

"Only a dealer. And not your bottom of the rung dealer either. Those wasters will have cut it to nothing ten times over by then. I'm talking about a *proper* dealer. Someone at the higher end of the chain."

"Such as?"

"Like none of them. He was a customer, money in the bank. What dealer had reason to want him dead?"

"I'd like to know the answer to that, wouldn't you? Just give me a name, Debbie. Someone who might be able to get gear like that?"

"You think I've got a death wish? Leave it out. They killed him, didn't they? I'm not up for getting topped just yet, believe me."

"Just give me a clue if nothing else."

"Here's a clue for you: There's the door. I've told you everything I can. Even if you nick me, I'll still tell you nothing. Because I'm innocent and I want to stay alive."

Palmer nodded and slowly turned away for the door. Debbie Tranter followed her all the way. When the front door was opened, what passed for fresh air whistled in from the tower block staircase. Palmer looked back, still blocking the way.

"Did you love him, Debbie?" said Palmer. "If you did, then help us."

The woman's chin crumpled. The question had taken her by surprise.

"Bitch," she said.

Palmer stepped out of the way as the door was slammed in her face. She sighed.

"Well played, DS Palmer," she muttered. But as she reached the fire door, behind her, the letterbox of Tranter's flat snapped open.

"You want a clue, do you? Try Leigh. That's where all the good champagne comes from these days."

The letterbox snapped shut and Debbie Tranter's blue eyes disappeared from view.

Leigh. Leigh meaning gangster Alex Galvan, or maybe the other new pretender on the block – the big man looking after the warehouse in Leigh while his paymaster, Patrick Ferber, served time. Neither was a prospect to be relished. And Palmer was sure they didn't need to open any more cans of worms. Hogarth had opened plenty enough already. But in terms of 'champagne' dealers, they were the closest fit. It was hard to know if Hogarth was going to be pleased, or disturbed when he heard the news. The case was beginning to open up for them. Shoe leather and a spot of luck had paid off in lieu of any scientific evidence from the boffins. But from the look of things, the case was going to get harder before it got any better.

Before she left the estate, Palmer took one last recce of the first-floor platform around the food bank. By now the queue was huge, stretching along one whole side fence, so she stayed on the other side of the building, and studied the faces from afar. No joy. She walked away and pushed up onto her tiptoes to look through the food bank's high windows. She peered into the hall. It was busy – the seats were lined with volunteers while Gordon, the big manager

stood at the front, waving hands like shovels as he gave a talk. Yes, he was a preacher alright. Looking around the hall, Palmer scanned the silent faces for any sign of her young niece. But the girl was nowhere in sight. The cheeky faced Alan Healy gave her a nod, and a few others looked up, including Gordon the manager who gave her a sleepy smile and a wave before he called out, "She's not here."
Palmer nodded and mouthed the word thanks, before she blushed, ducked her head and retreated to her car. She scanned the streets in all directions as she went. Her niece was nowhere to be seen. It wasn't good that she was out of contact. But maybe it was better still that she wasn't anywhere near the Refuge.
It was the thinnest of silver linings.
But it wasn't enough to ease her mind.

Sixteen

Palmer was still out and about, leaving Hogarth waiting alone in the office. Thankfully, Melford hadn't yet popped his maudlin head around the door to request an update. Besides, the man would try Palmer as his first port of call. Hogarth trusted Palmer as much as anyone else in his life. He knew the DS would be true to her word and say nothing unless he crossed a certain line. Thankfully, they had become close enough that Hogarth had a rough idea of where that line might be. Remembering his temptation to hurl the boiling kettle into Drawton's face, Hogarth realised he'd come dangerously close. Palmer was one of the few forces that kept him in check. The DS had more uses than she realised. He knew she was out on the street, hunting for her little scamp of a niece. Hogarth couldn't blame her for using a little work time to assuage her worries, especially seeing as the girl was getting dangerously close to the newest focal point of the murder case.

But waiting for Palmer was taking a toll. Hogarth needed air, and he needed to scratch a certain itch. The itch that kept coming back, time and again. Drawton had met Ollie Halstead. No matter what he had promised Palmer, it needed to be followed up. He decided the best way to play it was to tell her what he intended to do. He grabbed his keys, opened the office door and made a quick scan of the faces out in the main office. Most of the uniforms were out on the street, only the managers and the desk jockeys left behind. Hogarth took a careful stroll towards the main reception.

Better walk through the public exit than risk passing Melford's office at the wrong moment. That pleasure could wait.

Hogarth decided to take a sweep along Queensway to see if he could find Palmer. It stood to reason that she would check the only place her niece had shown an interest. He took the first turning off the large Queensway roundabout and slowed to a halt outside the bakery on the corner of Coleman Street which bordered the tower block estate. Like much of the area, the bakery had seen better days, but the food inside couldn't be faulted. Having skipped breakfast Hogarth decided on a cream finger doughnut and an egg roll to keep him going. He parked his Vauxhall Insignia on the double yellows and got out, fishing in his trouser pocket for change. But before his eyes had even found the shiny buns in the shop window, he noticed Palmer's dented Corsa sitting by the retractable bollards by the edge of the estate. Hogarth smiled. He'd called it right. Palmer was on a manhunt.

"Good luck with that," he muttered, knowing he'd soon be embarking on one of his own. He decided to leave her to it. She was worried. He would handle Drawton by himself. For peace of mind, he had already called Ivan Marris, the forensics man, to double-check on the condom type used in the rape before the murder. Marris had been unequivocal. The chemical profile was a match for Durex. Common as muck. But it was also the brand Drawton kept in his bathroom cabinet. The DNA samples had proved to be scarce and those few found were virtually useless. The beach hut door had been left open to the sea and the elements, so the high waves and salty sea air had access to scrub most of the evidence away. Dickens and crime scene had been dutifully thorough at the beach hut, but now he was busy with Robbins' flat, Dickens was no longer returning Hogarth's calls. Quentin the pathologist was still hard at work on Kevin Robbins' corpse. None of them would have been quite so careful with a standard drug overdose, but this one could be related to the Brimelow case. Everyone involved wanted a result. None more so than Hogarth. But first, he needed a little sustenance to keep him going.

The place was cheap as chips. Three eighty got him a cream doughnut and a large egg mayo bap. A feast fit for a king. As Hogarth pocketed his change and took his spoils back to his car, he stopped dead on the pavement, staring straight ahead. His mouth fell open. A young mother with a buggy waited silently for Hogarth to move aside, but he failed to notice her. The girl shook her head, turned her buggy and moved past him. Hogarth carried on staring, his heart thudding hard in his chest. Through the bars of the high blue fence across the street was a disturbing sight. A stick-thin figure stood beneath the grimy, cream painted wall of Haycock Tower. He was standing close by the big green wheelie bins which held the block's rubbish. They were full to bursting, lids angled high with all the rubbish they contained. It wasn't so unusual to see various oddballs hanging around such places, waiting to conduct deals, or meeting up with their drinking friends, but the stick man's eyes were angled up at the first-floor platform occupied by the play park and the food bank. It was Drawton, no doubt about it, and unless he was mistaken, there was a pair of binoculars around his neck. Hogarth narrowed his eyes and forgot all about his hunger. He carefully opened the side door of his car and deposited his paper bags onto the front passenger seat. He closed the door and locked the car, making as little sound as he could then stuffed his hands into his pockets and kept watch from across the roof of his car.

"What brings you here, Mr Drawton?" Hogarth whispered to himself. Like a GPS calculating a new route, Hogarth began to formulate a new version of Drawton and Ollie Halstead's friendship. Drawton as an admirer of the younger man's mind, with Ollie Halstead a cold fish, hard to handle because of his conditions, whatever they were. Which meant Drawton would have to work to get the man-child on side. Which explained why Drawton might have been lingering at the foot of the estate, staring up at the food bank, hoping to catch him. But it was a risky business for a man like Drawton. This was a place where his class and bearing would have made him a joke, a pariah, and a victim all at once. Or were there other reasons for Drawton skulking around? Hogarth's eyes narrowed by another degree. He watched Drawton staring up at the platform, pressing close to the side of the block so he wouldn't be easily seen.

Hogarth pondered his hand. Confront the man... or watch and learn. Perhaps a spot of watch and learn would enable him to eat his food and get him a better result. Inside the car was a better option for hiding too. He got into the Insignia and pulled the door shut with a gentle snick. The egg roll came first, big and creamy and sloppy, just the way he liked it. Drawton stayed where he was, using his binoculars occasionally. Hogarth finished his roll, but his fingers were covered in mayonnaise and there was nowhere he could wipe them. He leaned past his rear-view mirror to reach for an old napkin stuck on the passenger side of the dash. The mirror showed his chin was smeared with the stuff. "Bloody hell, Joe. You eat like a dog." He eyed Drawton, making sure the man stayed put while he cleaned his fingers. They still felt greasy, but the visible mess was gone. He leaned close to the mirror and wiped his chin, once, twice, three times, but the mess was persistent. It only seemed to move around his chin. Eventually, he screwed up the soiled napkin and tossed it into the passenger footwell to be dealt with in his next clean-up, whenever that was. He looked through the fence. The space occupied by Drawton was empty. The man was gone.

"Hold on a second," said Hogarth, eyes wide. He leaned his head back against the rest and strained to look behind the building. Next, he craned forwards over the steering wheel, to see if he had walked to the front of the building. But Drawton wasn't anywhere in sight.

"Shit. You're joking!"

Hogarth hustled out of his car and slammed the door behind him. He rushed across the street in a lumbering half-jog. Between the bollards he went until he had a clear view of the busy food bank side of the platform and the front of Haycock Tower. If Drawton was anywhere around, Hogarth should have seen him. Hogarth looked up at the miscreants and the needy waiting in the queue outside the Refuge. One or two looked back at him. But Drawton was not one of them.

"What the hell did you come here for, Simon?" he muttered, furious with himself, still scanning the grounds of the estate – the car park, the street beyond. All empty. There was no sign of the man. Three slow swipes of a dirty napkin and he had vanished.

Good work, Hogarth, he thought to himself. The sighting had made him feel ill at ease. Until recently, Drawton had almost begun to seem predictable. A cartoon-like, upper-class pervert, totally out of his depth, his depravity making him sail dangerously close to the rocks. The rocks being not just people like Hogarth, but people on the street too. People like those in the food bank queue, if only they knew what he had done. Maybe Drawton was experiencing a new lust because the man certainly seemed to be pushing past his comfort zone again. Whether he was looking to mould, groom, or educate Ollie Halstead, or begin the search for another innocent victim, none of it bode well. And it made Palmer's hunt for her niece seem an extremely wise move. He found himself hoping Drawton didn't find her first. Still hunting, Hogarth strode through the dim, dark tunnels of the derelict garages beneath the food bank. He tried each lane without success, then he looked across the street and up at the back of the Refuge. Above him, he heard the queue give a few ironic cheers as they were finally allowed into the building. When Hogarth was done, nothing had changed. Simon Drawton had been and gone, like a cartoon ghost. Hogarth hurried back to his car, glaring at Haycock Tower's full wheelie bins as if Drawton might pop out at any moment. But Drawton would never stoop so low as to hide like that. Hogarth frowned, climbed back into his car, ignored his cream doughnut, and started the engine. He looked along Coleman Street, but there was still no sign of the man. Though he did notice one thing. Palmer's car was gone. Hogarth turned out into the street and barely waited at the junction before he pushed out into the traffic. He was a man in a hurry, but he didn't fancy his chances of seeing the man on the street. Hogarth's phone buzzed in his jacket, but his mind was too wired for a discussion of any kind. He wanted only one thing: Drawton.

Seventeen

Hogarth didn't answer her call. Which meant he was busy getting his daily treatment from the DCI, or he was chasing the boffins for something new – a thankless task at the best of times. That wouldn't take long. Palmer's blood was up. She was worried about Aaliyah, and she wasn't going to find her through sheer luck. She had to trust the girl would call her eventually. And if she was intent on playing with fire, Palmer also had to trust that the girl would stay safe for the time being. It was still before midday. Not many psychopaths plied their trade in the daytime, and so far, Aaliyah had always come home. Provided she kept that up, Palmer believed she could push on with the job. But it wasn't easy. She found herself tense, the tiny muscles around her eyes and temples tight with worry. But work was the only distraction available, and with the high quality of the heroin in Robbins' flat, and Debbie Tranter's words ringing in her ears, she had made the brave decision to travel to Leigh. With Hogarth not taking calls, she was going there alone.

The contrast between Leigh and Southend was stark. Though Palmer rarely thought of herself as a snob, she found herself relieved to be somewhere away from the tower blocks and grim concrete of central Southend. She eyed the shop parade with its artisan bakers and the coffee shops which charged the best part of a fiver for a spiced latte. Splashing out on something nice seemed like a necessary comfort, but only provided she was brave enough to do what she'd come here for: to get an answer on one of the so-called champagne dealers. She had already decided that an honest answer was unlikely, but something coded might be possible. Especially if the dealers knew that the murder of an innocent girl was involved. Nobody wants that kind of PR. Especially not the likes of Leigh's flash criminals. Palmer had two landmarks in mind. One was Galvan's opulent corner house overlooking the Leigh estuary. The other was a warehouse tucked behind a residential side street. A warehouse that had been converted into a secret home without official permission, and then forcibly converted back again after a malicious tip-off from none other than DI Hogarth. The result was a brief but violent episode between Hogarth and the criminal, Patrick Ferber, which resulted in Ferber doing time. From the sentence he received for his involvement – and for his drug dealing – Palmer reckoned Patrick Ferber was still inside. But he had proved to be a man with substantial influence. Though she was sure most of the man's ire would be saved for Hogarth she had to be careful.

Today there was no need for any subterfuge in her approach. Palmer's old car was disguise enough. She took the narrow turning for the warehouse, bumping up the driveway into the smallest of lanes until it took her out into a space marked by a now full-grown hedge. Behind it, she saw the warehouse. She followed the hedges, pulled into the driveway and parked in front of the roller shutter door. The big dog inside was already barking its head off. If Ferber's man was home, he would know he had guests. Palmer took a nervy breath as she knocked on the shutter door. She waited a while and knocked again. She heard the dog come at the nearby pedestrian door in full-throated savage mode. Palmer moved to the door but stepped back as it opened, relieved to see the dog was restrained by the big blond-haired man who acted as Ferber's manservant, bodyguard, and chief dealer. The man's small eyes flashed as he recognised her and the door began to close as quickly as it opened.

"Wait," she said. "This isn't about you, or your employer. This is about information relating to a young girl's murder."

The door wavered, then the big man filled the door. He pushed the dog behind him and blocked the gap with his body. There was a look of intrigue etched on the man's face.

"What information?"

Palmer took a second to ready her pitch.

"You *have* heard of the murder in Southend?"

The big man shrugged. "People are always dying around here."

"The victim was a girl. She was a Christian girl who volunteered—"

The big man nodded and finished Palmer's words.

"—yeah, at the food bank. I know the place. It's in the middle of a *very* busy area."

The way the man said the words, Palmer imagined he was thinking of profitability rather than the traffic.

"You know about it?"

The man nodded again.

"I read the local rag like anyone else. It's mostly trash, but I pay attention to some things. She was killed in a beach hut. The bastard gutted her like a fish."

Palmer nodded. The article in The Record had certainly splashed enough gory details to keep the pages turning. They had managed to run follow-up articles for a whole week on the back of it. But Palmer wanted the man motivated to share.

"As you may be aware from the press, we believe it was a sexually motivated crime. There's reason to believe she was assaulted before the murder."

The man shook his head, his frown showing his disgust.

"Find them and hang them. Or chuck them into the prison yard for the inmates to sort out. It wouldn't last long… I don't see why you're here, though. My employer – all of us, in fact, have nothing to do with anything like that."

Palmer didn't reply about the number of other deaths likely caused by Ferber's businesses. Across the decades, the tally was likely to be in the thousands. Locally, maybe already in the low tens or twenties. In the drugs business, life was cheap - and death was always the only product on sale.

"With due respect, we know what you sell," she said. The man stiffened. The door started to close. "Wait. I'm only looking for a name. A link in the chain."

The man frowned at her as if she was an imbecile.

"You think I'm giving you any names?"

"Listen for a moment, please. This involves high-grade heroin. From what I've been told, it was near enough pure. This heroin was given to someone in Southend. Given not sold," she said with emphasis. The big man narrowed his eyes. Palmer went on. "The quality suggests it came from one of two likely sources. And the strength was so potent as to be toxic. As a consequence, the man who received this gift is dead."

The big man looked away. Behind him, the dog shoved at his side. He pushed the dog back and it whimpered.

"Gear like that? Uncut? That's too good to give away. That should have been cut down, diluted, made into multiple wraps. That's the whole business. That's how the scumbags make their dough. Someone giving away a pure sample like that… that's madness. The bottom of the rung smackheads buy their shit for a tenner. Maybe twenty-five if they've just had their giro and they're splashing out on a bumper wrap. By the time the heroin gets down to their level, it's been cut to crap. You know what I'm saying?"

Palmer nodded. "The value of the heroin given to this man was unreasonably high for a free gift."

"It's like giving away the crown jewels. That's what this stuff is to them. Treasure. Anyway, the end user should have known his shit. Most junkies know what to do with this stuff. He was sitting on a gold mine." The man frowned in thought. "Maybe that's why they gave it to him. To make some money. Instead, he injected it pure? That's not a smart junkie."

"The dead man wasn't a regular user."

"That's for bloody sure! Now he's a dead user."

Palmer nodded.

"Sorry," said the big man, shaking his head. "We don't deal drugs, never have, and if we did, I wouldn't allow anyone I know to give away product for nothing. A businessman makes money, he doesn't give it away."

"Maybe not… unless he wants someone dead. Someone who won't see it coming."

"No way. That's a very expensive way to kill someone. People in this town, some of 'em would do it for a ten-pound bag."

"You know an awful lot about drugs for someone who claims to know nothing about it."

The man shook his head.

"This conversation is over. But if you want to stay around, you can always play with the dog…"

"No thanks, I'm going. Just one last thing. If a dealer was paid the right amount for the high grade or pure heroin how much might it have cost?"

"How would I know?" said the man.

"In theory," said Palmer.

"In theory. Okay. Between one hundred to two hundred. How big was the wrap?"

"Standard issue. Medium small. Like a larger twenty-five pound bag," said Palmer.

"Two hundred then, give or take. Theoretically. Because we don't deal, remember. This is an honest business."

"So you say. Do you know anyone I could speak to? Anyone who might have access to that kind of product?"

"You mean people who cut it down to sell?"

"Yes," said Palmer.

"Don't be stupid. Listen up." The man leaned out of the door. Palmer spied the drooling dog eyeing her from a gap in the shadows. "Now this is the truth. The person who sold that wrap had nothing to do with us. Nothing. And you're not fitting us up with anything."

"No fit-ups here, we're after a killer."

"I'm still telling you, it's not us. None of us. If I hear any different, I'll deal with it."

"But that won't help us, will it?" said Palmer as the door began to close.

The man's voice was still audible through the door.

"You're looking for an idiot. Someone who takes risks we wouldn't. I think you know where the idiots live around here. Adios."

The door slammed. Palmer heard the man stomp away from the door, dragging the dog, barking in excitement, at his side.

I think you know where the idiots live around here. Either a throwaway line to put her off the scent or a hint that his local rivals were to blame. Red herring or not, Palmer had no alternative but to take the bait. Look on the bright side, she told herself. You got through that one unscathed. One more roll of the dice until a posh coffee and an expensive lunch.

Hogarth drove another circuit around the top end of town, hoping to see Drawton on one of the main pedestrian crossings towards the town centre, or making his way over the footbridge that arched across Queensway. Instead, he saw a rogues' gallery of the usual suspects going about their business. Some were already clutching a Refuge food parcel, all in the same give-away grey and purple carrier bags, like a badge of honour. Hogarth put his foot down and headed across town. Perhaps Drawton had been a quick mover too. He knew the thin man often preferred to walk around town on foot, but he also kept a two-seater Smart car which he used for the occasional jaunt. Having followed the man a fair number of times, Hogarth knew Drawton used the thing rarely, but when he did, he was the type of man who liked to park the front bumper against the kerb to show off how small and neat his car was. It used to be one of the ways Smart car owners showed off their car's USP. By now most Smart car owners had gotten over that kind of showing off, but not Drawton. Hogarth floored the accelerator, beating a red light and making it all the way to Westcliff before he was forced to use the brake. He was impressed with himself. He turned the familiar left past The Cricketers and was soon slowing along the snaking road which he had visited the night before. Though his late nights and whisky drinking probably still showed on his face, he was no longer tired. Hogarth got out of the car with a spring in his step, from an urgency built on intrigue. He looked around. The Smart car was nowhere in sight, and Drawton's house looked quiet. A curtain twitched at the nearby manse, but when Hogarth glanced at it, nobody was there. Bloody ghosts everywhere, he thought. Ghosts, but none that talked. He approached Drawton's front door, hoping the black Smart car might pull up before he knocked. But it was no good. There was no answer, either. He'd drawn yet another blank. Hogarth wasn't having it. He pulled out his phone and dialled Drawton's number. His call went straight to voicemail.

"Simon, it's me. Your old mucker, Hogarth. I've just seen you on your travels, old bean. I thought you might want to talk to me about it before I get impatient and do something you regret, so give me a call. There's a good man."

Hogarth hung up and looked around the driveway, but his mind was elsewhere. He dialled again and got through to Palmer.

"Palmer. You found her yet?"

"No, she's still playing hard to get."

"There's years of that to come."

"Not for me, there isn't. If she plays these games again she's off back to Rayleigh."

"You'd send her packing? You're too soft for that."

"If it was to protect her from herself, I'd do it in a heartbeat."

Hogarth crumpled his chin and nodded.

"Yes... you probably would."

Hogarth considered Palmer's plight. Her niece was putting herself in a dangerous place, and after seeing Drawton at large, Hogarth also knew it was the worst possible time. But he didn't want to worry Palmer – she was stressed to high heavens as it was.

"Where are you then?"

"Between stops," she said, hesitantly.

"It's not like you to answer a call when driving," he replied.

"No," she said, still hesitating. "But I thought I should in this instance. I'm visiting old friends up in Leigh."

Hogarth pondered her words a moment before his eyes widened. "What the hell are you doing?"

"Don't worry. I'm just knocking on doors."

"Sue, what's going on? That's a damn silly thing to do by yourself."

"It's okay," she said, the lie evident in her voice. "The first one went well enough. Ferber's man at the warehouse gave me some insight into the value of the heroin we found in Razor Robbins' flat."

"Ferber's man? What?! Now you just bloody hold on before you knock on any more of those doors. I'll be with you in ten minutes. I'm in Westcliff. Ten minutes. Wait for me."

"What are you doing there?"

"Same as you. Knocking on the wrong doors. What are you playing at anyway?"

"I turned up something while I was looking for Aaliyah at the Queensway Estate."

"Such as?"

"Robbins had an on-off girlfriend named Debbie Tranter. I bumped into her snooping around outside his flat. She knew all about his drug habit and his affair with Helen Brimelow."

"And? Is she a suspect?"

"Not for my money. She's the kind who wears her heart on her sleeve. Has a vicious crack-face when she loses her temper with it. If she was involved, I think I would have copped a lot more than a mouthful."

"And you're still out there looking for more trouble?"

"Not exactly. If Galvan tells me what we need to know, I'll be treating myself to a coffee on The Broadway. Maybe a cake too. If you hurry, I might buy you one."

Hogarth looked at his car, thinking of the filled finger doughnut in his car. He could always save that for after dinner.

"Galvan won't see you," said Hogarth. "His boys won't even answer the door to a copper. They can smell us a mile away. It's a dangerous game either way." Hogarth strode back to his car, his stomach growling at the prospect of another bite. He opened the door and got in. "Sue? You still haven't told me what you found."

"You were right. Robbins was clean. Debbie Tranter said he was far too vain to risk taking heroin regularly, but he still liked a hit now and then. Taking it and leaving it gave him the illusion of control. The girlfriend confirmed what Suitcase told me. She said Robbins liked to think he was better than everyone else."

"What else?"

Hogarth started the engine and pinched the phone between his ear and shoulder as he turned the car out onto the street.

"He never loved anyone but himself. According to Tranter, there was no way he would have ever topped himself, and especially not for a lost love. Sounds like you were right on that score too.

"Go me. But I won't pat myself on the back yet."

"You know what this means though?"

"Yes. The OD had to be a set-up…"

"And I don't think it was one of those 'assisted-death' ODs we sometimes get. Murder by a friendly heroin needle."

"Heroin friends sometimes kill for pathetic reasons. But no, I can't see it. Dickens would have given us a steer on that. We probably would have seen the signs ourselves."
"I don't think it was an accident either."
"What are you getting at?" said Hogarth.
"The heroin we found was very high strength – forensics or pathology should soon verify that. It was strong enough to have been cut down and sold on again and again."
"Probably. But how come you sound so sure?"
"Debbie Tranter – the on-off girlfriend – she used her key to get into Robbins' flat soon after he died."
"She found the body?"
"Yes. And she didn't call it in."
"Then she's put herself on the suspect list right there."
"Agreed. But she won't stay there for long – not if we can find whoever supplied that heroin."
"How come you know it was so potent?"
"When Debbie Tranter found Robbins' body she took some herself. She strikes me as more of a crack fiend than a fan of the brown stuff. But she still tried some."
"But she lived to tell the tale,"
"You're jumping the gun," said Palmer. "Debbie Tranter didn't inject. She smoked the stuff. She said she chased some to get over the shock of finding her boyfriend's body."
"Always an excuse. She took a chase because she's a junkie."
"Either way, she said the stuff was so strong even just a smoke made her feel like she was going to collapse."
Hogarth nodded.
"But why are you in Leigh?"
"Because she said this stuff came from a champagne dealer. By which she meant, someone higher up the food chain,

someone who gets hold of raw product and cuts it down. That makes a lot of sense, if you think about it."

"Dangerous waters, Palmer."

"Then you'd better bring some water wings," she said.

"I can do better than that. I'll tell you what I found too."

Hogarth held his tongue.

"What is it?" said Palmer.

"On my way. Tell you when I get there. And you're buying, remember."

"Nothing more than a cuppa and a sandwich."

"That'll do nicely. Now just wait."

Eighteen

Good to his word, ten minutes was all it took before Hogarth pulled up behind Palmer's Corsa, not far from the ornate garden wall of Alex Galvan's corner property with its enviable sea views. Hogarth joined Palmer on the pavement, hitching his trousers by the belt, stretching out his spine from all his tension behind the wheel.

"You fronted Ferber's man all by yourself? Hardly sensible. That bastard almost had me finished down at Chalkwell last year."

"I called you first, but you didn't pick up."

"So you went on without me anyway." Hogarth shook his head.

"It's not as if you've never made a few rash moves here and there. Maybe I'm taking my lead from you."

Hogarth grinned. "I should have known it was my fault. It didn't sound like you got too much from Ferber's goon. Just a bit of fluff about high-grade heroin before he pointed you in the direction of his enemy, Galvan. He could have been blagging the whole time."

"I don't doubt it. But I still learned more than I knew. After that visit, I'm almost convinced that Robbins was given super-strength heroin in the knowledge he wouldn't be able to handle it."

"Which would mean... it was given to him by someone who knew him *well*... well enough to know he was a part timer who wouldn't be able to handle it."

Palmer made a subtle seesaw motion with her head.

"It's possible."

"Probable, even," said Hogarth. "But the Kevin Robbins I've heard about doesn't sound inclined to share his secrets. He certainly wasn't someone open to sharing."

Palmer made a non-committal face, but she knew he was right. But Debbie Tranter's version of events left Palmer feeling the woman was telling the truth.

"Debbie Tranter would have known all of that, but she didn't kill him, and she didn't kill Helen Brimelow. You think the murders are linked, don't you?"

"You know I do," said Hogarth. "You think so as well. It's too much of a coincidence otherwise, and as soon as the papers catch wind that he was sleeping with Helen, they'll see it too. Then the pressure from on high will really start to land on us. We need to join these dots, pronto."

"Then forget Debbie Tranter. She's a different dot entirely. Helen was sexually assaulted by her killer, remember."

Hogarth nodded, grimly. "Quentin already confirmed signs of penetration. Marris confirmed the condom type this afternoon. Durex, the common or garden variety. Unless Debbie Tranter happens to be a man on the sly, that does rather leave her lacking one key attribute."

Palmer rolled her eyes. "You see why we have to follow the heroin angle?"

Hogarth crumpled his chin and gave a grudging nod. "Because it's all we've got."

"But it's a good *all we've got*," she replied.

He jangled the change in his trouser pockets and looked down the hill towards the shining water of the estuary far out and far below where they stood.

"You had something for me too," she said. "You said so on the phone."

Hogarth considered holding on to his news but decided it would only cause upset later if he did. He took a deep breath before he spoke.

"I saw your car at Coleman Street. I must have missed you by a split second or two."

"You were there?"

"Yeah. I guessed where you were but I couldn't see you. But guess who I saw while you were there?"

The look on Palmer's face said she wasn't in the mood for playing games but the mischief in Hogarth's eyes still burned bright.

"Simon Drawton."

"No way," said Palmer.

"Exactly. But there he was, standing right under Haycock Tower staring up at that food bank like Oliver Twist waiting for his second bowl of soup. Hungry is how he looked too. But not for food."

Palmer's face tightened. "I don't think he did it either."

"So why was he there? Maybe he was looking for his so-called kindred spirit, Ollie… Perhaps they've already struck up a friendship, or Drawton would like to build one. Makes me shiver to think what those two might talk about over fava beans and a light Chianti."

"Don't even joke," said Palmer.

"If we can't joke, then it's time to pack it in. Your niece will be alright, Sue. Killers don't hit on girls in broad daylight, even around there." But even Hogarth knew his voice was less certain than before.

"It won't be broad daylight forever though, will it?"

Hogarth couldn't disagree. He scratched the corner of his lip with a fingernail and nodded towards Galvan's property.

"This is your idea. What's your approach?"

"Knock the door and see what happens," said Palmer quietly.

"My, my. You really *have* been taking notes, haven't you?"

Palmer managed the thinnest of smiles.

"I wish she'd call."

"She will. But only when she wants something. Come on. Time for a spot of door knocking. If you change your mind, we can always claim to be JWs."

Palmer and Hogarth started a slow walk down the hill, both staring out to the brightly lit water as the breeze picked at their hair.

"Care to know what I found in Drawton's medicine cabinet?"

"You went back again?"

"No. This is something I remembered. Do you want to know or not?"

Palmer shrugged. "Do I want to?"

"Durex," he said. "The common or garden variety... now when was the last time you think that Hooray Henry got laid?"

Palmer remained blank.

"Exactly. Now I wished I'd checked the packet to see if any were missing."

"It's still not him."

"You don't know that, Sue."

"And you can't prove it is."

"Not yet. In the meantime, let's keep joining those dots. I wonder where Ollie Halstead is today."

"He wasn't at the food bank," said Palmer. "I asked. One of the managers said he might have been over the office with his brother."

"Running that place looks like a thankless task. Carrying the extra burden of his psychotic brother, on top of that… well, it's no wonder Freddie Halstead broke out with a very nasty case of excessive tattoos."

Palmer looked at him.

"All that stress has to come out somewhere. Some people shave their heads when they lose it. Some people drink too much, some take drugs. I suppose a hip young church worker like him had to resort to tattoos."

"He's only a few years younger than you," said Palmer, smiling. She looked out to the water, as something in Hogarth's words began to percolate before it fell out of sight, settling deeper in her mind. She didn't know what it was but knew it was something all the same.

Hogarth knocked on Galvan's door and rang the doorbell at the same time. The man who answered was a classic Galvan goon. Shaven-headed, mid-forties to fifties, in a smart suit but from a shop rail rather than a tailor. It was a little ill-fitting around the chest, and a little too short in the sleeve. He looked at them, taking both in from head to toe, before his attitude changed by a few degrees. He knew they were police. His cold pale blue eyes told their own story.

"Is the organ grinder at home?" said Hogarth.

"Funny. But the organ grinder doesn't take unsolicited visits."

"To be expected in your line of work. You never know who might show up at the door or what they might be carrying."

Behind them, the front gate slammed into the clasp with a thunk and a rattle. The goon at the door looked past

Hogarth as he and Palmer turned their heads to see a young woman approaching. She wore a short black dress and a jacket covered in pink and red flowers. She was blonde and holding her car keys and her handbag in one hand. For a moment she looked a picture of demure, innocent beauty. In the next, she seemed to sense a problem and instantly slowed her pace.

"It's okay, Jenny," said the goon. "These two are just leaving."

"Jenny, now, is it?" said Hogarth, offering a grin like a snarl. "Last time I was around here, Alice Perry was taking up all your employer's spare time."

"Alice who?" said the woman. Hogarth moved out of the way as the young woman gingerly stepped around him.

"Never mind, Jenny. He's trying to wind me up, not you."

"Not true," said Hogarth. "I was just making an observation. I've got plenty more where that came from. Words of wisdom from someone who knows wee Alex better than most."

A shadow passed by the nearby window, while the perplexed young woman wavered about what she should do. A moment later, the front door opened wider and Alex Galvan appeared beside his man, a good half foot shorter than his goon, but neater and smarter too.

"Harassing young girls, now, Inspector?" said Galvan, meeting his eye. "The last resort of a very sad human being."

Hogarth's eyes flashed at Galvan, taking in the now thinning hair, shaven to a buzz cut in an effort to limit the damage to his appearance. His face was tanned, and his stubble had been cut and trained to match the angles of his face.

"Actually, I couldn't agree with you more," said Hogarth "You know, Alex, you're looking more like the lost member of Bros every time I see you."

"Piss off, you sad old bastard. Jenny, come in. Ignore these two. They're nothing to worry about. Not unless you really have got something worth talking about? If you have, I'll call my solicitor."

Jenny tried to offer them a smile by way of goodbye before she stepped into the house and disappeared behind Galvan. They heard her heels fade away on the stone floor.

"She's a step up on the girl from The Record," said Hogarth.

"Alice Perry let me down," said Galvan, his eyes passing over DS Palmer's face. "She let herself down too."

"I'm surprised you didn't run her out of town," said Palmer.

"I'm a practical man. We had a discussion and came to an arrangement. End of story. Now before I close the door, what is it you two actually want? Because this already feels like a waste of time."

Palmer cleared her throat.

"It's not about you or your businesses."

Galvan arched an eyebrow.

"It's about the opposition then? Got more intel for me, DS Palmer? The way you're going I might just put you on my Christmas card list. Let them in then, Barry. We'll talk in the kitchen."

The goon stepped aside and pointed them towards an open door almost dead opposite the entrance.

"Now stop the mouth," warned the man, just as Hogarth passed him.

"Stop the face," replied Hogarth.

As they settled into their sturdy wooden seats Galvan was nowhere to be seen. They sat at a long rustic dining table in a stone-floored kitchen. Beyond them was a wide picture window looking out over Galvan's landscaped garden.

Galvan returned and blocked the view. He sat down before them.

"Spit it out," he said, ignoring Hogarth and looking at Palmer.

"This is about the murder of a young girl. She was found in a Southend beach hut."

"The Brimelow girl," said Galvan, in his faux hardman's voice. He shrugged and made a dismissive wave of his hand. "I can assure you, that's nothing to do with me."

"We didn't think so. But there's been another death since. This one was a drug overdose. A man who happened to be an infrequent user was given an amount of high grade – or even pure – heroin. I'm told the amount he had was equivalent to around two hundred pounds of street drug." Galvan took a moment's pause. His eyes shone with thought. "Maybe more, depending on where it came from. But so what? Why bother me with it? Junkies die all the time. I don't see you running around for all of them."

"We think this death could be connected to Helen Brimelow's murder," said Palmer.

"And then there's the heroin itself," said Hogarth. "High grade or pure, either way, it sticks out like a sore thumb. Nobody gets gear like that on that estate. By the time the end user gets it, it's been through five different dealers or more and it gets cut down and diluted by every one of them. In the end, they're not injecting heroin much at all, but whatever they're given."

"Nothing to do with us, then is it?" said Galvan.

"Don't worry. Those six degrees of separation will keep you safe as houses," said Hogarth.

"I wasn't worried in the first place," said Galvan.

"Only we think someone higher up, maybe two or three degrees away from the source supplier, sold this package on," said Palmer. "Which would explain the high quality. But not the reason."

Galvan narrowed his eyes in thought and bit his lip.

"You're trying to tie this to me?"

"No. I don't believe this involves you," said Palmer. "All we want is the name of someone high up in the central Southend supply chain. Someone who has good quality gear. This person may have been asked to deal direct to the market place."

"Any name I give you, you'll hang out to dry."

"Not in this instance, Galvan," said Hogarth. "Our priority is the man who raped and killed that girl. It was a sickening attack. Everyone needs him off the street."

Galvan nodded and narrowed his eyes again.

"Why does the dealer have to be someone I know?"

"Don't play dumb. We know who you are and what you do," said Hogarth.

"And because the opposition said they didn't do it," said Palmer.

"They would though, wouldn't they? You mean Ferber's warehouseman, or someone else?" said Galvan.

"We protect all our sources of information. They will remain confidential," said Palmer.

"Message received," said Galvan, with a nod and a smile. "She's a smart cookie, Hogarth. I reckon she could do better than you."

"Plenty of people wouldn't disagree with you," said Hogarth.

Galvan rubbed his nose and leaned across the table. "Give me your number. You'll get a call within an hour. That call will be from a withheld number, so don't bother to trace it. If our guy can help, he will. If he can't, you just won't get the call." Galvan smiled. "It wasn't the opposition anyway. Not over that way. We're in the ascendancy now. Ferber's been chased out."

"Boasting to a cop is never a very bright idea," said Hogarth. He looked at Galvan's goon, and the look on the man's face said he was inclined to agree. Hogarth smiled. "Memories like elephants, all of us."

"I'm helping you because Palmer here is the one worth talking to. If it was just you, I would have slammed the door in your face."

"The feeling is mutual, Alex."

"But Palmer here is the one who wins, get me?"

"If you come through with good information, we might all win," she said. "Let's wait and see, shall we?"

The two men eyed each other across the table, while Palmer pulled a business card from her jacket. She planted it on the wooden surface and slid it towards Galvan. He eyed the card and nodded.

"Thank you, DS Palmer. One hour, maybe less. Now, if you don't mind, I've got a guest waiting for me."

The small man stood up from the table and pulled his shirt cuffs down before he gave Palmer a nod of goodbye.

"We'll talk in future," he said.

Palmer opened her mouth to rebuff Galvan's statement, but he was in no mood to hear it. He strode out of the room with the business card in hand. They listened as he shifted gears into a friendly, fawning welcome before a heavy door was closed and muffled the volume to almost nothing.

"That's it. Out," said the goon. Hogarth grinned at him.

"Thanks, Barry. You've been a real star."

Palmer gave Hogarth a look, but he ignored her until they were out on the doorstep. There, the big man shut the door on their backs and left them to it.

"*We'll talk in future?*" said Hogarth.

"Don't," said Palmer. "I didn't ask him to say that."

"Either Galvan's got you down as his next dolly bird, or another copper in his pocket."

"But I don't think so, do you?"

"Which one?" said Hogarth.

"Neither," said Palmer, firmly. Hogarth chuckled as they walked down the front garden path. "You want lunch or not?"

"A free lunch in Leigh? Of course I do."

He was silent a moment as they turned away from the estuary views back to their cars. When he spoke again, his eyes were aimed at his brogues, his voice quiet.

"You did though, didn't you?" he said. "You got something from nothing."

"Like you told the man himself, we'll see."

"So where are you taking me?" said Hogarth.

"Anywhere I don't need to remortgage before we place an order," she said.

Hogarth nodded. "That narrows it down a fair bit."

They left Palmer's car on the hill and got into Hogarth's Insignia. Finding a space for one car never proved easy on the swish Leigh Broadway, but parking two cars would have used up all the time they had.

Having seen how busy the cafes were – with rarely a free table in sight – Hogarth and Palmer were forced to beat a hasty retreat into the familiar burgundy and brown confines of a Costa Coffee.

"No calls to the mortgage broker today," said Hogarth.

"Sorry," said Palmer. "I tried."

"It's fine. I'll have an Americano. But in a cup, not a soup bowl."

"And food?"

"Any toastie will do."

Palmer nodded and made off to join the short queue. Hogarth stared out on the busyness outside – well-heeled men and women marching around spending money as if they had nothing better to do, clutching fancy boutique bags with logos emblazoned on the side. They did the same job as a man with a sandwich board, only instead of earning a salary, they had to pay for the privilege. But this end of town, being flash was compulsory if you wanted to fit in. The wives had to spend hubby's London salary somewhere. Hogarth was being mean, churlish - jealous, even. But he was grumpy because of a lack of sleep, upset he had lost Drawton before he could work out the man's game, and now he was irritated at himself for playing the fool in front of Galvan. Palmer had been understated and calm. Galvan might have wanted to use her in future, but he doubted whether the little gangster would ever genuinely make it work. Galvan had been right about her. One day she would gain enough confidence to see she was destined for bigger things. Shame she didn't see it herself but give her time… Hogarth sighed and pulled his phone from his pocket. There were two missed calls on the screen. One of them was from Palmer, much earlier, but the last one was from none other than Simon Drawton. *Drawton!* Why hadn't he noticed? It must have been all the fun and games with Alex Galvan and his man Barry. He'd been so busy jousting that he'd let Drawton slip through his fingers again. As he fumbled and tried to return the call, his phone started to vibrate and ring in his hands. He twisted it over in his haste, and almost dropped the damn thing to the brown laminate floor. He managed to save the phone and put it to his ear.

"Yes?"

A prim woman from the table in front looked back at Hogarth. He glared and she quickly looked away.

"Who were you expecting?" said a female voice. It wasn't Drawton, after all. It was Andi. His heart stopped accelerating. He put a hand on his head and dragged his hair back.

"Andi! You called me back. I wasn't sure you were going to."

"I wasn't sure either, but here I am. So, you want to give this thing another go?"

Hogarth smacked his lips, thinking of the clock ticking since his last contact from Drawton.

"Joe?"

"Yes. Yes! Of course, I do. I need Barking's finest to keep me in order."

"What's the matter? Or shouldn't I ask?"

"I'm in the thick of it here, as always." He lowered his voice and eyed Palmer as she slowly advanced in the queue to pay.

"It sounds more like you're in a coffee shop," said Andi.

"No flies on you are there Detective Andi?"

"I've been learning from the best, so he tells me. So, who are you with?"

"DS Palmer."

"Coffee with Palmer? You *sure* it's strictly platonic between you two?"

"Strictly business. We're just recovering after a visit to one of Southend's local kingpins."

"Oh," said Andi. She sounded impressed, but Hogarth wanted her off the line. But he also wanted her to stay in his life, at least for the time being.

"Shall I come round tonight? Or did you want to stay around mine?"

Stay around her place? That was a development. Maybe absence did make the heart grow fonder.

"What is it?" said Hogarth. "You got a lightbulb that needs replacing?"

"Oi! Don't knock a gift horse in the mouth. Not many gentlemen have darkened my door."

"Glad to hear it. But I'd better stay local for now, if you don't mind. This case is taking more turns than my old satnav."

"Fine. But you'd better get a bottle in, and I don't mean that awful orange pish you waste all your money on."

"Tizer? I never touch the stuff."

"I mean it, Joe. Get a nice red. And a takeaway."

"Yes, milady."

"And one word of advice."

"Just the one?" said Hogarth.

"No more late-night walks. When I stay with you, I want you to stay too, okay?"

"Yeah. I get it, Andi. I've gotta go."

"Yeah, yeah, I get the picture."

Palmer had placed the food order and the barista was busily clattering their coffees together.

"Andi – I'm looking forward to it, okay?"

"Good. Go on then, enjoy your lunch. But not *too* much."

Hogarth snickered down the line before he ended the call. The phone buzzed again as soon as he was finished. There was a fresh text message on the screen. A message from Drawton.

Need your help. Please call me back.

As Palmer deposited a heavily-laden tray on their small table, she met Hogarth's eye.

"Who was that?"

"The call was Andi – from Barking."

Palmer gave a nod. The tone of Hogarth's voice suggested further inquiry was off limits. He saw Palmer's guarded response and shook his head.

"I thought we were finished," he explained. "Turns out I've got a temporary stay of execution. But that's not what I'm thinking about. Look at this. This just came in."

Hogarth spun his phone screen around on the tabletop and pushed the device towards Palmer. She frowned at the screen as Hogarth retrieved his coffee cup.

"Drawton? He's asking *you* for help?"

"Exactly... makes me wonder what his game is."

Hogarth took a slurp from the cup and managed to swallow the molten liquid down before it burned his mouth. He winced and put the cup back on its saucer.

"Now, how exactly do I play it?"

"Why would he ask you for anything? He's got friends in high places. They could send in the army, police, navy, even the Revenue if he deemed it necessary."

"I'm assuming he wants the kind of help officialdom can't supply. Something more than sweeping his crap under the rug."

"What like?"

"I don't know, that's the problem," said Hogarth, his eyes glazing as his thoughts took him away. "What do I do best?"

"You've sometimes been known to employ renegade tactics. You think that's what he's after?"

"Only sometimes, eh? Drawton knows first-hand what I'm like. Perhaps this is a trap. Maybe he worked out that I got into his house.

"You said you were careful."

"Maybe not careful enough – I could have left a thumbprint on his cabinet door, or left his fountain pen out of place. The man's a prissy know-it-all. Maybe he wants to gloat as he makes his complaint."

"Not if he thinks you'd like to hurt him as much as I know you do."

"Men like him, they don't care. He's born of a different class. The entitled kind. They always think they have what it takes to win, even against people like me. No, I'm not about to walk into a trap. I think I'll leave him waiting a while longer. Until he shows his hand."

Two slim cheese and ham toasties arrived on plates with napkins. Hogarth eyed his and was glad he'd eaten the egg mayo roll beforehand. If not, he would have been left hungry. He bit the cheese and ham and immediately gave Palmer a funny look.

"Tastes a bit off to me," he said.

Palmer looked at her sandwich.

"Sorry. I must have picked up two vegan ones by mistake."

"Vegan?!"

"Fake ham, fake cheese. I'm trying to cut down on meat."

"Not picked up one of your niece's fads, have you?"

"No," said Palmer, sounding defensive.

Hogarth took another oversized bite to consider the taste of the food before he dropped the sandwich back on his plate in disgust. He picked up his bag of posh crisps and got stuck into them instead.

"Have you considered the possibility that Drawton might actually need help?" said Palmer. "You might want to call him back."

"Help? He'd never ask me and with good reason. It's got to be a trap of some kind, and I don't intend to take the bait." Palmer gave Hogarth a doubtful look as she took another bite. The strange, rubbery pink ham that hung from her sandwich offended Hogarth's eye, but he tried to ignore it. Instead, he wondered whether he was making the right call. It wasn't often that he ignored a call for help, even from a scumbag like Drawton; it went against the grain and wasn't easy, but a cool logic told him to stick to his guns. He picked up his last clutch of salt and apple-cider crisps and Palmer's phone began to ring. The timing wasn't great. Palmer had just stuffed a lump of fake cheese and ham into her mouth. She pulled her phone from her pocket and picked up her coffee to wash down the food. The coffee was still boiling hot. Her eyes bulged and she handed the phone to Hogarth as she started to cough.

"Was that the coffee or the plasticine sandwich?

"Neither," she croaked, putting a hand across her mouth. "Answer it. And no wisecracks," was all she could add. No number or name showed on the screen.

Hogarth dabbed the answer button and put the phone to his ear.

"DS Palmer's phone… Sorry. I'm afraid she's indisposed. This is her colleague, DI Hogarth. We were expecting your call."

When she saw the caller hadn't instantly hung up, Palmer gave Hogarth a nod of support. She knitted her eyes shut and swallowed before she offered to take the phone.

"DS Palmer's ready now. Would you like to speak to her?"
"No," said the curt male voice in Hogarth's ear. He shook his head at Palmer and she withdrew her hand in irritation. The caller's voice was muffled. Hogarth imagined the man was trying to disguise his voice with a cloth over his mouth, or the back of his sleeve.
"Talking to one of you is enough."
Hogarth narrowed his eyes, detecting an obvious disdain for the police in his words.
"You know what we were after?" he said.
"Yes," said the stranger. "But I didn't make that deal. The man you want to speak to is Brian G. He's the one."
"You're giving us a name? I thought we were getting actual intel. Something we could use."
"Listen. I've spoken to Brian. He'll tell you whatever you need. But before that, we both need to know he's going to be safe from arrest. He had nothing to do with the man who died. Or the girl."
"He'll be safe so long as he's innocent."
Palmer nodded. They both waited. The man at the other end was silent for a moment, then sighed in resignation. "He is innocent. Now you stick to your end of the bargain. Be at the Gannymede in half an hour. Miss the time slot and there'll be no call-backs, you get me?"
"I hear you. Thirty minutes. The Gannymede. We'll be there."
The phone went dead and Hogarth handed it back to Palmer.
"We've got a meeting?" she said.
"Yeah. At the pub on Sutton Road. And seeing as you at least attempted to buy me lunch, I might go the whole hog and buy you a drink. But I best not tell, Andi... I think she's getting jealous."

Palmer raised her eyebrows and picked up the second half of her sandwich. "Jealous? Of me?!"

Hogarth nodded with a low chuckle. "I know. The girl's got a screw loose. Just as well she has other attributes which more than make up for it."

Palmer shook her head. "I don't think I want to know. I'm not Simmons."

"Thank God for that. But I was only talking about her sparkling personality."

Palmer didn't believe a word. They ate the rest of what was edible and hurried their drinks down before they returned to the hustle of Leigh Broadway. Now there was no time for sightseeing or for posing. They had an appointment to keep.

Nineteen

The Gannymede was the pub on a street corner not far from the bakery where Hogarth had bought his egg mayo roll, just a two-minute walk from Coleman Street, Haycock Tower and the rest of the estate. By Hogarth's estimation, they were early. Having deposited Palmer back by her car, he was the first to arrive, but so as not to put off their host, he waited near the Co-op car park, trying his best not to look like CID. Palmer soon arrived. She opened the door of her Corsa and got out.
"Is he here yet?"
"Don't know," said Hogarth. "I didn't want to go in without you. I thought if he clapped eyes on my ugly mug, he might run out again."
"It's not that ugly," said Palmer, managing a smile. A spot of banter helped take the edge off the tension. The way the days had been lately, banter was becoming their daily bread.
"Maybe not. But with a glamour puss like you, Palmer, we'll keep him glued to his seat."
"Now I know you are talking rot," she said.
The banter helped, but Palmer was just as bad at hiding her feelings as he was. Behind the smile, he saw the tension, especially around her eyes.
"Let's get this done, then you can get on chasing your niece."
"I'm that transparent, am I? She's causing so many problems lately."
"That's the nature of family, isn't it?"

The Gannymede had corner saloon doors, much like their other favourite across town, The Sutland Arms. Only these saloon doors were better maintained. The pub inside wasn't quite as grim either – no sticky dark wooden floors, no dark wooden walls – but even so the place lacked character. The kind of place you'd use only if it was your local – a concept Hogarth wondered about. Did people have locals anymore? A couple of messy looking waifs were leaning against a quiz machine, their faces brightly lit from the screen. They were cradling half-empty pints, smiling, and munching peanuts. Their smiles dropped when they saw Palmer and Hogarth walk in through the second set of doors. The pub was painted mostly red and green. There was a pool table, a dartboard, dark wooden tables, and a bored-looking barman flicking through a tabloid at the bar. He eyed them and stiffened. The man had overgrown grey-brown hair and a drinker's nose. Red and swollen. So far, the nose was a curse Hogarth had managed to avoid.

"He's not here yet," muttered Hogarth.

Palmer nodded. They went to the bar and Hogarth ordered drinks. The classic Archers and lemonade for Palmer. Hogarth eyed the optics ranged behind the barman, and disapproving of their whiskies, he prodded their standard-issue ale tap.

The barman offered them no smile. No patter either. He gave Hogarth his change and walked back to his newspaper, glad the ordeal was over.

"That's a man who's happy in his work," said Hogarth as he pocketed the change. His sarcastic words were plain to hear. The barman pulled a sour face and shook his head as they walked away. Hogarth caught the look and smiled.

"That one was for the hospitality trade," he said aloud as the picked a table by one of the pub's few concrete pillars. The table gave them a clear view of the double doors and provided enough distance that the scallywags on the machine wouldn't cause any trouble. They supped in peace. Hogarth checked the time on his phone as Palmer looked out of the window towards the Co-op car park, searching for their visitor.

"Think it'll be a no show?" said Palmer.

"If it is, then at least we can enjoy a drink. Has our lord and master chased you for an update yet?"

"Not yet," said Palmer coyly.

"Then no doubt, he'll grab you when we get back. I think I'd rather spend the afternoon with the barman, thanks."

"Heard anything else from Drawton?"

"No. Chances are he's worked out I'm not falling for it, so the trap's been called off."

Palmer pursed her lips and raised her eyebrows.

"Don't panic. I'll drive around his house afterwards – without calling first. If there's a genuine problem we'll sort it out then. Hang on… Who's this?"

Hogarth's eyes focused on the saloon doors. A man in a black anorak and a blue and red baseball cap walked into the porchway. He peered through the window of the second doors until his eyes reached their table. The man was narrow faced, had bulging eyes, stubble, and olive skin. Hogarth sensed he may have seen the man before, though they certainly hadn't crossed swords directly. Southend was a small town with a lot of people, and the ponds he swam in, he was bound to have passed every shady face at least a once. They watched the man's jaw tighten as he opened the door and made his approach. The barman looked up and nodded at him; the newcomer gave the slightest of nods back. The lack of a positive response made the barman inquisitive and he frowned at their table as the man joined them. Hogarth noted the look. He turned the back of his chair towards the barman, to hide as much of the meeting as he could.

"Brian?" asked Hogarth.

"I didn't know there was going to be two of you," he whispered.

"I spoke to your up-line," said Hogarth. "It was always clear there were two of us. Don't panic. This isn't about you."

"Isn't it?" said the man.

Hogarth jutted out his bottom lip and shook his head. "But it is about an unusual transaction you made."

"I don't make any transactions. And if I did, I certainly wouldn't be talking about them to the Old Bill."

"Fine. Whatever you say," said Hogarth. "But you're here, right? That's a start. I take it you don't want a drink?"

The man shook his head and leaned back in his chair, hands in pockets like a sulking teen.

"Not from you, I don't."

"Good man. You've saved me four quid I didn't want to spend. Now, seeing as you don't do transactions, how about we do this as a theoretical?"

Hogarth glanced at Palmer. She gave a nod.

"Theoretical?" said the man, struggling with the concept.

"Yes, Brian. Here goes. Theoretically, if you were a dealer, which – for now – I accept you aren't…. but if you did deal, and you had happened to have a strange transaction where a certain person asked for a certain type of high grade—"

"Leave it. I know why you're here. This is difficult enough as it is."

Palmer nodded. She gave the man a look approaching sympathetic.

"We know you were forced to come here. Your bosses aren't happy with you for what happened."

The man sighed as if Palmer had touched on one of his current headaches though, from the look in his dark eyes, it wasn't the only one.

"It's not just that. But yeah, maybe that too. They don't like anything different. Anything memorable. For this exact reason. It always leads to trouble. I should never have agreed to it…"

"The deal?" said Hogarth.

The look in the man's eyes said Hogarth was right.

"But you did agree to it because the person who bought this from you – in theory – offered you a very nice sweetener, didn't they?"

The man shifted in his seat. He looked as if he was struggling.

"If you've got a bad tooth, you pull it out. Once it's out, the pain stops. Tell us what we need to know, and we're done."

The man met Hogarth's eyes. "I don't know, man. It's not that simple."

"Why not?"

"Because it will look bad. You won't believe me."

"A man like you? Looking bad? And telling lies? I'd already trust you with my life."

The man shook his head in disdain.

"Come on, Brian. Why can't you tell us?" said Palmer. She looked at Hogarth. "Is it status? Did they give you the impression that there would be consequences?"

Hogarth saw where she was going and nodded with enthusiasm.

"Or did they give the impression that they were untouchable in some way?"

"Status, yeah. They have status. Untouchable, I don't know about that. But no one's going to like it when I say—"

"I know the bastard already. Just say it," said Hogarth.

"You know him?" said the man, wide eyed.

"Say it!"

"Look. He came up to me on the estate. I was passing through, like always. Going between the blocks..."

"Plying your trade," said Hogarth.

"Minding my own business," said the man, correcting him. "When he approached me, I tried to move faster, to get away from him. I don't like no chatting when I'm busy, especially not with people like them. You never know what they want, or what they're gonna say to you next."

"People like who?" said Palmer.

Hogarth had a picture in his mind of a pampered, privileged member of the well-heeled classes In the next moment, the image in his mind was shattered.

"Church people, man."

"Church?" said Hogarth, frowning as his mouth dropped open.

"Yeah, man. I know what they do in that place. Some of it's good, yeah, but all that patronising crap about God, the devil... all of that... I can't do it. You know, they almost had me going for a while. I went there years back when the place first opened, back when I was young. I wanted to believe in something back then. But after what happened, well, now I'm the one who's seen the light."

Hogarth's mind raced. He looked at Palmer, then back to the man at his table.

"Explain yourself," snapped Hogarth.

The two men at the quiz machine glanced over their shoulder. The barman looked up from his tabloid.

"We should stay calm," said Palmer.

Hogarth nodded.

"I warned you. I said you wouldn't believe me. It was the guy who seems to be the head man, these days. The cool one with all the tattoos. Freddie, his name was Freddie."

Hogarth fell silent, but he felt as if he had been winded by a serious punch in the gut. He looked at the froth on top of his ale, then back at the man in the hat. The man met his eye, waiting.

"Freddie Halstead?" said Palmer.

"Yeah, man, whatever. It was him. You see why this is sensitive? That man will lose his job. But I can't worry about that now. Think about it. If he's buying stuff like that, pure product, it can only be because he's dealing. I got it straight away. And think, he's got a captive market in there. It's almost genius. But listen. That didn't come from me. I'm nothing to do with any of it. Theoretical, right?"

"Theoretical," said Palmer, looking at Hogarth, waiting for his agreement. But she saw his eyes were drifting, his brow falling low over his eyes.

"Theoretical," said Hogarth, eventually, but his word was barely a whisper. "Why couldn't you say his name? Why didn't you tell us at the start? Or is this all some more half-baked bullshit you cooked up on the way here?"

"It's not bull, man," he said, already backing away from the table. "I didn't want to say a word, remember? I'm telling you the truth."

"Then why all the struggle?" said Hogarth. "These are church people. It's not as if they're intimidating."

"Course they are, man! I don't like religion. I'm not superstitious, but come on. They've got God behind them. No one needs all that kind of thinking in their head. You cross them, who are you crossing exactly?"

"I didn't think you believed, Brian."

"Less than I did before, that's for damn sure. We done now?"

Hogarth and Palmer exchanged a lengthy glance and the man called Brian nodded to himself, taking his cue to leave.

"We're done. Theoretical, remember."

The man turned away and strode out of the pub doors without a nod or a goodbye to anyone.

Hogarth picked up his beer and knocked back half of it in one go.

"He could be lying," said Palmer.

"That's what you're saying," said Hogarth. "But it's not what you're thinking. I had it all wrong... and I've had it wrong since the start."

"No, he could still be lying. Like you said, he might have made it up."

Hogarth shook his head.

"No. It's too wild to be a lie. If he was lying, he would have come up with something else. *Anything* else."

Hogarth picked up his beer and downed the second half right down to the foamy dregs. He set the glass back down on the table, his mind racing as his eyes traced over the well-varnished wood grain beneath.

"Maybe Freddie *is* dealing," said Palmer. "We could have stumbled onto a separate crime. He always did look too cool to be a preacher, after all."

Hogarth met her eyes. He looked stern, but she knew most of what she saw was self-recrimination. He shook his head. "That would be another coincidence though, wouldn't it? And you know what I think of them."

"But Ollie's the one with the issues," said Palmer. "His brother."

"Then it's beginning to sound like it runs in the family, doesn't it?" he said, rising from his chair.

Hogarth looked pale, his tiredness had caught up with him in one sudden hit. He put the heel of his palm to his forehead and looked out of the window.

"Bloody hell. And then there's Drawton... I was going to have him hung, drawn and quartered at the top of the high street. But if it wasn't him, then what the hell did he want?"

Palmer shrugged. She stood up and drank down half her drink. She left the other half on the table.

"I'm beginning to think you need to return his call."

"Yeah," said Hogarth. "I'll do that. Then we'll go and find good old Freddie. You're right. This could still be a pack of lies. We need to keep our focus. This case has been going all over the place."

But Hogarth's words sounded empty. He felt sick to the stomach and knew he couldn't blame it on the vegan sandwich. He'd missed things the whole way through. Doubt ridden, he wondered whether Drawton *had* set him a trap. Even if he had, the way things were now, Hogarth knew he had no choice but to walk right into it.

"I need some air," he said. He turned for the door, then snapped his fingers like he'd just remembered something. "Your niece. You should find her. Halstead can wait a while longer. If Brian was telling the truth then right now, Freddie Halstead doesn't know anyone's onto him – which means we've got some time to get ourselves in order. Make sure you use it to get your niece out of the way before we swoop."

"The case takes priority."

Hogarth shook his head.

"Not this second. It will soon. But right now, family comes first."

Palmer took a deep breath as her mind returned full force to the worries she had been pushing aside all morning. She felt more anxious than ever.

"What will you do while I look for her?"

Hogarth shrugged. "I'll see if Drawton really does want my help or not… by walking into his trap." As he spoke, he saw Palmer wasn't even listening. Her mind was already elsewhere.

"Don't worry, Sue. You've still got time on your side. This killer doesn't strike in the day, remember?"

Palmer remembered the line from when Hogarth last used it. It hadn't provided much comfort then and gave even less now. She sighed, formed a crumpled smile and offered it to Hogarth by way of goodbye.

"Don't get into any trouble," she said. "You know why."

"That's not for me to decide, is it?"

Palmer nodded once more and walked out into the street. Hogarth paced to the pub window as he tried to compose his thoughts. He watched Palmer climb into her Corsa and check her appearance in the rear-view mirror before she started the engine and drove off.

Hogarth's mobile vibrated in his pocket as the barman noisily snatched the left behind Archers and lemonade and the empty pint; the exaggerated clink of glass was a signal for him to leave. As Hogarth didn't like being told what to do, he stood gazing at the phone screen but it wasn't Drawton, at least not from his usual mobile. It was another 'no-caller ID' Perhaps a nuisance call centre wanting to sell some service or other. That would have been a relief. But he doubted it. Hogarth put the phone to his ear.

"Yes?"

"Hogarth," said the gruff voice. Hogarth frowned, failing to place it. But it certainly wasn't Drawton's plummy tone at the other end.

"Yes?"

"I've got something for you. Not sure if it's any good, but you can be the judge of that."

It was John Dickens, the brusque-mannered lead of the crime scene team Hogarth braced himself for a revelation. After the news on Freddie Halstead, he both hoped for one and he dreaded it.

"We found something. It was tucked into the side of the deceased's armchair. Like it had slipped out of his pocket."

"Robbins?"

"Who else?" said Dickens. "It's soiled with all the usual crap people drop down their sofas, and with some of Robbins' bodily fluids, I expect. He died in the chair after all."

"I get the picture. But what is it?"

"It's some kind of Bible tract. There's something there about turning away from a life of addiction and having the scales fall from their eyes."

"That'll be from the Refuge food bank. Bound to be…"

"But from what I heard, I didn't think he was a regular at the place. Didn't have much time for the whole thing, did he?"

"Who've you been speaking to?" said Hogarth.

"You spend a day or two picking around a dead man's home and you get talking about all kinds of things. And then information from your lot eventually seeps in, it's like osmosis."

"Like a bloody sieve more like."

"Either way, I'm calling to tell you what I found."

"Thanks, John. Anything else I should know."

"Yes, this is the important part, Hogarth. The tract leaflet. There's a note on it. Handwritten. It could be in the dead man's writing, though I can't be sure."

"Go on. What does it say?"

"It's just a fragment. But it sounds like an appointment to me. Food Fayre eleven am tomorrow F."

"That's it?"

"Yeah. And it's written Fayre, as in size of offering, quantity of supply, rather than 'all's fair in love and war."

"Food Fayre? Never heard of it."

"You don't know the place? It's pretty good, actually. It's a caff along the side of Victoria Plaza. Small place but it's always quiet and spacious upstairs. Nice deep filled bagels. Cheap too."

"Nice advert, John. I'll have to give it a go sometime."

"Sounds like Robbins already has," said Dickens.

Hogarth's expression darkened. "You said 'eleven am tomorrow' and then what?"

"Just one letter. F. As in F for Foxtrot…"

"F for Freddie," said Hogarth.

"That's it, but it's Foxtrot in the phonetic alphabet," said Dickens, not picking up on Hogarth's meaning. Hogarth headed for the pub doors.

"Was there any evidence of visitors there, John? Recent ones?"

"As in the last week – since the man's death?"

"No. Well, maybe. What about before that?"

"The floor's not been cleaned in an age. There are plenty of footprints, with shoes and without – it would have been a brave soul who went without shoes in there. It was a lady's foot from the shape and size of it."

"Thanks. Anyone aside from her?"

"Older prints, mostly. Predating the murder by some time, though Marris will have his own opinion."

Hogarth nodded, drawing his own conclusions. Halstead hadn't visited Robbins' home in recent times. But why would two men like them ever meet? They would have hardly known each other from the food bank. So how come Halstead even knew him to offer him the deadly gift – supposing it were true? One man worked his days and evenings in the busy food bank and church, his spare hours supposedly eaten up by serving his brother's special needs… the other was known as a violent scumbag, the virtual enemy of all things good and holy, and a selfish loner to boot. Their paths should never have crossed. Robbins was unlikely to have ever been near the food bank for longer than it took to make a deal or threaten someone in the queue. The only logical place where the two intersected was with Helen Brimelow. The café meeting only made sense if Helen Brimelow was the cause of their meeting. But it still seemed unlikely that they would go for a chat over a roll and coffee. Hogarth shook his head, his mouth downturned.

"I'll leave you with that, then, shall I?" said Dickens, listening to dead air.

"What?" Hogarth came back to the present. "Oh, yes. Good work, John."

"I can already hear the cogs spinning," replied Dickens. "Good luck, Hogarth."

The crime scene man ended the call and Hogarth stood on the street corner, watching the traffic as he gathered himself. *Halstead... or Drawton?* It was then that Hogarth remembered his own words: Halstead could wait. He was still sure there was a Drawton connection there somehow, but now Ollie seemed less likely to be the link. He intended to confront Halstead before the day was out. But before that, he needed to be sure, absolutely sure, that they weren't being taken for a ride. And for that, another meeting with Simon Drawton was unavoidable. Hogarth curled his lip at the thought.

Twenty

Palmer was struggling. Finding her niece was a good idea, but the trouble was Aaliyah didn't want to be found. Palmer's mind had been sent spinning back to all the mischief she herself had gotten up to as a teen – especially the times she tried to keep out of contact from her mum and dad. Sometimes, rules had been broken. A trip to London on the train with a friend, back when she had only been allowed to London with her parents. And later there came the other kinds of risks, those involving the excitement of meeting a boy, one who she knew her parents disapproved of. It had ended in a kiss and fumble and the boy thinking he was entitled to go too far. Palmer had broken away and had gone home with her tail between her legs, with a new unwanted secret to keep. Knowing Aaliyah as she did, she hoped a kiss and a fumble would be the limit of it. But with who? None of the service users at the food bank, surely? In any case, if that happened her sister would never forgive her.
Aaliyah still wasn't answering her calls. Palmer's calls were going straight to voicemail, but she didn't wait to leave a message. Aaliyah's phone was off. Or out of battery. Either way, Palmer was beginning to worry, daytime or not. The girl liked shopping, so there was always a chance she might find her down the high street, browsing through the rails at H&M and New Look. But there were only a few fashion stores left on the high street. After that, Palmer was out of ideas. Cafés? Pubs? *No.* The only place Aaliyah had taken any interest in lately was the food bank. She decided to try again. There was another virtue in going back to the Refuge.

Looking for Aaliyah was a good pretext for an impromptu meeting with Freddie Halstead. If he was the man who supplied Robbins – if he was Brimelow's killer – then he would be working hard to keep up his act of the caring community worker. It was an opportunity to inspect the man at close quarters. It was the smallest of silver linings. Better still, she hoped to find Aaliyah in the food bank, after having duped big Gordon into letting her stay. The girl certainly had the gift of the gab – another trait she'd gotten from her mother.

Palmer drove around the block and turned right onto Coleman Street. She passed the bakery and slowed when she saw a car was waiting behind the bollards of the tower block estate. As the bollards lowered to give the car access, Palmer accelerated and drew up almost bumper to bumper with the car as it went through the gate. Her Corsa just made it. Palmer watched the bollards slowly rise behind her. The woman in the first car shot her a mean look in her rear-view mirror, implying 'you're not a resident' but Palmer ignored it. She drove along the car park and pulled up beside the white Transit van she had seen Gordon unloading before. Up on the first floor, an untidy mob of smokers leaned over the blue railings. Most of them were clutching the grey carrier bags dispensed by the food bank and had already enjoyed a plate of food. They looked in no hurry to leave. Some looked down at Palmer as they chatted, only one or two bothering to pass comment. Even if she looked like a cop, this lot had seen it all before. Palmer noticed a woman with tied-back hair and glasses weaving between the groups with a vague air of purpose. She was holding a clipboard and there was a white lanyard around her neck. Palmer climbed the curving slope to the top of the platform and approached the sprawl of people. A few looked at her, but Palmer ignored them and made her way to the clipboard woman, listening to the questions she asked as she approached.

The woman was offering help with benefits or housing problems. No one seemed interested.

"No takers this afternoon?" said Palmer.

The woman stopped in her tracks and looked at Palmer, taking in Palmer's suit, hairstyle, and face. When she offered a smile, Palmer saw she had been accepted as another professional.

"No. No one's got any problems around here, can't you tell?" The woman made a sweeping gesture with her pen which took in the thirty or so people ranged around them. Palmer smiled. The lanyard said the woman worked for an agency called Family Mosaic. Her name was Ellie Turner.

"I'm looking for someone," said Palmer. "I don't suppose you've seen a girl with long brown hair, bit of a violet tint in it. She's dressed like a fashion doll. Bit too young to be in the food bank if I'm honest, but she might have blagged her way in."

"You're with the police, I take it?"

"That obvious, am I?"

"I know the look. And you're looking for someone in there, that tells its own story. There are plenty of girls in there who look borderline this morning – anywhere between fourteen and twenty-one, but they're usually old enough."

Palmer gave a knowing nod. "Any that match my description?"

"Sorry. 'Fraid you'll have to go in and take a look. Don't worry. Gordon will help you. He's lovely."

"Oh, I'm not scared of getting bitten," said Palmer. "I'm just trying to save time. This is a personal matter. The girl I'm looking for is my niece."

"Oh. I see," said the woman. "Probably even more important you see the manager, then."

Palmer nodded.

"Thanks anyway." She turned for the door, passing a trio of scruffy older teens as they bundled out with their food parcels, one of them lighting a roll-up as he went.

Palmer turned back. "Excuse me," she called.

The Family Mosaic woman turned around. "Yes?"

"You said I should speak to Gordon. But is anyone else in today?"

"You mean the project manager? Zack's not been in for months. I think Freddie must be over at the office. They've got an office in town, close to Warrior Square."

Their brief chat was interrupted as one of the street homeless from the high street shuffled between them and began talking at Ellie Turner. Palmer turned away and walked into the food bank. A man with a sweat-glossed face and Victorian-style sideburns asked her for her name without looking up from his computer.

"Can I speak to Gordon?"

The desk man looked up at her, appraising the suit and the hair the same way as the agency woman had before him. His bearing changed immediately.

"Gordon, yeah. I'll see what I can do. Where you from again?" When the man stood up, Palmer saw he was dressed in a suit which looked somewhere between Victorian and nineteen-eighties' bank manager. The food bank seemed to offer a home to waifs and strays of all kinds.

"The police," said Palmer.

The Victorian's brow wrinkled. He leaned into a doorway on the back wall and called out, "Gordon. There's a woman from the police out here. She wants a word."

The word police went off like a klaxon in the confined space. Those nearby poked their heads around the corner and stared at her. As Gordon emerged from one door, another couple of heads followed, snakelike, around the edges of the doorframe. As ever, Gordon was grinning again, wiping his hands on a tea towel. Palmer wondered if his face did anything but smile.

"You again," he said with a friendly air. "Thought it might be."

Gordon looked as if he was about to say something else but stopped when he noticed the surrounding volunteers and needy watching and listening.

"Let's talk in the office," he said, thumbing the door behind him.

Palmer followed him. Being led to a private office in a food bank, Palmer suddenly had the sense of being a woman in need like all the rest of them, someone ready to offload her cares to a friendly face. She felt the panic for her niece begin to boil up inside but managed to bring herself back to order as Gordon closed the door behind her. Instantly, she saw the room was less an office than another messy storage room with a couple of leather sofas chucked in, along with a dated cream computer.

"Sorry about that. The walls have ears in this place," said Gordon. He dropped his big frame into a sofa, and Palmer watched the leather cushions sink deep beneath him. He picked up a mug from the floor, sipped it and made a face. "I made that two hours ago," he said. "Right then. I take it you didn't find that niece of yours."

"Not yet," said Palmer.

Gordon's smile slipped but mostly stayed in place. "She wasn't in before – when you looked through the window. I double-checked. Everyone who was here was in that room, and I know all of them."

"I'll bet you do," said Palmer. "From what I see, you run the place all by yourself."

Gordon grinned. "Oh, I wouldn't say that. Zack made the place what it is. And Freddie works his socks off to bring the people in. He keeps the community aspect going."

"Whereas you just do all the actual work?" said Palmer.

Gordon's grin widened.

"It's a labour of love."

"Because of your faith, I take it?"

"Look around. This is what the church should be. It's biblical. Helping the needy, preaching the gospel, showing God's love as it really is, not in some cold and remote stone building."

Palmer smiled at the man's words, but she needed to fish for more.

"The other managers feel the same about the place too, do they?"

"I know they do. We all show it in different ways."

"How does Zack show it?"

The truth was Palmer wasn't interested in Zack at all, but the question would help her segue to the next.

"Zack shows it in his preaching."

"And Freddie Halstead? How does he show it?"

"In the work he does. He loves the community stuff. Though he does a lot of paperwork, too, these days."

"Community? Paperwork? Compared to what you do, those sound like two very dry words to me."

"Paperwork, maybe. Yeah, I can't stand it. That's not for me. But community, no. That's what this place is for."

Palmer nodded, recalling Halstead's talk at the memorial service. As she remembered it, the bespectacled church pastor had pushed him to speak. He'd seemed reluctant. At the time she had imagined he was shy. Now she wondered if there was another reason for his reticence. How could anyone deliver a eulogy for his victim?

"If you like, you can take another look round, see if you recognise your niece among the service users. It's really busy at the mo. I suppose she might have snuck in under a false name."

"Does that happen?" said Palmer.

The big man shrugged. "This is Southend. Anything can happen, right?"

Palmer flicked her eyebrows up and nodded. "Yeah. You can say that again."

Gordon heaved himself up and picked up his cold mug. "I'll take you down to the café. I could do with a fresh brew anyway. I keep some good stuff in the cupboard, if you want a cup."

"Good stuff?" said Palmer.

Gordon nodded. "Don't worry. I meant coffee. I've got a tin of Illy. I make it strong too."

"Now you're talking."

As the big man put his hand to the door, Palmer called him back. "Just one thing. Before we go."

"Yes?"

"Kevin Robbins," she said.

Gordon finally lost his smile. "Yeah. The estate's just lost another one. It's a real shame. From what I hear, he was close to…"

Palmer frowned and shook her head. "Close? Close to what? I thought he never came near the place."

Gordon's smile slowly returned.

"That's what he wanted people to think. There's a good few like that. The bolshie estate mums who are too proud to come here, but whose families need the help and call us for a parcel on the quiet. Then there's the others who can't come to the building, you know – beaten wives whose exes come in here, that kind of thing. We deliver to them if needed."

"But Kevin Robbins had money, as I heard it. He didn't need the place."

"*Everyone* needs this place," said Gordon. "Some people realise it, and some people don't. For some it just takes time. Razor was one of those."

The confused look on Palmer's face forced Gordon to explain.

"Razor was a loner, okay. He pushed everyone away. Always acting aloof and cool. A lot of people fell for it, all the acting hard and fronting people. He was a troublemaker, granted. I had to usher him away from the food queue a few times, to stop him intimidating people. But I saw right through him, to the scared, frightened, naked little man beneath. He was hurting, just like the rest of 'em."

Palmer shook her head, frowning. "So what happened with him? You said you provide for people that won't come in? How did you provide for him?"

"Like you said, Razor didn't need the food. Was too proud for that. Always strutting around the place, he was. But he still lived in Haycock Tower. Part of Freddie's job is meeting with people on the estate. He gets paid by the church and by a community agency to do just that."

"Family Mosaic?" said Palmer, speculating.

"No. Stepping Stones, I think. But that's not the point. The point is, Freddie is like Carlsberg."

Palmer shook her head.

"Freddie gets to the places other churches can't reach."

"You're saying Freddie visited Kevin Robbins?"

"Part of Freddie's job is to try and connect with as many people as he can. He's a community worker here. He has to go to all of the tower blocks on the estate. Like me, Freddie knew Razor was close."

"There you go again. Close to what?"

"To his shell cracking apart. Close to giving his life to Jesus," said Gordon.

Palmer's mouth dropped open.

"You're kidding?"

Gordon grinned. "Course not. You'd never believe the people we have in here, giving their lives. It changes them from the inside out."

Palmer nodded, but her mind was already processing, her eyes darting around the room.

"You're in shock, aren't you?" said Gordon, chuckling.

"How long has Freddie been meeting with Kevin?"

"A while now, I think it was every fortnight or so. Whenever Razor wanted a catch-up. Which basically meant, whenever he was feeling lost or wanted to ask about the faith."

"Did Freddie ever instigate those meetings?"

"Maybe now and then. But that kind of work, spiritual work, that has to be done slowly; softly softly, or you spook 'em. That's how it was with Razor. Like I say. He was close. It's such a shame he OD'd before he could make the commitment."

Palmer's mind raced with permutations of dates, opportunities, possibilities.

"Do you know if anyone else here got close to Kevin Robbins?"

"Me occasionally, but mostly it was Freddie. Then you told us about him getting close to Helen, now that was a real shocker."

"You never knew that? Never had an inkling?"

"I knew Helen had a caring heart, that's all. If I ever saw her talking to a service user, I knew she was reaching out, fulfilling her calling. But I never saw her with Razor, no. If I had, I would have warned her. He liked the ladies too much. Razor was Freddie's job, no one else's."

Freddie's job, no one else's…

Palmer swallowed.

The big man seemed to sense Palmer's unease, but maybe out of respect for her profession, he didn't ask. He opened the office door and led her out into a busy, narrow corridor. They seemed to be swimming against the tide of people as they walked to the free café and Gordon pushed the heavy door. The big hall was even noisier then she had expected. A cloud of steam billowed from the kitchen catering kettle, and every brown leather seat was taken, with a surplus of guests standing by the remnants of the food on tables, and in the corners.

Gordon laid his hand on Palmer's shoulder and moved close so she could hear him.

"I'll get you that coffee, okay?" he said, raising his voice to be heard.

"Wait, Gordon. I think I need a word with Freddie. Is he still over at the office?"

"Probably," said Gordon.

"What do you mean, probably?" she replied.

"He hasn't made it over here this morning, so probably, yes."

"You mean you don't know if he's there or not?" said Palmer.

"It's a work day, so he'll be somewhere, but he hasn't rocked up here yet. I'm guessing he'll be doing that paperwork. He gets a lot of that, you see."

Palmer's brow fell low over her eyes. Her mouth stayed open. Gordon raised a finger as if to say, *wait,* before he walked away to leave Palmer looking out over a hall full of noise, steam, smells and colour. Her mind worked overtime as her eyes scanned the faces around the hall. She found Suitcase, studiously avoiding her eye. Next, she found the missionary man, Dennis Corby, sitting beside a troubled looking woman, smiling as he spoke. She saw Middle-Eastern folk, Africans, Asians, and working-class whites mingled close together in the one hall. The place was a melting pot of poverty of all colours and creeds. Palmer almost caught wind of the excitement her niece must have felt for the place. Amid all the chaos, she sensed a kind of unity. But it was fleeting. She guessed a teenage newcomer might have sensed adventure too. But as hard as she scanned the chairs and tables, Palmer saw no sign of Aaliyah. She looked back at the food serving table. Ollie Halstead was absent too, but perhaps the other volunteers would know where he was. Palmer cut between the tables, squeezing between seats until she reached the food serving table. A matronly woman with white hair and piercing blue eyes looked at her from the other side of the table, ready to tell her to join the queue along with everyone else. Palmer interrupted her train of thought.

"Ollie Halstead not in today?"

"Ollie? No, he's not. Which is a blessed relief. He's hard work that one. Harder to deal with than this lot," said the old woman.

"I bet," said Palmer. "No sign of Freddie either?"

"No. Not a dickie bird. Who shall I say was asking?"

"Don't worry," said Palmer, shaking her head. "I'll keep looking, thanks."

"Something happened, has it?" said the old woman, her eyes dropping to Palmer's suit.

"Nothing yet," said Palmer.

"Then that's a relief too," she said. Then, armed with a set of stainless-steel tongs, the old woman walked away to serve the next in line.

When Palmer turned she bumped into Gordon.

"Steady!" he said, chuckling. The man stepped back and Palmer saw he had two mugs of steaming coffee, one in each hand.

"I'm sorry. I really need to go."

The man nodded. "Yeah. I know. Your niece. Do yourself a favour. Drink this before you get on your way. You look like you could do with it."

Gordon handed Palmer her coffee and as she took it, Palmer noticed that Gordon had slipped a small square of glossy-feeling paper into her palm along with the mug. For a moment, she almost believed the man had slipped her his telephone number. Then she remembered that was unlikely. Palmer opened her palm and saw a bright white leaflet with a red sun and a gold cross on it. There was scripture written across the front.

"You never give up, do you?" said Palmer.

"Not in my nature," said Gordon. "Drink your coffee and keep that tract. You never know when you'll need it."

You never know, indeed, thought Palmer. She was glad to slide the paper into her pocket, safely out of sight. She gave Gordon a careful, pursed-lipped smile, and sipped her coffee. The stuff was searing hot and as strong as any cup she'd ever had. As soon as it was drunk, she would need to find Freddie Halstead. And no matter what Hogarth had said about having plenty of time before dark to find Freddie, Palmer was no longer content to wait. Her niece was AWOL, and it seemed the case was changing at a rate of knots.

Twenty-one

Hogarth parked his car on the snaking lane directly outside Drawton's house. This time the man's signature Smart car was sitting on the driveway. Even if Drawton had wanted to evade him, to get into his car and drive off, Hogarth had blocked him in. He wasn't going anywhere. Hogarth looked across the street. The small wooden-clad infant school was in full swing. Little kiddies were running around behind the green wire fence, screaming their heads off and having a whale of a time in what looked like a mud garden full of big toys and a pretend kitchen. A couple of young teachers – one of whom looked young enough to have been at secondary school herself – were kneeling by the children to help them play. Hogarth looked at the house and tried to scan for movement, but he couldn't see a thing through the thick net curtains. He walked to the front door and used the big brass knocker. For added effect, he snapped the letter box and rang the doorbell. He waited and looked back at the kids and all their busy innocence. He was too old to envy them. He didn't want to go through school and puberty all over again, no thanks. Instead, he pitied them. One day they would realise what the world had become. He hoped they would also see a way to navigate it. To sift the good from the bad. It was a survival strategy that had kept him alive and sane after twenty years on the front line… though sane might have been overstating it. Still, Drawton's door hadn't yet opened. Hogarth knocked and drilled the bell, then bent down and opened the letter box. This time he peered inside and called out.

"Drawton. International Rescue has arrived! The Thunderbirds are on your doorstep, so open the bloody door!"

Silence.

"Open it, Drawton. I know you're in there, so stop dicking me about."

Remembering the kids across the street, Hogarth looked back, but their noise was such he doubted whether they would hear if he swore his way through the tune of Hickory Dickory Dock. He wasn't impressed with Drawton. Chasing up Freddie Halstead would have been a far better use of his time than this. Drawton had thwarted him once, now he was trying to ruin an even more pressing case.

"Listen up, you snivelling little…" But Hogarth didn't bother to finish his sentence. He'd read the man's text message but remembered he hadn't bothered to listen to the voicemail. Now seemed like as good a time as any – just as a precaution, if nothing else.

He dialled 901 and waited. The voicemail started with a series of breaths, hurried and light, as if Drawton had been out running or felt unwell.

The message kicked in: "Ho… Hogarth… Why won't you pick up, damn you? You hound me… hound me for months… now you won't accept my calls…"

"Get to the point, you bastard," Hogarth replied, but he was already fascinated. There was something off about Drawton's voice. He sounded panicked. Faint. It was highly unusual.

"Listen. I'm in grave danger. I didn't kill that girl. I know you didn't believe me, but I told you the truth. Something that someone told me… it got me thinking… thinking that I might know who might have done something like that… who might have had the chance, and the reason… the urge…"

Hogarth grimaced. Now he was listening. He turned and looked hard at the solid grey wall of the net curtains behind the glass. The message went on.

"I had an inkling… so I pursued it. He called me today. The man I suspected. I wanted to know for sure, so I went to see him again… But… he tried to… he tried to kill me, Inspector. I'm hurt. I think I'll be fine, but I need to speak to you. You've got to stop him or someone else will die, I know it… I felt it on him… That urge…"

The man's voice was slow and croaky by the time the voicemail timed out. Hogarth stared at his phone and then the door. He stepped back and peered up at the upstairs windows, but there was no sign of Drawton, no sign of anything at all. He checked the missed call notification on his phone. The notification was an hour and a half old, but the damn things came in whenever they liked. Sometimes a notification would come in a full two days after the call had been made, which did nothing for his reputation as a cop with a scruffy attitude. Scruffy, no. Attitude, yes.

"Drawton, you'd bloody better be in there," said Hogarth. He thought about the back way in, through the neighbouring garden, but broad daylight and a covert break-in weren't easy bedfellows. Best all round that he saved his aching body, and made his foot do the work instead. Hogarth moved close to the door, took one pace back, lifted his leg as best he could, and slammed it hard and full against the Yale lock. The red door shuddered in the frame. The noise of his boot echoed from under the porchway. It was loud enough to draw eyes from across the street. A moment later, as he prepared another kick, Hogarth sensed a face appear in the big bay window of the nearby manse. He caught sight of a woman with a short puffy bob of dark grey hair watching him with a shocked face. Hogarth ignored her. He pressed his hands against the edges of the porch wall and booted the door as hard as he could. On impact, it felt like he'd failed, like the damn thing was going to hold, but at the very last, the fibres of the wood gave in. The wood creaked, split, and the door shuddered inwards. Hogarth took a breath and pulled a hand back through his hair. He looked inside, listening. The fridge clicked and hummed in the kitchen, but otherwise there was only silence.

"Drawton! You wanted help. I'm here," he called.

There was no reply. He took another deep breath and began a steady door-by-door search. The front room was empty, sparse and clean as the last time he'd seen it, and the time before that. He walked to the kitchen and stepped onto the cork tiles. Nothing. He was about to back out when a flash of red caught his eye in the big white cottage-style sink. Hogarth paced across the kitchen and found the folds of scrunched up kitchen roll dropped into the sink. They were blotted with blood like bright red ink. The sink was full of them, and the wooden stand where a roll of paper had stood had been knocked over on the surface. Hogarth frowned and looked back to the stairwell. He noticed more blood on the cork tiles.

"Drawton!" he called. Still no reply. Hogarth rushed out to the hallway and was about to pass the front door when he saw the teachers gazing and muttering from behind the mesh fence across the street. Hogarth pushed the door to the frame and set off up the steps. Now he was in a hurry. By the top steps, he found spots and spatterings of blood on the wooden floor. There was plenty of it.

"Drawton, where are you?"

The bathroom was the first door he went to. He opened the door and saw the medicine cabinet had been left open. A small green first aid box and all its contents had been spilt across the black and white floor tiles, beside another trail of spattered blood. Hogarth's eyes followed a vague trail of plastic and paper bandage packaging across the landing towards an open door. His stomach turned in anticipation of what he was about to find. He set his face hard, his eyes flinty, and walked into Drawton's bedroom. There was Drawton, sprawled out on his back across one corner of his bed. His shirt was soaked in blood, as was his face. A bloom of bright red had spread outward from his face and head. But Drawton had got himself home. He had been able to make it this far. But that didn't mean the man wasn't dead...

Hogarth strode to the edge of the bed and pressed his fingers against the man's wrist. There was a pulse, a weak and irregular pulse to Hogarth's mind, but at least the man was alive.

He let go of Drawton's hand and watched his head turn limply from one side to the other. His dry lips parted and his eyes opened, but barely. Without his spectacles, the man's eyes looked small and molelike.

"Can you hear me, Drawton?"

The reply came out as a weak whisper. "H... Hogarth."

"What the hell happened to you?" he said.

Drawton coughed and tried to smile. "I tried to play detective." His words were barely audible. "It's not as easy as it looks..."

Hogarth looked at the man's face. His nose was broken, his lip split, and one of his eyes was swollen and puffy. There was almost certainly internal bleeding. Drawton might have been a sick criminal, but now he was also a victim. More than that, he was a key witness. Hogarth needed him to live. He dialled for an ambulance and made the call as quick as he could. As soon as he was done, he texted Palmer. The search for her rogue of a niece was going to have to wait.

"Who did this to you?" said Hogarth.

Drawton looked at him, blinking, a faint smile on his face.

"Tell me!"

"I beat you to it, didn't I, Inspector?" said Drawton. "You know, I met someone who is as close to being a psychopath as one is ever likely to meet. I thought it was him... until I realised his limitations... but his brother..." Drawton coughed so hard he was forced to roll over on his side. As he rolled, Hogarth watched a fresh slick of blood sluice from the man's hip, instantly soaking into the duvet. Hogarth's eyes widened. When Drawton rolled back to look at him, Hogarth had the impression he looked worse than before. Hogarth didn't ask for permission. He pulled the man's shirt tails high and saw the gaping wound just above the belt.

"Freddie Halstead? He did this to you?"

"Well done, Inspector. You worked it out, too. Bravo. You see, it's not always the quiet ones. Sometimes it's the ones who only do good to compensate for the wickedness inside... the ones who are avoiding what they are... No one can avoid that forever, Hogarth... not when it's everywhere they look."

"Speaking from experience there, Drawton?" said Hogarth.

"You know I am, Inspector. But I always knew about my little problem. I never hid it from myself. That's how I've managed so well."

"Managed so well?" said Hogarth. "Managed to avoid justice, you mean? You hid behind your friends, and they got you off, but I saw you for what you are. I always have, and I always will."

The man coughed and Hogarth saw another trickle of blood spill to the bedsheets, a small red wave breaking on a white shore. Grim faced, Hogarth picked up the bandage from the floor and pressed the wadding pad hard against the wound to staunch the flow. Drawton wailed in pain.

"What were you doing there, Drawton?"

"Doing where?"

"I saw you today – at the Queensway Estate, peering out from beneath the tower…"

"I'd worked it out… I was looking for him…"

"Halstead?"

"They're much more alike than they seem, you know. Appearances can be deceiving, but as the Good Book says, you shall know them by their fruit. His is rotten, Inspector. All of it. As I guessed it would be, last night I got an inkling… but today, I saw everything as it is…"

"What happened?"

"I was going to follow them, see what I could see… but it turns out my little chat with him last night, well, stirred something."

Hogarth blinked. "You visited Halstead?"

"Twice," said Halstead with a wheeze. "The first time it was my own choice. But today, he invited me. I warned him to stop. But he said, 'I can't stop'…and as soon as he said that I knew I was in trouble, deep trouble."

"What else did he say, Drawton?"

"Nothing else. But I know it, Inspector. I know he's going to do it again. He's going to kill…"

The faint words caught in Hogarth's mind. He swallowed on a dry throat.

Drawton's eyes turned bleary and his head lolled to one side. "Hold on, man!" said Hogarth, shaking his shoulder. "Hold on!" The shake revived him enough to turn his head. "An ambulance is coming."

"I'll be fine, Inspector," he said, in more of a murmur than a whisper. But Drawton's eyes rolled back as he lost consciousness.

Hogarth willed the man to live. By the time the ambulance crew arrived, nothing would stir him. He called them upstairs and barked at them from the landing.

"He's in the bedroom. Simon Drawton, fifty-three years old. He's been badly beaten about the head and face, likely concussion, but he's been stabbed too. The wound is to the abdomen, I can't tell how bad it is, but he's been bleeding heavily."

The two-man paramedic team moved in. The smaller man slid in and took Hogarth's place at his bedside. He opened a paramedic bag. Outside, a police siren drew to a halt.

"Jeez, this one's in a bad way," said the smaller man, checking Drawton's pulse.

"Just keep him alive," said Hogarth. "He's a key witness." Hogarth moved to the door.

"You don't need to tell us," said the larger man. "Keeping 'em alive is what we're paid for."

Hogarth nodded and slid past.

"I've got to go. My colleagues will join you shortly."

"Oi, where are you off to?" said the big man.

"To stop a killer," said Hogarth. His eyes burned with a fresh intensity. For the first time, he knew for sure. The man

had been right beneath their nose the whole time, hiding in plain sight, clothed in modern-day holiness, and all the while – a killer. A sheen of sweat shone on Hogarth's brow. His heart was beating hard and fast. Finally, he was close.
He skipped down the steps with Drawton's faint words still echoing in his head.
"He's going to do it again… He's going to kill."
Hogarth shook his head as he made his way back to his car. He had to stop Drawton's prophecy from coming true.

Twenty-two

His brother was going to be well catered for. For today at least.

A large carrier bag full of supermarket sandwiches, three giant bags of crisps, and two family size bars of Dairy Milk sat by the sofa. It was enough food to last Ollie through two whole days, maybe three. And then there was a delivery of a new PlayStation game coming. It was coming by next-day delivery. It was the one Ollie had been on about for weeks. A new release that kids half his age were raving over – laser beams and space magic on an epic scale across the universe. A game like that might keep Ollie going for days. There was more food in the fridge too. Pasties, pies, sausage rolls. All easy to eat without any preparation. The fruit bowl was full as well but Freddie knew his brother wouldn't bother with that. What mattered was that his brother would be able to go on without him for as long as it took. Because after his chat with the stranger, Freddie knew that everything was about to come apart. The weirdo from the Baptist church had been on his mind all night. All his innuendoes and thinly veiled threats. It had given him hours of worry and denied him any sleep. By morning, Freddie had made his decision.

He woke up early and got to work, using the same tactic he believed the stranger had deployed against him. His first gambit, a search of the online records at Avenue Baptist, proved less than fruitful. But after fifteen minutes, he found his first clue. A photograph in a newsletter. The stranger had been photographed manning a tombola at the church fete. The caption beneath said his name was Simon. Later in the same leaflet, Avenue's pastor had given special thanks to named volunteers, and there had been only one Simon mentioned in the whole leaflet. His name was Simon Drawton. From there, it was easy, and the excitement of the inevitable started to build.

He dug deeper into Google. He used combinations of name and surname, town locations, church names and regular calendar events. Freddie knew the church language inside out, both formal and informal. Soon after, he'd found not one but two separate listings with Drawton's name and mobile number. They may not have been careful with his contact details, but Avenue had been careful in how they used Drawton. In newsletters, he wasn't once named as a senior volunteer. Clearly, he wasn't trusted. But he still helped with their regular events. Twice he had been named as an event coordinator. His name and number had been given in the church minutes, and those minutes had been published for the whole congregation to see. Published to the web, they were available to everyone else as well.

Freddie tested the number before breakfast, withholding his own when he dialled. He had listened as Drawton picked up the call and ended the call just before the man spoke. Before he went any further, he had decided to plan out everything else. All of it. His whole day. Everything needed to happen in the right sequence, or he knew he would lose, and this time he would lose forever. Drawton came first, obviously. The man needed to be dealt with in a way that kept him out of the picture long enough to complete what he had in mind. There was no way Freddie could work today. Work was over. But that part was easy too. The bosses trusted him. They had never tracked his movements minute by minute.

His work environment was built on trust. Trust was always the weak point, and his one advantage. He planned to milk it for as long as he could, every second used up until all trust had finally run out.

With the rest of his day organised he called Drawton to a face-to-face meeting. Drawton didn't seem surprised. In fact, the man seemed to imagine it was a cry for help. A desperate plea for clemency. Halstead fought to hide his smile as they spoke. He already knew exactly how things would play out, and there would be no clemency involved. They met outside when Drawton pulled up in a Smart car outside Halstead's flat. At first, they had talked in Drawton's car and the man lectured him and he listened, all the while feeling the gentle weight of the knife in his pocket. When the conceited little man had said his piece, Freddie was more than ready to finish it. Drawton didn't know when he'd said enough. His words were like an invasion of everything that was private and personal and sacred. Of everything he'd said and done, this was the man's worst mistake.

"I know what you did to that girl, Freddie. I know it was you. I can see it in your eyes. I recognise the hunger in you."

The hunger? It wasn't hunger. Freddie knew what it really was. He was unwilling to dress it up.

It was an all-consuming, all-pervasive need to act on how he felt. The need to feel skin on skin, until all his problems and worries were utterly gone. A wonderful oblivion. For months at a time, he had been able to resist temptation, simply watching as the people all around him gave in to their basest desires whenever they liked. But his life was not theirs. It had never been easy to live with so many burdens and not have any of the outlets he used to depend on. And meeting anybody when so many rules were in place proved impossible. The few women he'd met seemed content to toy with him. And Drawton, the pompous invader, wanted to end the only pleasure he'd had in years. Why? Because like all the rest, he thought it made him good.

But that wasn't part of Freddie's plan.

"Let's walk," he'd said. "I need some fresh air."

Drawton had looked at him, hesitated, but then agreed, as Freddie knew he would. Because he'd been quiet and compliant, Drawton thought he was the one in charge. Freddie let him continue to believe he was in charge as they walked down leafy Kings Road… as Freddie bided his time for a moment when the traffic had cleared… when the nearby pavements were as good as empty. He hadn't had to wait long. They weren't far from his house when the silence came, and the gap in the hedge by the big stone church presented itself like an invitation. An invitation Freddie Halstead could not refuse. He moved in a flash. He subdued the man with his fists, fast and brutal. It felt good. Freddie knocked the man down, battered him half unconscious and dragged him onto the gravel behind the hedge. Then, when Freddie knew there was no energy left for the man to scream, he drew the knife. The knife was intended to put him out for the count. As he plunged in the blade, he didn't care if the man lived or died. He knew nothing about Simon Drawton, other than the man was a typical nuisance. One Freddie needed gone, so he could prepare for something much, much better…

Sweet release.

As every year had passed, each new chance flirtation in the church had taken him by surprise. The women had all been off limits. Forbidden fruit. But the need had risen up in him more strongly, like a volcano about to erupt. He always fought to hold on, to control himself, and he had almost succeeded, until Helen.

Sweet, beautiful Helen. The young girl had flirted like all the rest, but innocently. Her sweetness had barbed him, left thorns in his flesh, memories he couldn't erase. Her suggestive eyes had stayed long in the mind, teasing him at night, persuading him there was a way he could have her and keep his job. But every morning, he knew it had been a lie. She had been too young, too innocent. The price was just too high. So, he had denied himself, and kept away, telling himself she was still his. It was a perfect love, too perfect to ever happen.

And it had stayed that way until he found she had given herself away so cheaply. After he lost his temper and took her to the beach, it was only a matter of time before Razor had to go. And the heroin idea had come to him as foolproof inspiration.

Each and every time he'd seen the police detectives flailing, desperately clawing for clues it had given him more confidence.

He was going to survive.

He was going to get away with it.

And that had been true, all the way up until Simon Drawton. And now, with that problem gone, nothing could ever be the same again.

He wasn't going to get away this time.

His fate was upon him. The fate he deserved. But if it was still in his power, he would have one final chance at tasting life. The very best of life, before it was over.

One last sweet oblivion before the final curtain.

His knife had been cleaned. It was back in his jacket pocket, an unused Durex pouch in the other. There was no need for gloves this time. His car keys jangled in his hand.

"Have a good day, Ollie. If you get hungry, there's plenty of food in the fridge."

His brother stayed silent until he opened the door to leave. Then he paused the video game and looked back at him. The look in Ollie's eyes glued him to the spot.

"There's plenty of food around, mate. Enjoy. Look. I've got to go."

It was true; he had to leave. As far as he knew, Drawton's body was still silently bleeding away mere yards down the street.

His brother nodded at him, and a sly look filled his face.

"I know what you're doing, you know," he said.

"Why? What am I doing?" said Freddie, trying for a smile.

"You're not going to work. It's too late for that. It's almost eleven."

"Maybe I'm working late," said Freddie. "I work late sometimes."

His brother shook his head, turned back to the screen, and resumed his game.

"It's that girl. You're going to do something you shouldn't, aren't you?"

Freddie sighed.

"What makes you think that?" he asked. His heart started to race as he waited for the answer.

"Don't worry," said Ollie, staring at the characters fighting on the television screen. "I won't tell."

Tears welled up in Freddie's eyes and spilled over his lids. They weren't so different after all, were they?

"Thanks, Ollie. I always knew I could count on you."

Freddie Halstead closed the door on his flat and walked out of his old life, knowing he would never come back. Things would never be the same. Because today was still going to be the day that the sky fell in. But first, he had one last chance to live.

He walked downstairs, out into the street and looked across the street to the big cold grey church opposite. If he crossed the street and looked down the side of the church, he wondered if he would still see Drawton's body. But he dared not look. He didn't want to be distracted by fear of being caught. This was his moment. He was committed. He was excited. And finally, he wanted what had been promised by those sweet young eyes.

Freddie made the call. As good as her word, the girl answered without delay.

"Yes?" said Aaliyah.

"You ready?" he said.

"Of course. I can't wait," she replied.

Halstead grinned.

"Neither can I," said Freddie. "Neither can I."

Twenty-three

"You've not seen him?" said Palmer "He's not called in at all?"

"No," said the girl at the desk. Palmer had long since assumed she was the secretary of the church office. In keeping with the rest of the church, the girl was younger than she might have expected. She looked to be in her mid-twenties and dressed in style. The office was modern and bright, furnished in Ikea and bleached wood, but Palmer only noticed these things in passing, because for the most part, she could only think of her niece.

"But surely you'd know where he is," said Palmer. "He's a full-time employee."

"Yes," said the girl. "But the food bank staff work differently to us. They run the outreach and so we mostly see them later in the day. In fact, it's not uncommon for us to go a day without seeing them at all. But we know when they're at work. We send emails to them and speak by phone, for instance."

"Emails and phone calls?" said Palmer, pouncing on the woman's statement. "Has Freddie emailed or called then?"

The girl made a downturned line with her lips and checked her screen. She clicked the mouse a few times before looking back at Palmer, the young woman matching the seriousness in her eyes.

"No. He hasn't yet. Why? Is something the matter?"

Palmer didn't know where to start. She floundered, open mouthed, thinking of her niece and the man she'd seen run the memorial service for a girl he had raped and killed. It was awful. Almost too shocking to be put into words. Palmer didn't try. Instead, she wondered where she might try to find the man, her niece, or where either of them might be. A pale wooden door at the back of the office opened and a man in spectacles and grey cardigan walked out, brandishing a set of A4 papers.

"Emma, would you mind copying these for me? They're the handouts for tonight's Alpha. I'll need about twelve, if all they turn up."

The look on Emma's face made the man pause. His smile faltered and he looked at Palmer.

"I remember you," he said. "You were at the memorial service for Helen. The policewoman…"

"You're the pastor," said Palmer, but she was in little mood for small talk.

The look on Palmer's face must have discouraged him. The pastor's smile faded. "Is everything all right?"

"No," said Palmer. "No, I don't think it is. I need to find Freddie Halstead, and I need to find him now."

The pastor frowned.

"Why? Is Freddie in some kind of trouble?"

Palmer took a breath, stiffened her back and her mouth became a firm line.

"I need his address and contact details. How long has he worked here?"

The pastor's brow dipped over his eyes. He laid the documents down on top of the photocopier and put his hand to his chin.

"Three years, at least. I've known Freddie for longer than that. He's a recent convert, of course. But he's full of fire and passion for the Lord. That's why he's here."

Palmer nodded once, but her eyes drifted back to the woman behind the desk. Just like Helen Brimelow, the young woman knew how to put a fetching outfit together, and she seemed self-assured enough to not need to hide her figure for the church.

Freddie Halstead was a newcomer to the faith. That explained the tattoos. The church had come to save the lost, that was the story, was it not? Maybe Freddie Halstead had been lost before he had been saved. Lost to what, she wondered. And how deep had that conversion really been…

"Do you think he truly believes in what you do here?" said Palmer.

"Yes, of course," said the pastor, but Palmer noted a moment's hesitation in his voice. A fraction of a second, but enough to be heard.

"But?" said Palmer.

"No buts," he said. "I saw him in his early days. He was so keen to learn. He wanted a new start, he had so much love to give, a heart ready to serve but it was all locked up inside him, just waiting to come out. I never knew how quickly he'd rise, but he was always led by a burning urge to serve."

"So, this was a new start for him?" said Palmer. "What did he do before?"

"Anything and everything," said the receptionist. She spoke with confidence, her dark eyes meeting Palmer's as if there was more to say. "He worked in sales and in the stock market when he was younger, but he hated it. He's had tons of jobs. I even think he was even a trainee teacher, once. I don't think he ever stuck at any of them. I always got the impression each job stint lasted only a few years."

"A few years?" she said. A few years and then something happened, she thought.

The pastor looked unsettled. "There's really no reason to think that Freddie has done anything…" It was clear where the preacher was going, but when the man saw the look in Palmer's eyes his face paled. The man was unable to finish his sentence.

Palmer turned to the woman in the chair.

"You seem to know him pretty well. Did Freddie ever give you cause for concern?"

"Not really… I mean, he was so persistent, so passionate in the early days of his faith… I mean, he was pretty full on. But that was a good thing, wasn't it?"

The pastor nodded his agreement. But Palmer sensed there was more.

"Anything else? Anything that might have worried you about his… conduct?"

Palmer's eyes lingered on the secretary with a cool hint of suggestion. She hoped the pastor wouldn't notice. His spectacles were a little too rose tinted for Palmer's liking. Palmer saw the girl blush and knew she was onto something. The young woman brushed a loose lock of brown hair from her face and glanced away for a moment before she looked up, composed once more.

"I think he was still coming to terms with some aspects of the work here."

"Aspects?" said Palmer.

"It's not like a normal job, is it?" said the girl. She looked at the pastor as if she were about to say something which might have disturbed him.

"No, it's not," said the pastor "We have to deal with all kinds of things here that other jobs never throw at you. You couldn't begin to imagine. But then this isn't a job, is it, Emma? It's a calling."

The girl nodded.

"A calling that requires you to leave certain things behind?" said Palmer. "Do you think a forty-year-old man might have found that challenging?"

The girl met Palmer's eye and nodded carefully. She saw they had an understanding. Something had happened between them, maybe something minor, maybe a brief affair, but now was not the time or place to open a can of worms without good reason. One can was more than enough to be dealing with. Whatever had happened between them, Palmer gathered the young woman hadn't been entirely against it… if she had been, Freddie Halstead would surely have been forced to leave his post a long time ago, well before his standard three-year itch. Shame for everyone that he hadn't. A shame for Helen Brimelow. Shame for Aaliyah… Palmer stopped the thought in its tracks before it could paralyse her. With Halstead missing, she needed to be fleet of foot, ready to act. Most of all she needed to stay calm.

"His address then, please. And anywhere else he might be likely to go." She looked between the two of them. "Anywhere at all. This is very important."

Within a minute, Palmer had been given a couple of print-outs and another small list of Freddie's possible locations. Armed with the information, Palmer nodded her thanks to the receptionist and turned to make her way to the stairs and the exit below.

"Wait," said the secretary. "If Freddie turns up here, what do we say? What should we do?"

"Call me," said Palmer. She pulled a business card from her purse and handed it to the receptionist. "Call me, and don't say a word."

"That's a bit of a tall order, isn't it?" said the pastor.

Palmer gave the man a blank look. "If you must say anything, tell him we're doing follow-up inquiries with all the food bank managers. That's true enough. I had my first proper chat with Gordon this morning."

"He's a good man," said the pastor.

Palmer nodded. "I'd say he's the best you've got."

She turned for the stairs and jogged down towards the office door and the street.

Once the door had slammed behind her, the pastor looked at his secretary and raised his eyebrows.

"I think she's got Freddie wrong, don't you?"

The young secretary offered an affirmative noise, but her dark eyes misted over. She frowned in silence before the spell was broken by some sheets of paper landing on her keyboard.

"Those are for tonight, erm. Twelve copies, remember."

The pastor walked back to his office. He shut the door behind him, and the silence returned.

Twenty-four

Palmer saw Hogarth's text when she got into her car. Simon Drawton had been badly beaten and stabbed in the gut and Freddie Halstead was the one who'd done it. The crosshairs of the Brimelow case were converging over Halstead, but unbelievably, it was Simon Drawton who had got there first. When Palmer's old Corsa pulled up outside the vast grey stone Methodist church on the corner of two, once-proud Westcliff streets, she found Hogarth standing beside the old building, looking along a narrow strip of ground at its side. Palmer frowned, wondering what he was playing at. Hogarth gave her a wave, car keys still dangling from his hand. His Vauxhall Insignia was parked at an odd angle, left mounting the pavement outside the church's double yellow lines, and directly opposite was the big old house where the Halstead brothers lived. Palmer got out, smoothed her suit and looked at Hogarth. He looked wired, much as he often did when they were closing in on a suspect. Palmer hoped he would be the Hogarth she needed him to be. Not the moody, hungover man he'd been of late, but the man of keen insight and determination to get the case over the line. More importantly, she hoped he would help bring her niece home safe. Aaliyah was at risk. She didn't how she knew, but she still sensed it. Hogarth was directing her attention to a patch of blood on a grave, spilling out onto the paving stones near the church. It had dried onto the ground leaving a thin dark trace.
"See that?" he said.

"Blood," said Palmer.

"Has to be Drawton's. And there's more of it down there," he said, pointing to the line of gravel between the church wall and the hedge. "And some across the street. It disappears there, probably where he got into his car. I think he only just made it home."

"Will he live?"

Hogarth puffed his cheeks before he answered. "The paramedics couldn't say. Let's hope so."

Hogarth's sharp eyes looked across the street towards the old house swathed in overgrown hedges on all sides. It was the kind of house that belonged to another era. The roof of the property peeked just above the top of the unkempt hedges. It was a vast townhouse of reds and browns. The kind of place that should have kept a mad old woman in the attic. But by now the relic had been subdivided into smaller flats, its history all but gone.

"Drawton visited Freddie," said Hogarth.

"Twice?" said Palmer.

"The first time he came here, he suspected Halstead was Helen's killer. But when he came back, he found out the hard way."

"How did he work it out?"

Hogarth looked at Palmer, his words sticking in his throat as he saw the quiet panic behind Palmer's eyes.

"Same way we did," he said. "Because of the group therapy. He wanted to know more about Ollie Halstead, because of the things he said, because of his behaviour. When he met Freddie here last night, I think he recognised something even darker in him."

Palmer took a deep breath and shook her head.

"Hey, Sue," said Hogarth. "I know she's not been in contact all day but that's hardly unusual, is it? And she's been to the food bank – what? – twice? Freddie Halstead worked in the same place as Helen Brimelow for months before he killed her. They got very close for that to happen. Your niece has only just met the man."

"I don't think he gets close to people… you don't get close to someone and kill them."

Hogarth shrugged. "We don't know how his mind works. Don't start drawing conclusions yet, Sue. Not about your niece. Keep calm and save it for when you give her a rollicking tonight. She'll deserve it."

Palmer tried for a smile.

"But what was Drawton doing here in the first place?" said Palmer. Her eyes drifted to the big house. The address from Halstead's employee file.

Hogarth shrugged. "Who knows? He's undergoing all kinds of therapy and other commitments, probably as a trade-off for the favours the brass and his bigwig friends did for him. Either the therapy started working and he felt guilty and needed to make amends…"

"Or…?" said Palmer, meeting his eye.

"Or, he lied through his teeth and recognised what he really came here for. Kindred spirits, remember? Maybe he came here looking for one and instead found two. Shame for him one of them was on a very short fuse."

"Shame," said Palmer.

"I don't believe Drawton knows anything about guilt or remorse. He tried to tell me he did, back when he was drowning in his own blood. By then I had the feeling he wasn't talking to me, but the man upstairs. Making his plea bargain."

"You'd never believe him no matter what he said," said Palmer.

"I can't disagree there. But from this point on, we need him. Let's get on with it. If we're lucky, Halstead will be holed up there biting his fingernails."

They crossed the street and dove between the two high hedges on either side of the non-existent gate. The front garden should have been spacious but was enclosed on all sides by more overgrown greenery, including the lawn. They were halfway down the path when a thin grey cat emerged from one of the borders, its tail in the air like a question mark, its blue eyes already settled on Hogarth as it approached. Hogarth had been set to ignore the thing, but it moved towards him anyway, blocking his way until it weaved between his legs, curling its tail by his knee.

"Bloody things always seem to go for me," said Hogarth. Palmer nodded, her troubled gaze landing on the cat's rigid back. At the base of the cat's tail, she saw a raw pink wound where the fur had been scraped away. She looked closer and strained her eyes.

"Forget it," said Hogarth. "It's been in a fight."

"No," said Palmer. "That's not a scratch. That's a burn. Someone's hurt that cat on purpose."

Hogarth narrowed his eyes at her then dragged his leg away from the cat and set off for the house. Palmer followed.

They found a brown plastic rectangle of intercom buzzers mounted by the big, battered door. Hogarth eyed the numbers, but he saw the door had been left ajar. He pushed it open and peered into a dim, empty hallway which rose high towards a distant ceiling. The first flight of the staircase was on his right. A bicycle leaned against the railings, chained to them. The door had nudged an unsightly stack of junk mail, leaflets, and blank envelopes aside, along with some free newspapers.

"First floor," said Hogarth. The place smelt, but it certainly wasn't as bad as Robbins' flat. The odours were of old food, full bins, and the essence of the big house itself, at least a century old. TV noise, music, and subdued chatter filled the air, but it was all low-volume, filtered by the doors and walls of the flats. The wide stairs creaked underfoot, but the place was alive with noise. There was a stained glass window in the wall halfway up the staircase, something left behind from a previous era, meaningless scrolls and sunlit hills. At the first floor, Hogarth eyed Halstead's door – number four – then he looked back at Palmer. She nodded, her breath held vicelike in her lungs.

They knocked on the door. The white gloss paint had turned yellow with age. There was no knocker, just a Yale lock and a fisheye lens embedded in the wood. Hogarth pressed his ear to the door and heard something like a cartoon explosion, followed by another, then some hammy dialogue in an American accent.

"Sounds like he's watching something. Got the volume too loud," said Hogarth.

A strange cartoon-like noise followed. Electronic, cascading. Palmer shook her head. "Sounds more like a video game to me."

"One more knock," said Hogarth. He thumped the door and waited, but no one came. No one even moved.

"Hard to tell if anyone's in there," said Palmer.

"Someone is," said Hogarth.

His eyes narrowed and his mean thin mouth took on a hint of a smile. "Stand back," he said. Palmer did as he asked.

Hogarth moved back and aimed his shoulder at the edge of the door frame. This old gloss door looked nothing like the one on Drawton's house. Hogarth threw his shoulder at the wood and it gave in one sharp crack. The door flew open, smashed back on the wall and Hogarth charged inside. He was forced to put his hands out to stop him from hitting the wall opposite. Hogarth looked into a tiny doorless kitchen, once white, but now grimy with age. He saw a calendar on the fridge loaded with dates marked 'Refuge'. The front door had shuddered back to halfway, blocking half the flat from view as it almost touched the narrow hallway wall. Hogarth's eyes were drawn into the room on his right. Hogarth found himself looking into a large gold and terracotta wallpapered front room. In the centre was Ollie Halstead, looking up from his seat on the sofa, game controller hanging from his hands. The man's mouth was open, his serious eyes temporarily stunned. On the giant TV screen, a bare-chested warrior waited for instruction, his knees bouncing, back arched, and ready for action. Hogarth looked at the torn food wrappers on the floor; the spilt fizzy drinks. Halstead blinked at them both before he turned away.
"You're disturbing me," he said.
Hogarth straightened his back and shook his head.
"Tut, tut," said Hogarth. "Bad old us."
Palmer walked inside and closed the door as best she could. She left Hogarth in the front room and turned towards the previously obscured parts of the flat. She passed a small bathroom and looked inside. The fittings were cheap and old fashioned. There were two other doors dead ahead. Palmer pushed one open, and the smell of stale man-air came at her as thick as a wall.
"Don't you go in there, that's my room."

Palmer didn't protest. She walked on. She opened the door to Freddie Halstead's bedroom and found a plain room with a double bed. Bar a few dubious posters, there wasn't much in it. She saw a Jansport rucksack dumped on one side, several spare pairs of Converse pumps in different colours, and a pair of cherry-red Dr Martens boots. Palmer looked around, desperate to find something. She did a three-sixty of the room. Trendy winter coats hung on one wall. On another, were posters. She took a look. Each was a poster of a scantily clad girl with a big chest and tattoos on their bodies. Palmer winced as she noted that both women had colour-tinted hair. One of them had hair the exact same colour as her niece. Above the bed, almost directly opposite the girly posters, was a single crucifix mounted in the centre of the wall. It was black and silver and could have been chosen for its ornate value as much as its faith value.
She heard Hogarth padding down the short corridor. "Crucifix on one wall, naked girls on the other," said Hogarth. "Looks like ideal church vicar material to me, though I don't think everyone would agree." He walked directly to the man's wardrobe and threw it open. There were few clothes in it, mostly T-shirts and jeans with little promise. Next, he tore the duvet away from the bed and tossed it to the floor as a statement of intent. They needed to find every secret the man had kept hidden. Hogarth pulled open the drawers of the chest and tipped them out on the bed. He prodded the socks and boxers away until he found few things of note. An old unused wallet, empty but for a National Insurance card. At the bottom of the drawer, he found a photograph of a brunette girl in a smart little dress. She was smiling and making goo-goo eyes at the camera. The

girl was sitting under one of Southend's unlikely palm trees, down on the seafront. Besides the photograph were a couple of folded notes written in two very different female hands. The notes looked old, their folds well-established.

"Palmer, take a look at these will you?" he said.

Palmer joined Hogarth by the double bed. She was about to tease one of the folded notes open with her fingernail when she saw the photograph.

"Hang on. That's Emma, the church secretary," said Palmer. "She looks a couple of years older these days, certainly older than she is here."

"Looks like our Freddie likes to keep mementos. I'll keep looking."

Hogarth flipped the note and opened it, taking a risk of leaving prints.

"Love Sharon," said Hogarth. "Sharon?"

Palmer shook her head. Palmer abandoned the first note and picked up the second. He was less careful this time. He peeled it open and looked for the name.

"Another one. This is from a girl called Lauren."

Palmer shook her head. "The one in the picture is called Emma."

"Three of them, eh? Three keepsakes from three different fancy ladies. Still, they're no good to us."

Hogarth scanned the note. "Bit Barbara Cartland, lots of heat and light but no final pay-off. Doesn't look to me like he scored with any of them… Could leave a man very frustrated, that…"

"As if that's an excuse for anything," snapped Palmer.

Hogarth dropped the note. "It's no excuse. Not unless you're a man like Simon Drawton."

Palmer studied the photograph of the girl from the church office. Her eyes were on the person taking the shot, not on the camera lens. And the look in her eyes was keen. Yes, there had been something going on there… at least a hint of attraction. Something had happened between them, maybe not much, but something. Funny… The girl had seemed far too sensible for that. But desire did things to people, no matter how sensible they were.

"I don't think he got anywhere with the secretary either," said Palmer. "Not the way she tells it."

"No. But… based on these notes… and from the way she's looking at that camera, I'd say they probably got very close to it."

Palmer nodded. "We think they all refused him then?"

"Ultimately, I'd say so. These letters look more like near misses than anything else… sounds like the church secretary was another. Sounds like Freddie Halstead has been hitting brick walls wherever he looks. Add to that the obvious chronic 'issues' in the family, and maybe he's always been a disaster in waiting."

"We don't know that his brother's issues are in the family," said Palmer.

"Not hard to make the leap though, is it? After what he's done to Drawton? There's more than something in the water in this place."

Hogarth eyed the bed. He groaned with effort and bent double to look beneath it. In the dingy gap beneath, he saw a mess of discarded socks, screwed-up boxer shorts, and a fancy old sweet tin, the giant kind which Hogarth's nan used to send him for Christmas. There was plenty of dust around too. The carpet under the bed was thick with it, but Hogarth noticed something else. There was no dust on the sweet tin, or around it. And there was a dust-free scrape mark in front of it. Hogarth knelt and thrust an arm under the bed, straining and stretching as far as he could until he managed to tease the tin closer and slid it free.

"I think we've got something here," said Hogarth with a hint of excitement. He used his fingernails to prise the lid off. When the lid popped away. Hogarth saw a single porn magazine, with some other folded notes tucked beneath.

"Halstead has a thing for girls with tattoos," said Hogarth.

"And dyed hair," said Palmer, ruefully.

Hogarth picked up the magazine by the furthest corner, delicately hoisting it between finger and thumb. He tossed it onto the bed. The thinnest, smallest corner of white paper was left poking from between the pages, but neither of them saw it. Their attention was already on the two handwritten notes beneath. Hogarth took both and handed one to Palmer. He began to peel the second open, handling the thing like it was toxic.

"Don't much fancy this," said Palmer, handling her note much the same as Hogarth. But she already recognised the handwriting. It was the same as the one in the drawer. It was another note from Sharon.

"I keep telling myself to buy some hand gel," said Hogarth. Hogarth pulled the note open and laid it out on the bed. The writing was scrappy, slanted, and with plenty of clunky gaps between the paragraphs. It looked hastily written. There was a heading at the top, underlined as if the content was going to be important. The writing certainly belonged to a man. Almost certainly Halstead himself. Hogarth scanned the sheet.

The sheet was titled: *Phone Call From Helen.* There was no date. Just the heading and the writing. Hogarth read the short blunt paragraphs detailing lurid promises of flesh on flesh and various carnal delights which Hogarth had no time for. But he was interested to read that Helen Brimelow had been the one making the promises – if the note was a true account of a real call. But there was no account of Freddie's replies. Hogarth wrinkled his nose.

"What do you think?" he asked.

Palmer laid the note from Sharon aside and read the phone call transcript.

"Halstead wrote this?"

Hogarth nodded. "There's no way of telling if that call ever took place, or whether it's just a warped sexual fantasy. But seeing as he's kept it with his dirty mag, I'd say he's pretty fond of it."

Palmer made a face.

"And the other note there?" he asked.

"More of the same," said Palmer. "More hot promises from the woman called Sharon. Flirting and kisses. A little more heated than the previous note, but still nothing too sordid. I'd say they were pretty keen on each other though."

"But no sign that they were having sex?" said Hogarth. "This Christian lot make playing hard to get into an art form."

"Is the lack of sex important?"

"It would be to him. And maybe to us, depending on how sex-starved he seems. This is a forty-year-old man we're talking about. He's got posters on his walls like a horny schoolboy, he's keeping a porn magazine under his bed, love letters from the closest thing he's had to a girlfriend. This isn't a normal person, Sue. He might have seemed normal enough in the food bank. He puts on a good front. Either he's had an affair with one of these women and he's had an outlet for all this – which means he's broken the rules of his job. Or he's not had an outlet, and he can't handle it. Either way, he's not the man he presents himself to be. He's getting close to people he shouldn't touch. After what he did to Drawton, it feels like - we've had a time-bomb ticking right under our feet."

"I feel sorry for the rest of the people at the food bank," said Palmer. "They don't deserve any of this."

"No one did."

"But I've seen it at work a few times now. It's an odd place. But it moves you somehow."

"You're not going to buy one of those, are you?" said Hogarth nodding at the crucifix on the wall. Palmer rolled her eyes.

Hogarth's gaze fell back to the tattooed dream girls on the cover of the porno mag and his eyes widened when he saw the piece of paper sticking out from between the pages. He picked up the magazine, shook it by the spine and watched as a single rectangle of paper fluttered free. It was relatively small. Ten or twelve centimetres long by five or six wide. Hogarth turned the tiny white sheet over and his eyes flickered with shock. Palmer took a sharp intake of breath.

"Helen Brimelow!" said Palmer.

"She was such an innocent little girl… to those who knew her least," said Hogarth. "Including her father…"

"So it seems," said Palmer. "So, they got it on then? Her and Freddie?" Hogarth had picked up the photograph. He scanned the background details behind the girl's promiscuous pose. She stood in a room with walls painted pale pink. There was a fuchsia framed mirror in the background, and the curtains had a floral print.

"No, Sue. Look. This was taken at her home…"

Palmer eyed the background and nodded. "Yes, that looks like her bedroom alright."

"This gives a good bit of credence to Freddie's telephone transcript... but, if this is all he's got to dwell on from their time together... A mucky selfie and a self-transcribed dirty phone call..."

Palmer ended his sentence for him.

"Then their flirting probably ended before it got much further."

"Yeah," said Hogarth. "Or else he'd have plenty more material than this."

"But it looks like he got closer to the act with Helen than the others."

"A hell of a lot closer," said Hogarth, scratching his temple. "Which must have made it all the more frustrating. Look at that image. The way she's looking down the camera. The girl is offering him everything on a plate, but assuming this ran true to form like the others... then sweet young Helen changed her mind... and instead, she ends up swooning over a local villain like Kevin Robbins instead of everyone's church hero. That must have been a hammer blow to Halstead's ego, not to mention his libido. If it's true, the girl went from an almost affair with the food bank leader, to jumping into bed with a council estate hard man. That's some taste in men, the girl had. But is it true? Is that why he killed her?"

Hogarth looked at Palmer.

She swallowed. "It's the clearest motive we've had yet."

"Yes. Yes it is, isn't it?"

Palmer frowned. "Maybe there's not so huge a difference between Robbins and Halstead."

Hogarth arched an eyebrow. He looked at the photograph one last time, shaking his head as he thought of David

Brimelow and how he'd take the news. The girl didn't deserve what had happened. Neither did her father.

"Go on," said Hogarth.

"I spoke to Gordon – one of the other managers at the Refuge. He said that Robbins wasn't nearly as hard as he made out. Gordon said although Robbins rarely frequented the place, Freddie still got to know him because of his community outreach work."

Hogarth arched an eyebrow. "Go on."

Palmer summarised what she had learned from Gordon. Hogarth narrowed his eyes, processing what Palmer had told him.

"Freddie Halstead visited the blocks for the outreach work… He got to know Kevin Robbins and talked to him about God, the life, the universe and everything. Robbins showed some interest, so they kept meeting. Presumably, because our local saint…" Hogarth eyed the posters of the tattooed girls before continuing, "was then doing the Lord's work, before he started batting for the devil. Poor old Robbins should have stayed curious at a distance. He might be still alive if he had."

"I don't know about that," said Palmer. "I think getting to know Helen may have been the thing which made him curious about the faith."

"We'll never know now, though, will we?" said Hogarth, narrowing his eyes. "That's why Robbins died though, isn't it? It's Helen. He got closer than Freddie ever could."

"Not just closer," said Palmer. "Helen and Robbins were genuine lovers. I think the thought must have tormented Freddie. Maybe Robbins even let it slip during one of their coffee and chat meetings. Seeing how desperate he was for these other women, if Helen Brimelow egged him on and then spurned him for someone like Robbins—"

"Someone that Halstead – for all his espoused holiness – might have seen as cheap and nasty and disposable?"
Palmer nodded. "Then it would have burned deep."
"After all these knockbacks, then to lose his prize right at the last, yes, I dare say it would…"
"It's still no excuse," said Palmer in a whisper.
"People like Halstead, people like Drawton… they've never needed an excuse."
"Drawton?" said Palmer. "If Halstead killed Helen Brimelow and Kevin Robbins, you'd have to say he's even worse."
Hogarth crumpled his chin. "To me, they're just shades of the same poison. Drawton would have got worse too, given time and opportunity. He won't get that with me. If he manages to live through this, I'll still be around to watch him."
Palmer picked the photograph of Emma the church secretary from the chest of drawers.
"Helen Brimelow… Gordon," said Palmer, "the whole church, in fact… Halstead's tarnished them all."
"No," said Hogarth. "The only thing he's tarnished is himself. The food bank will go on because people need it. And in this town, that will never ever change. I take it we think Halstead gave Robbins the heroin himself?"
"That makes sense, doesn't it?" said Palmer.
"But Robbins must have thought that odd."
"Odd, but still plausible from a man who sympathised with him, talked to him, encouraged him, believed in him. I'm sure a practised sermon-giver like Freddie Halstead would have found a way to explain the reason behind the gift. Perhaps as a final dance with the devil before he renounced old ways and stepped into the light?"

"Maybe," said Hogarth. His thoughtful grimace turned slowly to a sneer. "But we'll get the truth from the horse's mouth."

Hogarth walked back to the front room, where Ollie Halstead was still busy on his PlayStation. Hogarth peeled the control from the man's tight little mitts as the muscled barbarian on the screen charged at a squadron of sword-wielding goblins. This time, the game scenery had changed. The on-screen heroes were surrounded by an Aladdin-esque desert world. Ollie was glued to the screen as if he was a living part of the action. Hogarth walked towards the electrics and switched them off at the wall.

"Hey! That's the furthest I'd got."

"How tragic. I'm sorry. Where is he?" demanded Hogarth.

"Where's who?"

"You know who, Ollie. Your big brother, Freddie, the tattooed preacher."

Hogarth's eyes fell on the haul of shop-bought supplies spilling from the carrier bags at Ollie's feet. There was enough junk food to keep him going for days. Palmer saw it too. She turned away abruptly and headed back to the kitchen.

Palmer opened the fridge and saw packet after packet of plastic-wrapped sausage rolls, steak slices, pasties, and cheap filled sandwiches. She shook her head, slammed the fridge door and walked back into the front room.

"Where has he gone?" she demanded, her booming voice filling the room, taking them both by surprise.

"I don't know. He didn't say," said Ollie. He picked up a handful of crisps and began to eat, crunching noisily.

Hogarth picked up the rest of the bag and took them away.

"Simon Drawton came here, didn't he?"

Ollie carried on eating his crisps.

"You know who he is, I know you do. Did you see what your brother did to him?"

Ollie met his eye and crunched his crisps louder still. When he had swallowed the last of them he gave his answer.

"I didn't see him, but I knew he was here. I know his voice."

"They argued, did they? Maybe not the first night, but the second. Ollie, did you see what your brother did to him?"

Hogarth's nostrils flared. His lip curled.

He lowered his voice. "You know, don't you? Maybe you didn't see him, but you're smart. Conniving even. At the very least, you know Freddie hurt the man. He hurt him badly."

Ollie said nothing. He reached for another bag of crisps from the carrier bag. Hogarth kicked the whole bag away from his hand.

"Now you listen to me, you're going to tell us where he's gone because if you don't, I'm going to make sure the men in white coats lock you up and throw away the key. I'll call every criminal psychiatric specialist I know to make sure of it. You might not go to prison, Ollie, but I'll see to it that you lose your freedom. In those places life means life."

Hogarth watched Ollie suck the crisp flavouring from his fingers.

"He's my brother," said Ollie. "I promised I wouldn't say." His eyes settled on Palmer a moment before he turned away then he looked down at his feet. Neither of them could see his face but when Ollie spoke, it sounded as if he was smiling. "But I do know one thing," he said. He angled his head towards Palmer, but not enough to meet her eye. "I know he's going to break the rules again."

Hogarth and Palmer exchanged a glance. Hogarth narrowed his eyes, and Palmer's mouth fell open.

The room was so quiet that they could hear the sounds coming from the neighbours' apartments. The sash windows were both wide open. From outside, they heard the coo of a wood pigeon and the howl of a cat.

"Bloody cats," said Ollie. Hogarth noticed the man clenching his hands so tight his knuckles turned white. Hogarth grimaced.

"I mean it, Ollie," said Hogarth. "You're going away. For good." Hogarth put his phone to his ear. Palmer was already headed for the door.

"Sue. Wait!" We need this place secured, uniforms, crime scene the works."

"You heard what he said just now. You know what he means," she said. "I can't wait."

Hogarth looked at Ollie then Palmer. He ducked down to the skirting board and flicked on the electrics for the PlayStation, hoping the game was enough to keep him in place.

"Neither can I," said Hogarth. He jabbed a finger close to Ollie Halstead's face. "You just stay where you are and play your bloody games and eat your crisps." When he reached the door, he pointed back at him, and called, "And stay away from those cats." This time Ollie looked at him. Hogarth held his gaze for the merest moment before he turned away. As Hogarth moved out into the hall, Ollie Halstead picked up his video controller, with obvious relish.

"Thing is, where do we go next?" said Hogarth. "We can't waste time." His phone was pressed to his ear. His call was connected and he recognised the voice of PC Matthews at the other end.

"Don't worry," said Palmer. "I've already thought of that." She pulled out the sheets of paper from the church office and thrust them into Hogarth's hands.

Twenty-five

Halstead's employee profile had been bolstered by a hastily-typed set of notes provided by Emma, the church secretary. The employee profile stated that Halstead had worked at the church for just over three years – in a voluntary capacity at first – before being taken on in a permanent role for a mere ten hours per week at pay just above the minimum wage. Hogarth had given the information the briefest scan, but now the paperwork was back in Palmer's hands as he drove his Insignia, with the DS at his side. Hogarth glanced at Palmer as she scanned the sheets with a dedicated and serious eye. They were headed across town to the address of the agency that had co-funded Halstead's outreach job alongside the church. They had a few minutes to go before they arrived.
"What makes you think he'll be there?"
"Back when he first started, Halstead used to have two offices; the church office, and one at the Stepping Stones Community Group. Stepping Stones put up fifty per cent of the money for his salary. I suppose they'd make a claim to him as much as the church did."
"Not that anyone will want to claim a stake in him now."
"No," said Palmer. "Emma said that the Stepping Stones outfit had lost their funding since. Changes in grants, funding agendas and all that. The result is that their office has been left virtually empty since. The volunteer bureau owns the tenancy, but they're not using it."

"Leaving Freddie Halstead with keys to a nice empty space... but then why didn't he take Helen Brimelow there instead of the beach hut?"

"Because he wanted to get away with it," said Palmer. "Remember, he almost did, didn't he? The office isn't a dead cert, but it's got to be checked. It's not worth checking the beach huts, is it?"

Hogarth pursed his lips and shook his head. Halstead would never go back there, he was sure of it... and any new potential victim, at least anyone who knew of Helen Brimelow's fate would never have gone there with them. Not unless she was a stupid, willful little girl... like Palmer's niece. But that was very unlikely. Palmer's worries were in the ether, filling the entire car, and they were catching hold of him too. Hogarth wondered if their focus was going awry because of it.

"She'll be fine, Sue. Honest. This is what teenagers do. They mess you about and sulk about it when you tear a strip off them. And you know what? When she comes home, it'll all be your fault."

Palmer looked at him from the corner of her eyes.

"And you're an expert in teenagers now?"

"No, but I am a copper, and an expert in blaggers. I can tell what she's like already. Besides, I was no angel myself."

"Now that I can believe," said Palmer.

"I bet you were a good little girl. Let me guess, head prefect, and you tidied your room every night and ate all your greens because your mum said so."

"Something like that. Until I noticed boys."

"Bet you were no wild child though, were you?"

"Not quite."

They drove in silence for a moment as the car cut across a road which bridged over the rail tracks between Southend Central and Westcliff. They were getting close now.

"My point is, he's on the run after what he did to Drawton. And teenagers have chronically short attention spans. It says so in the papers. Your niece has probably moved on from the food bank and found some other dodgy way to pass her time. Making you suffer along the way is just an added bonus."

"You don't know that. You heard what Ollie Halstead said back there. He said Freddie is going to break the rules again. And the way he said it... Ollie must have known about some of the other women. He often volunteered at the food bank alongside Freddie. He would have seen some of those encounters up close. Damn it, he was even there the first time Aaliyah met Freddie, working behind the food counter."

"Was he?" said Hogarth.

"Yes. You were there too, remember."

Hogarth's eyes misted before he gave a nod. "The memorial."

Palmer shook her head. "Yes. I was there when they met. There were no obvious vibes between them, no obvious sexual chemistry. I saw them talking, that's all. They exchanged a few words. But Aaliyah's smart. She knows I would have picked up on any flirting... but she might have taken a liking to him then."

"You're her aunt, Sue. She would have blocked you out from all that stuff."

"So now you're trying to worry me?"

"No," said Hogarth. "I still think she'll be safe. For now, anyway. I was just agreeing. She's smart."

For now. Those two words drew Palmer's eyes to his face. Hogarth sounded far less certain than before and they both knew it.

"He's on the run, Palmer. He's got just one chance to get away from us. If he blows it on trying to score with another girl…"

"But he's burned every bridge he ever had. He attacked Drawton right around the corner from his own flat. He left the man for dead."

Hogarth fell silent.

"He killed Helen Brimelow out of nothing but lust. He raped her and then he killed her for it, in the most brutal way he could. The people who work with him, all of them, they've only known him for a few years. It's clear to me, from the pastor down, they never really knew him at all. But we do now, don't we?" said Palmer. "We saw who Freddie Halstead really was the day when we opened that beach hut door."

Hogarth clenched his jaw.

"Yes, we do. He only got away without suspicion because of his position. Don't worry. We'll have him before the day is out." But Palmer wasn't worried about Halstead getting away. Once the media caught hold of him, Freddie Halstead wasn't just going to be just a local story. There was every chance he would be a pariah on a national scale, global even. There was no chance of escape. But there was still a chance that he would cause much more harm before they caught him. Enough of a chance that Palmer couldn't rest for a second.

They arrived on a street lined with old-fashioned offices, set in smart stone and brick buildings, with an almost stately appearance. The train station lurked close by, hidden by the cutting and the high wall which kept it out of sight. The sound of trains and passenger announcements laced the air along with the caw of gulls from the nearby seafront. It took them a hurried moment to locate the building Stepping Stones had once occupied. In the end, the empty sandstone block above a narrow office window gave a hint: a clean imprint had been left on the stone where the signage had been removed. The Stepping Stones name was now a ghost captured on the masonry. The agency windows were dressed floor to ceiling with white slatted blinds. The place looked mostly dark inside, apart from one light left on at the back. Hogarth thumbed the buzzer by the door and stepped back to look through the glass beyond.

"Can't see anyone in there," he said.

"That light could just be a break-in deterrent," said Palmer. She looked at her watch, marking time in her head, still willing herself to be wrong, for her niece to return her call. She fought the urge to call her sister. What would she say to her anyway? *Aaliyah's been missing all day. I think a killer might have lured her away...* There was no value in that. None at all. But the weight of the thought bore down on her, growing heavier with each passing moment.

Hogarth pressed his face to the grimy glass and banged on the window. "Hang on... Somebody still uses the place," said Hogarth, eyeing a bright green cheese plant sat by a desk. The plant looked healthy. There was a desk calendar on the desk beside it. The kind mounted on a cardboard pyramid stand bearing some company logo. A corporate gift, or similar, like a business card on permanent show. Hogarth squinted and angled his head to get a look. Yes, the calendar even seemed to be set on the right month and year. Hogarth banged the glass harder still. Sure enough, a side door opened at the very back of the office. A bald man poked his head out of the door, his mouth a small inquisitive circle. Hogarth wasn't in the mood for delay. He pulled his ID from his pocket and pressed it to the glass, filling a gap in the blinds.

"Police!" Hogarth watched the man smack his lips and pull the rest of his corpulent body out of the office. The man gingerly weaved through the front desks, unlocked the door, and opened up. He was small and dressed in a tank top with a yellow button-down shirt underneath. He was a mulish looking type.

"We're looking for Freddie Halstead," said Hogarth. "We believe he has access to this office."

"Freddie?" said the man. He looked between them, already shaking his head. "Can't say I know anyone of that name.

"He used to work here. Part of the Stepping Stones lot."

"Oh, they're gone now. Long gone. I'm only here to stocktake what's been left behind by them and the others."

"And you're from?"

"Neil Vernon. I work at the volunteer bureau."

"And how often do you come here?" said Hogarth.

"Every day at present." He gave a shrug and a hint of a smile. "Truth be told, it's much quieter than the madhouse I normally work in. I can get some peace and quiet in here. Until we give up the tenancy, that is."

But Hogarth wasn't listening. He looked at Palmer and she gave him a nod. It was time to go. They had already learned everything they needed from the man.

"Thank you for your help, Mr Vernon."

By now Vernon was intrigued enough to lean his head out of the door after them.

"Is there a message – if this Freddie character turns up? Anything you want me to tell him?"
Hogarth unlocked his car and pulled the door open before he looked back.
"Don't worry, that's not going to happen, Mr Vernon."
Without further explanation, Hogarth gave a single nod, got into his car, and shut the door. The little man looked at Palmer, but her mawkish face was a closed book. She ignored Vernon's eyes and got into the passenger seat. The little man watched them as they carried on down the narrow street towards the bowling green and the well-preserved houses of the conservation area.
"Odd little chap," said Palmer.
"I wouldn't want to see what else he gets up to all alone in that office. Could be enough to give me even more nightmares." But Hogarth's attempt at levity missed the mark by a wide margin. He saw Palmer was still pursed-lipped, staring straight ahead through the windscreen.
"Where next?" said Hogarth.
Palmer scanned down the church secretary's list. "She's given me his mother's address. But that won't be it."
"No," said Hogarth. "Not unless he's going totally Norman Bates. Assuming he's on the run, alone, knowing we're after him... he's not going to take trouble like that back to his dear old mum's house."
"I don't think he's going to be alone either."
Instead of reassuring Palmer, Hogarth opted to pause for breath instead.
"Okay then. What's next on the list?"
"It's the last of the three," said Palmer, the strain showing in her voice.
"Which is?"

Palmer studied the notes, assessing as she read. She shook her head.

"Well?"

"The secretary said he sometimes went onto the pier when he was depressed or needed time to think or pray."

"When he was pining for someone, more like."

"She said he used to dabble with a fishing rod. Spent a few hours angling off the pier."

"He's definitely not going fishing today."

"No. And walking out there, a mile over the water, isolated and exposed like that. That's not running away, that's waiting for capture."

"He'd go there alone," said Hogarth.

Palmer gave him a questioning look.

"There's no coming back from this one," said Hogarth. "He'll know that. The only reason he'd go out on the pier is to top himself. He wouldn't go there with a prospective kill, especially not a sexual one."

"Why not?" said Palmer.

"On a bleak winter's day, maybe the pier would be isolated enough to consider. But look. It's not cold out, and the sun's breaking through. There will be other people around."

"But not many. There never are until summer."

"Not many, but enough. Trust me. If he goes there, he's going to end it all."

"So?"

"It means we can skip it because if he drowns himself, he'll have done us a favour. We'll drag him out afterwards. If he does that he solves our problems for us."

"Then you don't want to check?"

"You said it yourself. We can't afford to waste time. If Ollie's threat had any substance, then we have to concentrate on stopping the man from killing again. We rule out the pier until we get a witness report."

Palmer narrowed her eyes before she gave a nod of acceptance. The nod became more emphatic as she went on.

"Which means we'll have to pay a visit to his mum's house," said Hogarth. But he said it with a sigh and an air of resignation.

"But that doesn't work either," said Palmer. "Like you said, he won't take this trouble to his mother."

"Then where next? We've already exhausted what we know," said Hogarth. He slapped the steering wheel. "Maybe there are some other places connected to the food bank. Other buildings, warehouses, lock-ups…"

"And, if he goes to any of those, will he still be alone?"

"If he's intent on topping himself, probably."

There was an unspoken *if* in Hogarth's words. Palmer picked it up and ran with it.

"But if Ollie was right, there could well be someone with him. If he's going down anyway, does it matter where he takes his next victim?"

"Sue, what's important here is we find him."

"Then where do we start?"

"Back at the Refuge food bank?" said Hogarth. "Your mate Gordon. He's bound to know if there are any other work venues to try."

"Poor Gordon will be broken by this."

Hogarth jutted his chin. "A lot of people will be. That part is only just about to start."

He changed gears and pushed the Insignia faster, accelerating through a traffic light in the moment before it flashed to red.

"Nice car," said Aaliyah.

She looked at Freddie. He looked tired today. There were lines around his eyes that she'd never noticed before. But then she had only just met the man. Seeing him close up brought home the detail. He was handsome and well built. Just a bit older than she had imagined. His hairstyle, tattoos and clothes helped a lot. Besides, his age wasn't exactly a turn-off. Older men were fine, providing that they kept themselves in good order, and Freddie had certainly done that. Her eyes dropped from the lines in Halstead's profile to his muscular, tattooed neck, and the bulges of his biceps as he gripped the steering wheel. Freddie looked across at her, his eyes wide. A smile drifted across his face, showing his teeth. He looked keen. But his smile was also a little hard, like he was nervous. Him, nervous?! He spoke to whole gatherings of people, he ran church services, he worked on the frontline with drug dealers, gangsters, and hardened criminals. How could he be nervous because of spending time with her? A grown man? But, if he was nervous, she decided it was sweet. There was the slightest hint of sweat shining on his brow. He tapped his fingers on the wheel as he drove. Bounced his knee. Occasionally, he looked at her, his smile enigmatic.

"How did that happen?" she asked, eyeing the scuffs and grazes on the top of his knuckles.

"Oh… that's nothing. Must have scraped my hand while moving some food donations around at work. The job is always a lot more manual than you think it is."

Aaliyah nodded, impressed. She was young, but she'd had a job of sorts, helping on a market stall. But she'd never had to do much lifting. That was all done by the stall owner, Graham. She hadn't liked the job much and it had only lasted a few weeks. She tried to imagine everything Freddie had to do. All the responsibility on his shoulders. He was a proper man. *A catch*. To have someone like him even interested in her was amazing. He looked at her again and she saw it. A spark of lust in his eyes. It wasn't just in her imagination. It was real. He wanted her. A burst of excitement rose from her stomach and had her talking again. "I can't believe we're together like this," she said. It was thrilling, being on a secret journey with an older man. She had no idea where they were going, no idea where it might all end. Although, she had secret hopes… Her aunt was going to kill her when she got home, whenever that was. But she would never find out where she had gone, or who she had been with. That little secret would be hers and hers alone.

"You're a brave girl," said Freddie. Smiling, he reached out and rubbed her cheek with his thumb. Aaliyah leaned into his hand, thought of kissing his palm, but decided not to. She didn't want to make the wrong play too soon. It might have been a turn-off for him. She wasn't playing kids games now. This was for real. Every play had to count towards the bigger picture.

"Brave?" she said. "No. You're the brave one, working in that place, day in, day out."

"It's a job," he said, with a shrug.

"No. It's more than a job."

"Okay. It was a passion, at first. But after a while, it's still just a job. You get used to it. And you don't realise what you're giving up, until much later. But this is all new for you, isn't it?"

"What is?" said Aaliyah, a coquettish look in her eye.

"You know," he said.

She knew. She smiled.

"You're brave, especially after what happened to poor Helen. You were there at the memorial service, weren't you?"

Aaliyah frowned a little. Why bring that up now? Maybe his job had numbed him to such concerns. Because of its frequency death had lost some of its taboo.

"Yeah, I was there," she decided to say.

"A lot of our female volunteers stopped showing up after what happened. But you, you're made of stronger stuff."

"I just know what I want," she said, trying to sound sassy and older than her years.

"That's why I like you."

His words were enough to keep her smiling as they passed the seafront. Aaliyah watched the gentle waves and the far distant shore as she tried to think of something to say. Something cute. Something sexy. Just be yourself, she thought. Enjoy the journey. Enjoy his company. See where it leads.

"This *is* what you wanted, right?" said Freddie, her silence making him glance over.

"Of course, it is, silly. Or else I wouldn't be here."

"Just checking you hadn't changed your mind," he said.

"No," said Aaliyah, pursing her glossy lips.

"Good," said Halstead. "Because I hate it when that happens."

Aaliyah supposed he was joking with her, so she laughed, but the sound rang false to her own ears and she stopped. A hint of colour showed on her cheeks. She was embarrassed that she didn't understand his wit. Perhaps he would realise she was just pretending to be smart, that she was too immature to consider spending his time on. For a moment, Aaliyah felt the prickle of tears behind her eyes. But then his hand landed on her black tights covered knee and squeezed. She looked up and saw Freddie gazing at her, earnest and sincere. His eyes were intense. Full of passion.

"Don't worry, Aaliyah," he said softly. "You're doing fine. Just fine."

Freddie was a good man. Aaliyah laid her hand over his and squeezed tight. Yes, he really felt for her. And now she knew for sure, she had no reason to fear. She wondered about his job. What he would say to them about her... but thinking of her aunt, she knew exactly what he would do. When it was over, they would be the only ones to know. It would be their secret, theirs alone. Theirs forever.

They decided to call ahead to the food bank so Gordon would know they were coming. The building would still be busy, and they had no more time to waste. Hogarth was driving. Palmer sat in the passenger seat, phone pressed to her ear as she scanned the streets for signs of her niece up to no good. There had still been no message, no text. No word at all. When Gordon picked up, his voice brought her back to the present.

"Gordon speaking."

"Gordon, it's Detective Sergeant Palmer here. I need another word. It's urgent, I'm afraid."

The man's reply came slowly. He paused to shout an instruction at someone, and Palmer pulled the phone away from her ear.

"Got some lungs on him, hasn't he?" said Hogarth.

Palmer put the phone back to her ear to hear Gordon speaking – this time to her.

"Sure, no problem. What's the issue anyway?"

Palmer hesitated as she formulated her response. "It's Freddie Halstead. We've spoken with staff at your head office. He didn't show up at work today. We're concerned about him, Gordon. Have you got any other venues, warehouses, places of work he might go to?"

"Venues? Well, we've got two little workshops over on one of the industrial estates. We teach work skills there. And there's a storage unit over in Rochford. For excess donations... but he doesn't ever go there. That's more my job."

"We'll need all the addresses, and keys if you have them."

"I'm telling you, Freddie barely knows those places. This estate is his business. The stock units and the workshop are more my department."

"But he has access to them?" said Palmer. "And he's got keys?"

"Yes," said Gordon but he sounded confused. "But I mean it, he won't be there." The big man chuckled as he spoke and Palmer recognised the man's mild irritation. He was busy and they were adding to his burden.

"Fine... so where will he be, then?" said Palmer.

Hogarth looked around from the steering wheel. "We need to check no matter what he tells you. We need those keys."

Palmer nodded, but waited, listening as Gordon took a moment to think. Palmer pulled the phone away from her ear as he raised his voice again.

"Listen up, you lot! Has anyone seen Freddie on their travels this morning?"

Silence, so Gordon repeated himself. "Anyone? Has anyone seen Freddie?"

More silence. Hogarth looked at her, his eyes sharp, waiting. Palmer heard a distant, muffled reply the other end of the line and her heart started to beat a little quicker.

"Where?" said Gordon. There came another muffled response, too distant for Palmer to discern.

"You're sure about that? This is important."

This time she was able to make out a slightly clearer reply. "Yes. I know his car."

"You say he was with someone."

Palmer's eyes flared wide.

The other voice replied again. This time he was closer. Whoever he was, the man sounded disgruntled at being asked for any further detail, but his words were clear. "I don't know. Some girl or other. Probably one of your church lot."

"Hello," said Gordon as his loud voice came back on the line. "Turns out one of our lot saw him a little while ago. He was driving, and there was a young lady in the car. He thinks it could be one of the church team."

Palmer felt a sharp shot of adrenaline fill her body. She shifted in her seat and eyed Hogarth. He nodded. He was still listening in as best he could.

"When was this exactly?"

"Hold on," said Gordon. His voice lowered as he pulled the phone away.

"When did you see him?"

"Fifteen minutes ago," came the reply. "Maybe twenty. Something like that."

"Where?" said Gordon. Palmer nodded in approval.

"Heading down towards the seafront. Bombing it, he was. Like he was late for something. Or showing off."

Gordon stopped asking questions. Palmer felt him trying to process where his colleague had been going, and who might have been in the car with him.

"It's not like Freddie to bunk off work. There's got to be a reason for it. Have you tried the office? They're bound to know what's going on."

"But they don't, Gordon. They don't," said Palmer, edginess creeping into her voice. Hogarth shot her a look. Palmer understood. He didn't want to raise the alarm or reveal their hand ahead of time. If there was still a way of Halstead being alerted that they were onto him, it had to be prevented.

"He won't be at those warehouses or the office. Not if he's headed to the seafront. They're in the opposite direction, behind the town."

"I understand."

"What's going on?" said Gordon.

"We don't know yet, Gordon," said Palmer. "But as soon as we do, you'll be the first to know. One more thing. Can you get me a description of the girl in the car?"

Gordon pulled the phone away and conveyed the message to his witness. Since the last question, the witness had moved back out of audible range. Palmer strained to hear the faint, garbled response, but it was useless.

"He says she was young. Had straight dark hair."

"Was it coloured? Tinted or dyed?"

Gordon passed the question on. Hogarth grimaced at the wheel. Palmer watched his knuckles pale as his grip tightened.

"He doesn't know. Dark, is all he knows. Here – you don't think it was your niece, do you?"

Palmer was unable to answer. Hogarth offered to take the phone from her, but she managed to compose herself.

"I don't think so," she said.

"Don't worry," said Gordon. "If she's with him, she's in safe hands."

"Thanks, Gordon," said Palmer, her voice almost failing. "We'll need the name and number of that witness." Her heart was racing. Her mind flashed with an image of Aaliyah being driven somewhere, innocent, unknowing... just like Helen Brimelow.

"Yeah, sure, his name is—"

Palmer cut the call before Gordon had time to answer. She turned away and stared out of the window, avoiding Hogarth's eyes.

"I know, I said too much."

Hogarth kept his eyes on the road. "No. It doesn't matter."

"You think it does," she said.

"Not now, I don't. It'll be no use trying those warehouses, will it?" His question was rhetorical, his mind already made up. Hogarth pulled off the main road, heading towards the hospital end of Westcliff, and the leafy streets beyond. Palmer realised where he was headed. Freddie Halstead's mother's house was all they had left.

"Stop," said Palmer. She looked around and Hogarth met her eyes. She was close to tears, but there was something else there too. Something steely, angry, determined.

"Fine," said Hogarth. He turned away from the traffic, mounting a kerb, letting the cars behind him pour away towards the hospital and the A127 arterial road beyond.

"So, we know he's with someone," said Hogarth. "A girl. Which is just about the worst-case scenario. The pier is on the seafront, but we both know he's not going there. We should have questioned them all much harder than we did.

We interviewed the volunteers well enough, but those church leaders... we gave them an easy ride. The church gave us a blind spot. If we'd grilled them we'd surely have known about Halstead before. Weeks, we've wasted, just to get here... two dead bodies and the man's still at large."

"Take me back to the church office," said Palmer.

"But you've already been there."

"Yes. But that was before we saw that photograph."

"We haven't got the time for more interviews! He's on the run with another girl."

"But we haven't got any choice, have we?" said Palmer.

Hogarth wrinkled his nose, took a deep breath, and shook his head.

"No," said Hogarth. "I don't think we have."

He looked in the rear-view mirror, turned the steering wheel and performed an aggressive U-turn in front of the following traffic. He was now facing the wrong way on a one-way street. One car howled its horn at him, long and loud. Hogarth flicked a switch on the dash, and the blue lights hidden behind his Insignia grille began to flash. Immediately, the traffic made room without complaint. Hogarth stayed close to the kerb but hit the gas. At the nearest junction, Hogarth pulled out into the fast-flowing traffic heading towards the centre of town. He felt Palmer's nerves and tension at his side. Truth was, his own sense of foreboding was creeping ever higher. He'd made himself and others a few promises about this killer. If the bastard managed to kill again, he would have failed by every measure he had set himself. And if he managed to kill Palmer's niece, Hogarth knew it would be the end for both of them. The team would be finished. Palmer would be broken, and Hogarth suspected he would have to walk away from the force. It didn't bear thinking about. And yet, the thoughts wouldn't leave him. He put his foot down, and his speed crept past forty. Palmer knew he was speeding, but there was no complaint. They were running out of time, and Palmer was running out of hope…

Halstead's car pulled into a perfect space at the back of the single line of parked cars, tucked behind the very biggest vehicle he could find. His car was invisible behind the giant red Toyota Hilux. Aaliyah looked at him from the passenger seat, smiling. He glanced at her, smiling but saying nothing. He needed to check one thing before he could begin. Freddie opened the door, and got out of his car, and peered over the top of the Hilux's gleaming bonnet, down the entrance lane towards the busy road in the distance. The cars at the end passed quickly, following the winding road as it took them on their way. Just one was trundling down the access lane towards them. An old purple Micra. It indicated and turned into one of the empty spaces farther back. Halstead saw there was an old lady behind the wheel. No. He had nothing to worry about. They were all alone. At times like these, he thought, the freedom the job had given him was a blessing. He was a free agent. *Times like these*, he thought, realising this would be the last time of all. He took a sharp breath and took a moment to look up and around. The sky was crisp and blue. He heard the sound of a small aircraft growling somewhere overhead. Behind his car were the wide-open fields which trailed away to another distant wood. Much nearer, directly in front and on the left, was his destination – a broad expanse of quiet leafy woodland. The fields behind were deserted but for a few dog walkers. The single row of car parking spaces was virtually empty too. As things stood, everything looked even better than he could have hoped. He knew he deserved no such luck. He was no longer entitled to all the things he used to pray for. But he could still hear the voice of his Christian co-workers echoing in his head.

"If you make things happen yourself, that's you playing God. And that never works. You're doomed to fail. You need to wait for Him."

Playing God. Making things happen. Love. Sex. Death. He had made it all happen because he had endured enough. He had seen chance after chance at happiness pass him by. Was it any wonder he had grown impatient? Yes. He had played God more than once. *That never works,* said a voice. *And you're doomed because of it…* Yes, he knew that well enough. He knew the flipside of Godliness, and where it would take him. But there was no way out of it now… The door on the passenger side of his car opened and slammed. Freddie looked around to see Aaliyah's girlish smile and violet-tinted hair looking radiant in the afternoon sun. She leaned her chin on her arms like a fashion model posing for the camera.

"It's lovely here," she said. "I haven't been to a wood like this for years."

"Didn't your mum ever take you?"

"If she did, I don't remember it. Still, who cares? I've got you to take me, haven't I?"

Halstead felt his loins stir and a warmth tighten around his throat. She was pretty as a picture. She was too young for him, too sweet. But he still needed her.

"So, where are you going to take me?"

"On a nice little walk. Then we'll stop for a bit and take a rest together."

"Will we now?" said Aaliyah.

"Yeah. I know somewhere really nice. Somewhere special."

"Sounds lovely," she said.

"It'll be even more lovely with you there." Freddie watched her blush, saw her eyes widen, and enjoyed the sparkle of desire he saw reflecting his. Helen Brimelow had let him down. But this girl looked far more promising. She was still in the earliest stages, still wanted him, still thought he was a catch worth having. Maybe that was where he had gone wrong before. He should have acted earlier, taken them when they were keen, instead of wringing his hands about the rules and commandments. Did this one have to die? Did he have to make it worse? Freddie hadn't yet made up his mind.

He locked the car, walked around the other side and offered the girl his hand. She took it gladly, meshing her fingers through his. Slowly, swinging their joined hands, they walked along the lane towards the wooden visitor centre café and the woodland beyond. There was no hurry. This was the last one. He wanted to enjoy every moment. No one knew where he was. No one could stop him now.

Twenty-six

Hogarth had parked in the loading bay across the street from the church office, directly beside the NatWest bank. He left his hazard lights on in hope that the traffic wardens would leave his car alone. They stood in the upstairs church office, crowding around the secretary's desk. The young woman was seated and a choir of discordant female voices sang behind a nearby door on their left. They had seen a group of women through the small door on their way up the stairs. The women were singing a modern church song, and Jesus had already cropped up a few times in the lyrics. It was the only word Hogarth had recognised. There were three other desks in the office, each with its own computer, but it seemed only the secretary was at work today. Palmer eyed the door at the back where the pastor had emerged from on her previous visit.

"Those addresses didn't help then?" said the secretary. She gave Palmer a sheepish look before meeting Hogarth's weary eyes. She tried to offer them a smile as she stiffened in her chair. It was the kind of smile Palmer imagined Emma had used many times before in her line of work. When the girl's glance landed on Palmer's face again, she must have seen something of the ugly flood of emotions careening through her system, because her smile wavered.

"Has something happened?" she said.

"No," said Hogarth. "But it might."

The young woman's perma-smile fell away quickly. She turned to Palmer for elaboration.

"One of the volunteers at the Refuge saw Freddie driving away from town with a young female passenger about twenty-five minutes ago. He was headed for the seafront. It seems he was in a hurry."

The secretary's face flashed with concern.

"But I gave you a list of the places he likes to go to. And his mother's house, though he doesn't visit there much these days. He always said she let them down. They don't get on as well as they did."

Palmer opened her mouth and looked at Hogarth for permission. He nodded for her to proceed.

"We have grave concerns about Freddie. It's a matter of urgency that we track him down, the sooner the better."

The secretary's eyes flitted between Hogarth's and Palmer's faces. Her eyes widened. For a moment she blushed. In the next instant, her face turned pale, and she clasped her hands over her nose and mouth. She looked in shock.

"Is your boss in, Emma?" said Hogarth. "The pastor?"

The young lady started to rise from her seat. "Yes, he is. I'll get him for you."

Palmer raised her hand. "No. Not now, thanks. It's you we wanted to speak to. Just for a minute or two."

The girl looked between them again, her mouth hanging open. She nodded once, and slowly sank back to her seat.

"Is the pastor likely to disturb us?" said Palmer, eyeing the closed door.

"I don't think so. He's working on one of his talks at the moment."

Palmer nodded.

"Emma," said Palmer. "I'm going to have to ask some very personal questions. I don't have much choice in the matter.

And we need to find Freddie Halstead right away, so the more you can tell us the better. Do you understand?"

"I think so," she said.

"I need you to be honest. We need the truth."

"I understand. But surely he's not the one who—"

Hogarth cut in. "Now's not the time for speculation, miss. Please just answer the questions. Time is of the essence here."

"We visited Mr Halstead's flat today," said Palmer. "We searched his room and found some personal mementos. Among them was a photograph of you, taken a year or two back. It made us think you might have had a personal relationship with Freddie – outside of work."

Emma stared back at Palmer, her dark eyes steady and inscrutable. It took a moment before she answered.

"We became friends soon after he joined the staff here. Within a year or so, we were quite close, yes."

"How close, miss?" said Hogarth. She met his eye for a second before directing her answer to Palmer.

"We became close confidants, about work, staffing issues, and all that – then it became social, about music, faith, and the deeper things of life."

"Did you become intimate?" asked Palmer.

The young woman's face turned red as quickly as if Palmer had flicked a switch.

"We might have kissed once or twice… I suppose we talked about things going further, but… in the end, I decided against it. He was only a year into the job and I have a career here. Sex on the job isn't allowed, this is the church. Sex outside of marriage was out of the question."

"That was what he wanted?" said Palmer.

Emma paused before she gave a nod.

"You had to turn him down?"

"I value my job. It's more than a nine to five for me. It's a matter of faith."

"I get that, Emma. So you turned him down. How did he react?"

"It didn't go well for months after that. We eventually got back to speaking terms, I suppose. Became closer again, but nothing like before. I had to turn him down once more after a Christmas party. After that, he stopped asking."

"Thanks for being so honest. After that, did he ever say or do anything that disturbed you?"

The girl shrugged. "He was very pushy. But aren't all men pushy when it comes to sex?"

Palmer made no comment. "And afterwards?"

"He gave me the cold shoulder. It wasn't nice. And daggers across the office."

"How did you react?" said Hogarth.

"I thought he was being very immature. I thought it was beneath him. Certainly beneath our line of work. For a time, I even questioned his faith. I wondered if, being so new, it had been wise to recruit him after all." The girl looked down at her fancy shoes. "Maybe I should have discussed all this with my employer first, seeing as something's happened…"

"Forget about that for now," said Hogarth. "This is urgent."

Palmer sensed his words were for her as much as the secretary.

"The reason I'm asking about your relationship is because we're worried about where he's taking that girl. We tried the places you gave us before. Stepping Stones was a good one, but we drew a blank. The rest aren't likely, not if he's with company."

"No, probably not," said the secretary. "May I ask who he's with?"

"It's not relevant right now, miss," said Hogarth, firmly. "But you can still help us. Think. Can you name anywhere else he might have taken her? Anywhere at all?"

The girl shook her head, her eyes staring into the middle distance. "No. Not really. What happened between us was years ago."

"Please, Emma," said Palmer. "We're looking for somewhere he knows well. Somewhere private enough where he might take a girl for sex… somewhere he knows he would have access to at short notice, and at any time."

The girl looked suddenly upset. The bluntness of Palmer's words had hit home. "I can't believe it. I can't believe it's him. It is, isn't it? I feel sick…"

Hogarth shifted raised a hand.

"Miss… please focus. Can you think of anywhere at all where Freddie Halstead might take a girl?"

The secretary shrugged and shook her head.

"He has the keys to a few of the storage units. And the work skills workshop."

"We've considered all that," said Palmer. "He'd be at risk of getting caught there. We need somewhere where he'll feel comfortable getting intimate… somewhere he might feel able to make a getaway if he had to."

Emma looked at her. Palmer met her eye. "We know you two were close. You kissed. Those moments had to be private."

"Yes. It happened once in my house… my parents were away."

Palmer grimaced at the possibility but soon dismissed it. Aaliyah was dumb, but not dumb enough to take Halstead to her flat. Halstead already knew she was a police officer. Using her flat would have been inviting disaster.

"Somewhere else…" said Hogarth, rolling his finger at the young woman to speed her up.

"We kissed in his car."

"Where were you parked?"

"In the car park downstairs."

"That doesn't work," said Hogarth. "Somewhere else. Was there another time? Another place?"

"Yes. We went walking on the beach."

"No," said Palmer. "There must be somewhere else you can think of. Somewhere he might take her."

They watched as the young woman's cheeks turned a deep shade of red. She looked down at her hands and twisted a ring on her finger. Palmer saw her hands were shaking.

"A life is at stake. Whatever you can tell us will help."

The young woman nodded.

"The time we came closest to something happening… the closest to crossing that line… was when he took me to the woods. It was all his idea. He drove us there and we went for a nice walk. There was nowhere else for us to go, you see. I lived at home, he had his brother to think of. I was crazy to even think of doing it, but he'd been on at me for so long, and I liked him back then. So that's where we went. And I almost went through with it. Thankfully, I came to my senses just as he started getting heated. I realised I would have lost everything, my job, my faith, my self-confidence, my self-respect, all for just one crazy moment. So I stopped it all. I called it off and asked him to drive me home."

"Where was this?" said Hogarth, narrowing his eyes.

"Belfairs Woods. He seemed to know the wood very well. He said there was a comfortable, little copse not far from the beginning of the trail."

"Where exactly?" demanded Hogarth.

The girl met his eye, this time her gaze was cool and even. Hogarth thought she looked relieved.

"Not far from the visitor centre, right at the start."

Hogarth and Palmer exchanged glances.

"Thank you, miss," said Hogarth. "You might just have saved a girl's life."

The girl nodded and watched as Hogarth disappeared down the stairs. Palmer lingered for a moment more.

"Thank you," she said again. Something about the look on Palmer's face and the firmness of her voice struck the girl as meaningful. Palmer ran down the stairs, hurrying after Hogarth. As the exit door clicked into the lock, Emma's eyes filled with tears. She closed her eyes. Thinking of the unknown girl seated in Freddie's car, she started to pray.

Twenty-seven

Before they reached the woods, the air had been mild and pleasant. Now, beneath the canopy of trees, they were absorbed into a cool brown world of twisting branches with a root-strewn floor of hard mud, barely softened by the last of the recent rain. The cool beneath the trees made Aaliyah shiver. She wrapped her arms around herself and looked at the endless trees ahead. There seemed to be two or maybe three paths laid out before them. Not true paths, but trails. One was a fun route marked with sculptures and coloured signposts, designed to inspire children. The sign for the adventure trail lay dead ahead. In the near distance, a couple of women walking tail-wagging dogs had stopped for a chat in the middle of the trail. On the left-hand side was a narrow trail meandering off in a different direction, destination uncertain. On the right was a wide track with large trees bordering each side, some trunks hooped with faded white paint.
"This is the main path," said Freddie, nodding at the adventure trail and the dog walkers dead ahead. He looked across at her and saw the goose pimples on her neck, the slight discomfort written in her eyes. It was impossible not to note the beauty of her youth. And even better, he noticed the way the girl tried to orchestrate a smile every time he looked at her. He saw her willingness to please and felt a heady sense of excitement. He knew what was to come. Maybe he could now break the first taboo. He would let her know this was to be more than just a walk. He stepped closer

and slid an arm around her shoulders and pulled her close to his side.

"Hey," she said. "You can't do that, silly." But her words were silky and conspiratorial and she slid an uncertain arm around his back and stroked his spine.

"Why not?" he said, gazing into her eyes. He didn't try to hide his hunger for her.

"Because of your job."

"Does that mean you want me to stop?"

The girl looked at him, her face close. He saw where she had applied just a little too much make-up in the effort to appeal to him. He noted the keen, almost desperate look in her wide black pupils. Even through the material of her jacket, he could feel her heart beating faster.

She shook her head and kept her eyes on his.

"No, I don't."

Freddie smiled at her.

"Do you know why we came here, Aaliyah?" he said.

"No. Not really."

"Come on. Are you sure…? You don't have the slightest inkling?"

The girl blushed as he raised an eyebrow at her. Knowing he'd seen her embarrassment, she chuckled.

"Maybe… maybe I hope that…"

"Hope what?" he said.

"Hope that this is what it feels like," she said.

"What feels like?" he asked.

"When a man and a woman are about to… *you know*."

Halstead felt his own heart start to thud a little faster. He nodded.

"But, Freddie, what happens after?" she said. "What about your job?"

"You want to worry about that now?"

The girl shook her head and turned to face him. "No. I suppose I don't."

"I didn't think so," he replied. They turned to face one another and he put his arms around her. Aaliyah threaded her arms around his neck. She leaned up and kissed him as passionately as she could. There had been other kisses in her life, but not many had been good. Aaliyah wanted this to be the best she'd ever had. She invested in it – everything she had. When the kiss broke, she was red faced, her heated eyes glued to his. They leaned close together as they turned back onto the path, like new lovers, walking with her head against his chest, her arm around his back.

"Which way do we go?" said the girl, her voice almost cooing. "This path or the other?"

"Neither," said Freddie. "I know a special little place, just for us. Come on. Follow me."

Halstead turned them away from the main path, taking them through a hint of a path toward the left. It was a trail she hadn't even noticed until he'd taken it. Aaliyah looked down at the undergrowth. As she picked her way along, keeping close to Freddie, she saw the path wasn't clear. It was bordered on either side by thickening foliage. But there were signs that other feet had walked this way before. And as they moved on the sound of chatter and dogs barking grew quieter with every step. Instead, there was birdsong, the crunch of leaves and twigs beneath her feet, the sound of her breath, and the racing of her heart. Every sense seemed elevated. It was unbelievable. But here she was. She couldn't wait.

As Hogarth's Insignia pulled up outside the wooden building of the wildlife visitor centre, a man in a green polo shirt and grey workman's trousers appeared from the side of the building. There was a white safety helmet on his head and clear plastic goggles. A heavy-looking petrol strimmer hung from a strap over his shoulder.

"You can't park there, mate," said the man. "That's a loading only area."

Hogarth offered a smile which looked like a grimace. "Police business," he said, sharply.

The man stiffened and seemed about to restate his complaint, despite Hogarth's status. But Hogarth saw it coming and raised a hand to stay the man's tongue. "We're looking for a man and a young woman. We believe they might have arrived here half an hour ago, maybe longer. The man is middle-aged, but he styles himself younger. Bearded. Tattoos. Rockabilly hair."

The strimmer man was already shaking his head, but Hogarth continued. At his side, Palmer was already looking around, getting her bearings. The woods looked vast. On their right the trees stretched for untold acres, enveloping fields and a golf course, before they went onward, beyond the distant boundaries of Southend, into the edge of the neighbouring towns in Castle Point, some three or four miles away. The expanse was intimidating. The logical, cynical detective inside her head told her that they had no chance of finding Freddie Halstead before something happened. But it was a verdict every other part of her couldn't accept. She ground her teeth and wheeled around, using her hand like a sun visor over her eyes, staring back across the green and the golf course to another stretch of wood in the distance.

"Is she alright?" said the man with the strimmer, looking at Palmer.

Hogarth looked at Palmer. Palmer looked at the man, her thoughts only just returning to the present.

"I'd be a whole lot better if you answered the question," snapped Palmer. "Have you seen them? The couple – the young girl and the older man."

The man looked at the lines of stress on Palmer's face.

"No. I can't say I have. But then again, I've only been working around the play areas the last hour, cutting everything back."

Hogarth grimaced. Palmer shook her head and breezed past him, striding into the cool white and blue interior of the visitor centre.

"You still can't leave that car there," said the man "We have work vehicles turning, deliveries and all sorts."

"You stick to your job and we'll stick to ours," said Hogarth, one eye on Palmer's back as she strode deep into the interior, passing a gift shop area of wooden planters and bird boxes, as she headed towards a café at the back of the building. Hogarth followed her in. The place was a big open affair, the ceiling high above. The centre was filled with a din of child noise and chatter, knives and forks landing on plates, and the squawk and gurgle of a coffee machine. Hogarth saw Palmer talking animatedly to an older woman in a navy blue polo neck. The woman shook her head, but Palmer wasn't taking no for an answer. Hogarth arrived at her side to catch the end of her question.

"…she has a purple tint to her hair. Her hair is very straight. She's very young and very trendy. About five foot six…" But the woman shook her head again.

"No. I don't think I can help you. We've only had the mums and children in, and the older walkers. Not many either.

"You might remember the man," said Palmer. "He's dark haired, bearded, about five foot nine or ten, slicked-back hair, covered in tattoos, dresses young but he's aged about the forty mark."

"Doesn't ring any bells with me either, I'm afraid. Sorry, I can't be of any help."

Hogarth tapped Palmer on the arm. He spoke quietly, carefully. "We don't know if he's with your niece. You can't jump to any conclusions, or else we'll get duff information. We just need to find *him*. The church secretary could well have given us a false lead. Just because he brought *her* here, doesn't mean—"

Palmer gave Hogarth short shrift.

"He's here, I'm telling you," she said.

"What? How—?"

"While you were talking to the groundkeeper, I saw it."

"Saw what?"

"The same car I saw outside the Refuge. A sporty hatchback. It was parked there every time we visited, every time except today."

"Hatchback?" said Hogarth, not following.

Palmer nodded. "It's parked outside right now, at the nearest end of the parking bays. We didn't see it on the way in because it was parked behind a huge four by four."

"There are a lot of cars in this town, Sue."

"It's his," said Palmer. "I know it is. And Aaliyah is with him. She would have texted me by now, I know it."

Hogarth crumpled his chin but didn't express any of his doubts. The woman in the polo shirt had already moved on. She picked up a few empty plates from the tables and returned to the kitchen door by the service hatch. Once she was inside, Hogarth watched through the hatch as she said something about them. Palmer saw them looking and met their gazes.

"They wouldn't have come in here," said Hogarth. "We need to get into the woods. If they're in there, someone in there will have seen them."

Palmer nodded, but her eyes were on the kitchen door as it opened and a woman with a mop of curly brown hair and thick glasses looked her way.

"A man with a beard and tattoos, you say?" said the woman. "That's who you're looking for?"

"Yes," snapped Palmer.

The woman nodded. "I think I saw them a while back. I was taking some stuff out to the bins. I caught sight of them as they headed along the path, by the log piles. They had their backs to me. I thought they looked like a nice young couple."

"He had tattoos?" said Hogarth.

The woman nodded. "On his neck. His jacket must have covered the rest."

"You're sure about that?" said Hogarth.

"She's sure," said Palmer. "Which way did they go?"

"Along the main trail, directly into the woods. There's a trail with sculptures and signs. You can't miss it. That was at least half an hour ago. They could be halfway around by now."

The woman watched them as they exchanged a glance. "What is it anyway? What's happening?"

"We're not at liberty to say. Thanks for your help, madam," said Hogarth.

"One thing," said Palmer. "The girl. Did she have coloured hair?"

"The hair was dark. Brown, I think. Sorry."

Palmer nodded and moved away. The front entrance doors were a good way behind them now, but the back doors opened out onto a patio of wooden decking set with chrome bistro tables. A few were occupied by some well-wrapped walkers. Palmer marched back out into the sunshine, the breeze picking at her hair as she went. Hogarth narrowed his eyes and followed. He walked out into the bright day as Palmer stepped down off the patio and headed back for the paths and trails.

"Wait up!" said Hogarth.

"I knew it. It's Aaliyah. She's here. He's taken her with him," said Palmer. "I should never have let her anywhere near that place! I could have stopped her. I could have insisted that we didn't go to the service that night. That's when it happened. It must have."

"When what happened?"

"That she got talking to Freddie Halstead – when he started cracking onto her."

"Aaliyah is seventeen years old. You can't control a person that age – especially one like your niece. And she met Halstead before remember? She met him at the memorial."

"But it was busy then. They didn't have the chance to talk. Not properly. No, it must have happened after that…"

"Calm down. You need to focus. Theorising like this won't help anyone. You have no idea when they got friendly…"

They rounded a corner behind the café, passing a log pile, and found themselves walking along a path of crushed white cockleshells. Ahead of them was a painted sign set in a small grassy triangle, bordered by split logs. On the other side, a few walkers were coming back the other way, one or two slipping on their sunglasses as they emerged into the daylight.

Palmer stopped in her tracks. "Please, just stop," she said.

"Stop what?"

"Stop trying to reassure me. Please. I know, alright. I know when it happened. They could have only got close at that church talk. I took my eyes off her for five or ten minutes, while I was talking to Suitcase. The man's a predator. He saw his chance and he took it. I know it's her. Silly girl. She's probably enjoying the sense of danger. The risk. She'll think it's cool, won't she?!"

Hogarth looked at the state of Palmer. Whether she was right or wrong, it was going to do no good arguing with her. He gave her a firm nod.

"Either way, we've got to find him before we can stop him. If you're sure that was his car—"

"I'm sure," said Palmer.

"Then we need to call it in."

Palmer was walking again, and Hogarth moved after her, as they walked under the shade of the first trees.

"I'll call it in when I know she's safe. Until then, I'm not stopping for a thing."

Hogarth's nostrils flared. He strode after Palmer with renewed vigour, determined to follow her every step of the way.

The wildlife trail led them into a place where the tree trunks were set out like pillars in an old church. All around them, beyond the first pillars, were walls of densely packed tree trunks of all different varieties. Immediately before them was a space of dappled light on dry soil; a few walkers and the sound of barking dogs nearby.

The path was clear. There was an arrow sign pointing them dead ahead to where the trees closed in, but the trail was still wide enough for two whole families to have walked side by side. Another trail to the right looked wider still.

"Which way?" said Palmer. Immediately, her mind set to answering her own question. She looked left and right, not bothering to wait for Hogarth's answer.

"Not there," said Hogarth nodding to the right. "That's too big. Too public. The church secretary described somewhere secluded."

"A copse with a private space," said Palmer.

He could almost hear her fear as she spoke.

"That way leads back to the pitch and putt and the stables," she said, nodding to the broadest path on the right. "That's the bridleway."

"You know these woods?" said Hogarth, sounding hopeful.

"I knew them a lot better in my youth. That was well before this adventure trail was put in."

"Can't be that different, surely?"

"It's a forest, isn't it? Trees grow all the time. Everything changes constantly," said Palmer.

"But the old paths would have been kept, new signs or none," he said. "Unless you've got any objections, then let's keep going down this path."

"No," said Palmer. "They won't have followed the trail. There's far too many people for what he has in mind."

"But we need to start somewhere."

"She said it was near the house. There was a white house back there."

"There may be other houses further on," said Hogarth.

"Only the private ones that border the park. We can't get this wrong. We have to find her now!"

Hogarth eyed DS Palmer. He knew she was on the cusp of losing it. So far, she was holding it together, but only just. For a change, it seemed he would have to be the one to keep things on track. He toyed with the idea of phoning in for help. But if he delayed, he knew Palmer would stalk off on her own.

"Your call then. Where do we go?" he said.

Palmer bit her lip. She looked back towards the start of the trail, then nodded on towards the woods ahead. It was the same direction Hogarth had suggested – the trail – but he didn't say a word.

"This way then. But we need to look for a quieter path as soon as we can find one."

Hogarth nodded. "Fine. This way it is."

They walked deeper into the shade, and for the first time, Hogarth felt a pang of worry.

Halstead pushed aside the final branches until they were in the smallest of clearings. It was just as he'd last seen it, the place he'd found by chance the first time around, two years back. The place he had found for him and Emma. At the time it had seemed perfect, but the way things had ended that day had been anything but. The copse was semi-circular, almost eye-shaped, facing onto a high fence of upright logs. Just beyond the top of the logs was a big house, but every window was hidden from view by the fence and, so long as they were quiet, no one would know a thing. She would have to be quiet, right to the end. He knew how to make that happen but he didn't want to think about that. Not yet. Because first there was pleasure to be had. Especially since she hadn't been schooled with the same barriers to enjoyment as Sharon or Emma, or even Helen. He liked the girl and it seemed she liked him even more. What if he kept her instead of killing her? Was there a way? She was pretty and sweet as anything. There was so much trouble to come. He'd attacked Drawton, left him for dead so close to his home. In hindsight, it seemed rash, but silencing the man had bought him precious time. Time… time was tightening like a noose around his neck. All he could do was block it out, postpone the end as long as he could, making his final fantasy last. At least this time, it would be no fantasy. At the end, there would be a genuine consummation. As much as he had adored her, Helen had shown no love for him. Surprisingly, maybe this one would be the best of all.

Aaliyah found herself standing in the tiny, eye-shaped copse, edged with trees on one side, and a log fence on the other, and gazed up at the canopy. She spun around with glee. She looked at the firm mud and the mossy looking ground just beside the fence. The moss was spread out, soft, spongy, dry, and pale green. As far as these things went, it almost looked cosy. Aaliyah smiled.
"It's so pretty in here. And this place… it's like a den. So quiet and cosy."
Halstead nodded. His heart was thumping now. He was feeling nervous like he did when he was with Sharon during those first tender moments, like he had been around Emma when he brought her here. Like with Helen, on their last walk along the beach.
"This is our place now," he said. "Yours and mine."
"I like that." Her voice shook with nerves. She looked at him and he saw her shaking.
"Don't be scared," he said. "There's no need to be scared."
"I'm not scared," she lied. "I'm with you."

"Good. Because I want this to be perfect. A truly perfect memory. One that lasts a lifetime."

He walked towards her and slid his arms around her slender waist.

"Does that mean... you and me... here... now?"

"Would you like to?"

The girl blushed. He felt her heart racing in her chest. She chuckled.

"It's so open here. What if...?"

"No one comes here, Aaliyah. All we have to do is be quiet and this will be our special place forever."

He looked at her, waiting. Was she going to deny him at the last? Like Emma had? He stared a little too hard, and he saw a question in her eyes, but he quickly changed tack and smiled. His smile softened her eyes. The girl smiled back.

"Our *special* place?"

"Yeah. You want that?"

"Yes, I think so. But then... what happens next? Between us? See... there's you and your job to think of... and I'm just seventeen. I'll be in eighteen in four months, of course, but until then..."

Freddie blinked away his irritation. A voice in his head warned her not to ask too many questions. Warned her not to spoil it.

"Then it stays our secret, because it has to. Our special secret. Besides, the job doesn't matter anymore."

"Doesn't matter anymore?" said Aaliyah. She pulled back a little and looked into his eyes.

"But that's your life. You help all those people."

"Do I?" Freddie considered his words carefully. "Slip of the tongue, that's all. I mean that none of it matters compared to you."

The girl nodded, but she looked less than convinced. Warning bells rang faintly in his mind.

"I don't want to get in the way of your job. I don't want you to lose your job just because of me."

"But you do still want this?" he said, squeezing her hand, willing her to say yes.

She looked down at the mossy bed covering the ground then back at him.

"I think so," she said. "But I don't want to get used either, Freddie."

"Used?" said Freddie, frowning. "I don't think I've ever used anybody." Lies, now lies were his only recourse. The man he was once – that man would never have used anyone. Besides being a loving brother, he had become a humble servant, a man thirsty to make the best of what remained of his life after a misspent youth. That man had walked into the church office seeking an answer to every one of the problems that had dogged him all his days. For a year or more, he worked hard and with zeal. Back then he had been sure that he'd found the answer. But then the old Freddie had come back with a vengeance. Only the new rules he found himself constrained by had made everything worse. He found he had an insatiable lust for women, but his job, the faith, the rules, all of it had prevented every chance of fulfilling his desires.

"Not this time," he muttered.

"What?" said Aaliyah. "

Freddie looked at her, surprised he had spoken aloud.

"Nothing," he said.

The girl looked at him, desire still showing in her eyes, but now it was tempered by something else. A hint of doubt. Maybe he was causing it. But it couldn't happen. Not this

time. He couldn't allow it. The girl's voice started uncertainly. "If we... *you know*... do this... then I want us to be close afterwards. Very close. Even if it's just our secret."
"Close," he said, nodding. "As close as can be. I promise."
"That's what you want too?" she asked. "To be together?"
He laid a hand on her shoulder softly, squeezing gently. "What I want right now... is you."
The girl nodded, but she was scared too. It was thrilling... but almost too much. She'd come this far already... it was too late to go back, wasn't it? But who was this man anyway? He was attractive, yes, but he was so much older than her. Stop. It needed to stop. She had gone too far too fast. He was betraying his job for her – his God – if he believed in one. What else might he betray, if he could do that?
"Freddie," she said, laying her hand on his.
"It's okay," he whispered, nuzzling her ear. "It's okay." His hand slid from her shoulder and pulled the edge of her jacket down from her arm. Aaliyah let loose an involuntary gasp, and her eyes raked through the tree branches in search of the light, and prying eyes. Yes, it was too late. She had come too far. She had no defence against him. She would have to go through with it.

"Excuse me, sir," said Hogarth. He stood in front of a stick-thin dog walker, blocking his way, forcing him to engage. "Have you seen a young couple? Young girl at any rate. She has long dark hair, she's pretty and well dressed. She's walking around the woods with a man who has tattoos and a beard."
"Can't help you," said the man curtly, stepping around Hogarth.
"Wait. Did you see them or not?" Hogarth snapped.

The man looked at him, shocked by his tone, and shook his head. "I haven't seen anyone like that at all."
They let the man go. Hogarth watched Palmer as she picked her way at another possible path away from the edge of the adventure trail. Palmer shook her head and turned away, dismissing the gap as another misleading dead end.
"No good," said Hogarth. "None of this lot we've passed have seen them."
Fuelled by anguish, Palmer met his eyes with defiance. "But they are here somewhere. That's his car. The woman in the visitor centre saw him."
"But nobody else has. Are you sure about that car?"
Palmer looked hurt by the question. "I'm not deluded. I know that car, and if you hadn't tied yourself in knots about Simon Drawton for the last three weeks, you'd probably have noticed it too."
"Point taken," said Hogarth, frowning. "But I wasn't altogether wrong about Drawton, was I? There was a link. Drawton knew something was up with Ollie, and it led him to Freddie. There was a connection in the making."
"You were intent on making one anyway."
Hogarth let her have another free hit without responding. She needed to let off steam and he was a suitable target. But they still had to find Halstead before another disaster occurred. Hogarth rubbed the back of his neck and peered back down the path they had followed.
"It's okay. I agree," said Palmer, reading his thoughts. "They came off the path back near the start. That's where the house is. We should go back and take another look at the first of the ways off the main trail."

Hogarth nodded. "We'll ask a few people as we go. They may have finished whatever they came here for and left already."

But his words were hollow and he knew it. If Halstead had come here, it was for one thing only.

"We need to hurry," said Palmer. She marched back the way they had come, looking left and right with every step.

Two minutes of retraced steps passed before the first of the mini-trails opened on their right.

"They will always be on this side, wherever they've gone. The other way leads to the play parks, the golf club and the stables. This way leads to the house."

"You're sure?"

Palmer nodded. "If they wanted to go further over that side, there's a different car park. They'd have used that, instead.

"If you're sure, then we really need to call some help."

"No. I have to keep looking. I can't do anything else until I find her."

Hogarth nodded. "Then I'll call it in."

He pulled his mobile free while Palmer prodded her way into another possible trail.

"We should try this one," she said, looking him in the eye.

Hogarth saw Palmer was also trying to tell him something else.

"What?"

"There's another path further on. A possible way into the deeper woods right back at the start. We need to try them both, but—"

"But you're worried about something happening before we reach them."

Hogarth nodded.

"Fine. I'll take this one and see where it leads. I'm going to make one call, then I'll call you. We'll keep in contact the whole way. Just in case."

Palmer mumbled in agreement and gave him a passable look of thanks before she went on her way. Hogarth watched her, a grim sense of foreboding weighing in his chest as Palmer walked away. But she was a good copper. She'd gotten through plenty of scrapes both with him and without him… and though this one was certainly different, he had to trust her. Hogarth turned to the narrow gap in between the trees, spying the hint of a track Palmer had seen before him. But it didn't look promising. Hogarth pushed himself through the gap, a branch pulling at his hair and chafing his back.

"Should have bought a bloody machete," he mumbled. As soon as he was onto a wider path, he put his mobile to his ear and made the call to the station.

"Dawson. Just the man. DI Hogarth here. I'll need a couple of squad cars despatched to the visitor centre at Belfairs Woods, and make it pronto. Two of you to stay by the visitor centre, and two of you to follow the wildlife trail."

"Sir. What's going on?"

"No time to explain now," said Hogarth bending a branch out of his face. "Just get on it, and when you get to the woods, keep your ears open all the way."

Hogarth cut the call before Dawson could ask anything more. He ducked past another scraping branch, dialled the number for Palmer, and put the phone to his ear.

Not far away, Palmer was following a clearer path, her eyes glued to the hard brown soil. Her phone vibrated in her jacket pocket. She picked the phone free, saw Hogarth's name on the screen, and hit the green call-answer button as she walked. With her eyes still on the screen, the toe of her shoe caught on a tree root, and she stumbled forward. She managed to right herself at the last moment, but her phone fell from her hand. It landed on the hard soil and cartwheeled against a tree. The thud of the impact made Palmer wince. She bent down, picked up her phone and saw the screen wasn't just cracked – it was shattered. It was a lifeless black.

"Hello?" she said, trying to speak into the mouthpiece. But there was no answer. The phone was dead. There was no choice but to press on without it.

Ahead, she made out the roofline of a house just visible through the endless trees. She also heard a mumble of conversation, though she could tell little more than that. It could have been people from the distant house. It could have been Freddie Halstead. Heart thudding against her ribs, fear attacking her nervous system like a billion needles, Palmer pressed on, hoping for the best, while the cop in her could do nothing but expect the worst possible outcome. If that happened, she would leave the force. She would be finished. There was more faint noise ahead and to her right. It sounded like a mumbling, but she supposed it might have been a conversation, the words distorted by the innumerable leaves, branches and trunks. It was certainly a furtive kind of talking. Palmer wove between the trunks, stepping carefully now over the stretching roots, and as she got closer to the source of the chatter, she slowed and watched where she put her feet. Instinct kicked in. The instinct to hide and listen. But even though Palmer couldn't quite make out those voices yet – not clearly – she knew the tone well enough. They had spoken with Halstead before. And as for her niece, she would have known that voice anywhere. Except… she sounded different. Silken and honeyed… but laced with fear. Palmer's ears pricked, and the adrenaline already pumping through her veins flooded every part of her mind, body and soul.

"Did you hear that?" said Aaliyah.
"Hear what?" said Freddie. He brushed the hair away from her face and tucked it behind her ear, laying a soft kiss on her forehead. Her skin was cool to the touch. Her hands were on his waist, but limply, as if her mind was elsewhere.
"I heard something just now. A thud. And then a crunch. Someone could be coming."
"No. No one's coming, Aaliyah. This is our space. Yours and mine. And we don't have to leave until we want to. Not ever."
She looked at him, her smile wavering. Hoping her feelings were down to nothing but nerves, she gave him a crooked smile. "You're so sweet. I never had you down as a romantic. More of a rock'n'roll preacher."
"I can be so many things, Ali."
"I'm sure," she said, her voice small.
"Would you like to find out?"
They kissed again. But as his hands pressed over her figure, she pulled away and dabbed at her lips. She regained her poise and put her hand back on his hip. Dutifully.
"How does this work?" she said.
He chuckled. "Don't you already know?" he said, smiling. The girl blushed. "That's not what I meant. I meant with you… your religion…?"
Freddie narrowed his eyes. "First my job? Now my religion?" His mouth flickered with barely hidden irritation

but he worked to overcome it as best he could. But her words were familiar, like the words Sharon had used when their coffee meetings started to wither away. Like Emma had said that day in this very place, and just as Helen had flung his job in his face during their last walk on the beach… threw it in his face, even as she was screwing a junkie. In the end, everyone was a hypocrite…

"It doesn't matter," he said.

"Freddie, I'm only thinking of you," she said.

But the look in her eyes said she was thinking about a lot of things. The earlier heat was receding. He knew it. The passion had already faded from her touch. Maybe he could rekindle it with a kiss, reminding her why they had come this far. He tugged the rest of her jacket down from her shoulders and tossed it to the floor. Aaliyah's eyes followed it to where it fell – by the soft mossy carpet on the ground.

"We could lay there," he said. "It looks comfortable."

"I'm cold," said the girl, shivering. She rubbed her arms.

"Let me keep you warm then."

Her smile flickered but instantly fell away. "I'd like that. I think."

"So would I," said Freddie, "so very much…"

He kissed her and gently steered her towards the moss, and Aaliyah went where his hand directed. His other hand tweaked the shoulder strap of her vest, pulling it down from her shoulder.

"I want to, Freddie, but not like this," she said. "Please, Freddie. Let's just walk. We can do it later. Or another day. We can get a hotel room and a lovely warm bed, and we'll stay there all day and all night. I promise."

But the look in her eyes said the hotel visit would never happen. She was getting cold feet. Not again. It was torture, all these false promises, these false women, playing with him because he was supposed to be safe. Off limits and safe. Once, he used to play along. But now he was neither of those things. Today, he had finally torn himself free of every obligation. And after what he had done to Helen, Robbins, and Drawton, there was no way back. His sacred commitment had been blasted away in a moment of sin, worthy of nothing but the worst damnation. There was no way back for him. The faith might have said he could repent, but in the earthly world, he knew he would never be forgiven. He would pay the worst price. Didn't he deserve to taste the prize that went before it?

"It's just nerves, Aaliyah. That's all. But I saw the look in your eyes that night. I know what you want, darling, and I'm going to give it to you."

"Wait, Freddie, please. Not like this. I've changed my mind. Anywhere but here."

"Where then?"

"The hotel. Like I said."

"I gave up work for you today, Aaliyah. I risked getting the sack, just for you. You're saying this *now?*"

The young girl saw the anger flare in his eyes and reached for him. Freddie took hold of her wrist and looked at her small hand. He turned it over to look at her palm. She winced at the discomfort in her shoulder. Halstead traced a finger over her soft skin and smiled at her gently.

"I made a commitment to you by coming here. You made a commitment to me too. Nothing's going to get in the way of that now. Not this time."

Aaliyah frowned and looked into his eyes. "Not this time?"

Freddie said nothing. He squeezed her arm and his eyes sparked with sudden fire. He lunged towards her, pushing close until his face blotted out the light. He saw her open her mouth, saw the hideous fear in her eyes – like the fear he'd seen in Emma, and the final terror in Helen as she realised what was about to happen.

It was all happening again. So be it. He slapped a palm over the girl's mouth as the first squirm of a scream escaped her lips. Aaliyah's eyes rolled, blinked, turned wild, as he forced her down to the moss, tearing at the straps of her vest. "Shh!" he said. "You wanted this, remember…?"

They were garbled whispers, but the tone told her everything. First there was secrecy, intimacy. Then there was a muted chatter of discussion, perhaps an argument. It was happening, just as she'd feared. Palmer moved in, sliding between obstacles of branches and roots, avoiding every one of them until she caught her first glimpse of the man's back. She had to keep moving to see it, peering over one branch, and through a mesh of other branches. But she saw it. She recognised the curling wings tattooed around his neck. The curling emblems of smoke and fire. It was him, Freddie Halstead. She couldn't see Aaliyah. His body had hidden her from view but Palmer was able to make out a hint of her girlish fingers tucked around his waist. The horror of it all struck her hard, like a punch deep into the gut. This man was more than twice her age. He was muscular, and forceful. He was a true predator. And a killer to boot… Palmer felt sick with the knowledge, her senses swirling with rage and fear. Halstead's voice was quiet as he spoke but there was no mistaking the menace there, lurking beneath.

In front of Palmer's eyes, the couple broke apart. Something was happening. Palmer looked at the tangled branches all around her. She had come away from the path to try subterfuge, but the result was that every way forward was blocked by a wall of branches. They were probably passable. But before she managed it, Halstead would certainly know she was coming.

"I took risks for you. All you have to do is love me. That's all. Give me what you promised!"

His voice was hard now. He was getting angry. If he was armed, there was every chance he might hurt the girl before she even got there. Palmer turned her head and looked back. She needed to surprise him. But there was no time to find another route in. If she left Aaliyah now… No… it didn't bear thinking about. Palmer looked at the branches all around her, seeking the least-worst option. There had to be a way. Her eyes darted to Halstead's back. Her ears locked onto his every word.

Palmer took a deep, sharp breath. There was one possible way in, ahead and to her right. It was a bad option, but the only one. It would take her towards the side of them. Halstead would hear her, then he might see her coming, but there was no other choice.

There was a noise like a gasp and a stifled scream. Palmer's eyed widened and she started to move without thinking. She lunged forwards, branches scraping her face, tearing at her blouse, shredding her tights as she moved in.

"You wanted this, remember?!"

His words sounded like a death sentence. Even as the branches drew blood from her legs, there was no pain. Even as she battered her ankles across roots and low branches and stumps. Nothing. Just pure determination. Palmer gritted her teeth and put her hands out as she reached the final barrier – a flimsy group of tall saplings. She yanked them aside and thrust herself through into the smallest of clearings. The three of them were pressed between a high wooden fence, and the wall of trees stretching around behind them. Halstead stood up and away from his prey. His eyes wide, his mouth dropped open. He seemed surprised, and briefly afraid. But not for long. Palmer looked down at her niece. There were wild tears in her eyes, silent apologies pouring from her as their eyes connected. She was sorry. She was deeply ashamed. Palmer felt every bit of it. Palmer shook her head at Aaliyah, hoping the girl understood. None of this was her fault. In the final reckoning, Halstead was the guilty one – guilty on all counts. She looked at Halstead as his eyes moved beyond her, checking the wall of trees for other hidden threats. But aside from the usual forest noise, it seemed there were none.

"You bastard," said Palmer. "You sick, evil bastard. You're going to go down for a very long time for what you've done. To think you, a holy man, killed that poor girl…"

"What?" said Aaliyah. She started to scrabble away from Halstead, but he moved to block her way.

"You killed Helen Brimelow… we know you did. You killed Kevin Robbins because you were afraid he'd work out what you did to her. You gave him that heroin, Freddie. You knew it was too strong for him. Both murders were premeditated. And even after that, you stayed on in that job, pretending to grieve, eulogising, preaching, deceiving all those good people you work with, all the people who believe in that place and what it stands for. You took advantage of all of that and you used it as a shield."

"You're not my judge," sneered Halstead.

"But you will be judged, Freddie."

"No doubt about that," said Halstead. "Just not today. Not by you…"

Halstead's eyes flitted to the trees. He licked his lips, bared his teeth, and launched himself towards Palmer, swinging a punch at her face while trying to seize her by the jacket. "No… you don't!" she said, gritting her teeth and evading his striking hand. Allowing him to grab her, she used the momentum to hit him full in the face, as hard as she could. Her fist was shocked by the impact, but she felt a satisfying snap beneath her knuckles. Halstead's nose popped. His beard was instantly drenched with a flow of blood. He groaned and shoved Palmer to her knees. He lashed a kick in Palmer's direction to warn her off. She stumbled back and blocked the way to her niece.

"I'm sorry," Aaliyah whispered in Palmer's ear. "Sorry about everything."

"Don't be," said Palmer. She reached back and squeezed the girl's hand. Freddie Halstead blinked the pain away and shook his head.

"You've only made things worse." He drew the knife from his pocket and looked into Palmer's eyes.

"You're alone, aren't you?"

Palmer said nothing. She looked at the tip of his blade, knowing it was the one that almost cut Helen in two. Halstead seemed able to read her mind. He nodded and started to move in. They were pressed against the wooden fence now, kneeling together, as the man closed in. There was no way out. She had one hope left. Halstead's overconfidence. She hoped to exploit it with the only gambit she had left.

"Help! Over here, help!"

"Help?" said Halstead, pausing. "No one knows this place. This place is mine. No one's coming to help you here. If I were you, I'd learn to pray…"

Hogarth tried Palmer's phone for the seventh time. He had reached the end of his nominated rat run. It was a dead end of course. He'd spent near on ten minutes playing the king of the jungle, pushing branches aside, bending them out of the way only to have them thwack back into his face, as he navigated his way towards what turned out to be nothing more than a mud crevasse with a pathetic looking stream cutting through it. He lowered his phone and peered at the running water and the stones at the bottom, clean and shiny. There was not a fish in sight, just clear cold water. Not even a tiddler. For some reason he found himself reminded of Gerald Gilmot, but Gilmot was worth forgetting at the best of times, so Hogarth put the man out of his mind. Perhaps the water had reminded him, or maybe the frustration of having even more time wasted. Time was the one commodity that could never be replaced, and yet again here he was, spending his down empty rabbit holes. Beyond the waterway, there was a mesh fence and another section of the wood. Maybe it was a boundary thing – one council to the next. Either way, it was a dead end. He gritted his teeth and pressed the call button again. No joy. Palmer's phone was going direct to voicemail. He gave up and slid his phone away.

Get rid of Simmons, and Palmer suddenly decides to start imitating him. He knew why, of course. Her niece had proven a distraction for weeks. The Brimelow case was difficult enough without her being tested in the home department. Credit to her, Palmer had held up okay, all things considered. Hogarth tutted and started to weave his way back towards the main trail, dodging the odd twig that had connived to slap his face on the way in. Just as he was about to step out into the main path, he heard something. A squeak of panic. A snapping of branches. A shout. Hogarth was already moving before the sound came clear in his head. "Palmer..." he said. A shot of adrenaline kicked him into gear. He broke out onto the adventure trail, shoving by a hefty looking man with a little black pooch. The man was shocked and his dog didn't like it one bit. He yapped at Hogarth as he raced down the trail back towards the entrance. Hogarth's eyes raked across the trees, and he saw another crevasse in the mud, hidden only by a sprinkling of trees. He heard the water and looked over his shoulder to follow the curved waterway as it made to cross the path further ahead. A sign behind the nearby trees gave the waterway a name. Prittlewell Brook... *Really?* he thought. *His* brook... *his* late-night walk. It had followed him here, and it was miles away from the concrete version he was used to. He was still amazed. The place he visited to clear his mind for his unsolvable case had found him right here. He hoped it was significant, and yet he prayed it wasn't. Palmer had been calling for help, and there was no denying the utter panic in her voice. Hogarth pushed on as fast as he could until he found the first narrow gap which seemed to offer a path away from the woody clearing. Hogarth shook his head, not knowing if he'd already missed his turning, but another shout soon snapped him to his senses.

It was Palmer, but this time she was telling someone to stay back... Hogarth's eyes widened, and he plunged headlong into the narrow gap and broke into a run, as best he could.

The trees stung his face, body, arms and legs as he pushed on. But he didn't stop. He could not risk a wasted second.

"Stay back!" said Palmer.

Halstead shook his head. "Can't do that, sorry. I don't want to hurt you. In point of fact... I didn't want to hurt anybody. I wanted to serve people. I wanted to be part of what the Good Book talks about. Helping people. Doing the stuff. Seeing miracles in action. Being a true believer. But I never knew all the shite that went with it. The people stuff. The rules. The religious stuff. It was all so nice at first... all so happy. It was like being part of a commune. A kibbutz. There was much love and joy everywhere I looked. But in the end, people let you down. No one lives up to who they pretend to be."

Palmer was only half listening. Her eyes were on the blade in Halstead's hand but she'd also spotted a narrow gap in the trees. She thought about pushing her niece through the gap to save her life. But doing so would probably cost her a knife in the back. Most likely a deadly wound. It would have been a worthwhile gesture, the last gift of a life well lived in many respects. But surely, she had more to offer the world still. If she had to do it, she would. But for now, let the man talk – let him try and justify himself. Anything to buy her a few moments to find another way out. But he was spouting so many self-righteous lies that she could barely stand it. Palmer's anger was just too much to keep inside.

"You're not talking about your job, Freddie. *You're talking about you!* I've seen that place at work. I've seen it at its best. I've been there and seen and felt what it's like when people that I know as hardened criminals come in, drop their guard, and lighten up and act like nice people. They become human. Friendly even. No one was faking that, not when I was there. No one, except you."

"No! I poured my heart and soul into that place!"

"Like Gordon, you mean? No. I've seen your little notes. Your mementos from Sharon, Emma and Helen. Your work was only ever about you. Your self-image. What you wanted to be, how you wanted to be seen, what you could get from it! The others who work there, people like Gordon, they're the soul of the place, not you! You stole it from them! Because of you and what you did, the women on that estate walk around in fear! Because of you, people like Sharon stopped volunteering! Because of you, young Helen Brimelow, a girl who was just finding her way in the world, a good, sweet Christian girl—"

"There was nothing Christian about her. She was a slut!" The man jabbed the knife at her.

"A slut, why? Just because she wouldn't sleep with you? Because she saw something in a man you thought was below you? Is that why she had to die? Because she insulted your self image?"

Halstead opened his mouth to speak but said nothing. He was sweating now. His nose was misshapen, blood pouring through his moustache into his mouth, staining his teeth. He looked down at the point of his blade.

"Among all of those volunteers, among all that good work, you were the one true bad apple."

"That's just not true!" he said.

"Isn't it? Your legacy might yet close the place down. All because you're a selfish, jealous, evil man, drunk on lust. Was this what you wanted when you joined them? To help the cause, or bring them down?"

"I… I wanted to help."

"And? Have you helped them? Did you help Sharon? Or Helen, or Kevin? And what about Gordon who really does pour his heart and soul into the place every day? Tell me. What was your contribution, Freddie? Because from what I've seen, all you've brought is blood, and heartache, and poison…"

The man's eyes filled with tears. The knife wavered in his hand.

"You don't get to judge me. You don't! There's only one judge in this life."

"And when the time comes, what do you think he'll make of you?" said Palmer. She squeezed her niece's arm behind her back and tugged her gently towards the gap in the trees. It was a subtle gesture; she hoped her niece would understand.

"No," she murmured.

Palmer tugged again, insistently.

"The man upstairs? You know what he'll do," said Freddie, baring his teeth. "And so do I."

"And is that what you wanted, Freddie?" said Palmer. She met his eyes across the top of the knife.

Tears ran down his cheeks. "But this is the only way."

Palmer shook her head. "It's your way, Freddie. No one else's. It's yours."

Palmer stood up from her crouching position. She grabbed her niece by the shoulder and hurled her towards the gap. The girl staggered and fell through it, landing on her hands just beyond the first boundary of trees. She heard a crunch just behind her and turned her head in panic, then looked up. In front of her, she saw a grim, dark figure desperately sucking air into his heaving chest. Hogarth put a finger to his lips, but he saw the girl was too panicked to obey. Her eyes were wild.

"He's going to kill her! He's going to kill her!" she wailed, with a shaking voice.

He saw Halstead approaching Palmer, knife in hand. Palmer was backed against the log fence, just a few feet away. She was as good as dead unless he did something. He saw the girl's torn clothes. Her hair. He recognised her. It was Palmer's niece. She had been right the whole time, and he had been wrong. Having heard most of her accusations against the man, he knew she was right about them all. The man had desecrated something special. If not something holy, then something good, at least. And God knew the town needed something good. Not more darkness and poison. He saw only one way ahead. Taking a risk. So far, the man hadn't bothered to think about what the girl had been raving about. Probably writing her off as losing it. Good. Hogarth lifted a foot and stepped past Aaliyah into the outskirts of the small clearing. His feet clear of the roots, he knew he had one good chance. That was it. One. He took a breath.

"I'm going to kill you," said Halstead. "That was my life."

"But what about their lives?" said Palmer. "If that place closes, that will be on you. And what happens to your brother?"

Halstead shook his head. "I can't... I can't..."

Hogarth watched the blade waver up in the man's hand. The man was a proven killer. There was only one way it could end. *But not on my watch.* Hogarth lunged out of the dim light at the outer edge of the clearing. He charged, long arms stretched, fists out, hoping to parry the knife when it came, but mostly to charge the bastard out of Palmer's way. He caught a flashing glimpse of Halstead as he turned. Saw the knife flash his way. Hogarth lowered his head out of harm's way and smashed both fists into the man's torso, charging full on until he'd rugby-slammed the man against the bark of the furthest tree. There was a bone-crunching thud, and he looked up to see Halstead shocked and winded, a splatter of blood from his nose falling through the air.

"Get her out!" shouted Hogarth. "Get to safety!" he called as he glimpsed the knife coming at him from the side. Hogarth raised a blocking arm, to spare himself a knife in the face. The knife was blocked, and held up in the air, leaving Halstead exposed. Hogarth saw a fist coming at him from the right. He swatted it away and fixed on his opening. His chance to establish control. It was grim, but he took it. He slammed his forehead against Halstead's unguarded face, and the man cried out in pain. What was left of his nose had been hammered again. Immediately the knife dropped from his hand and fell to the soil. Hogarth felt the other man's blood on his forehead. He swept a kick at the knife, sending it sliding away across the ground. He let go of Halstead and the man slumped down against the tree. There was blood in Hogarth's hair, and on his face but for almost three weeks, the monster had hidden right in front of them, using faith as his mask and his shield. A little blood on his face was nothing.

Hogarth remembered Helen at the beach hut that awful morning. He remembered her body on the slab at the mortuary as Ed Quentin made yet another incision. He remembered her father, broken, tearful, and pining for suicide.

"You've ruined so many lives, Halstead. Prison's too good for you."

The man groaned. Hogarth slammed another angry punch into the man's gut before letting him crumple to the floor, coughing his guts up at the foot of the tree.

"But prison is what you'll get," said Hogarth. As he read the man his rights, the distant sound of sirens echoed through the trees. He held out a hand towards Palmer. She was crouched with her niece by the edge of the small clearing. She nodded and offered him the handcuffs. Hogarth met her eye and gave her a nod by way of an apology. It was his admission that Palmer had been right. Justice had been done. Justice of a kind, at any rate. The only kind available. But the damage had been so great, there was still no telling how things would end.

Epilogue

It took twenty-four hours before the blur of the Brimelow case reached any kind of calm. When it came, Hogarth seized it with both hands. First, DCI Melford had given them his usual thanks for capturing the killer, but his praise was almost as faint as it was quick. The inference being that he would have done a better job if he'd been the one on the street. Every mitigating circumstance had been deleted from Long Melford's memory. But Hogarth reckoned he knew the real reason for Melford's bad mood. The brass and the local council didn't like the fact that the killer had come from a church. The less devout amongst them would have been preening, but the police had always benefitted far more from the presence of the food bank than they had ever cared to admit. The council had long benefitted too, but both organisations loved to blame the food bank for trouble on the estate as and when it suited them. With the cruel spotlight of the red top press focused on the Refuge, there was a genuine fear that the place would fold, leaving a black hole only crime could fill. Whatever his problem, by the end of the meeting Melford seemed to remember his manners. He ended with a word of praise for each of them, but Hogarth refused the credit.

"Tracking Halstead like we did is due entirely to DS Palmer here, sir."

Melford didn't seem unwilling to believe him. *The grim old bastard.*

"Very good, then, DS Palmer. I'll see to it that your good work is remembered. Well done. Now you'll both need to make sure this case is absolutely watertight for the CPS. You can bet the defendant's solicitor will be making a great deal of the damage done to Freddie Halstead's face."

"But not enough to get him a grain of sympathy from any jury," said Hogarth. "The witness statements are good enough to damn him alone."

"Someone needs to start remembering how we do things here, Hogarth. One day, you'll cost us a conviction. And when that happens, don't think I'll be able to protect you."

No fear of that, thought Hogarth. Despite the favours he'd already done the neurotic DCI, Melford wasn't grateful for any of them. But so long as the arrests came and they were followed by successful prosecutions, Hogarth knew he was safe enough. For now, at least.

After Melford, they went where they often went at such times – to the bar across the street. The soulless place frequented by the staff from the local internet firms, the job-club staff, courthouse clerks, and all the other people Hogarth didn't want to associate with. They went because it was close, and it served what they needed. A drink to cheer another scalp. For a short while, they sat in comfortable silence. Hogarth looked at his beer and the whisky chaser waiting at its side. Palmer watched him studying them.

"This one got out of hand, didn't it?" he said, meeting her eye.

"Don't they always?"

"Not like this," he said, giving her a crooked smile. "At the woods, I should have been in the firing line, not you."

"It was my niece. What else could I have done?"

Hogarth nodded and picked up his pint. "I'm just saying, that's all. This one came far too close."

"I can't disagree with that," said Palmer, picking up her Archers and lemonade. She thought of Aaliyah terrified and shaking on the woodland floor and blinked the memory away. She sipped her drink and concentrated on the fizz.

"So, did I almost let Halstead slip past me because of Simon Drawton?" said Hogarth. "That's what you think, isn't it? That's what Melford thinks, clearly."

"Melford is worried because the brass are on at him about the estate. They're worried about an uptick in crime if the Refuge closes. As if they have to worry about it! We'll be the ones lumbered with it."

Hogarth flicked his eyebrows.

"But they're right. If it closes, the council had better shut the whole estate down like they've promised."

"I hope it stays. But from now on, that's a matter for media and politics."

Hogarth curled his lip at Palmer's pronouncement. She was right and he knew it.

"It's not your fault, you know," she said. "Neither what happened in the woods, nor him getting past us for so long. He was smart. He used latex gloves when he raped and killed poor Helen. The elements got rid of most traces, and he didn't leave any other evidence. He never ran. He never put a foot wrong until he blinked and gave Robbins those drugs. If he had kept his cool – if he'd never tried any crime again – this probably would have gone down as unsolved."

Hogarth shook his head. "You saw the notes. He was always building up to something. That kind never stop. He would have only got worse."

"Then no matter what Melford and the rest say behind closed doors, it's a good job that we got him."

Hogarth offered a grim smile. "I'll drink to that." And he did. "How is she?"

"Aaliyah? She's still shocked. Keeps apologising. Keeps crying. She knows she had a very near miss."

"What now for the girl?" he said, supping his beer.

"She's spoken to her mum. So have I. Not pleasant. I got it in the neck for a whole hour. It goes without saying that my sister never thanked me for saving her life. She's ordered the girl to go back home."

"But will she go…?" said Hogarth, cradling his beer while a bunch of lesser-spotted office numpties guffawed and slapped each other's backs at the bar.

"Yeah. She's going back tonight. She was packing her stuff when I left her today. She says she'll be safer in Rayleigh, but I think she's resigned to leaving because she feels she let me down."

"Which she did. Would you have her stay?"

"If she wanted to. For a while. But I can't say it won't be a relief to have my place back."

"I can imagine."

"But my sister and I… I think we've just crossed the Rubicon. A lot of things we said to each other can't be unsaid."

Hogarth nodded. "But what does Aaliyah say?"

"That I saved her life. I've seen another side of her since the woods, you know. She's got the potential to be a good young woman. Better than her mother, that's for sure."

"Then you did a good job, Sue. No matter what your sister said."

"Sounds like what I said about you and Melford."

"Yeah," said Hogarth. "Except I can't give Melford the cold shoulder for the rest of my life. I'll have to wait for retirement for that little blessing."

"At least Gerald Gilmot can't blame you for the murders anymore…"

"That's true," said Hogarth, thinking of the brook at the woods, and the brook at the end of his street. "I think I might skip my late-night walks for a bit, seeing as Gerald's moved in down there. He's harmless enough, but he's spoiled the therapeutic effect of a gentle stroll by the brook."

"I'm sure Andi will be pleased."

"She might be, at that," he said.

"You two getting on okay?" ventured Palmer.

"Oh, I don't know yet. The case almost finished things for us. She was supposed to come around last night, but well, the case turned, didn't it?"

"She'll forgive you for that. That's police work."

"She already has. She's coming around tonight."

"Pleased for you," said Palmer, but she didn't sound it.

"Don't be. I'm not sure if either of us are the long-term type."

"One of these days, you might surprise yourself," she said. But to Hogarth, she sounded unconvinced.

"That doesn't happen much," he said. He raised his pint glass. "To you, DS Palmer. To your niece, as well. And to all ungrateful bastards everywhere."

Palmer clinked her glass against his. "To the team," she said.

Hogarth sipped his beer. Uncanny. As they finished their toast, Hogarth's eyes drifted to the blind-slatted window, just as two PCSOs in their blue-striped helmets walked past on the way back to the station. The one nearest the window was none other than Ecrin Kaplan, the girl on the fast track to becoming a constable proper. Beside her was another young woman who arguably deserved promotion just as much, Bec Rawlins. But budgets being what they were, only one would

get the nod this year. Palmer followed his gaze and saw Kaplan just before she disappeared from view.
"You're right," said Palmer. "I think she'd do a good job with us."
"Then it's up to you to persuade Melford to let us have her. If I ask him, that would kibosh it for all concerned."
"Fair point," said Palmer. "I'll ask on my next visit."
"On your next snitching mission," said Hogarth, with a teasing smile. But Palmer frowned and shook her head.
"I've never done you a disservice."
"No, Palmer, I really don't think you have."

Soon after, they parted, each one desperate for a rest from the case which had eaten them from the inside out for almost three weeks. Palmer wasn't just shell shocked, she was emotional, too. Before Aaliyah's taxi came to take her to Rayleigh, the girl gave her aunt the biggest hug she had ever received from her in all her years.
"I'm sorry," said Aaliyah.
"I'm sorry for what's coming," said Palmer. There'll be a court case. We're hoping for a confession, but there's no sign of it yet. The court case will be hard, but I promise I'll be there."
Aaliyah nodded. "I'll do it. He has to go to prison for what he's done."
Palmer nodded, hoping for the best, saying nothing more. They hugged once more, and Aaliyah promised to stay in touch. For the first time, Palmer felt inclined to believe her.

Physically spent, exhausted in more ways than one, Hogarth rolled over in his bed. He clapped a hand over his forehead and sighed out loud.

"You're not gonna have a cardiac on me, are you?" said Andi. Hogarth was well into middle age, unfit, and tired as hell. He looked at the woman in bed beside him, irritated at her comment. But her broad smile soon made him see the funny side.

"Don't flatter yourself," he replied.

As their laughter faded, Hogarth's mobile buzzed by his bed. He tutted, frowned, and picked it up, squinting at the screen.

"You're not going out again, are you?" said Andi, sharply.

"No," he croaked. "I'm giving up late-night walks. See? If you stay here more often, I'll have found a different healthy habit."

Andi looked at him, raising her eyebrows.

"Was that an invitation?"

Hogarth narrowed his eyes before he realised what Andi meant. His words had been no more than an off the cuff joke, but there was no way to back out without offending the woman. Instead, he sat up and put the phone to his ear.

"DC Simmons?! What the devil would you want at this time of night?"

"It's not that late by your standards, guv," said the young man in an apologetic voice.

There was an awkward silence between them – water under the bridge – gone but not forgotten.

Simmons cleared his throat. "I just wanted to say congratulations, sir. On the collar today. It was a big one."

"Then you should congratulate DS Palmer," he replied. "That's who deserves it."

"Not the way she tells it. She says you nutted the scumbag into behaving himself."

"As if I'd do that?! Come on, Simmons, that's not how the modern police service operates these days."

Both men laughed. "That's all I wanted to say, guv. Just well done."

"Thank you, Simmons. And good luck over there. Remember, from now on, head down, nose clean, and don't trust any of the snakes on that team either. Don't become one of them."

"I'll try my best. Take care."

Hogarth hung up, and Andi nestled closer, lifting his arm and placing it around her shoulders. He saw she was still grinning from ear to ear.

"I will, if you want me to."

"Will what?"

"Move in," she said.

Hogarth kept his smile fixed in place. He said nothing. She kissed him again and rolled up on her elbow. She laid a hand on his chest and looked into his eyes.

"If we're going to be an item, I think I'd better road test that ticker of yours, hadn't I?"

Hogarth smiled. "Oh, If you insist, Andi… if you insist."

The next morning.

Simon Drawton sat up in his hospital bed. There was a cannular in his hand and a monitor by his bed. This morning the nurses had paid him far less heed than the day before. He supposed it was a good sign. He was out of the woods but trapped in a hospital bed, without a clue as to what had happened in the world outside since his ordeal. Some of the hospital beds had TVs set on a little metal arm, allowing them to swing towards the bed-bound patient. He looked back at the wall and saw he had one too, but they required a card payment to work and some assistance to get started. The few staff he saw were too busy to assist. Irksome, but he would have to wait his time like a good citizen. Which of course, he was. Especially now.

After lunch, Drawton's screen was still blank and he was more than bored. But when the ward doors opened, he finally saw a friendly face. If not friendly, then at least it was smiling. There was no way to know how much of the man's smile was real and how much was false because this man smiled by profession.

His visitor was dressed in an immaculate suit – no tie – as had been the style for a while now. Drawton thought a shirt without a tie vulgar, but he said nothing. The man was carrying a punnet of green grapes – did anyone in the entire history of hospital stays ever really want green grapes? A bottle of Lucozade and a bar of chocolate were held in the man's other arm. It was Green & Blacks, not the cheapo stuff the plebs enjoyed. Good man, thought Drawton.

"James?" he said, forcing a smile to match that of his visitor.

"Simon," replied James Hartigan MP. The MP put the grapes, Lucozade, and posh chocolate down on Drawton's bedside trolley. He stayed standing, opting not to take the blue wooden-framed armchair at his side. Clearly, this was a business visit. Of course it was. James Hartigan had always been business and little else.

"What can I do for you, James?"

"I suppose should be asking you that, shouldn't I?" said Hartigan. He made a flourish with his hand. "Given the circumstances…"

"But?" said Drawton.

"But, seeing as you asked. Tell me what happened to you. I want to know everything. And especially, I want to know exactly how DI Hogarth had a hand in what happened to you."

Drawton looked at the men in the beds nearby. Most of them were oblivious, but he lowered his voice anyway.

"Whatever else he's done to me, this wasn't his fault. It was a man called Halstead."

"The man who's been arrested for murder?"

Drawton nodded, his eyes gleaming.

"Hogarth got him?"

"Yes, but we both know he's no hero, don't we?" Drawton narrowed his eyes before speaking again. "What do you want, exactly, James?"

The man's smile never wavered. "Seeing as I've helped you, I thought maybe you'd like to return the favour. Tell me how Hogarth was involved in how you got hurt."

"But James, he wasn't involved."

The MP's smile wavered.

"Then seeing as how the man likes to pay you a little visit, perhaps we could organise some way of inviting him round. When you're back on your feet."

"You want me to try some form of entrapment on the man? But, James, I've just tried to help them—"

"Simon, he hates you. No one mentioned the word, entrapment. Heaven forbid. But remember this. That man will never let you off the hook. You need to remember that, don't you?"

Drawton frowned, receiving a hint of a threat from Hartigan's eyes without a single word of coercion being uttered. The man was a master. It was done with bright eyes and a wicked smile.

Drawton's face tightened. "James... what exactly do you want me to do?"

To be continued in The Deadly Gaze – out now!

Thank you for reading DI Hogarth's The Deadly Kiss. If you enjoyed this book I would be honoured if you could post a short review to let other readers know. Thank you very much – I really appreciate your help.

And if you'd like to get some more highly rated novels, boxed sets, novellas and short stories for free, then simply join the Readers' Group at SolomonCarter.net. It's free to join and once you're in I'll send you links to lots of cool stuff. You can quickly and easily unsubscribe at any time.

All the very best,

Solomon:)

The DI Hogarth Deadly Kiss Series

1. The Deadly Kiss
2. The Deadly Gaze
3. The Deadly Mind

More thrilling books by Solomon Carter

The DI Hogarth Darkest Lies series – The first DI Hogarth series

1. The Darkest Lies

2. The Darkest Grave
3. The Darkest Deed
4. The Darkest Truth

The DI Hogarth Secret Fear series – the second DI Hogarth series

1. The Secret Fear
2. The Secret Dawn
3. The Secret Sins

The DI Hogarth Poison Path series - the third DI Hogarth series

1. The Poison Path
2. The Hunter's Path
3. The Cinder Path

Long Time Dying

The first thrilling adventures featuring Eva Roberts & Dan Bradley, private detectives

1. Out with A Bang
2. One Mile Deep
3. Long Time Dying
4. Never Back Down
5. Crossing The Line
6. Divide and Rule
7. Better The Devil
8. On Borrowed Time
9. The Dirty Game
10. Only Live Once

11. Behind the Mask
12. The Dark Tide
13. Lucky For Some

Luck & Judgment

The second thrilling series featuring Eva Roberts & Dan Bradley, private detectives

1. Luck & Judgment
2. Truth Be Damned
3. The Sharp End
4. Don't Go Gently

London Calling

The third thrilling series featuring Eva Roberts & Dan Bradley, private detectives

1. Rite To Silence
2. London Calling
3. Promise To Pay
4. The Pressure Zone

The Final Trick

The fourth thrilling series featuring Eva Roberts & Dan Bradley, private detectives

1. The Final Trick
2. Taste of Death
3. The Danger Room
4. Killers and Kings

Harder They Fall

The fifth thrilling series featuring Eva Roberts & Dan Bradley, private detectives

1. Harder They Fall
2. The Stone Girl
3. Harvest of Blood
4. Last Man Standing

Between Two Thieves

The sixth thrilling series featuring Eva Roberts & Dan Bradley, private detectives

1. Between Two Thieves
2. Cuts Both Ways
3. Play With Fire

Into The Shadows

The seventh thrilling series featuring Eva Roberts & Dan Bradley, private detectives

1. Into The Shadows
2. The Devil Inside
3. No Other Way

Also by Solomon Carter

The Last Line thriller series – espionage, international adventure and all out action with Jenny Royal and The Company

Black and Gold – Vigilante Justice short read series featuring Simon 'The Man in the Mask' and Jess. Crosses over with the adventures of Eva Roberts and Dan Bradley, private detectives.

Roberts and Bradley Casebook – segmented short read series available in novel format as 'complete box sets'. Continues the PI storyline onward from Long Time Dying until Luck & Judgment

Flesh and Blood

Rack and Ruin

Two Wrongs

THE DEADLY KISS

The Deadly Kiss The DI Hogarth Deadly Kiss Series Book 1

First published in Great Britain in 2021 by Great Leap

Copyright © Solomon Carter 2021

Solomon Carter has asserted his moral right under the Copyright, Designs and Patents Act 1988, to be identified as the author of this work.

This book is a work of fiction and except in the case of historical fact, any resemblance to actual persons living or dead, is purely coincidental.

All rights reserved. No part of this e-book publication may be reproduced, stored in a retrieval system, or transmitted in any form or by any means, electronic, mechanical, photocopying, recording or otherwise, except by a reviewer who may quote brief passages in a review, without the prior written permission of the author.

Printed in Great Britain
by Amazon